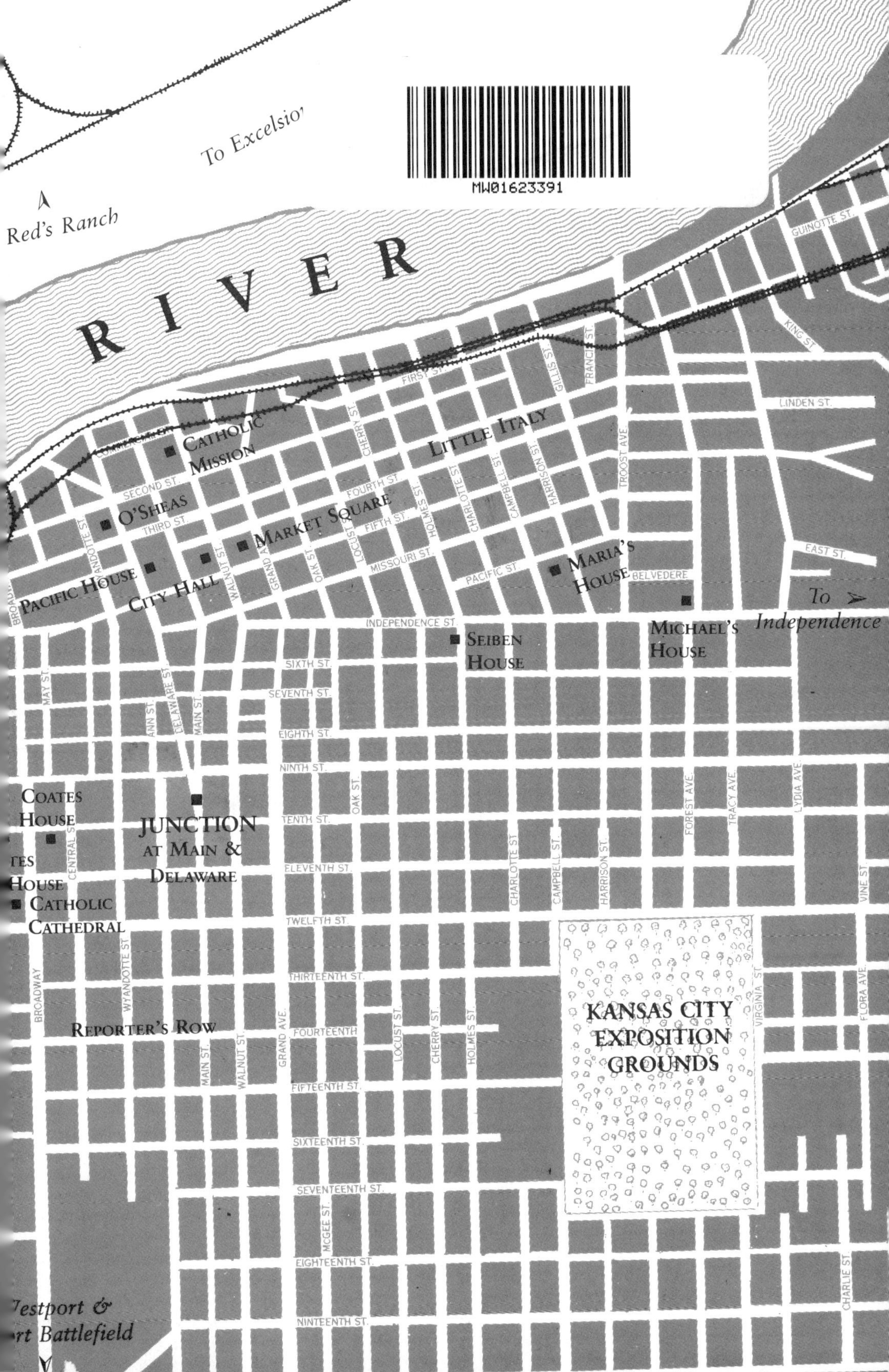
MW01623391
To Excelsior
Red's Ranch
RIVER
GUINOTTE ST.
KING ST.
LINDEN ST.
FIRST ST.
GILLIS ST.
FRANCIS ST.
CATHOLIC MISSION
LITTLE ITALY
SECOND ST.
FOURTH ST.
CHERRY ST.
TROOST AVE.
HARRISON ST.
CAMPBELL ST.
CHARLOTTE ST.
HOLMES ST.
O'SHEAS
THIRD ST.
MARKET SQUARE
FIFTH ST.
LOCUST ST.
WYANDOTTE ST.
OAK ST.
GRAND AVE.
WALNUT ST.
MISSOURI ST.
PACIFIC ST.
MARIA'S HOUSE
BELVEDERE
EAST ST.
PACIFIC HOUSE
CITY HALL
To Independence
INDEPENDENCE ST.
SEIBEN HOUSE
MICHAEL'S HOUSE
SIXTH ST.
SEVENTH ST.
MAY ST.
ANN ST.
DELAWARE ST.
MAIN ST.
EIGHTH ST.
NINTH ST.
OAK ST.
FOREST AVE.
TRACY AVE.
LYDIA AVE.
COATES HOUSE
JUNCTION AT MAIN & DELAWARE
TENTH ST.
CENTRAL ST.
ELEVENTH ST.
CHARLOTTE ST.
CAMPBELL ST.
HARRISON ST.
VINE ST.
CATHOLIC CATHEDRAL
TWELFTH ST.
WYANDOTTE ST.
BROADWAY
THIRTEENTH ST.
KANSAS CITY EXPOSITION GROUNDS
VIRGINIA ST.
FLORA AVE.
REPORTER'S ROW
FOURTEENTH
MAIN ST.
WALNUT ST.
GRAND AVE.
LOCUST ST.
CHERRY ST.
HOLMES ST.
FIFTEENTH ST.
SIXTEENTH ST.
SEVENTEENTH ST.
MCGEE ST.
EIGHTEENTH ST.
CHARLIE ST.
NINTEENTH ST.
Westport & Battlefield

# GULLY TOWN

A Novel of Kansas City

by G. P. Schultz

GULLY TOWN



Manufactured in the United States of America

First edition

Shadow Mountain Press
P.O. Box 1153
Lake Forest Rural Station
Bonner Springs, Kansas 66012

This book is a work of fiction. Ficticious incidents, characters and names are superimposed upon an actual setting of time and place. Any resemblance to persons living or dead is entirely coincidental.

Library of Congress Catalog Number: 90-61046
ISBN: 0-9626324-0-6

# Dedication

*For those in my Kansas City family who already have crossed the great river: Jack, Irene, Loren, Scott, Vic and Dorothy.*

*For my grandsons, Eric and Jeff, who begin a new generation.*

*And for all the joyful reunions and tearful good-byes that collectively formed a city's heritage, this book is also dedicated to the preservation of Kansas City's Union Station.*

## Table of Contents

# Acknowledgments

I would like to thank the following individuals and organizations for their assistance in the research and production of *Gully Town:*

Andrea Warren, for her encouragment, her critiques, and for editing *Gully Town*.

The staff of the Kansas City, Missouri, library.

The Jackson County Historical Society.

*The Kansas City Star* and the *Kansas City Times* for the generous use of their records.

Fred L. Lee, editor of *The Battle of Westport*.

The Elms Hotel in Excelsior Springs, Missouri.

Art Brisbane.

The Staff of the Johnson County library.

Mary Ellen Buck — The University of Missouri at Kansas City.

Susan Coman and Carl Brune — Coman and Associates, Tulsa, Oklahoma

Anne Thomas — editor, Tulsa, Oklahoma.

Photographs are courtesy of the Jackson County Historical Society and the Kansas City Library.

The Battle of Westport map, courtesy of the Westport Historical Society.

*Gully Town* has been a ten-year project. My thanks to everyone who took the time to help.

# Author's Note

Gully Town is a historical romance spanning the years from 1861 to 1915. The setting is Kansas City.

Although the name Kansas City was not generally in use until the 1870s, for continuity the name Kansas City appears throughout the novel.

With the exception of certain Civil War officers and other notables from history, the characters in Gully Town are fictitious. Although a work of fiction, the story plays out against a background of actual events, locations, and natural disasters. Every effort has been made to remain true to the historical record. The few liberties I have taken are as follows:

- The Front Street Massacre is a loose enactment of the Belt Line Massacre
- I have combined certain scenes from Troost Park and Electric Park into one location.
- The electoral process is my own creation.
- O'Shea's tavern and Lattas restaurant are fictitious.

Kansas City
*April 1990*

# 1

# Border War

August 9, 1861

Red Farrel slowed his horse to a gallop and looked over his shoulder. A cloud of dust was visible in the distance. "They're still behind us, Uncle Jesse!"

The other man turned to look, then pulled his horse close to Red's. "We've got to reach the Trinity before dark, Red. How's your horse holdin' up?"

Red touched the lather on Catto's neck. "He's tired."

"We've got about an hour's lead on the posse. We'll rest a spell when we get to the river." Jesse spurred his horse. "Let's go!"

The boy sighed, then coaxed the stallion back into a run. They were moving into the bright sun scorching the east Texas prairie, heading west from Nacogdoches. The posse had been on their trail all day, unshakable. Hours later, when the sun was a sliver above the land, they slowed again.

Jesse grinned. "There it is Red, over there!"

The horses smelled water and sprinted ahead as Jesse pointed to a sandbar jutting out into the water. They rode down the river bank. Unsure of the footing, they dismounted and carefully led the horses out onto the sandbar. Red and Jesse fell on their knees and plunged their faces into the cool water of the Trinity. When Red finally came up for air, he pulled the two horses away from the water and led them back to the river bank. Jesse followed. As Red wiped his face with the bandana around his neck, Jesse took pouch and paper from his shirt pocket. He glanced nervously over his shoulder as he rolled a smoke. Water glistened on his face and hands, burned brown by the Texas sun. The cigarette, wet from his fingers, dangled from his lips as he struck a match on his boot heel to light it.

Red squatted on the river bank. He watched his uncle drag on the cigarette.

"They're makin' up time on us, Red."

The boy looked behind him at the wide expanse of prairie. "Yes, sir," he answered.

"I got us in a real bind."

"You did what you had to, Uncle Jesse."

Jesse slowly shook his head. "I just didn't figure on the deputy sheriff. It was bad luck that he was in the bank."

He took a final tug on the cigarette, then flipped it into the river. Red watched as it floated downstream.

"I guess you know what we have to do?"

Red nodded.

"It's our only chance," Jesse said solemnly. "The way this posse holds the trail, there must be a Texas ranger with them. When we get in the river, I'll head south. You ride north. Down river I'll get out and leave a trail they can follow to the west. You stay in the Trinity as long as you can. The posse will check tracks for at least two miles up and down the river."

Jesse saw the downcast look on Red's face. "We've rode the trail together for a long time, Red. You're fifteen years old. It's time you were on your own."

The boy nodded.

"You still have a chance for a good life somewhere else."

Red bit his lip. He looked away. Jesse put a hand on his shoulder. "We'll meet up again on the trail some day."

"Yes, sir."

"Now listen. Stay with the Trinity until nightfall. When you leave the river, head north into Indian territory. You'll have to pass through the Choctaw and Cherokee nations, so keep your wits about you. The Indians are supposed to be civilized, but keep an eye out for renegades. Further north you should be okay. The Confederacy captured Fort Smith in April, so you don't have to worry about Yankee troops. When you leave the Indian territory keep headin' north."

"What will you do, Uncle Jesse?"

He smiled. "I think I'll help Jeff Davis win the war. "Let's go!"

They mounted up and rode out into the water. Jesse glanced at the boy. Red was lean and tough. He had been well seasoned by the Texas prairie and was as good with horses as anyone Jesse had ever seen. He had found the boy wandering along the trail in the Red River country back in 1849. Red was about three years old and had either been lost or abandoned. They had camped beside the trail for two weeks, waiting for someone to come back and claim him. But no one did.

Red had followed Jesse from one Texas bunkhouse to the next. It was a hard life for a youngster. Red had grown up watching and learning from the man he called "Uncle Jesse." He had learned how to ride and rope, and how to handle a Colt revolver. But more importantly, Jesse had given the boy the ability and the will to survive. Red had watched Jesse remain steadfast through violent storms, stampedes, starvations, and Indian attacks. Jesse's resolve had carried them through impossible situations that Red had given up as hopeless. More than once, looking at Jesse's smiling face, he had felt guilty that he had wanted to give up.

Three years ago, on a cattle drive across the Mexican border, bandits had jumped them as they drove cattle down a narrow canyon. Two of Jesse's four men were killed instantly. In the confusion of the cattle stampede, Red, Jesse, and the other two men escaped out of the valley and into the rocks above. The bandits had bungled a perfect ambush and left themselves no escape route.

For three days, without food or water, the men faced each other across the canyon. Any movement was instantly answered with gunfire. On the third night Red was awakened by a piercing scream as a man fell into the canyon below. In the darkness one of the bandits had tried to work his way across the face of the canyon wall. On the fifth day Red and the other two men could take no more. They were delirious from the heat and from lack of water. The two men tried a dash from the shelter of rocks and died under withering rifle fire. In the middle of the sixth day the cries of "You die, Gringo!" had changed to "We talk, Gringo!" Jesse had remained silent, watching, always watching the rocks across the canyon.

Red became too weak to move. He propped himself against a rock and waited for the inevitable. He knew Jesse would die before giving in, and had resigned himself to death.

On the seventh day, mad with thirst, the bandits broke cover. Jesse methodically shot each one off the canyon wall. Then he picked up Red from the baked earth and carried him five miles to water. Jesse Farrel was a hard man. More than anything, Red wondered how he would survive without Jesse's resolve.

Red extended his hand. There were tears in his eyes. "Good-bye, Uncle Jesse."

Slowly, avoiding his eyes, Jesse shook his hand. "Good-bye, Red. Take care of yourself." He turned his horse away and started moving quickly down river. Red watched until he was out of sight.

The summer of 1861 had been a dry one and the water was low. Red worked his way up river until he found a spot where some rocks allowed access out of the water. He rode next to the river until dusk and then headed north toward the Oklahoma Territory.

After dark, feeling very alone, he rode into a stand of pine trees. He unsaddled the stallion and stretched out on a bed of pine needles. Thankful for the clear skies above him, he pulled his hat down and closed his eyes.

* * *

*The sun was blood red on the horizon. He was riding low in the saddle with the wind whipping at his face. He slowed the stallion to find his way. In the distance he could see clouds of dust in all the colors of the rainbow. Behind him the posse relentlessly pursued. Far ahead he could just make out the ranch house he and Jesse had labored so long to build.*

*"Come on, boy!" He urged the horse ahead. But it was taking an eternity for the stallion's hooves to strike the ground.*

*Behind him the posse was closing the gap, but the more he encouraged the horse, the more its gait slowed. He became frantic as the posse closed in around him. They rode black horses and wore black flowing capes. He could hear laughter above the pounding hooves. Ahead, the sun had ignited the prairie. He was riding away from the laughter into a wall of flame.*

*"Uncle Jesse!" he called.*

*Jesse appeared from out of the din. He was riding straight into the wall of fire. Red had to warn him. "Uncle Jesse!" he screamed.*

*Jesse continued on. Faster. Faster.*

*"Uncle Jesse!"*

*Jesse turned slowly toward him. He had no face.*

*"Uncle Jesse!"*

* * *

Red bolted from sleep into a sitting position. His heart pounded. He was covered with sweat. In the distance a coyote gave a mournful howl. Red took a deep breath and looked around. The stallion stood calmly next to him. He reached over and rubbed the horse's leg. He no longer had Jesse or Texas, but he still had Catto.

Two years ago Jesse had taken Red to see an old Indian trader he knew, swearing that the Indian was the best judge of horses in the territory. They sat on the top rail of the corral and watched the old Indian move about, preparing for the sale.

Red recognized the Indian's markings. "I thought all the Cattos were on a reservation on the Brazos River," he said.

"You're right," Jesse replied. "Gray Fox left the tribe. He's too proud to stay on the reservation."

"What does Catto mean, Uncle Jesse?"

"It's short for Kadohadacho Confederacy. The Kadohadacho were fierce warriors. There just weren't enough of them. They were outnumbered and suffered heavy losses to the northern tribes, mainly the Osage. Kadohadacho means 'real chiefs.'

Catto is another form of the word."

Gray Fox signalled that he was ready.

Jesse turned to Red, a grin on his face. "For your birthday you can pick any horse you want. But you won't get any help from me."

Red was elated. "Do you mean it, Uncle Jesse?"

Jesse nodded.

Red knew this would be a test of his ability to judge horses. Gray Fox handled only quality stock. Red was assured a good horse, but if he picked right, he would have a great horse.

Gray Fox began parading the horses around the corral. Some of them were smartly groomed; others were covered with dirt and grime. Red would have to judge each one on merit rather than appearance. Gray Fox praised each horse with equal intensity. Sometimes he would rush a horse past and Red would ask for another look. The show and the exchange of wit were more important to Gray Fox than the exchange of money.

Red spotted a brown colt in the back of the corral. Throughout the sale he watched the young horse move about next to its mother.

"Many good horses," Gray Fox chanted.

Red watched and waited for the colt.

Gray Fox slyly separated the colt from its mother and paraded the young stallion past next to another mare.

Red's decision was confirmed. This was the horse he wanted.

Gray Fox stood in front of Red and Jesse with his arms folded across his scrawny bare chest. "Many good horses," he said.

"Have you made up your mind, Red?" Jesse asked.

The boy nodded. "I'll take the brown colt."

The smile left Gray Fox's face. He put his hand up to his ear.

"No hear," he said.

Red pointed to the colt. "I'll take that one."

The old Indian jumped off the ground. "No sale! No sale!" he said angrily.

Jesse jumped off the fence into the corral. "We had a deal, Gray Fox. You said any horse we wanted."

"No sale! No sale!"

"I've told my friend here that the Catto are a proud and honorable people," Jesse said. "Great warriors. Their word is good."

Gray Fox stared at Jesse. The old warrior knew he was beaten. He turned and walked reluctantly across the corral to get the colt.

Red jumped into the corral. He moved his hand over the stallion.

"He's a beauty, Red," Jesse said. "What will you call him?"

Red looked admiringly at the colt. "He's a Kadohadacho Confederate, which makes him a chief. I'm going to call him Catto."

* * *

It took Red Farrel three days to reach the Red River. He crossed over and looked back into Texas. "I hope you made it, Uncle Jesse," he whispered softly.

He turned Catto away from the river and began traveling to the northeast until he reached the military road connecting Fort Towson with Fort Smith in Arkansas. For several days he stayed on the road, hiding in the woods at the sound of approaching horses. The country was rugged and gave him plenty of cover. He wasn't taking any chances. He was hiding from lawmen, renegade Indians, and Union troops.

He left the trail after four days and skirted around Fort Smith. A few days later he crossed the Missouri border and continued north for the next week. The country had flattened out, making travel easier. Late in the afternoon of the fifth day, Red noticed a band of black clouds building in the west. He rode out of a patch of woods into a meadow. The stallion was restless so he let him run. Watching the trail ahead and glancing at the approaching storm, he failed to notice a group of men on the other side of the meadow.

Then a glint of blue uniform caught his eye. He pulled the reins to the right and veered Catto away from the men. Rifle fire exploded and bullets whizzed past the speeding horse. The cover of trees was just ahead.

Red felt a tug in his left leg. The pain registered a moment later. He reached for his leg and almost fell off the stallion. He frantically rode into the woods. It was all he could do to hold the reins. He pulled to a halt and looked down at his blood-soaked pantleg, then tore off his bandana and forced it between his leg and the saddle. The bullet had entered from behind, half way up the thigh. He grimaced from pain as he tied the cloth above the wound. He knew if he got off Catto he would never get back on.

A bolt of lightning flashed in the sky. Red steadied Catto. Thunder rolled. He moved the stallion ahead as the first sheet of rain arrived on a gust of wind, drenching him.

Several hours passed. Finally he rode out of the woods onto a trail. The stallion plodded along. Red fought to keep his eyes open. The loss of blood was making him weak. He put his head down on the stallion's mane and closed his eyes.

Red slept until Catto came to a halt. He opened his eyes. The rain had stopped. In front of him, a gang of men blocked the trail. He moved Catto ahead. The men came in and out of focus. Two men rode out of the woods and stationed themselves on either side of him. The man on the right reached over and lifted Red's Colt revolver out of his holster. Red felt chilled to the bone. The landscape was spinning in the dusk. The other man took the reins from him and the stallion came to a halt. The men up ahead rode toward him. They stopped in front of him, blocking the trail.

"Where you headed, boy?" An older man with a beard stared at Red.

"Kansas City," Red answered.

"Kansas City? There's nothin' in Kansas City but a bunch of goddamn Jayhawkers." The man leaned over close to Red. "You're a Jayhawker, ain't you, boy?"

"What's a Jayhawker?" Red asked. From behind him he heard the hammer on a pistol click back. Everything started to slip away. Red fell out of the saddle into the mud. He looked up. The men seemed far above him. "If you shoot me, don't hurt my horse," he said. He passed out.

When he regained consciousness he was in bed. Rain was beating on the roof. Red felt the warmth of the covers around him. He fell back to sleep.

When he opened his eyes sun was shining through the curtains. He looked around the cabin. Four men and an older woman were eating at a table in the kitchen. He could see the front door. He tried to get up. Pain shot through his leg, making him groan.

"He's awake, Adam."

The men got up from the table and walked over to the bed, looking down at him.

"Good morning."

Red nodded. He clenched his jaw against the pain. The spokesman was clean shaven and had a dignified air about him.

"My name's Adam Quint. What's yours?"

Red looked at him warily. Adam Quint was of average height. His clothes were clean and well pressed. He had wavy black hair that shone almost blue in the light. His blue eyes were penetrating, but friendly.

Red knew instantly that Adam Quint was a fair man, but a man who would tolerate no nonsense.

"My name's Red Farrel."

"Where you from, Red?"

"Texas."

"You were right, Ben." Adam looked at the older man standing next to him. "Ben could tell by your Mexican saddle," Adam explained.

The older man had skin the texture of old leather. His beard was stained with tobacco juice and his clothes and boots were covered with a thin layer of dust. His receding hair was unkempt and exposed, as if waiting for the return of his hat.

"Is my horse okay?" Red asked.

"Yes. He's in the barn. You're a long way from home, Red. How old are you?"

"Fifteen."

"Why did you leave Texas?"

Red looked at the men suspiciously.

"You can tell us the truth," Adam said.

"My uncle raised me," Red began. "We ran a small ranch in east Texas. A band of renegade Indians burned us out. They shot the stock they didn't steal. Uncle Jesse had every penny he'd saved in that ranch. With the war and hard times, we couldn't find work anywhere. Uncle Jesse decided to borrow some money from a bank."

"At the point of a gun?" Adam asked.

Red nodded.

"Where's your uncle now?"

"To lose the posse we split up at the Trinity River. Uncle Jesse said he was goin' to join the Confederacy."

Adam pointed to Red's leg. "Who shot you? That's a fresh wound."

"There were some men hidin' in the woods not far from here. I saw a flash of blue through the trees and took off. They opened fire on me."

The older man of the foursome rubbed his beard. "It was probably Doc Jennison and his gang. I heard they were raidin' across the border again. You're lucky to be alive, kid."

"Where am I?" Red asked.

"Independence, Missouri," Adam answered. "Those men you ran into were friends of ours. They brought you here."

The old woman got up from her chair and walked over to the bed. She tied a white scarf over her head. "Young man, you stay off that leg for at least ten days. You're lucky the bullet missed the bone."

"Yes, ma'am," Red answered.

"Come on. One of you boys take me back over to my place." She paused at the door. "Let me give you some good advice, young man. When that leg heals, you get out of this part of the country."

Ben followed the old woman out the door.

"Who is she?" Red asked.

"Hester Quint. She's my aunt," Adam answered. "Ben Collins is the man who followed her out. These two are Luke and Jason Cooper."

The two young men appeared to be in their early twenties. Each stood about six feet tall. Their bulging upper arm muscles were a testament to hard farm work. Locks of light blond hair streaked their foreheads, complementing teeth that flashed against full, tanned faces. The Coopers were handsome men.

Red shook hands. "You two look alike," he said.

"Just remember that I'm the smart one," Jason answered. Luke swatted Jason's shoulder with his hat.

Adam headed for the door. "We have to leave, Red. You're free to go anytime you wish. But I strongly suggest that you stay here and rest."

The three men left. Red listened as they mounted up and rode away. He rested his head back on the pillow. Where would he go? For now it was enough to be warm and off the trail. He quickly fell asleep.

When he opened his eyes again, he was immediately aware of the cabin. His stomach growled.

Ben stood next to the bed. He held a steaming bowl in his hands. "Hungry?" he asked.

Red nodded. The pain in his leg had subsided.

Ben sat down on the bed. "A bowl of my stew and you'll be up and around in no time." The old man placed the spoon between Red's lips. "Careful, it's still hot."

Red sipped juice from the spoon.

"Feel well enough to feed yourself?"

"Yes."

Ben propped him up in bed. He handed him the bowl of stew.

"How long have I been asleep?" Red asked.

"Two days."

Red started devouring the stew.

Ben laughed. He grabbed Red's arm. "Hey, slow down. Give your belly a chance to wake up."

Red rested his head back on the pillow.

"How's the leg?" Ben asked.

"Stiff and sore."

"Just like your pecker used to be, Ben," Jason said, as he moved up next to the bed. His brother Luke laughed.

"Don't pay no attention to these two, Red," Ben said. "One's just as ornery as the other."

"Looks like you're gonna live, Tex," Luke said.

Red smiled. The hot stew was beginning to fill his stomach. "How far am I from Kansas City?" he asked.

"Far enough," Ben answered.

Red grimaced as he tried to make his leg more comfortable.

"You'd better leave that leg alone," Ben suggested.

Red finished the last few bites of stew. He handed Ben the empty bowl. "Do you know where I might find a job?"

The three men laughed. "A job?" Jason asked.

Red nodded.

"Excuse us for laughin', Red. But there's no work on the Kansas-Missouri border. Most folks are just tryin' to stay alive. Haven't you heard about the border war?"

Adam Quint came in. "Hello, Red. How do you feel?"

"Much better, thanks."

"He's already lookin' for work," Ben said.

Adam smiled. "We have to leave for a few days, Red. You'll be safer over at Hester's place. Can you stand a ride over in the wagon?"

"Yes sir."

"Ben, take Jason and Luke and bring the wagon around to the front of the cabin," Adam said.

The four men carried Red outside and gently placed him in the wagon bed. Red raised his head. "Don't forget my horse," he said. Jason tied Catto to the back of the wagon.

* * *

Hester wiped Red's forehead with a wet cloth. Red opened his eyes. "Where is everyone?"

"Except for Jake here, everyone's out on a scouting party."

Jake, Hester's invalid husband, held out his hand. Pleased to meet you, Red."

"Same here." Red shook hands.

"How long have you been on the run, Red?" Jake asked.

Red rubbed his eyes. The ride over in the wagon had given him a fever. The events of the past few weeks were all running together. "I don't know," he answered.

Hester wiped his eyes with a wet cloth. "From the looks of you, I'd say you've been on the run all your life. We'll let you get some rest."

Red sat up in bed. "I don't have any money to pay you."

Hester shoved him back on the pillow. "When you're up and around I'll see that you earn your keep."

"I thought you told me to get out of this part of the country."

Red caught a glimpse of amusement in the old woman's eyes — eyes that seemed to defy the hardships of life on the prairie. She shuffled about, ignoring the infirmities of age. With just a hint of gray, her light brown hair belied the wrinkles in her face. Her hair looked soft to the touch as it flowed into a tidy bun at the back of her head.

Hester grunted. "I haven't changed my mind about that, either. Now close your eyes and get some sleep."

* * *

At the end of the week Red was well enough to put some weight on his leg. After two weeks the leg started to heal quickly.

He limped around the farm helping Hester with the chores. He became very fond of the old couple. Under Hester's supervision and with three good meals a day, he lost the wild look of a fugitive. In the ensuing months, as he became stronger, Red took excellent care of the house, barn, and surrounding land. He always carried Jake over to wherever he was working so the old man could supervise. In his younger days Jake had been a ranch foreman in Montana country. Jake Quint knew most everything about running a ranch. With Red's strong back, they became a team that could handle anything.

Before long, Red was once again astride the brown stallion. He loved to entertain Jake with feats of horsemanship. The old man would screech with delight as Red tore past the cabin on Catto. Jake would grab his rifle and pretend to shoot Red out of the saddle. Hester always scolded them both for this foolishness.

The cabin was located southeast of Independence in a place called Crackerneck. It was in the heart of bandit country, insulated from the border war. No Kansas raider had dared venture into the area known as bushwhacker country.

Every week Adam Quint or one of his men would drop by and leave several horses at Hester and Jake's place. Adam had noticed the transformation in all the livestock since Red's arrival; the young man had a special way with animals.

Red still had pangs of homesickness when he thought of Jesse, but he was becoming more accustomed to his surroundings. With pockets of forests and undulating hills, this land was not unlike eastern Texas. He had become good friends with Luke, Jason and Ben. Adam Quint was friendly enough, but he remained somewhat reserved while the others were the type of men Red had been raised with. Rugged men who were comfortable on the range. Men who were self-sufficient, who faced danger easily, yet tempered their existence with a keen sense of humor.

* * *

Red leaned back and rested his elbows on the top step of the porch. Evenings were his favorite time of the day. Hester began softly singing "In the Sweet By-and-By" as Jake accompanied her on the guitar. An oasis of light on the prairie, the clearing seemed to hold back the darkness gathering in the surrounding forest. Above, against a faint glimmer of stars, a hawk glided its last circle of the day.

"Here we go, Red," Jake called.

"In the sweet," Hester sang.

"By-and-by," Red and Jake came in on the chorus.

"All together, now."

"We shall meet on that beautiful shore."

No church congregation sang with more enthusiasm than the trio in the small cabin in Crackerneck.

When he called good night to Hester and Jake before drifting off to sleep at night, Red felt for the first time in his life that he had found a real home.

* * *

On a clear night in mid-September, Red was awakened by the sound of approaching riders. He wiped sleep from his eyes and went outside. Moonlight bathed the area around the cabin. Adam, Ben, and Jason rode into the clearing. Hester walked out onto the porch in her nightclothes.

"What's going on, Adam?" she asked.

"Luke doesn't feel well, Hester. I need Red to ride with us."

"Where are you going?"

"I don't have time to explain."

Hester moved off the porch and stood next to Adam's horse. "Red's just a boy," she protested. "He's too young to get involved in this war."

"Red, go get your horse," Adam said sternly.

"Yes, sir." Red ran to the barn. He saddled the stallion.

Hester let out a sigh of frustration as she watched Red mount up and follow the men into the night.

Jake called to her from the cabin. She walked back inside. "Don't worry, Hester," he said. "Red will be all right. That gray-eyed youngster is a tough one."

She nodded. "Maybe that's why Adam came back to claim him," she said.

* * *

The day was starting to break. The small band of men had ridden for twenty miles.

"Where are we headed, Ben?" Red asked.

The grizzled old cowboy spat out a stream of tobacco juice. "We're goin' to Osceola. General Lane came over the border yesterday. He's sackin' towns and killin' everyone in sight."

"Who's General Lane?"

Ben contemptuously spat out another stream of tobacco. "Murderin' devil that leads the Jayhawkers."

Red raised the question he had first asked on the trail. "What's a Jayhawker, Ben?"

"You'll find out soon enough." Ben spurred his horse to join Adam at the head of the column.

They spent the night on the trail. The next day they passed burned-out cabins on the outskirts of Osceola. The residents of the little town scattered in fright as the gang rode through the streets.

The men reined the horses to a halt. Red looked around at the charred buildings. The invaders had destroyed the small community. When the town's residents realized Adam and his men were not Jayhawkers, they filtered back into the street and went back to work sifting through the ruins.

Adam approached a man. "How many men did Lane have?"

"Hundreds. They came into town shooting down unarmed men. It was cold-blooded murder. After looting us, the general ordered them to burn every building."

Adam looked around at the devastation. "Where are they now?"

"Back across the border. They burned every building between here and Butler. I don't understand it. They even killed men who were pro-Union. It don't make no sense at all."

Red turned away. He looked down the street. A group of women were milling about. He rode toward them. As he moved closer he saw a row of bodies in the street. Hammers and saws played in the background as the carpenters made coffins.

A woman grabbed his boot. "Why did they do this?" She cried, tears streaming down her face. "John and I arrived yesterday from Ohio. He never hurt a soul in his life. Why did they do this?"

"Red!" Adam was waving for him to follow.

"I'm sorry, ma'am." Red removed the woman's hand from his boot and rode after Adam. For the next several hours the little group followed Lane's march back to Butler. Red moved his horse up next to Adam. "Why did Lane attack the town, Adam? There were no soldiers in Osceola."

"Soldiers have nothing to do with it, Red. Lane, Tennison, Montgomery and the rest of the Jayhawker scum raid indiscriminately. They figure if you live across the border you're a rebel. You can be as blue as Abe Lincoln, but if you live in Missouri you're fair game. War and the slavery issue gave every cutthroat in Kansas the opportunity to plunder and kill with immunity."

"Don't you fight back?"

"We do. The Jayhawkers have Federal troops in Kansas City and along the border to back them up. We have to retaliate with small bands of men that can strike quickly and fade away. Osceola will make the difference. Every man in Missouri will be ready to fight after the word spreads."

Following Lane's trail of devastation to the Kansas border, the band of men reached Independence the next day. They dismounted in front of Hester and Jake's cabin. Hester was preparing the evening meal. She shuffled outside to the porch. Her eyes met Red's and she smiled. "You all look famished. Come inside and get some food."

Luke and Jason carried Jake in and set him at the table. While Hester cooked, Adam related the events of the past few days.

"You're right, Adam," Jake said. "Every man in Missouri's gonna have his back up about this. Osceola will heat up the border war for sure."

"Such a waste," Hester said. "Adam, you got to quit this foolishness and get back to teaching school."

"You were a schoolteacher?" Red asked, surprised.

"Yes. All of us were employed until the border war started. Ben and his brother were partners in a blacksmith shop. Then his brother was killed and his business burned by the Jayhawkers. Jason and Luke lost their parents in a raid on their farm by Jennison's redlegs. Every man here has a reason to be fighting."

Hester carried a platter of chicken to the table.

"Hester, you're the best cook in Missouri," Adam said.

"You say that to anyone with food in their hands," Hester replied. The men laughed.

After the meal they went outside to smoke and chew tobacco. Adam stayed behind to talk to Hester and Jake. Hester eyed Adam from her position in front of the stove.

"What's on your mind, Aunt Hester?"

"I was just thinking about what you said. Every man has a reason to be fighting. Every man except Red. You got no right dragging him into this war. He may look tough outside, but inside he has a lot of growing up to do."

"He can handle himself all right."

"Lord knows he's had to. Why don't you leave him here with Jake and me, Adam?"

"What makes you think I was going to do anything else?"

Hester stared at him.

"Remember the day Red first came to us, Hester?"

She nodded.

"When Red woke up the first thing he asked for was his horse. He still hasn't asked for his gunbelt."

She smiled. "Thanks, Adam. I don't know what we'd do without him."

Adam walked out of the cabin. "Let's go over to the barn and talk for a minute, Red."

The boy followed him. Adam leaned against the barn. He studied Red. "You're not thinking of drifting on, are you?"

"No, sir."

"You can have a good life here with Hester and Jake. We're all agreed the border war is going to ignite. I'll sleep better knowing you're here with them."

Adam Quint's quiet manner and rugged features reminded Red of Uncle Jesse. "I'll stay as long as they'll have me, Mr. Quint."

Adam smiled. "Then it looks like you got a home. We'll be doing a lot of riding in the weeks ahead. I'm going to keep a string of horses here. I wonder if once a week you'd bring them over to my place and bring the worn out ones back here to rest."

"I'll help any way I can, Mr. Quint."

Adam held out his hand. Red shook it. "And will you please start calling me Adam?"

Red laughed. "Yes, sir. I'll do that."

Red walked back to the cabin and took his customary spot on the porch steps. He watched as Adam and his men mounted up and rode off into the tree line. Back in the woods, a prairie chicken cooed in courtship. The sound mingled with the sound of clanging dishes as Hester cleaned up the kitchen.

Red watched Jake whittle methodically on a block of wood. "What're you makin', Uncle Jake?"

Jake held up the block of wood for inspection. "I ain't decided yet."

Red smiled. Jake always started on a large project like a horse or a cow. If he made a mistake he could whittle his way down to a dog or a cat.

In the pond down behind the barn, frogs began a rythmic chirruping against the dusk.

"I've been wondering about the border war, Uncle Jake. What started the fighting, anyway?"

Jake shook a firefly off the block of wood. It blinked away into the twilight. He pondered a moment. "Some say it's the slave question. Some states' rights. Same reasons the big war started. We just got a jump on the rest of the country."

"Why's that?" Red asked.

"I think Missourians and Kansans don't like each other. Everything else is just an excuse to fight. The end of the Civil War won't bring no end to the Border War. With all the people in the world to fight against, and causes to fight for, we end up fighting each other."

Red nodded his head at the irony in Jake's statement. It seemed unnatural for Americans to war against themselves. Jake dropped the block of wood and smacked his arm. "Let's go inside, Red. The skeeters are out in force."

Red yawned. "I'm ready, Uncle Jake. It's been a long day."

* * *

The seasons passed quietly and quickly. Once a week Red took the string of horses over to Adam's place. The guerilla activities of the gang had peaked during the summer. They helped Colonel Hughes of the Confederacy capture the Union garrison at Independence and rode with the Confederate cavalry in the defeat of eight hundred Union troops at Lone Jack, Missouri.

August was a scorcher. The intense heat reminded Red of the chase out of Texas two years ago. He took excellent care of the horses. When he took fresh ones to Adam's, the school teacher was ready with the books. He taught Red to read and write during weekly sessions. Not only did Adam enjoy teaching again, but he had a willing pupil in Red Farrel.

One day after the lesson, Red and Adam walked out onto the porch of Adam's cabin holding a recently published novel Adam had purchased from a passing wagon train, titled *A Tale of Two Cities* by Charles Dickens.

"Hey, Adam," Ben called. "Did you pound anything into that thick Texas skull?"

"I sure did. We may have an educated man on our hands."

"Well the Lord be praised. And I thought Texans could only absorb dirt and alcohol."

Red laughed with them.

"Do we need to replace any horses, Red?" Adam asked.

"I don't think so. Jason's bay gelding has a tender back, but with a week's rest he should be okay."

"My saddle's warped, Red. I'll replace it the next time out."

Red nodded. He looked at Ben. "If you run into a good blacksmith, your horse needs shoes."

Adam and the men howled with laughter. The former blacksmith shook his head and laughed with them. Red mounted the brown stallion.

"We'll see you next week, Red."

"Okay, Adam."

Red led the string of horses away from the cabin onto the trail. In the twilight he glanced at the first pages of his new book. The ability to read had changed his life. He now had the means to explore someone else's thoughts and feelings, to examine lives and life styles far removed from his own. He read every book that Adam could find for him. His favorites were Dickens, James Fennimore Cooper's *Leatherstocking* series, and Herman Melville's *Moby Dick*. When he finished each book, Red discussed the book's content and meaning with his teacher.

As the light faded, Red closed the book and tucked it in his saddle bag. As he rose up in the saddle he noticed a red glow above the trees on the horizon. A brush fire in this dry weather would be disastrous. As he moved further along the trail he realized the glow was coming from the direction of Hester and Jake's cabin. Throwing aside the rope attached to the string of horses, he shouted Catto into a run. Horse and rider sped along the familiar trail. Red was in a panic as he covered the last mile. The stallion burst out of the woods into the clearing. Red pulled Catto to a halt in front of the burning cabin. Jake was in his rocker, silhouetted against the flames. In an instant, Red was off the horse and running up the porch steps. He picked Jake out of the rocker and carried him off the porch. Blood from the old man's chest covered Red's clothes. He laid Jake on the ground. The old man was dead.

"Aunt Hester!" Hester had been sick in bed. Red ran into the burning cabin. The smoke was so intense, he couldn't see. He felt along the cabin wall until he reached the bed. He lifted Hester into his arms and carried her out into the yard.

"Aunt Hester!" He shook the old woman. The cabin went up in a whoosh of flames. Red looked at Hester and realized she was dead. Stunned, he sat on his knees and watched the cabin burn.

He didn't hear Adam and the men who rode into the clearing until Adam got off his horse. He stood silently for several minutes before telling Ben to bring blankets and shovels from the barn.

"I should have been here, Adam!"

"You were doing your job, Red. Don't blame yourself," he said gently.

"I should have been here," Red repeated bitterly.

The men carried Hester and Jake to the meadow while Adam went to the barn to get a lantern. Two hastily thrown torches lay on the ground outside the barn doors. The raiders must have been in a hurry, not to have finished the job.

Red followed the lantern's light over to the meadow. In a daze he looked back at the clearing. Flames still sputtered around the burned-out cabin. The smell of death and devastation fouled the air. Plumes of smoke billowed into the darkness before drifting across the face of the moon. With his shirt sleeve, Red wiped the tears off his face.

Adam sent messengers around to tell neighbors about the tragedy. Jake and Hester had many friends in the Independence area.

* * *

Red flinched at each stroke of the shovel as Adam began digging the grave. Lost in grief, he sat motionless beside the couple's bodies. He stayed that way, staring into the darkness until dawn.

The first rays of sun flickered through the trees and found the small gathering of friends and family around the grave site. Adam climbed into the freshly dug grave and the coffins were lowered to him. After he placed them side by side, he climbed back up and helped shovel in the dirt. When he was almost finished he held out the shovel for Red to take. The boy backed away.

"I know how you feel, Red," Adam said. "Hester and Jake were the only family you and I had."

Red stepped forward and took the shovel. He put the last scoops of dirt on the grave. Adam took off his hat.

"Dear Lord, we release this couple into your loving hands. They were decent, hard-working people and deserve a rest. Amen."

Red stayed at the grave site long after the last person left the meadow. He stared at the graves until Adam rode up leading the brown stallion. As Red mounted Catto and turned for one last look at the graves, he vowed to have his revenge.

* * *

In a blaze of red, Adam watched the sun begin its rise in the east. The light from the horizon slowly melted away the darkness. Adam reached over and lifted the globe on the lantern beside his chair. He blew out the candle. This was his favorite time of day. There was something refreshing about watching the sun come up. As a young boy he had followed his father out of the house in the morning darkness. He remembered the muffled, sleepy voices and ghostly images of field hands slowly moving toward the tobacco fields; the clink of metal as tools were unloaded from the mule-driven wagon; the slow, methodical rhythm of pick and shovel as the cultivating began. And then, as the sun revealed itself, the increased tempo of the work as the light seemed to chase away all fear and doubt and renew the human spirit.

Adam had been raised on a tobacco farm near Weston, Missouri. His mother and father, Samuel and Amanda Quint, were originally from North Carolina. They had traveled west to visit Samuel's cousins, Hester and Jake Quint, and to see what the western country was like.

Land was cheap, so to the consternation of Adam's mother, his father had decided to stay in this rugged country. A new life away from her family proved challenging for Amanda. Although from a genteel background and used to the social graces, she was determined to persevere. She helped Samuel clear fields and plant tobacco, and even found time to organize the ladies of Weston into a ladies club and a garden club. Samuel and Amanda were strong-willed individuals. The land provided a living grudgingly and most years were lean, but they managed a good life for themselves.

The Quints yearned for a child. They were near forty and had given up hope when Amanda became pregnant. When Adam was born they could hardly believe their good fortune.

Amanda taught her only son the social graces, and Samuel instilled in him that to be a gentleman was to be everything. Adam was educated at home as well as in the classroom. The Quints were ambitious for their only child and they wanted him to enter a university. Adam loved his parents. He listened and learned from them, but he also had a mind of his own. He was strongly independent, and he was always seeking out some unsavory children to run with. If there was a fight at school he was usually in the middle of it. He had a quick temper and a fire in his eyes that puzzled his parents. When trouble arose, which was often, they would futilely search their lineage for the offending ancestor. As Adam grew older he acquired a fascination for guns and he loved to ride any horse he could find. Adam was ten years old when Samuel gave him his first revolver. After his lessons and chores, Adam could be found out in the woods shooting rabbits or taking target practice. Samuel also allowed him the use of the plow horses to ride if he promised not to wear them out.

Through trial and error, Samuel and Amanda had realized that Adam could not be raised with old Southern values. He was a product of the West, and to tame him was to lose him. So the Quints compromised. Adam was allowed to pursue his love of guns and horses, and if it were not of a serious nature, they would turn a deaf ear to rumors of fights and mischief. Adam did his part. He was a good student and he was quick to learn. At the age of twenty-one, he fulfilled his parents dream when he earned a teaching degree from the College of William and Mary in Williamsburg, Virginia.

His ties to the West were strong and in 1852 Adam returned home to teach in a one room school house near Weston.

Samuel and Amanda Quint died in a cholera epidemic in 1854. Their deaths were a devastating blow for Adam. His parents had always been the focal point of his existence. The loss wounded him deeply. For the next two years he combined his school teaching duties with running the tobacco farm.

In the spring of 1856 events began to happen that would change his life forever. The state of Kansas had become a battleground for the slavery issue.

The people of Missouri claimed the territory as their own. They staked out land claims to hold the territory, and did everything in their power to make Kansas a slave state.

Free soil, anti-slavery forces supported by the New England Emigrant Aid Society were pouring into Kansas. These abolitionists felt that slavery was abominable and were determined to make Kansas a free state.

Like the majority of the people in Missouri, the Quints had never owned slaves, but they believed in a set social order, and they believed in states' rights. The Yankees from the North were not going to dictate to them or change their way of life.

In May a pro-slavery gang sacked the town of Lawrence, Kansas. In retaliation the abolitionist John Brown and his sons murdered five pro-slavery men at Pottawatomie Creek. These two events sparked the already simmering Missouri-Kansas border war. Armed marauders from Kansas started using the slavery issue as an excuse to burn and loot farms in Missouri.

* * *

On October 7th, 1856, Adam had locked up the school house for the day and gone home. He was grading papers in his study when he heard the hurried hoof beats. He strapped on his gunbelt, grabbed his rifle, and tore out the back door. He crept around the corner of the house in time to see two men on horseback throw torches into his barn. The barn was full of winter hay. Smoke and flames quickly filled the air. He heard a whoosh as torches were thrown from the other side of the house onto the roof.

Adam became enraged. Samuel and Amanda had poured their lives into this place. He pulled his revolver and turned the corner of the house. The two men had dismounted. They were carrying burlap bags to loot the house before it burned, and they were not expecting resistance. The two men saw Adam and went for their guns. Adam felt the kick of his revolver as the two men were blown backwards off the porch. Rifle fire zinged past his head. He crouched down and aimed at the mounted horseman near the barn. His years of practice had made him one of the best shots in the territory. He squeezed the trigger slowly, once, twice, and both men fell mortally wounded to the ground.

Their mounts bolted away from the burning barn and into the safety of the woods. Adam ran to the well for water. He worked with all his might to save his boyhood home, but it was useless.

Word of his exploits carried around the territory. This was the first time anyone had won a battle with one of the marauding gangs. As the raids on Missouri continued, his neighbors started coming to him for advice on how to protect their property. Eventually a group of concerned townspeople and farmers asked him to form a vigilante group to help protect the people living near Weston. Adam knew that if he rebuilt his farm he would not always be there to protect it. He also knew that his heart was not in farming. He had worked the place out of respect for his parents. Like his mother, Adam was an idealist. He wanted to teach, but if he could help end the border war he would be doing more for his fellow man. Adam leased his farm to some of his field hands and formed the vigilante group. After it became an effective force, he and a few of his loyal followers broke away from the group and moved to Independence. Adam wanted to be near the border where most of the action took place. He also wanted to be closer to Hester and Jake, his only living relatives in the area.

As a mental exercise, Adam kept a daily journal. Every morning at sunrise he would jot down his thoughts and feelings, and the events of the previous day. His mother had revered the written word and somehow this creative process kept her alive within him.

### FROM ADAM QUINT'S JOURNAL — AUGUST 19, 1863

*There is no letup in the heat . . . I keep searching the horizon for rain clouds, but none develop. To escape the sun we do most of our work before noon and after sunset. The deaths of Hester and Jake coupled with the heat have cast a pall over the men. They are irritable and ready for action.*

*Red has gone into a shell, and he will not discuss what happened to Hester and Jake.*

*The way Red handles himself we sometimes forget that he is just a boy. He is capable enough, but I worry about the war's long-term effect on him. Perhaps youth will work in his favor and after the war he can put all of this behind him.*

*Tomorrow we ride across the border. In the past, I've been reluctant to join William Quantrill's guerrillas. He's an ambitious man who would betray a friend if it suited his purpose. He has steel gray, unfeeling eyes, and the stooped appearance of a thief slinking away into the night. It is hard to believe that he was once a school teacher. I often wonder if men like Quantrill are products of the war or vice versa. His two lieutenants, George Todd and Bill Anderson, are fearless, cold-blooded killers. In spite of my reservations, we must avenge the deaths of Hester and Jake, and to be successful we must ride with these men.*

*The border war goes on and on. I see no chance of compromise or an end to the violence.*

* * *

For the next week the gang stayed close to the cabin. Reports of damage caused by the Kansas raiders continued to filter in.

Red sat alone at the end of the porch. After Jake and Hester's deaths he had kept to himself. Jason and Luke stood by the hitching rail watching Ben clean his Winchester.

"What do you think will happen, Ben?" Luke asked.

"I don't know. The Jayhawkers have killed over two hundred Missourians the last few weeks. The federals in Kansas City have been arresting women suspected of helping us. The building where they kept 'em collapsed and killed Cole Younger's cousin and Bill Anderson's sister. The feds say it was an accident; some think otherwise."

"What do you think, Ben?"

Ben spat out a stream of tobacco juice. "I think we've had about enough."

Hoofbeats sounded on the trail. Adam rode into the clearing. He dismounted and took a chair on the porch. They gathered around him.

Adam scanned the faces of the men. "We originally formed this unit on a voluntary basis. Tomorrow that changes. Incidents have happened on both sides of the border that are hard to justify. That's why I've steered clear of raiding into Kansas. Our struggles have been defensive in hopes the border troubles would cool down and we could get back to leading normal lives. That hasn't happened. After the incidents of the past week I'm ready to strike back. It's time the Jayhawkers learned they're not immune away from the border. Any man who doesn't want to go, step forward. We won't think any less of you."

No one moved.

Adam nodded. He got up from the chair and headed for the cabin door.

"What about me?" Red asked.

Adam turned and looked at him, then went on in the cabin. Red stared at the door for a moment before turning to leave.

"Red!" Adam stood in the doorway with Red's Colt revolver and gunbelt in his hand. He handed them to the boy. "From now on every man takes care of his own horse. Check your gear and get a good night's sleep. Tomorrow we ride across the border."

* * *

With the Colt heavy on his hip, Red kept the stallion in the rear of the vengeful army as it swept across the border into Kansas. He had never felt such an overwhelming desire for vengeance. He pictured Hester and Jake lying on the ground in front of the burning cabin. No cause justified the slaughter of innocent men and women. If he could have his revenge, perhaps the pain of losing Hester and Jake would subside. He wondered about these people who lived across the border. How could they commit such atrocities? They were as foreign to him as any tribe of Plains Indians, and seemed just as savage. He had witnessed the results of their raids on Osceola and Crackerneck.

Catto moved easily beneath him as the gang traveled across the rolling Kansas countryside. Kansas reminded him of Texas. A place where you could ride forever into the setting sun and never gain any ground on the horizon. The land seemed endless as it fell away into the dusk.

The sun was gone, but the air remained thick and sultry. Red's shirt was soaked, and sweat glistened off Catto's neck and shoulders.

The men around him were sullen, their faces determined, as though they were all being carried along on a wave of anger and frustration. This raid would make up for years of suffering at the hands of the Jayhawkers.

Dust from the pounding hooves of the more than four hundred horses rolled across the prairie. The column slowed as darkness closed in on the land. They halted a few miles west of the town of Gardner. A farmer was roused from his bed. The raiders needed a guide over the unfamiliar terrain. They continued on for a few miles. A shot rang out in the night. Red rode past the body of the farmer lying at the side of the trail. The sight made him turn away. He could not believe the gang had shot an unarmed man.

The gang stopped at another farm house. In the moonlight Red could tell it was a prosperous ranch. The barn appeared to be new; a freshly painted fence surrounded the front yard.

Gunfire filled the night. Inside the house a light moved away from the window. A rugged-looking man with black hair and mustache carried a lamp out onto the porch.

"Who's there?" he called.

"Get your horse and come with us!"

"Not without good reason," the man said.

"We'll burn the place. Is that reason enough?"

"Who is it, Father?" A beautiful black-haired girl came out of the house into the light. She stood next to her father.

Red moved the stallion up closer to the porch. The girl's violet eyes flashed in the lantern's light.

"Get back inside!" her father ordered.

"Don't go with them, Father!" she pleaded.

"I said get back inside!"

"Please don't go!"

A woman came out onto the porch. She forced the girl back into the house. The man got his horse out of the barn. He went to the head of the column.

The girl came back onto the porch. She picked up the lantern. In the light Red saw the anguish in her face.

"Father!" she called. Her voice was lost in the sound of the thundering hooves.

An hour passed before another shot rang out. Red looked down at the rancher's body lying in a gully beside the road. He had been raised by a Texas code that said every man deserved a fair chance in a fight. All his thoughts about a righteous crusade upon the people in Kansas ended. The pleas of the young girl stabbed at him over and over. She was his age, and now she was without a father.

Red moved the stallion through the throng of riders. He searched for Adam in the darkness, working his way to the head of the column. "Adam!"

Adam appeared from out of the mass of riders. He moved his horse next to Red's.

"They murdered those unarmed men, Adam. Why?"

"I said not to, Red, but they wouldn't listen. When we get to Lawrence, stay close by me. The Anderson and Todd gangs are getting out of hand. I won't be able to control what happens."

As the first grey light of dawn appeared on the horizon, the sleeping town of Lawrence came into view. Quantrill stopped the column. He sent scouts ahead. Quantrill became restless before the scouts returned. He ordered the men to attack. As the army of raiders swept into the tranquil village, gunfire and cursing ruptured the peaceful morning. Unaware they were under attack, the citizens of Lawrence came out of their homes to investigate the gunfire. Unarmed men were shot on sight.

Red swerved Catto to the right. An encampment of young recruits had been trampled by the horses. The bodies of shattered boys lay in the street.

The acrid smell of smoke drifted through the town. Red followed Adam along Massachusetts Street to the Eldridge House. A man held a sheet out of a hotel window. He was yelling down to Quantrill.

"Adam!" Red pointed down the street. A woman was trying frantically to get her furniture out of a house before a gang of men put it to the torch.

Adam intercepted the men. "Are you attacking defenseless women?" he yelled.

One of Anderson's bearded marauders held a torch. "We're not harming women. I got orders. We're going to burn this house."

Adam knew it was useless to argue. "Come on, Red."

Red jumped off his horse. He helped Adam and the woman move as many of her possessions as possible before Anderson's men threw in the torches.

"Red!" Adam pointed to the west. "I want you to ride up the hill and keep watch. At the first sign of approaching riders empty your rifle into the air."

"Yes, sir."

From his position high on Mount Oread, Red could see columns of smoke rise in the air and roll across the prairie. He was glad to be away from the killing. He could hear the random pop of gunshots as men hiding in the woods and fields were gunned down by the marauders. For the next two hours, he kept his eyes on the horizon. Around 8:30 he spotted a column of men in the distance. He took the Sharp's breech loader from his rifle scabbard and fired all seven shots in the air. He mounted the brown stallion and headed off the hill at a gallop.

Quantrill assembled the scattered gangs of men. They rode out of the burning town.

Red held his breath. The smell of burning flesh was heavy in the air. Red had made up his mind. When they returned to Independence he wanted no further part in the border war.

The gang retreated slowly to the east. They burned farms and plundered along the way. After a few miles, Quantrill moved them off the Santa Fe Trail onto the Fort Scott road. The hot sun took its toll as men and horses fell in the heat.

Red ducked when gunfire erupted from behind the column. The Jayhawk leader General Lane had escaped the marauders by hiding in the woods. He and his men had linked up with federal troops and were pressuring the column from behind.

Adam turned a portion of the men around to face the approaching enemy. Blue uniforms were visible on the other side of a cornfield. Adam waved the men forward, charging through the field. Red's revolver was in his hand.

The federal troops were making a stand. Red emptied his revolver as fast as he could pull the trigger. The federal troops were no match for the attackers and fell back. Adam formed up the men and headed them for the state line. When they finally reached the border, he separated his men from the others and headed back to the cabin in Independence.

Once across the border they stopped at the first creek, dismounted, and plunged into the water. Ben looked exhausted.

"Are you okay, Ben?"

"I'll make it, Adam." The old cowboy managed to mount his horse. The small band of men slowly worked their way home.

Red took the horses to the barn. He took off the saddles and wiped down the tired animals.

Adam came into the barn. "Go get some sleep, Red."

Red shook his head. "You go ahead. I'll finish with the horses and then stand guard on the trail." Red wiped the sweat from his forehead. He was covered with grime.

"You sure you don't mind?"

"No, I couldn't sleep anyway."

Adam leaned against a stall. I'm sorry about what happened, Red. I guess I was too full of hate to realize things might get out of control."

Red stopped rubbing the horses. "It wasn't your fault, Adam. We all felt the same way. I wanted revenge, too. Somehow it turned out all wrong."

Adam turned to leave. "You'll feel better when you're rested. I'll relieve you in a couple hours."

Exhausted, Red sat down in the hay. He covered his face with his hands. He could still hear the pleas of the young girl, and he could smell the burning flesh.

* * *

Retaliation was swift. From his headquarters in Kansas City, Colonel Ewing of the Eleventh Kansas Volunteers issued Order Number Eleven. Under the order's provisions, all persons living along the border in Missouri were required to abandon their homes by September 9, 1863, or be removed by federal troops.

"What does Order Number Eleven mean, Adam?" Red asked.

"It gives the federal troops license to clear the border of all inhabitants. They can murder, confiscate property, and burn homes with complete immunity," he said bitterly.

"They can do that and be within the law?"

"Yes. The raid on Lawrence put Ewing under a lot of pressure. The public and the newspapers are demanding drastic action. Just like in Lawrence, more innocent people will now be slaughtered and burned from their homes."

"Where will we go?" Jason asked.

"I think we should ride south. The raid on Lawrence proved this is no way to fight a war. We can join the Confederates in Arkansas. General Sterling Price is the commander. I knew him before the war. He and Colonel Jo Shelby were friends of my father. They are fair and capable men."

Everyone murmured agreement. "Before we leave let's board up the cabin and barn. If the place looks abandoned, maybe it won't be burned by the federals."

# 2

# CIVIL WAR

On September 15, 1863, Adam Quint's small band of men rode into the Confederate encampment near Arkadelphia, Arkansas. The Iron Brigade under the command of Colonel Jo Shelby had been fighting for two years throughout the state of Arkansas. The Colonel was considered to be one of the finest Cavalry officers west of the Mississippi. Always in the thick of the fighting, he had four horses shot from beneath him at the battle of Prairie Grove.

A guard led Adam through the campfires to the Colonel's tent. An aide greeted him.

"Would you tell Colonel Shelby that Adam Quint from Weston, Missouri, is here to see him."

The aide nodded. He went inside the tent.

"Adam Quint!" Immediately Colonel Shelby came out.

"Hello, Colonel. You remember me."

"Most assuredly." The Colonel shook hands with his left hand. "I took a bullet in the shoulder at Little Rock," he apologized. "How's the border war going, Adam?"

"Not well, Colonel. I'm afraid Order Number Eleven put us out of business."

"Yes, we heard about Ewing's proclamation. Were you at Lawrence, Adam?"

"Yes. But none of my men participated in the destruction of the town. After Lawrence, we decided to ride south and see if we could join forces with you. How's Old Pap?"

Shelby smiled at the nickname the troops had affectionately dubbed their commander, General Sterling Price. "The General's fine. I'm leaving now to meet with him and General Marmaduke. How would you like to come along?"

"I would, sir. Thank you."

Adam rode with Shelby to the Confederate headquarters at Arkadelphia. He was greeted warmly by General Price. After his introduction to General Marmaduke, Adam listened as Shelby unfolded a daring plan of attack on federal Missouri.

"What I propose is to make a series of raids that will prevent the federals from reinforcing Rosecrans at Chattanooga. After our losses at Gettysburg and Vicksburg, the citizens of Missouri need a boost of confidence in their fight against federal control."

"It's a bold plan, Colonel," Marmaduke said.

"I agree, General. We will be relying solely on the elements of speed and surprise."

General Price's aide folded the map.

"I'll take the plan under advisement and let you know in a few days, Colonel," Price said. The General looked at Adam.

"And what do you plan to do with this bushwhacker?"

Adam smiled.

"I lost a company commander on the Cape Girardeau-Jackson road," Shelby answered. "If you will approve Adam's commission, he can take command of a cavalry company."

"Consider it done." Price shook Adam's hand, smiling at his surprise and pleasure. "Good luck to you, Captain Quint."

Back at camp, Colonel Shelby's aide administered the Confederate oath to Adam and his men. Red spent the next week learning the cavalry's way of doing things. He sold his Mexican saddle to a farmer and replaced it with a skeleton saddle. He spent the last of his money on new bridle reins, halter, moss blanket, and stirrups.

On the morning of September 21, Shelby received the order to make his raid on federal Missouri. At dawn Red crawled outside the tent. Ben followed. They shivered against an early frost. The call to reveille sounded. The bugle carried across the woods and fields.

Jason and Luke crawled out of their tent. Luke yawned and stretched. "I'm not sure I'm cut out for this Army life, Ben."

The old man laughed. "You'd better get used to it."

They walked over to check the horses. Red rubbed the brown stallion's nose. A sergeant and two corporals walked up to them.

"Ain't you the new recruits?" the sergeant asked.

"Sure are," Ben answered.

The sergeant looked at Red. "This your horse?"

Red nodded.

The sergeant walked around the stallion admiringly. "He sure is a fine animal. It's too bad you have to lose him."

"How's that?" Ben asked.

"He's Army property now. A man with higher rank in need of a horse can claim him."

"What's Red supposed to ride?" Ben asked.

The sergeant pointed to a horse down the line. The animal had been ridden so hard he could barely stand. The two corporals laughed. One of them handed the sergeant a saddle. "We call this confiscating supplies." The sergeant started to swing the saddle onto Catto.

Red pulled his Colt revolver. "If that saddle touches my horse, mister, you're a dead man."

The sergeant laughed. Red pulled the hammer on the Colt. The sergeant, uncertain, looked at Ben. "He's bluffing."

"The only way you'll find out is to saddle the horse," Ben said. "To be truthful with you, the kid would shoot Robert E. Lee if he tried to take that horse."

"This is insubordination!"

Ben spat out a stream of tobacco juice. "Could be," he answered.

Red moved the Colt revolver. "Get away from my horse, mister!"

The sergeant backed away. Red put his gun back in the holster. He lifted his saddle off the ground and put it on the stallion. The sergeant walked away, muttering to his companions.

* * *

To execute the raid into Missouri, Shelby chose elements of three regiments: a battalion of scouts, a section of light artillery, and twelve light ammunition wagons. Adam and his men were assigned to the battalion of scouts.

For the next six weeks, moving by night and raiding by day, Shelby's small force wreaked havoc on the state of Missouri. They burned forts, bridges, destroyed telegraph wires, and tore up railroad tracks. Resistance by federal forces was limited to militia units that were no match for the seasoned Confederate troops.

The raids went smoothly until October 15. Shelby's force had worked its way into the center of the state at the town of Booneville. Federal militia under the command of General E. B. Brown had consolidated and were marching on the Confederate rear. Shelby decided to leave Booneville for Marshall. His scouts reported that one thousand militia cavalry were drawn up on a high ridge, prepared for battle. They blocked Shelby's path to Marshall. Shelby had no choice but to attack before Brown struck his rear.

The Confederate force charged into the militia cavalry. In a two-hour battle, Shelby's men doubled the federal left wing back into the right and drove them into Marshall.

Brown's militia, hot on the Confederate rear, caught up with Shelby. The federals surrounded the town. Badly outnumbered, Shelby decided to run for it. To confuse the enemy, he formed the battalion into a two-column front and retreated south. Skirmishes were fought until the brigade reached Hawkin's mill. That night, Shelby ordered the ammunition wagons sunk in the Missouri River.

For the next six days the battle-weary troops fought skirmishes all the way back to the Arkansas border. Pursuit ended at Clarksville, where the Confederate force crossed the Arkansas River. They continued on to the south.

The troops were exhausted and starving. The next week they were struck by an early snowstorm. They rode on into Arkansas and finally stopped on November 3.

In fifteen hundred miles of raiding, Shelby's force had killed or wounded six hundred federals and destroyed two million dollars worth of property and supplies. More importantly, faith in the Confederate cause was restored in the Missouri population.

The brigade remained in northern Arkansas through the winter as the men recuperated from the raids. As the months went by, the war seemed further and further away. Union and Confederate forces were looking east to the armies of Lee and Grant. The armies of northern Arkansas waited for orders to resume fighting.

* * *

From his position back in a stand of cottonwood trees, Red could see Union pickets lazily sprawled in the grass. He ran a cleaning rod through the barrel of his Spencer carbine. Ben lay next to him emitting snorting sounds as he slept. Pickets from both sides had tired of yelling across the creek at each other. Daily they discussed everything from the war to the weather. Red carefully pushed each of the 56-52 cartridges into the tubular magazine. He wiped off the stock. Across from him a bluejay landed on the lower limb of a sugar maple. The bird's screeching call shattered the solitude. Red took aim with his carbine. He simulated pulling the trigger. "Bang!" he said.

"Nice shot, Reb."

Red whirled around. A Union soldier stood behind him holding a pistol. "Lay that Spencer down nice and easy, Reb; I wouldn't want you to mess it up after all that work."

Red laid the rifle in the grass. Ben sat up.

"My name's Cal Petterson, boys." The soldier shoved his pistol back in the holster. "I didn't want you rebs to get itchy fingers and shoot Ma Petterson's boy full of holes." Cal squatted down next to Ben. He offered some tobacco from his pouch. Ben shook his head.

"I've been watching you two rebs for the last few weeks," Cal said. "I decided it was time to come over and get acquainted."

"Mighty dangerous way of meeting new friends," Ben said.

Cal smiled. "To tell you the truth, boys, I drew the short straw." Cal let loose a stream of tobacco juice.

"What can we do for you?" Ben asked.

"For starters, you can tell me who I'm talking to."

"I'm Ben Collins from Missouri. He's Red Farrel from Texas."

"Pleased to meet you. I'm from Springfield, Illinois. The boys and I have had our eyes on the stallion." Cal turned his gaze to Red's horse. "Have you ever raced him, Red?"

Red watched Cal warily. "No," he answered.

Cal rose to his feet. "Mind if I look him over?"

Red looked at Ben. Ben nodded. "Go ahead," Red replied.

Cal walked over to the horse. He moved his hand over the stallion. "Fine lines," he said. "Fine lines. About five years old, I'd say."

"That's right," Red confirmed.

Cal stepped back. As he scrutinized the stallion, he rubbed the scruffy beard on his chin. "He might be too old for what we had in mind."

"And what might that be?" Ben asked.

"We have a bay gelding that can run with anything on four legs. If your horse was two years younger it might be a fair race. We want to liven things up around here but we hate to steal your confederate dollars."

"I bet that would keep you awake nights," Ben said.

Cal Petterson smiled.

"What do you think, Red?" Ben asked.

Red rubbed the stallion's nose. "He's had a few months' rest since the raid into Missouri. He's stronger than ever. You have some decent ground to race on?"

Cal pointed through the trees. "We been racing around the meadow over there the last two weeks. The gelding's got no competition on our side of the creek."

"It'll have to be declared neutral ground," Ben said.

Cal nodded. "I'll bring the starter's gun; all other weapons gotta be left in camp. And no officers."

"What day?" Ben asked. "We'll need some time to get ready."

"I need three days to promote the race and take bets," Cal said. "We'll race Saturday morning at ten. How much you in for, Ben?"

"Twenty Yankee dollars."

"Whewee!" Cal shouted. "This race will make old Cal Petterson a rich man. I'm gonna call it the Mason-Dixon Sweepstakes. I'll see you rebs on Saturday morning." Cal turned to leave.

"How do we know this ain't a trick?" Ben asked.

Cal looked offended. "Hell, man. Everybody knows a horse race is more important than any goddamn fool war." Cal walked off through the trees.

Red and Ben laughed. "I guess we better get you ready to run a race," Ben said.

Saturday morning broke cloudy and cold. Hundreds of Confederate troops walked warily through the trees. The late frost on the grass was trampled underfoot as soldiers from both sides moved toward the meadow. Red and Ben met Cal at the creek. Cal squatted on the bank. He spit tobacco juice into the water. His breath made vapor in the morning air.

"Cold, ain't it?"

"Yep," Ben answered. "We'll need some time to warm up the horses."

"Okay, Ben. We want to take your money fair and square. Follow me." He led the way through the trees.

For the opposing armies, the Mason-Dixon Sweepstakes had become more than a release from the daily monotony of soldiering. With no battles to fight, the race took on added importance. As each individual soldier put his money on the line, he was also laying down some prestige for the cause. The Friday before the race, the area around the creek separating the two armies had been covered with blue and grey as the troops covered the final bets. Word of the upcoming event had filtered up through the ranks, but no officer seemed willing to step in and halt it.

Cal led them out of the woods into the clearing. Union troops covered the north end of the meadow. The south end was a mass of grey.

"Take him for a trot around the track, Red," Cal said.

Red mounted the stallion. As he rode past the south end, a cheer went up from the men. Red wondered how he had managed to get himself into this. He surveyed the ground as he rode along. The surface was worn enough to make a fast track. A sharp turn on the east side and a grade leading to the finish line on the west end were the only blemishes on the course. The second time around the track Red put Catto into a canter. He wanted the horse good and loose before risking him in a race.

The bay gelding galloped around the track. He moved up next to the stallion. The sleek horse was made for racing. The gelding stood as high as the stallion but had none of the muscular content. The animal's chest was smaller and it moved on long, angular legs.

Cal Petterson and Ben waved them toward the starting line. Jason and Luke broke out of the crowd of grey uniforms. Jason grabbed the stallion's bridle. He led him toward the starting line.

"That's some horse we're up against," Luke said. "He don't look like he's seen much picket duty."

"Damn Yankees," Jason replied. "They set us up for this one. That's a bonafide racehorse we're up against.

At the starting line Ben took the bridle.

"The horses will race twice around the track and finish here at the starting line!" Cal announced.

Red looked down at Cal. "Three times around the track," he said.

"Three times? I don't know about that."

"Three times," Red insisted.

Cal's cheek muscles squeezed some juice from the wad in his jaw. He knew the Mason-Dixon Sweepstakes had gone too far to call off. He spit. "Three times around the track!" he shouted. Cal handed Ben the starting gun. "Ben, you can do the honors." Ben took the Navy Colt. He raised it in the air. Red crouched low in the saddle. He knew his only hope of winning was to wear the gelding down and make up time in the sharp turns. A muscle twitched on the stallion's shoulder.

From their position high on an adjoining ridge, Colonel Shelby and Adam Quint heard the shot ring out. They raised their binoculars to follow the race.

The gelding shot out to an early lead. Red was surprised at the quickness of the horse. A cheer went up from the north side of the track. Catto was twenty yards behind as they went into the sharp turn at the east end of the meadow. The gelding slowed considerably to make the turn. It was what Red had been planning on. The racehorse was up against one of Jesse Farrel's best cutting horses.

The stallion shifted his weight, came out of the turn on the inside, and flashed past the gelding. The surprised Yankee corporal put a whip to the racehorse. A cheer went up on the south side of the meadow. Red was ten yards ahead. The gelding steadied. He easily made up the yards in the straightaway. He was back in the lead as they shot up the incline at the finish line. Red held Catto twenty yards to the right rear of the gelding as they made the gradual turn and headed back down the south side. Red knew he had a chance if he could keep within twenty yards of the gelding. In the sharp turn the stallion once again set himself. He shot past, while the gelding scrambled for his legs. Soldiers on both sides were leaning onto the track. They were screaming and waving their hats. The gelding came out of the turn and started making up the yards. He moved past the stallion and went back to a twenty yard lead. At the incline Red gained five yards on the gelding. That hadn't happened the first time. The gelding was weakening. Both horses thundered past the finish line.

They started into the final lap. The Union corporal looked over his shoulder. He needed more distance from the stallion if he was to retain the lead coming out of the sharp turn. He whipped the gelding frantically. The lead was forty yards. A light rain started to fall. Red coaxed the stallion on. He cut the lead to thirty-five yards as they went into the turn. The gelding hit the turn on wobbly legs. He was up against a horse that had earned his stamina in all kinds of weather and on every conceivable range. The stallion set himself. He charged past the gelding. The troops on both sides were in an uproar. As he came out of the turn onto the backstretch, Red looked behind him. The gelding was a game horse. He was making up the yards. Halfway down the backstretch, the gelding caught the stallion. He moved slowly past. At the home stretch he was five yards in front. The rain fell harder. The gelding opened the lead to ten yards.

"Come on, Catto!" Red screamed in the stallion's ear. As they hit the incline leading to the finish line the stallion was cutting the lead yard by exhausting yard. Fifty yards from the finish line Catto's head was next to the gelding's saddle. Twenty yards away they were neck and neck. The two horses flashed across the finish line nose to nose. A cheer went up from both sides of the track.

Red pulled on the reins to slow the stallion. The rain started falling in a downpour. He galloped Catto around the track and back to the finish line. Both sides were in a shouting match claiming victory. Ben grabbed the stallion's bridle.

"What a race!" he screamed excitedly. He shook Red's hand. The finish line was swarming with soldiers. Ben walked over. He conferred with Cal.

"How did you see it?" Cal asked.

"A dead heat. How about you?"

"The same." Cal rolled the tobacco in his cheek. He raised his Navy Colt in the air and fired a shot for silence. The crowd quieted. "The Mason-Dixon Sweepstakes is a draw!" Cal shouted. A cheer went up from the men.

As the crowd broke up and drifted away, the men in blue and grey intermingled before going their separate ways.

Cal walked over to the stallion. He shook Red's hand. "Best race I ever saw, Red Farrel."

"Don't you want a rematch?" Ben asked.

Cal looked over at the gelding. "I reckon not. The gelding gave it all he had. He won't be the same again." The rain fell off the brim of Cal's hat. "Good luck to you boys if we don't meet up again."

"Good luck to you, Cal Petterson," Ben said.

Cal grinned. "If my horse had won, where in tarnation would I have spent all my Confederate dollars?"

Ben and Red laughed. They watched Cal Petterson walk away into the falling rain.

Back at camp, Red wiped down the stallion. Rain beat down on the canvas lean-to above his head. He checked each of the stallion's legs. The horse was very tired, but free of injury.

Colonel Shelby and Adam Quint walked out of the downpour into the shelter of the lean-to. "Colonel Shelby, meet Red Farrel," Adam said.

The Colonel stepped forward. He shook Red's hand. "I want to congratulate you on a fine race."

"Thank you, sir."

"Your horse is a gamer, Red. Another few yards and you would have had him."

"Yes, sir, I think we would have."

"Captain Quint has told me something of your background. We're glad to have you with us. Congratulations again. We will leave you to your grooming."

Adam and the Colonel stepped back into the pouring rain. Adam walked Shelby back to his tent. The Colonel looked very tired.

"I didn't think I would live to say this, Adam, but if someone called this war a draw, I'd take it. Goodnight, Captain Quint."

"Goodnight, Colonel."

* * *

In the spring of 1864, Shelby's brigade, as part of Marmaduke's Cavalry Division, fought in the Red River campaign in southern Arkansas. They drove General Frederick Steel's ten thousand Union troops back to Little Rock in defeat. With northern Arkansas under control, the Confederate high command was clamoring for another raid into Missouri, this time to capture the state and bring it under Confederate control.

General Price's scouts informed him that most federal garrisons had been removed from the state. The high command felt that a successful campaign in Missouri would help offset Confederate losses in the east.

The order arrived in late September. The army was to move north along the line of the Mississippi River. They were to cut off all western and southwestern states and territories from the Union. General Price hoped to capture Kansas City and Leavenworth in the process.

Red mounted the brown stallion. His company waited as column after column of cavalry moved past. Adam gave the command and the company joined the seemingly endless line of grey.

The army crossed the border into Missouri. They moved slowly through the state. General Price was unsure of the size of the enemy he faced. The Confederate Army briefly threatened St. Louis and Jefferson City, but passed them by and continued on to the west.

On the 19th of October the army won a brief battle against Union forces at the town of Lexington, Missouri. Adam's company was kept out of the fighting. After the battle the army continued on toward Kansas City.

The next day, excitement filtered through the ranks as a vanguard of Confederate forces came in contact with Union forces at the Little Blue River east of Independence. Sporadic gunfire continued as the Confederate Army camped for the night.

After a meeting with the newly promoted General Shelby, Adam rode back to the company bivouac area. He conferred with his junior officers, and then made a short speech to the company. Later that night he gathered his companions around him.

"What's up, Adam?" Ben asked.

"We're in for a fight. Our scouts tell us that General Curtis and his infantry and artillery are well entrenched behind fortifications along the banks of the Big Blue River. Pleasanton's Union Cavalry is pushing us hard from the rear."

"We're in for a squeeze," Ben said. "The Missouri River is north of us."

"That's about it," Adam continued. "General Price hopes to break out to the southwest. Try to get some rest tonight. It may be some time before you sleep again. Tomorrow we have to cross *that* river."

Red wrapped a blanket around him to keep out the chill October night. The brown stallion nibbled at the grass. Red leaned against the trunk of a giant oak tree. Occasional gunfire erupted from the pickets of the opposing forces. Muffled voices, creaking leather, snorting horses. Red fell asleep listening to the sounds in the night.

At dawn Adam faced the mounted company. "We're going to be in the thick of the fighting. Keep your wits about you and good luck."

Red made one last check of his Colt revolver. The sun was burning the mist away from the Little Blue River. Adam gave the signal. The company started forward through the timber.

Gunfire began at a rapid pace up ahead as the advancing army easily pushed the federals away from the Little Blue and into the town of Independence. Adam's company continued advancing west. The federals retreated through Independence. It was obvious General Curtis was fighting a holding action and would make a stand against the Confederate Army at the Big Blue.

Shelby's brigade, away from the heavy fighting, remained on the southern flank of the army. A tremendous battle erupted from behind. General Marmaduke's brigade was trying to hold the Confederate rear as Pleasanton's Union cavalry struck them from the rear. Marmaduke's brigade retreated westward from Independence, trying to stem the tide. Pleasanton was forcing the Confederate Army into Curtis's guns at the Big Blue. General Price's only means of escape was to the south. The Confederate Army, in a giant wave, tilted in a southerly direction. Shelby's brigade was now the spearhead of the army.

* * *

Adam halted his company in a stand of cottonwood trees on the banks of the Big Blue. Both sides were firing heavy vollies across the river. "Cease fire!" The Confederate cavalry officers shouted. Shooting all along the Confederate line sputtered and died as the cavalry officers prepared the men for the charge.

It became so quiet that Red was conscious of the sound of water rolling over rocks. The army would have to break through at this point or be caught in a vise and slaughtered by Pleasanton's troops coming up from behind. A low whine shattered the stillness along the river bank. It carried down the river and through the ranks. The sound became deafening as it was taken up by the last unit. The rebel yell. The Confederate cavalry burst out of the timber into the river.

Red rode guerilla style on the side of the stallion into the river. It was shallow. He felt like he was in the water forever. Wounded men screamed and fell from their saddles. The brown stallion finally made it to the opposite bank.

Blue-coated men deserted the breastworks and ran for the woods. Red rode up the bank. Two Union soldiers turned to meet his charge. He instinctively fired the Colt revolver. Both men fell to the ground. Red reined the stallion to a halt behind a tree and reloaded the revolver.

The brigade had broken a hole through the Union line. The Confederate Army was pouring through the gap behind him. He coaxed the stallion ahead into the fight. Union soldiers were fading into the timber.

To keep his army from being cut in two, General Curtis pulled his forces back. Skirmishes continued throughout the day as the opposing armies, feeling each other out, pushed to the southwest. At dusk the Confederate line was spread along the bluffs overlooking the entrenched Union position at the village of Westport.

Shelby's brigade was now on the western flank of the Confederate Army. The brigade's western flank was exposed to the Kansas state line.

Adam moved his exhausted company back off the field into a stand of timber. Red slid wearily from the saddle. He sat down next to Jason, Luke, and Ben. Darkness was slowly enveloping the woods and fields. To the north, campfires glimmered in the night.

The mood of the company was somber. A number of men had been killed during the day. The creaking of wheels filled the night as Confederate artillery moved into place.

"Looks peaceful, huh, Red?" Ben asked.

Red nodded. Below the bluffs he watched Union campfires dance in the night.

"It won't be peaceful for long. We're in for a fight tomorrow. The Yankees in this part of the country were afraid the war might pass them by. We brung it right to them."

"Will they fight, Ben?"

"They'll fight all right. General Curtis has been suckerin' us in all day. We're right where he wants us to be."

"Can we beat them?"

"You're damn right we can. It just makes me nervous to have the whole state of Kansas on my left flank."

Red grabbed Catto's reins as Confederate artillery started lobbing shells at the campfires. The fires were quickly extinguished. The location of the village vanished in the darkness.

FROM ADAM QUINT'S JOURNAL — OCTOBER 22, 1864

*General Shelby came by earlier. He informed me that the Division lost 124 men in fighting at the Big and Little Blue Rivers . . . good men we could not afford to lose. Marmaduke's Division has lost about the same number. Colonel Shelby's scouts estimate that we face a force of about twenty thousand troops. Our force of ten thousand is well trained and ready to fight, but it is obvious we will have to fight a holding action.*

*Dusk is falling over Westport. Campfires are beginning to glow on the horizon. The peaceful scene is sometimes shattered by the flash of rifle fire from nervous pickets of the opposing armies.*

*Tomorrow is Sunday. Life for most of the noncombatants will go on as usual. Church services will be held, families will gather, and off in the distance this battle will mean little more than a distant roll of thunder as men are locked in a life-and-death struggle.*

*I sometimes wonder if fate put us here at this time and place or if man makes his own fate. Perhaps we are just players on the stage of history with no knowledge of the grand design.*

*Regardless, we must make a good showing tomorrow; our way of life depends on it.*

*General Lee's Army of Northern Virginia is bogged down in the Richmond-Petersburg lines, and the Union General, Sherman, is fighting his way toward Atlanta. If nothing else, we need a moral victory to ease pressure on the Confederacy.*

*I'm exhausted, but I must go talk to the men. They did fight gallantly the last two days, and I want them to know what they are up against.*

* * *

Adam came out of the night. He sat down with the men. He sipped at a cup of hot coffee before passing it on to Ben.

"What are we up against, Adam?" Ben asked.

"We have to keep the Harrisonville road open until General Price gets the wagon train past Westport and escapes to the south. General Marmaduke is fighting a holding action against Pleasanton at Byram's Ford, protecting our rear. Frankly, he's outnumbered and in trouble. General Fagan will fill the gap between our position and Marmaduke's."

"This brigade is facing the brunt of the Union Army," Jason said.

"That's true, Jason. We also have General Moonlight's brigade on our left flank to worry about."

"What are the numbers?" Ben asked. He flipped cold coffee out of the bottom of his canteen.

"We're holding the high ground, but they're two to one against us."

"That should make things about even," Ben said.

The men laughed nervously.

"Make no mistake about what we're up against," Adam continued. "General Curtis's victory at Pea Ridge was no fluke. General Pleasanton was a cavalry commander at Gettysburg, and Major General A. J. Smith's nine thousand infantrymen are veterans of Vicksburg." Adam noted their looks of concern. "Also remember that you whipped them today," he said.

Sporadic firing continued as artillery lobbed shells at imaginary targets. Red rubbed the stallion's nose to calm him down.

Adam rose to his feet. He motioned for Red to follow. They stopped at the edge of the woods. "I'm glad you made it okay, Red. The charge across the river was a rough one."

Red nodded.

Adam looked away into the blackness of the Westport plain. "It will be over tomorrow, Red. This battle will decide the war in the west." Adam moved off into the darkness.

Red walked back to the stallion. He tied him to a young cedar tree. The army had settled down for the night. He stretched out on his oilskin next to Ben. Leaves pushed by a southerly wind rustled across the ground. "It's awfully quiet, Ben."

"Yea," Ben answered. "Everyone's waitin' for the storm to break."

Red put his hands behind his head. He watched the stars twinkle above. "Do you ever think much about Cal Petterson, Ben?"

"I reckon I do."

"Sometimes I wonder how people so much alike managed to get themselves into this mess."

"I know what you mean, Red."

"This storm won't blow over, will it, Ben?"

"No, Red. This storm has to happen."

Ben sat staring into the night. "Goodnight, Ben."

"See you in the mornin', Red."

Red turned over on his side. He wished that his Uncle Jesse were with him. He had become very close to Ben, but no one could replace Jesse. Red was determined to find his Uncle after the war.

As he often did, he thought of the black-haired girl with the violet eyes. He could not seem to get her out of his mind.

Her face had been so beautiful in the lantern's light. He wondered if he would ever see her again. He fell asleep looking at those violet eyes and listening to the wind chase leaves across the ground.

* * *

Red's eyes flickered open. In the darkness the eastern sky was a blend of orange and blue. He shivered against the cold. He sat up and looked around at the fog-shrouded woods and frost-covered fields.

Ben stood over him holding a cup of coffee. Ben studied the young man. Red was of average height. He was on the thin side, but his arms and chest were well proportioned. Traces of blond streaked his brown hair and dark grey eyes dominated his narrow, tanned face. Red had a weathered look from life on the range, and his eyes appeared older and wiser than their years. Red was a man of the west who would never be comfortable in a city.

"If I could only sleep like you youngsters." Ben handed Red the steaming coffee. Red took sips of the hot brown liquid.

"Strong, ain't it?"

Red nodded. He looked around. "What's goin' on?"

"We're gettin ready to move out."

"Where to?"

Ben pointed toward Westport.

"We're goin' to attack?"

"Yep." He reached into his pocket. He pulled out an official-looking paper. "I want you to have this."

"What is it?" Red asked.

"A deed to my ranch north of the river. I signed it over to you. You'll need a placc to raise horses after the war."

"But it's your land," Red protested.

Ben smiled. He tucked the paper in Red's pocket. "Go saddle your horse, kid."

An hour later Adam formed up the company. The sun hovered just above the tree line, making the fog transparent. From his vantage point Red could see the rooftops in Westport. The landscape was dotted with the glow of Indian summer. Leaves of red and gold shimmered in the morning light. Rock fences crossed the ground leading into Westport. Union forces were well entrenched behind the barriers. Through the fog Red could see ghostly images moving about as the enemy prepared for battle.

The red and blue company battle flag waved slightly in the breeze. General Shelby rode to the head of the brigade. Somewhere in the rear a drummer chased the quiet with a steady beat.

Artillery began to fire. Red rubbed the stallion's neck. In the distance,

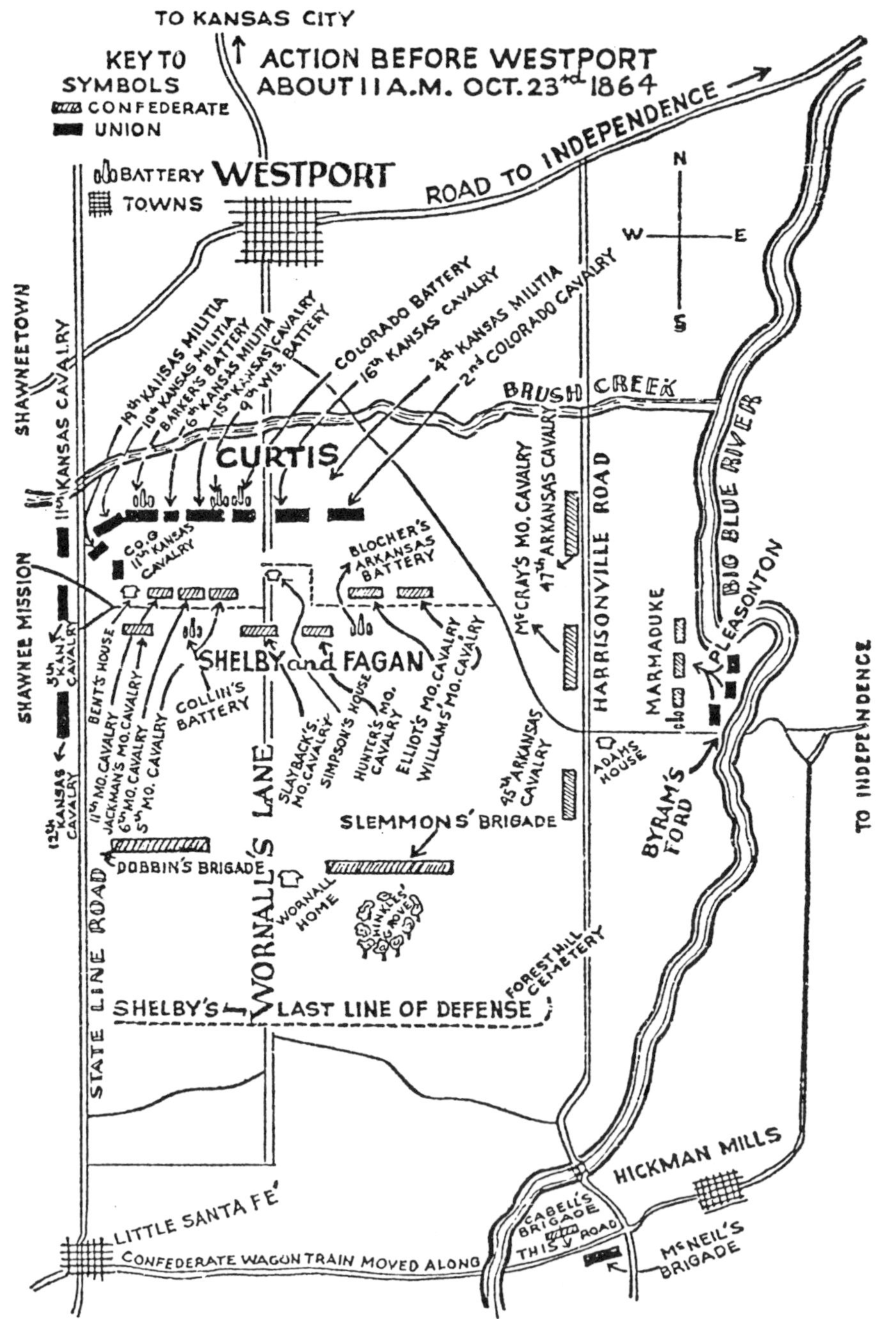
TO KANSAS CITY
KEY TO SYMBOLS
CONFEDERATE
UNION
BATTERY
TOWNS
ACTION BEFORE WESTPORT
ABOUT 11 A.M. OCT. 23rd 1864
WESTPORT
ROAD TO INDEPENDENCE
N
W
E
S
SHAWNEETOWN
11th KANSAS CAVALRY
19th KANSAS MILITIA
10th KANSAS MILITIA
BARKER'S BATTERY
6th KANSAS MILITIA
15th KANSAS CAVALRY
9th WIS. BATTERY
COLORADO BATTERY
16th KANSAS CAVALRY
4th KANSAS MILITIA
2nd COLORADO CAVALRY
BRUSH CREEK
CURTIS
BIG BLUE RIVER
CO. G 11th KANSAS CAVALRY
BLOCHER'S ARKANSAS BATTERY
McCRAY'S MO. CAVALRY
47th ARKANSAS CAVALRY
HARRISONVILLE ROAD
PLEASONTON
MARMADUKE
SHAWNEE MISSION
5th KAN. CAVALRY
BENT'S HOUSE
SHELBY and FAGAN
11th MO. CAVALRY
JACKMAN'S MO. CAVALRY
6th MO. CAVALRY
5th MO. CAVALRY
COLLIN'S BATTERY
SLAYBACK'S MO. CAVALRY
SIMPSON'S HOUSE
HUNTER'S MO. CAVALRY
ELLIOT'S MO. CAVALRY
WILLIAM'S MO. CAVALRY
45th ARKANSAS CAVALRY
ADAMS HOUSE
BYRAM'S FORD
TO INDEPENDENCE
12th KANSAS CAVALRY
WORNALL'S LANE
SLEMMONS' BRIGADE
DOBBIN'S BRIGADE
WORNALL HOME
HINKLE'S GROVE
STATE LINE ROAD
FOREST HILL CEMETERY
SHELBY'S LAST LINE OF DEFENSE
HICKMAN MILLS
LITTLE SANTA FE
CABELL'S BRIGADE
CONFEDERATE WAGON TRAIN MOVED ALONG THIS ROAD
McNEIL'S BRIGADE

puffs of smoke mushroomed into the air. The bugler blew the charge, and Shelby gave the signal to attack.

In Westport, the Union Army under the command of General Curtis had been preparing to move on the offensive. They were not expecting an assault on their positions by the outnumbered Confederates.

The Confederate cavalry companies started forward. In the distance, random shots were fired by the jittery Union troops. The cavalry picked up speed. Red could see the Yankee rifles positioned on top of the rock fences. A hundred yards away, Union troops fired the first volley.

Red felt the whine of bullets passing around him. Catto made it to the first barrier. In one graceful leap he crossed over. Red turned and fired into the mass of blue coats. The Union Troops scattered across the field. They fell back. Shelby urged his men forward, pressing the attack. The confederate charge was relentless. They moved ahead to the next fence, and the next. For the next few hours the brigades of Shelby and Fagan pushed the Union forces from fence to bloody fence. They pushed them off the bluffs, across Brush Creek, and back into the village of Westport. Confederate infantry and dismounted cavalry now held the high ground.

Red looked behind him at the battlefield. Men and horses were sprawled grotesquely in death across the terrain. Red took refuge behind a rock fence. Ben and Adam were next to him.

Shelby and Fagan's brigades now held the high ground in front of Curtis's entire army.

Smoke and the smell of powder hovered over the battlefield. To the south, Collin's Confederate battery was dueling with the Wisconsin Ninth and a Colorado battery stationed to the left of Westport. The troops were caught between the constant shelling.

"Here they come!" Adam shouted down the line.

Red looked over the fence. The Union Cavalry was charging at him. Artillery shells shook the ground. Red held the Colt revolver with both hands. He fired at the blue coats as fast as he could work the single-action revolver. Out of shells, he grabbed the Sharps rifle and continued firing.

The Union forces broke and fell back.

For the next hour the line of blue coats struck the Confederate positions time and time again. There seemed to be no end to them.

Finally the Confederates were pushed back across Brush Creek. Union forces were streaming out of Westport. Shelby's men retreated from the bluffs. They occupied positions behind the rock fences on the Westport battlefield.

Red lost all track of time. Dense smoke from the firing blocked out the sun. The battlefield was littered with the dead. He could hear the screams of dying men. The smell of blood and gunpowder tainted the air around him. He had lost track of Adam and Ben. He closed his eyes and gritted his teeth against the constant shelling.

"How you doin', Tex?" Jason and Luke dove to the ground next to him.

He was never so glad to see a familiar face.

The two brothers fired over the top of the fence. Jason ducked his head down. "Damn Yanks just keep coming!" he yelled.

To the east, General Pleasanton had fought his way through Marmaduke's position at Byram's Ford. His men charged into Fagan's brigade on Shelby's right flank. Fagan made a gallant stand but could not stem the tide. Pleasanton broke through. His cavalry assaulted Shelby's right flank.

A messenger rode into the melee. He spotted Adam Quint. "I have a message for General Shelby!"

"This way!" Adam led him through the smoke and bursting shells.

He found Shelby down the line. The General was reloading his revolver. He had lost his hat in the battle. "I have a message from General Price, sir."

"What is it?"

"He orders you to retreat. The wagon train is four miles to the south."

"I cannot retreat!" Shelby shouted above the exploding shells. "My wounded are on the field. I need reinforcements."

"There are no reinforcements, sir."

"Then get out of my way. I'll save this army yet." Shelby turned the Iron Brigade to meet the new threat from the east. The brigade stood its ground against Curtis's assault from the north and Pleasanton's charge on its right flank. Shelby's only hope was to keep his escape route open down the Harrisonville road. The Iron Brigade held firm, but Shelby knew the superior numbers of the enemy would soon wear him down. General Shelby bravely rode along the line giving the command to fall back. He moved the brigade further south in retreat.

* * *

"Watch it, Red!" Jason pointed to the east.

A squad of Union cavalry had crested the hill. They were moving at a canter toward the rock fence. The captain in front put his hand in the air, bringing his troops to a halt.

Red looked between the rocks. The Union cavalry was fifty yards away. Their horses milled about, waiting for the charge. More cavalry crested the hill to join them.

Red looked around. There were only eight men defending this section of the fence. Jason and Luke were busy reloading their weapons. Red licked his lips. His mouth was dry and his throat ached for water. His eyes were red and swollen from smoke and exhaustion.

Luke leaned his back against the rocks. He looked at Red. "You scared, Tex?"

Red nodded.

"Me, too," Luke said.

Red peeked over the top of the fence. "Get ready! They're comin'!"

The Union captain waved his men forward in an all-out assault. Horses' hooves pounded across the plain toward the fence.

"Now!" Red screamed.

Rifle and revolver fire exploded all around him. Red took careful aim at each target and squeezed the trigger. The Colt revolver jumped in his hands. He ducked as a riderless horse leaped the fence. The firing stopped. Red looked between the rocks. The first wave of Union cavalry had been badly mauled. They retreated back to their original position on the hill.

Red surveyed the line of defense. Three men were sprawled on the ground. The defenders were down to five.

"Here comes the infantry!" Jason shouted.

A battalion of Yankee troops advanced across the field toward the fence. Red and his companions opened fire at a rapid pace. The first line of infantry knelt down and fired a volley. Bullets whined through the rocks.

Jason screamed, falling to the ground. Luke bent over his brother. "He's taken a bullet in the stomach!" Blood gurgled out of Jason's mouth.

To halt the infantry's relentless pressure, Red kept firing over the top of the fence. He looked down the line. He and Luke were alone.

"Let's get him out of here, Luke."

Jason groaned as they lifted him off the ground. They half carried, half dragged him a hundred yards to the south.

Red collapsed on the ground. He was covered with sweat, dirt, and Jason's blood. He closed his eyes against the sun and tried to catch his breath. Something poked him in the side. Red opened his eyes. The stallion's nose nuzzled against him.

"Good boy," Red rubbed the stallion's nose.

Luke hovered over Jason. Red moved over next to him.

"It's real bad," Luke said.

Red heard the bugle call to the south.

"Shelby's forming up the brigade, Red. You better get out of here."

"I can't leave you and Jason."

"There's nothing you can do for Jason. I'll stay with him. Can I borrow your Sharps?"

Red slid the rifle from the scabbard beside his saddle.

Luke read the look of uncertainty in Red's eyes. "We're finished, Red. Go find Adam and Ben and get back into the fight." Luke held out his hand. "It's been a pleasure, Red Farrel."

Red shook Luke's hand. "Take care, Luke." He turned away and led the stallion back up the hill to the south. He held on tightly to the reins as artillery shells exploded all around him. He searched the lines looking for the company.

Adam Quint rode along the Confederate line offering encouragement. He looked to the south and spotted Red moving away from him. "Red!"

Red turned around and waved.

Adam rode up to him. "Red. Thank God you're safe. I've been looking everywhere. Where's Jason and Luke?"

Red explained what had happened. "Can we go back for them, Adam?"

Adam pointed to the north. The area Red had just left was covered with

Union troops.

"Have you seen Ben, Adam?"

"No. I've looked everywhere."

Red mounted the stallion. The Confederate cavalry moved a few hundred yards to the south.

General Curtis, sensing victory, ordered an all-assault on Shelby's position. Thousands of shouting Kansans came screaming out of Westport.

Shelby stopped the Iron Brigade and with shouted commands turned them around. They were going to make a final stand on the Westport plain.

The first wave of Union forces slammed into the Confederate line, reeling them back. The line stiffened and held. Wave after wave of blue coats hit the line and were turned away. The Yankees formed up for one final assault.

Shelby rode to the head of his brigade. "Mount up!" Adam rode to the head of the company. Shelby waved his pistol over his head. The rebel yell filled the air as the brigade charged into the surprised Union troops.

Red was at a full gallop when the stallion went out from under him. Red's face slammed into the turf, breaking his nose. Stunned, he rose to his knees. Blood flowed down his chin. A bullet tore into his shoulder, knocking him flat on his back. He struggled to get up. The battlefield was spinning.

"Catto!" he screamed. On his hands and knees he crawled back to the stallion. The horse's chest was a gaping wound. Red lifted Catto's head into his arms. A round of grapeshot hit Red in the side. He struggled to hold back the darkness that was closing in around him. Catto made a last gasp for air and was silent. Red passed out with his arms wrapped tightly around Catto's neck.

* * *

Adam Quint opened his eyes. Something was probing into his back.

"There, I've got it."

He heard the clang of metal into a tray. Adam gritted his teeth as alcohol was poured into the wound. "Where am I?" he asked weakly.

"The Wornall farm. We're using it as a field hospital," the doctor replied.

"The boy I brought in — where is he?"

"They're working on him in the other room." The doctor put a makeshift bandage on Adam's upper back. "That should hold you until we get to better facilities."

Adam slid off the bunk. He was very weak, but he managed to stumble into the next room. Several doctors hovered over Red. They worked frantically on Red's upper chest. Adam moved over to the table. With his handkerchief he wiped the sweat off Red's forehead.

Red opened his eyes. "They killed Catto, Adam."

"I know. I'm sorry, Red."

"What happened to Jason, Luke, and Ben?" Red whispered.

Adam looked away.

Red lost consciousness. Adam motioned for one of the doctors. The doctor helped Adam back to his bunk.

"Will he live?" Adam asked.

The doctor made a gesture of futility. "I don't know. He's lost a lot of blood, Captain. You brought him here just in time."

A Union officer walked up to Adam's bunk. "Captain Quint?"

"Yes."

"I'm Major Brewer. I've been placed in charge of this sector. I'll need your word that none of these men will try to escape."

Adam stared at the Union officer. "The war's over, Major. We have no place to go."

The Major cleared his throat. "No, I guess not," he said. He turned to leave.

"What happened to the remainder of the Confederate Army, Major?"

"General Price is in full retreat to the south."

"And Shelby's Brigade?"

"Are you a member of that brigade, Captain?"

"Yes."

"My compliments. Your brigade made a stand to the south. General Shelby held off our army for several hours with only a few hundred men. He finally managed to escape south. Shelby lost a lot of men. I'm afraid there's not much left of the Iron Brigade."

"I lost most of my company in the fighting, Major. Can the bodies be retrieved for proper burial?"

"I'm sorry. They're burying the dead in a mass grave on the battlefield. There were so many, you see."

"I understand, Major. Thank you."

Red was carried out of the operating room. They placed him on a cot next to Adam. Red was still unconcious. Adam closed his eyes against the pain of his own wounds. There was nothing he could do for Red except say a prayer, and wait.

# 3

# The Irish

July 3, 1869

A dense fog surrounded the two young men as they trudged along the wagon road that connected the city of St. Joseph with Kansas City. The morning's sun, fighting its way through the clouds, was slowly burning a path through the mist.

Big Jack Hannon stopped and yelled at his traveling companion. "It will be easy to catch a ride, he says! Just go out on the road, walk along, and in no time someone will come along and pick you up!"

The smaller Irishman moved ahead pretending not to hear.

"Why do I listen to you, Donavan!" Jack bellowed.

A flock of crows were frightened into flight. Their "caw, caw, caw" rose above the two men. The birds were invisible in the fog. Jack peered ahead through the mist.

At first glance he was a frightening spectacle. His huge head was supported by a short neck that seemed lost in his massive shoulders. Small ears and a thin mouth accentuated his broad, flat nose. His barrel chest and thick waist were supported by short, stocky legs, and his feet left tracks so large they required no signature. Jack's mere presence commanded respect, and any ground he walked on became his own. On closer inspection, his eyes gave him away. Set under brown bushy eyebrows, they were as blue as an Irish sky, full of compassion for his fellow man, and laced with the merriment of his ancestors.

In contrast, Kevin Donavan, his traveling companion, was of medium height. He had a fragile, almost feminine beauty. His muscles seemed ready to spring out at any moment and fill his angular frame. Kevin's face was narrow, with high cheekbones and locks of light brown hair curled above boyish brown eyes that darted mischievously about. He had a keen sense of humor, a quick temper, and a definite weakness for ladies.

Jack Hannon and Kevin Donavan had been raised in the Catholic orphanage in Limerick, Ireland. They were friends as only orphans who faced an uncertain future in a harsh world could be. Friends who would make any sacrifice for the welfare of the other. They had sailed from Ireland six months earlier to seek their fortune in America. Upon arrival in Baltimore, they had sought out the Irish quarters. After a week of drink and listening to stories of life in America, they were convinced that the path to success led west. They arrived in St. Joe after a long and difficult journey over land and water. The bustling city on the Missouri River was a major supply depot for wagon trains heading west. Tired of travel, they decided to look for work.

While a child in the orphanage, Kevin was constantly jotting down notes. Everything he thought significant was recorded on paper. Student and staff activities alike were put down for posterity. This kept everyone wary, and led Kevin on innumerable trips to the Mother Superior's office. On one occasion, a sister at the convent had discovered Kevin's breast and bottom lists, rating the physical attributes of female students. A severe reprimand would have been in order if the attributes of Mother Superior and the sisters had not been included on the second page. Kevin received the worst of all punishments: He was confined to his room for a week without pen or paper. Kevin's ambition was to become a newspaper reporter. It was his sole ambition. No other employment would do.

In St. Joe he applied for work at all the city's newspapers but was turned away for lack of journalistic experience. He finally took a job washing down horses at the stables while he planned his strategy.

His employment was short-lived. A young lady on the trip west with her family was found in the stables with Kevin Donavan, her skirts and petticoats raised in a compromising fashion.

Jack was at his job loading wagons at the general store when he heard a commotion erupt down the street. He was immediately suspicious of any activity coming from the direction of the stables. Kevin had a way of attracting trouble. Jack tossed a hundred-pound sack of flour onto the wagon. He started running down the street to see what was going on.

At the stables Jack pushed his way through the crowd. Kevin was in a corner of the barn surrounded by three men. "What's going on?" Jack asked the man standing next to him.

"That one took advantage of a young lady." The man pointed at Kevin. "Her father and her two brothers are going to teach him a lesson."

The crowd was clamouring for satisfaction. The father circled Kevin. He was holding a horse whip menacingly in his hand. His two sons rushed at Kevin. They ripped Kevin's shirt off of his back. Kevin struggled to get away but the two farm boys were too strong for him. They each held an arm as they turned Kevin around to receive the whip. The father moved forward and drew back his arm.

Jack let out a roar. He charged forward from out of the crowd and jerked the whip out of the man's hand. The two sons let go of Kevin and rushed at Jack. Jack stepped back and swung the whip. He cut the legs out from under one son, and hit the other with a solid right cross. Jack turned on the father and the crowd. He snapped the whip, screaming like a madman. The crowd scattered in fright.

"Run, Kevin! Run!" Jack shouted.

Kevin was already slipping out a side door. Jack tossed the whip aside and ran after him. At the edge of the city they darted into an alley and fell to their knees in exhaustion. When Kevin finally caught his breath he looked over at Jack. "Perhaps it's time we tried our luck in Kansas City," he said. The two of them fell on their backs in the dirt and howled with uncontrollable laughter.

* * *

Kevin walked back. He cupped a hand to his ear. "Did you hear that, Jack?"

"Hear what?"

"Listen!"

The slow steady creak of a wagon wheel could be heard moving along the road. "Which direction is he traveling, Kevin?"

"I can't tell."

A wagon came out of the fog on a beam of sunlight. An old man in a black coat and hat directed the horses. His lips moved over bare gums. When he saw the two men beside the road, he pulled the wagon abruptly to a halt. He put his hands in the air. "All I've got is vegetables!" he croaked.

Jack looked questioningly at the old man. "We don't want to rob you, mister."

The old man breathed a sigh of relief. He put his hands down. "Where you boys headed?"

"Kansas City."

"Gully Town, huh? Well, hop in. I'll give you a lift."

Kevin smiled triumphantly at Jack as they hopped on the wagon and sat next to the driver.

"I'm Jack Hannon. This is Kevin Donavan."

"Pleased to meet you. My name's Hemp Cotter."

"Do you make this trip often?" Kevin asked.

"Once a week. Ever week since the French had the big brawl on the river in thirty-one. I never saw so many dead people in one place. Why are you boys headed that way?"

"We're looking for work," Jack answered.

Hemp looked over at the broad-shouldered young man. "You should be able to get work in one of the packing houses down in the bottoms. What about your friend here?"

"He's a newspaper reporter."

Hemp squinted to get a better look at the thin, sandy-haired Irishman.

"Look hard, old man," Kevin said. "You can tell your grandchildren that you gave a ride to the best newspaper reporter west of the Mississippi."

Hemp flashed a toothless grin. "A man that's best at what he does usually ain't on foot."

"My big-hearted partner gave all our money away," Kevin explained.

The old man cackled. "Big hearted, is he. You boys had better pass on through Gully Town. It ain't no place for do-gooders."

"Why do you call it Gully Town?" Kevin asked.

" 'Cause that's what it is. I had me a friend who lived on Main Street. One day he woke up, walked outside, and found his building fifteen feet above the street."

"What did he do?"

"He jacked up the building and built underneath it, that's what. Two years later the same thing happened. Damndest thing I ever saw. He ended up with a three story building built from the top down."

Jack and Kevin laughed.

"Wouldn't surprise me if one day the whole damn town washed down a gully into the mighty Mo," Hemp said. He squinted at Kevin again. "Newspaperman, huh? What if they ain't hiring?"

"They'll make room for me," Kevin replied.

Hemp looked over at Jack. "Cocky, ain't he, Hannon?"

"You're a keen judge of character, Mr. Cotter."

Kevin stood up in the wagon. With a smile on his face he hooked a thumb in his vest. "The key to success for every great man is to take advantage of God-given opportunities."

The old man laughed.

"Will this wagon go any faster?" Jack asked. "Your horses will be sick from listening to his blarney."

"What's your scheme, Donavan?" Hemp asked.

"The Hannibal Bridge, my friend. It opens tomorrow. I'm going to write a story on the celebration."

"So is every reporter in Gully Town," Hemp countered.

"True, true. Only my perspective as an outsider visiting the city will be unique in the annals of journalism."

"St. Joe ain't very far outside," Hemp said.

"Origins will not be questioned when the editor of the *Kansas City Times* is clutching a priceless piece of art in his hands. And besides, work is the secondary phase of my expedition to Kansas City."

Hemp looked at Kevin questioningly.

Kevin moved over close to the old man. "Can you keep a secret, Hemp?"

Hemp nodded.

"I've had a hard-on all my life," Kevin whispered, "and I plan to take care of it in Kansas City."

Hemp cackled with glee. "He's a case, ain't he, Hannon?"

"He is that, Mr. Cotter, He is that."

The wagon creaked on for several hours in the morning sunlight. Hemp pulled the wagon off the main road. He drove up to a house dwarfed by two large barns. "I've got to stop here and get my horses checked," Hemp explained.

A man came out of the barn. He walked over to the horses. He lifted each of their hooves and checked the shoes.

"Now, listen," Hemp said. "I done what you told me. The horses are gettin' lots of rest and I've cut down on my loads."

The man looked at the big Irishman sitting on the wagon. "I'm not sure your horses would agree with you, Hemp." He walked back to the wagon bed. He held out his hand. "Hello. I'm Red Farrel."

"Jack Hannon. This is Kevin Donavan."

"Did Hemp waylay you on the trail?"

Jack laughed. "He was kind enough to give us a ride."

"Damn fools gave their money away to an orphanage," Hemp announced.

"Put those horses in the shade, Hemp. I've got some food and cold well water in the house."

The trio followed Red inside. "What's your business in Kansas City?" Red asked.

"They're busted and lookin' for work," Hemp answered.

"That's our story, all right," Jack agreed, laughing. "We figure Kansas City will boom with the railroad bridge opening across the river."

"You're right about that." Red passed around the plates. "Seven railroads will be connected by the Hannibal Bridge. I must admit I didn't think it could be done. That Swede . . . What's his name, Hemp?"

"Octave Chanute."

"Well, the man performed a miracle across the Missouri River."

"You don't seem too concerned for a man the railroads might put out of business," Hemp said.

Red laughed. "There will always be a need for good horses, Hemp."

As they ate, Hemp told Red all about his two traveling companions.

Red pushed his plate away. "I have a friend working evenings at the *Kansas City Times*, Donavan. His name is Adam Quint. Ask for him when you apply."

"I'll do that," Kevin replied, pleased.

"I wish I could help you, Jack, but I steer clear of the packing houses." The men walked out onto the porch.

"No need. You've been real helpful," Jack answered.

"If you'd like, you can have two horses and saddles on credit," Red offered. "When you get jobs you can pay for them. Take as long as you need."

"That's real generous. But Donavan and I will fare better on foot, to say nothing of your fine horses."

Red laughed.

"We won't forget your kindness, Mr. Farrel." Jack followed Kevin to the wagon. "Thanks for the meal!" They waved goodbye.

"Rest those horses, Hemp!" Red called after the old driver.

"Nice fella," Kevin said.

"He seems sorta scornful of the packing houses."

Hemp snorted. "No horse of Red Farrel's ever ended up in a packing house. When they get old he puts them out to pasture. Now let me tell you about the brawl the French had on the river in '31."

The wagon rolled on for another hour in the hot July sun. Then Hemp began to point. "There it is!" In the distance the bridge spanned the river, the engineering marvel of 1869. As the wagon moved closer, they could see men scurrying around the structure making final preparations for the next day's dedication. The waters of the mighty Missouri lapped at the piers, probing for any weakness in the foreign object in its path.

"I'll bet the first big flood washes her away," Hemp sneered.

Jack looked across the river at the city. Wooden buildings of every size and shape lined streets that sliced through the bluffs. He suddenly missed Limerick. Kansas City was a raw, dirty frontier town. Giant craters marked by piles of dirt were scattered throughout the city as the bluffs gave way to street crews. Commerce from the river pushed the city south, giving it a direction and creating new gullies on the horizon. The mountains of dirt gave way grudgingly, leaving the city perched breathlessly above the mighty waters of the Missouri. To Jack it looked as if a sculptor had begun the project, given it up as hopeless, and left the city scarred and covered in a permanent layer of dust. An expectant new mother in the throes of labor, Kansas City looked very young, and very tired.

"Over there!" Hemp pointed to a flat section stretching out to the right of the bluffs. "The west bottoms. Where the packin' houses are. Pretty, ain't it?" Hemp snickered. "Don't say you weren't warned aforehand."

Jack and Kevin jumped out of the wagon. "Thanks for the ride, Hemp."

"Good luck, boys. You're gonna need it."

They watched the wagon move off. Jack followed Kevin down the slope onto the bridge.

One of the workmen was walking about making an inspection.

"Do you mind if we cross the bridge?" Jack asked.

The workman stopped the inspection. He looked them over. "Do you think it's safe?"

"It's as fine a piece of work as man ever devised," Jack answered.

"If I could only dump a load of your confidence into the well waters of Kansas City, young man. I'm Octave Chanute."

Jack shook the famous engineer's hand.

Kevin was busy groping through his clothes for pen and paper. "Would you answer a few questions for me, Mr. Chanute?"

"Are you a reporter?"

"An aspiring reporter," Jack interrupted. "He's applying for a job at the new paper, the *Kansas City Times*."

"Well, young man, thanks to the kind words from your friend, I'm going to give you an interview on the eve of this grand event."

Caught up in the excitement of the interview, Kevin wrote furiously. He put down several pages of engineering jargon and special insights into the construction of the bridge.

"Here's your headline, young man. 'Octave Chanute Says Bridge Will Never Fall'."

"Wonderful! That's great! Thank you, sir."

"You're quite welcome. Good luck to you."

Kevin read his notes as he stumbled across the bridge behind Jack. They passed through the crowds gathered on the other side of the river. The citizens eyed the structure dubiously.

Kansas City was alive with people who planned to attend the dual events of Independence Day and the bridge opening ceremonies. Several hundred wagons were lined up along the levee waiting for the trip west. Five steamboats decorated in all their finery were tied alongside the dock.

The two Irishmen walked past the Gillis House Hotel, and over to Delaware Street. The smell of horse manure permeated the air. Residents of the town filled all available chairs along the boardwalk, waiting for reluctant breezes to wash across the river.

"I've got to find a place to sit and finish my story," Kevin said.

They continued on to Fourth Street, and stopped at a red brick building. The name "Pacific House" was spelled out above the door. "How's this?"

"Okay by me."

They walked into the shade of the three-story hotel and found the bar. "I've held enough funds back for two cold beers, Kevin."

"Bless you, Jack."

Jack paid for the beers. They found a table. Oblivious to everything around him, Kevin went to work on his story. Jack looked out the window at the bustling activity on the street. Kansas City, the last doorway to the west, was booming. Surely a man with a brain and a strong back could make it in this town.

"There!" Kevin put down his pen. He read the story over quickly. "I'm ready, Jack."

"Do you think the newspaper is?"

Kevin finished his beer. "Probably not, but I'm on my way. Where will we meet?"

"I'm going around the bluffs and try my luck in the west bottoms," Jack said. "Meet me here at sunset."

A buxom waitress brushed past the table. She smiled at the two young men. Kevin eyed the white flesh of her breast jiggling above the low-cut dress. "We've got to get some money, Jack."

"Keep your mind on the *Kansas City Times*, Kevin."

"I'm on my way, Jack. Good luck to you." Kevin left the building.

Through the window Jack watched him turn south and head for the Times building at Fifth and Delaware. He finished his beer and then went outside and walked back through the jostling crowds to the river, turning west through the narrow strip that separated the bluffs from the river. The west bottoms stretched out before him. The packing houses clung to the Missouri and Kansas rivers, as if seeking nourishment from the lifelines that snaked out of the plains.

The Missouri River flowed quickly past the bluffs into Octave Chanute's triumph, forever challenging the inevitable victory of the railroads.

Jack Hannon walked down from the high ground into the stench of the West Bottoms. He moved out of the way as a wagon sped past; the driver lashed at sweating horses. Dust drifted into Jack's already soiled clothes.

He sought employment at a flour mill. A mattress factory. A brewery. None was hiring. In the late afternoon sun he worked his way through the bottoms. He tried the lumber yard, stone and marble yards, blacksmith shops, and livery stables. Discouraged, he stopped a stoop-shouldered man passing on the street. "Excuse me, sir. I'm looking for work. Do you know of anyone who might be hiring?"

The man scrutinized the broad shouldered young Irishman. "Try Bendall's Packing House." He pointed down the street.

"Thanks."

The man nodded, moving on his way.

Jack continued on until he heard the sounds of milling cattle and snorting hogs. He passed by the animal pens, and entered the building under the sign "Bendall's Packing House." Passageways cut through the dungeon of a building in every direction. Puzzled, he stopped and looked around. He heard the sound of voices in an adjoining room. He turned the corner and approached two men. They stopped talking and looked him over. Jack noticed the blood-caked boots on one of the men.

"What do you want?" the man asked.

"I'm looking for work."

"Are you, now?"

"Yes, sir."

"Where you from?"

"St. Joe."

The two men turned away from him and conferred. "You're in luck, young fellow. When can you start?"

"Anytime."

"Good. I need a man for the second shift. Come with me."

With a grin on his face Jack followed the man out of the building into the sunlight. "What will I be doing?"

"Knocker," the man replied.

"What's a knocker?"

"Come with me!"

Jack followed the man back through a maze of animal holding pens. They stopped at the last pen. An animal chute funneled into the building. Cattle were packed tightly into the pen. Their heads plunged above the wooden slats. Two exhausted-looking men sat on the ground clutching sledge hammers.

"All right, you two! Get back to work!" the man with bloody boots yelled. "Here's a new man to share the load. His name's Jack Hannon."

The tired, haggard men nodded in Jack's direction. Bloody boots handed Jack a sledge hammer. "Watch a few times to get the hang of it."

The two men, sledge hammers poised, balanced themselves on the bottom railing of the pen. Their muscles quivered, ready to strike. The hammers went down with a sickening thud. Slats were raised at one side of the pen. The stunned animals were dragged over to a killing bed. A man shackled their legs and they were pulled into the air.

Jack clutched his sledge hammer. He followed the hanging animals into the shade of the building. A man stepped out of the shadows. With a flash of knife he cut the animals' throats. Blood poured onto the floor. Jack watched as the carcass vanished into the cavernous building.

"You've seen how it's done. Now get to work!" Bloody boots yelled.

Jack walked back to the pen. He climbed up on the lower rail. The sledge hammer felt light in his huge hands. The thud, thud, thud of hammers went on around him.

Above the heads of the cattle, the sun, in an orange glow, was settling into the western prairie. Tomorrow's bridge opening was a new beginning. The city, his adopted city, was poised and ready to usher in a new era. As he looked into the sunset, a wave of optimism swept over him.

"Hannon, are you going to swing that sledge hammer?"

Jack jumped down off the rail. He threw the sledge hammer into the dust. "Mister, Jack Hannon never killed anything in his life!" He was already running away from the pens, headed back to the levee.

A half hour later he entered the Pacific House. He spotted Kevin at a table back in the corner. The waitress with the low-cut dress sat on Kevin's lap.

"Jack! Over here!"

Jack walked back to the table and sat down.

"Would you be a dear girl and get us two beers, Sally?"

"Sure will, honey."

Jack looked exasperated. "Kevin, we're broke! Remember?"

"History, my friend. We are now men of the world."

"What are you talking about?"

"It seems the *Kansas City Times* has been waiting in eager anticipation for my arrival. After reading my story, the editor, on hands and knees, begged me to take his job and run the newspaper. Kind-hearted soul that I am, I assured the man his job was safe and that I was merely seeking a reporter's position."

"Kevin, it's me, Jack Hannon. Cut the blarney and tell me what really happened."

"Observe this sleight of hand." Kevin reached into his pocket. He laid fresh U. S. currency on the table. "An advance on my monthly salary."

"Well, I'll be!" Jack said respectfully.

Sally returned with the beers and sat down again on Kevin's lap.

"I'll have to confess, Jack. It wasn't easy. Thanks to our chance meeting with Red Farrel we now possess money for women, wine, food, and board. In that order."

"What happened?" Jack asked.

"My conversation with the editor of the *Times* went something like this: 'What do you want?' he asked. 'A job,' says I. 'Get out; I'm busy!' says he. The editor, oblivious that a man of letters waits at his doorstep, doesn't even bother to look up from his work. Back in the hallway I gather my forces, then plunge back into his office. 'It's you!' says he. I flash him my most disarming, Irish smile. The next thing I know two strong-arm types are dragging me bodily down the hall toward the street. As we pass a large room with people working, I yell out the name, 'Adam Quint!' And what happens?"

"Tell me."

"A man comes out of the room and says, 'May I help you?' 'Yes, I'm a friend of Red Farrel's.' Mr. Quint helps me to my feet. He takes me back to the editor. The editor reads my story, apologizes, and you're now looking at a member of the working press."

"Congratulations!" Jack shook Kevin's hand.

"You look pleased with yourself, Jack. Did you find a job, too?"

"No, I found out what I don't want to do. That was worth something."

Kevin held up his beer. "We have our grubstake so you can look for work in style. Let's begin the celebration. To our first night in Kansas City."

Sally and Jack drank the toast.

"Sally girl. Before I left home my dear mother said to me, 'Kevin, you will run into a blue-eyed woman so beautiful that you will be as putty in her hands. Struggle you may, but her charms will render you defenseless.' "

Sally giggled into her beer.

"Do you have a friend that might join us for a night on the town?"

"Sure. Her name's Wilma. She works over at Bob Poteet's Faro Bank on Missouri Avenue. We both get off work at eight o'clock."

"Excellent! Jack and I will get a room upstairs, bathe in the waters of the Pacific House, and meet you here in one hour."

* * *

The two Irishmen, freshly scrubbed, escorted Sally into Bob Poteet's. The proprietor was dressed elegantly. He wore a silk hat and carried a gold-headed cane. He graciously greeted them at the door. Bob Poteet escorted them to a table. "Are you gentlemen new to the city?"

"Yes, we arrived today."

"I'm honored that you chose this humble establishment for your first night on the town."

"You're very kind," Jack replied.

Bob Poteet went back to his position at the door of the saloon.

A girl approached the table. A radiant smile hid the plainness of her face. Straight brown hair fell down her back, decoration for a voluptuous figure.

"Hi, Wilma! I want you to meet Jack Hannon and Kevin Donavan."

"Hello." Wilma sat down.

Kevin took her hand. "The gods are generous. That I should be allowed to fall in love twice on the same day."

The girls laughed. They talked and drank for several hours. Kevin played the Faro wheel and managed to double his money.

In good spirits the foursome left Bob Poteet's. They walked over to the marble hall on Main Street. It was a favorite hangout of Wild Bill Hickok's. Kevin was immediately on the trail of the famous scout. He wanted an interview.

Kevin set a pitcher of beer on the table. "The bartender says Wild Bill won't be in today. He's umpiring a baseball game out at Fourteenth and Mcgee."

"Lucky for him," Jack said.

"I'll catch up with him another time. Now girls, what say we finish this last pitcher of beer and head back to the Pacific House."

The girls, both tipsy, looked at each other and laughed. "What would we do there?" they asked teasingly. "We're nice girls."

Donavan grinned. "Scoot your chairs over close to me, girls."

Sally and Wilma complied. Kevin leaned over and whispered to them. The girls giggled. Jack watched their faces as they moved their hands down Donavan's leg. Their eyes widened in disbelief.

"My god! His father was a mule!" Sally whispered.

* * *

In a room of the Pacific House, Kevin sat naked in a chair. He tipped a bottle of bourbon to his lips and drank. "This is heaven, Jack."

Jack and the two girls were in bed. Finished with Sally, the big Irishman was moving on top of Wilma. The girl was barely visible beneath him.

Sally looked over at Kevin as she stroked Jack's hindquarters. "You're a good friend, Kevin Donavan. Not many men would be content to play second fiddle."

"My dear," Kevin replied, if your charms were a journey down a mile-long road, my good friend would only complete the first quarter. I will soon sample areas unexplored by the common man."

Sally giggled.

"Will you shut up, Kevin!" Jack yelled. When he was finished he moved away from Wilma. Jack got off the bed. He dressed quickly.

Kevin jumped into bed with the girls.

"You go first," Wilma said to Sally.

Jack opened the door. He looked back. Kevin was already in the saddle thrusting forward.

"Oh my God!" the girls said in unison.

Jack walked downstairs to the bar. He ordered a beer from the bartender.

"New in town?" the bartender asked.

"Yes. I arrived this afternoon."

"How do you like it so far?"

Jack grinned.

The bartender laughed. "It is a lot of fun, ain't it? I'm John Connor."

"Jack Hannon, John." They shook hands. "If I can find work, Kansas City and I will get along just fine." Jack told John Connor of his experiences in the West Bottoms.

"That would be a tough way to make a living," John sympathized. He moved down the bar, serving drinks to his customers.

Jack sipped his beer contentedly.

John returned. "Say, Jack, I was just thinking. Have you ever tended bar?"

"No, never. Why?"

"O'Shea is looking for a man. He has a saloon down the street."

"Is it tough to learn?"

"No. Nothing to it. You're big enough to handle the rough stuff, and that's half the job. I'll tell you what. Since you're a fellow Irishman, step behind the bar, and I'll teach you the tricks of the trade."

"You mean it?"

"Come on back!"

Jack gulped down his beer. He rolled up his sleeves and stepped behind the bar.

An hour later Kevin walked slowly down the stairs behind the two girls. The threesome slumped into chairs at a table in the corner.

Jack put a towel over his arm. He approached the table. "May I take your order, sir?"

In a stupor Kevin looked up at him. "Sit down, Jack."

"Sorry, sir. I'm on duty. You look rather done in, sir. Perhaps it's the hot weather." Jack winked at the girls.

"What do you mean, on duty?" Kevin asked.

"I'm learning the bartending trade."

"You don't say. Well, you always were good with drinks. Bring us three beers."

"Right away, sir. Ladies, if I may be so bold . . . did Mr. Donavan perform up to your expectations?"

"He's the King of the Levee, he is," Sally answered.

Jack smiled at his exhausted companion. "Now there's a title men would kill for, Kevin Donavan."

Kevin looked at Jack with drooping eyelids. "Just bring the beers, my man!"

Jack laughed. He turned away.

The bartender worked with Jack until closing time. "You'll make a fine bartender, Jack Hannon. Tell Tom O'Shea that I recommended you."

"Thank you, sir. You've made my first day in the city complete."

Jack and Kevin escorted the girls to the door.

Sally whispered in Jack's ear. "Did his mother really tell him he would meet up with me?"

"Sally, my love, if he bumped into his mother on the street he wouldn't recognize her. We were both raised in the Catholic Orphanage in Limerick,

Ireland. We arrived in this grand country last year. Our employment in St. Joseph recently expired and here we are."

Sally giggled. "He's the devil, he is."

Jack laughed. "If you ladies will accept, Kevin and I would like to escort you to the bridge-opening ceremony tomorrow."

"We accept," Wilma replied.

Jack tipped his hat. "Goodnight, ladies."

The next morning Kevin was up early. He sat in a chair with his feet propped on the window sill. From his perch in the third floor window of the Pacific House he could see all the way down Delaware Street to the river. The levee was already bustling with activity. Drovers loaded cargo from a boat onto the dock as a caravan of wagons lined up along the street waited for the supplies. A light morning shower cooled the early morning breeze. Through the mist Kevin could see the slightly swollen Missouri River. The waters seemed to quicken pace at Kansas City as the Kansas River emptied into the flow.

Kevin's parentage was a mystery. As a baby he had been left on the doorstep of the orphanage. He had always enjoyed life with Jack and the sisters, so his origins were never a great concern to him.

Jack's mother had died of consumption shortly after his birth and a year later his father had drunk himself to an early death. At the age of two Jack was brought to the orphanage by relatives who could no longer afford to keep him.

Kevin pictured the view from his room at the orphanage back in Ireland. At an early age he and Jack had commandeered the prize room next to the bell tower, high above the streets of Limerick. Like kings in a castle they could look out at thatched huts and winding streets that were as old as the ages. Cast in shades of blues and greens, the village was surrounded by a patchwork of fields and fences. Limerick was beautiful, orderly, and comfortable. But there was no work in Limerick or Ireland.

The unfolding of western America was an exciting place to be. He was now blessed with work in his chosen profession, and Jack was at his side. But looking out on the scene below, as the mist turned to rain and the street turned to mud and the wooden buildings seemed to droop in the rain, Kevin Donavan knew that Kansas City was going to take some getting used to.

* * *

Jack moved jauntily along Delaware Street. O'Shea's place was a block from the river. Jack walked inside the tavern.

An older couple sat at one of the tables going over ledgers. "Sorry, we're not open for business," the man said.

"I would like to speak with Tom O'Shea."

"I'm Tom O'Shea."

"John Connor, the bartender at the Pacific House sent me to see you. He said there might be a position open here."

"That's true. There might be. Have you ever tended bar?"

"Yes, sir. John Connor was kind enough to teach me last night."

"You've tended bar for one night only?"

"Half a night, sir. But I've got the hang of it."

O'Shea scrutinized the young man. "And why should I waste my time with you? You'll work for a week and then head west like the rest of the drifters I've had the misfortune to employ."

"If I strike a bargain with you, sir," Jack said, "I'll not break it."

O'Shea looked into the eyes of the big-shouldered Irishman. He knew that Jack meant what he said. "Do you have a family, Jack?"

"No, sir. I'm an orphan, and I've no wife."

O'Shea's face softened considerably. "Jack, this is my wife, Connie."

"Pleased to meet you, ma'am."

Connie shook his huge hand.

"Should we hire him, Connie girl?" O'Shea asked.

Connie looked Jack over. "Yes. I think we should. He can start work after the holiday. Welcome to The Tavern O'Shea, Mr. Hannon."

At noon Kevin and Jack met Sally and Wilma at the levee. With the exception of the saloons, the town was shut down for the holiday. The bluffs above the bridge were swarming with visitors and townspeople. Kevin surveyed the crowd. Several thousand people congregated at the bridge entrance. "How many folks are here, Jack?"

"At least forty thousand, I'd guess."

"Oh, look!" Wilma pointed. A giant balloon was stationed in a field across the river.

"Will someone go up in that thing?" Sally asked.

"That remains to be seen," Kevin answered.

They worked their way through the crowd to a point halfway up the bluff. Sally spread a blanket on the ground. The bridge below was a stage set in the natural amphitheater of the bluffs. Mother Nature had provided a spring day in July for the ceremony. The river bottom and bluffs were void of heat and humidity. Below them, flags hung limply from the bridge in the windless afternoon. The crowd applauded as the postmaster and his wife drove a carriage across the bridge.

The steamboat *Marcella* approached in the channel. Four men rushed to the drawbridge and swung it open. The structure's huge arms rested on the piers. The crowd whistled and cheered as the steamboat passed underneath the bridge. The men rushed out and closed the drawbridge.

"Look! Here it comes!" Sally cried. On the other side of the river the train approached the bridge. It was decorated with flags and flowers. Two Pullman cars trailed behind the engine named "Hannibal." They had been sent by the railroad magnate to ferry local dignitaries across the bridge. The remaining ten cars were filled with cheering citizens who were waving flags from the windows.

A hush came over the crowd as the train crept onto the span. Octave Chanute's moment of truth had arrived. The flag-draped engine chugged

**Opening of the Hannibal Bridge — 1869**

confidently ahead, oblivious to the churning waters below. As the last car made it safely across, a great roar went up from the crowd.

"Look! Look!" Wilma shouted. Across the river the balloon started rising from its moorings. Up and up it came. It grew larger as it crossed the river. The spectators watched in fascination as the balloon passed overhead. Hypnotized, they watched until it was a mere speck in the east.

Sally clutched her hand to her chest. "Well, I never!" she whispered.

Jack put his hand on Kevin's shoulder. "We're embarked on a changing world, Kevin Donavan."

His friend nodded somberly.

"Come on," Sally said. "We're going to miss the parade." She gathered up the blanket. They moved down the bluff and were swept along in the crowd that was pouring across the bridge. With the rest of the populace they viewed the twelve beautiful floats that were stationed at Fifth and Broadway.

As the procession got under way, Kevin ducked into a saloon. He returned with two cold beers. Sally and Wilma snatched them from his grasp. They looked around. Satisfied no one was watching, they gulped the cold liquid.

"Damn!" Donavan grabbed the empty containers. He ducked back into the saloon. Jack blocked the girls from getting the refills.

They followed the parade over to Troost Avenue. At Evans Grove the procession halted. Three tables, each a hundred feet long, were lined up in the grove. They were covered with whole carcasses of meat, fried and roast chicken, stacks of bread, and plate after plate of fresh vegetables.

Kevin smacked his lips. "Jack, I think we have stumbled onto paradise." They tore into the massive display of food and drink.

After the meal and speeches by local dignitaries, they followed the parade back to Main Street. Most of the revelers retreated into the nearest saloon. Sally and Wilma had been on their feet all day. They held their shoes in hand as they walked slowly down Delaware Street to the Pacific House.

"I could not have imagined a nicer weekend," Jack said. "Would you ladies care to join us for a nightcap?"

Sally sat down on the boardwalk. She rubbed her feet. "If it's all the same to you, love, I think we'll call it a night."

Wilma leaned against the building, exhausted.

"Come on, girls. Don't let sore feet ruin the evening," Kevin said.

"It's not only our feet that's sore, Kevin Donavan." Sally rose to her feet. "Thank you both for a lovely evening." The girls moved up the boardwalk.

"Stop by O'Shea's tomorrow for a drink," Jack called.

Sally waved wearily.

"What's the matter with them, Jack?"

"You tell me, Kevin Donavan," Jack winked. "After all, you are the King of the Levee."

Laughing, the two men went into the Pacific House.

## FROM ADAM QUINT'S JOURNAL — JULY 7, 1869

*The July 4th celebration was something to behold. There were thousands of people who had come to see the opening of the Hannibal Bridge. I am sure the new railroad service will spur the city's growth. My editor, Colonel Ellison, is of the same mind. He wants me to write a column that follows the progress of the city. This could not have worked out better for me, as I routinely follow the city's progress in my journal.*

*I have accepted a full-time teaching position at the new Franklin School on Fourteenth Street. I am a fortunate man to be able to make my living from the things I love most, teaching and writing. And last week I met the most charming woman while on a newspaper assignment. Her name is Bonnie Morgan, and she has opened a small dry goods and millinery store at Missouri Avenue and Main Street. She has a lot of spunk, and say's that she is determined to make a success of her business. She is not a striking woman, but she has a beauty of her own and a most pleasing personality. In many ways she reminds me of my mother. I have asked her to dinner and she has accepted.*

*This entry would not be complete without mentioning two of the most interesting characters I have ever met. They are a couple of Irishmen named Kevin Donavan and Jack Hannon. They seem to enjoy everything immensely, and are wide eyed and excited about all that's happening around them. Colonel Ellison hired Kevin at the Times because he said the young man had such confidence and was so full of life that he could not bear to let him down. Jack Hannon is a huge, likeable fellow. I've never met anyone who put me at ease so quickly. I saw them both at the bridge opening ceremony and they were having quite a good time of it. They have recently immigrated from Ireland and want to settle here. They should fit right in as they are as wild and raw as the city.*

# 4

# MELISSA

Jack worked hard during the months ahead, quickly earning the confidence and respect of the O'Sheas.

Connie schooled him in the art of food preparation. Tom, a master bartender, taught him his trade. They gave him free meals and a room above the tavern. Every evening the three of them went over the ledger. Jack learned that food and drink could be a very good business indeed. Jack repaid his generous salary by increasing traffic through the tavern. The bulging nightly crowds proved Jack Hannon's ability to befriend any man willing. If a working man needed money to sustain him through hard times, he looked no farther than the bartender at O'Shea's.

Tom O'Shea had admonished Jack for loaning out his first two weeks' pay. "You'll never see that money again, Jack! At least charge them interest."

"That would be taking advantage of another's misfortune, Mr. O'Shea. They will pay back the money."

And they always did.

O'Shea's tavern and restaurant catered to working men. They came from the stockyards and packing houses of the west bottoms, from the railroads, cattle trails, and riverboats. Assured of good food and drink at a fair price, O'Shea's clientele was loyal and growing. Jack Hannon's reputation was also growing.

* * *

The first hot sun of 1870 burned away memories of the frozen river and the chill of icy spring rains. On April 7 the city seemed to awaken and stand erect, aware that the assault from Arctic winds was over. The townspeople were out in droves celebrating the warm weather.

Kevin Donavan sat at a table in O'Shea's tavern. Two young women who frequented the tavern sat with him.

Wanting to escape the crowd in the tavern, Jack stepped outside for a breath of fresh air. It was good to feel the warmth of spring once again. A mob of men burst out of an adjoining tavern and headed in his direction. One of the men spotted Jack on the boardwalk. "Jack Hannon!" He led a burly man with a handlebar mustache over to Jack. "Jack, I would like for you to meet the next heavyweight champion of the world, Otto Sollenburg."

Jack's face broke into a grin. "I must say this is a pleasure, sir." He shook the German's hand. "Would you honor our establishment by having a drink on the house?"

Otto accepted and Jack led the way into the tavern, where the German fighter enjoyed drinks and accolades from those around him. Otto turned away from the bar, a beer mug to his lips. He spotted Donavan snuggled up at a table with the two girls and immediately pushed his way through the crowd, stopping at Donavan's table. "These ladies I would like to meet," he said. Kevin had been nurturing the girls for the past few hours and was in his final summation of bedroom delights. He resented the interruption, but tried to ignore the burly German.

"These ladies I would like to meet," Otto said again.

"Sorry, they're already taken," Kevin replied.

The smile vanished from the fighter's face. "You will drink with me, yes?" He looked at the girls.

They eyed him nervously. "No thanks. We're with him."

The fighter flinched as if from a punch.

The tavern had quieted. Everyone was listening to the exchange. Otto Sollenburg realized his honor was at stake. "But you must drink with me," Otto said. "My name is . . ."

"It doesn't matter who you are," Kevin interrupted. "I am the King of the Levee."

"And that means what?" The German asked.

"It means, my friend, that when the good Lord put all that muscle between your ears, he compensated by putting it between my legs."

The tavern roared with laughter.

"You are a little Mick bastard!" Otto reached for Kevin.

Outraged at the slur on his ancestry, Kevin unleashed a looping right. It hit the fighter above the eye. Otto reacted as if stung by a fly; his massive arm came back to deliver a blow, but Jack grabbed him from behind.

"There will be no fighting in this tavern! You should be ashamed of yourself, Kevin Donavan."

"He called me a Mick bastard."

"In the heat of anger. Both of you apologize and be done with it."

The fighter pulled away from Jack. "A gentlemen he is not if he comes from Ireland," Otto said.

Jack's eyes widened in indignation. "You could say that as you're having a free drink in the house of O'Shea?"

"You're goddamn right!"

Jack took off his apron. "Mr. Sollenburg, if you will be so kind as to step into the street."

Jack and the German fighter were swept outside by the force of the crowd.

"Did he say Sollenburg?" Kevin asked a bystander.

"That's right. Otto Sollenburg, the heavyweight contender."

Kevin whistled softly. He reached for his holy grail of pen and paper and rushed out to the street. He heard Connie O'Shea yelling at her husband to stop the fight. Tom O'Shea pretended not to hear as he rushed outside to watch.

At twenty one, Jack was five years younger than the German. They were perfectly matched in size and weight, but Otto Sollenburg had the advantage of experience. "You can't do this, Otto!" The fighter's banty rooster of a manager screamed. He hopped around the circle that was forming. "We fight for the championship of the world in two weeks!"

"Out of my way!" The fighter pushed his manager into the crowd. He circled Jack slowly as the mob of men shouted for action. Otto kept moving, studying the Irishman. Suddenly he feinted with a right, landing a solid left jab to Jack's nose. Jack's head snapped back. Otto made the move again. Blood poured from Jack's nose.

"Watch the left!" Kevin yelled to Jack.

Stunned and partially blinded with pain, Jack watched the German's left. With a fluid motion Otto sent a right cross above Jack's guard into the jaw, and Jack went sprawling into the crowd. He got up warily and moved back into the circle.

The German faked a combination. He landed another right cross to the jaw. The punch buckled the Irishman's legs. Jack shook his head. He moved in again. The German faked a right cross and landed a short left jab to the solar plexus. Jack went back into the crowd, sucking for air as he fell to his knees.

Kevin leaned over him, writing frantically.

Jack finally got air into his lungs. "What are you doing Donavan?"

"I'm covering the fight."

"Covering the fight?" Jack was outraged. "I'm getting killed and you're covering the fight?"

"You're doing fine, Jack. Just watch out for his left and his right."

Jack stumbled back toward the German. He was rewarded with a left to the stomach and a chopping right fist to the kidney. The punches set him up for a left-right combination to the jaw, sending him back into the crowd.

Jack's face was swollen and battered. Blood continued to flow from his nose. No match for the German, his only hope was to land a lucky punch. Noticing that the German dropped his guard and moved to the left whenever he threw a right cross, Jack dropped his left guard and moved in to test his theory. The German hit him with a right cross, then moved to the left. Jack's eyes were swelling shut. To set up the German fighter he took several more left jabs to the face. Then he dropped his left guard and braced his right leg.

The German took the bait. He threw the right cross. Jack ducked. Aiming a foot to the left where he thought the German would be, he put all his weight behind a straight right. Otto walked into the punch. It landed with the sickening thud of a stockyard sledgehammer. The German went down on his back. The crowd roared.

Stunned, Otto Sollenburg rose to his feet. He shook his head trying to figure out what had happened. His manager and handlers stepped between the fighters.

Otto was furious. He charged at Jack, but his entourage held him back. "That's all, gentlemen! It was a good fight but it's over." Otto's manager and handlers hustled the German away through the crowd.

Jack was never so glad to see a man leave. Kevin and Tom O'Shea helped him into the tavern. Harry the bartender had to lend a hand to get him up the stairs to his room. Connie walked solemnly behind. She carried a pan of water, salve, and bandages. They laid Jack on the bed and Connie went to work.

"You could have been killed!" She admonished him.

From far away Jack could hear O'Shea and Kevin reliving the fight. It was the last thing he remembered.

When he awoke the next day, the early afternoon sun was shining through the window. Racked by the soreness in his body, he rose to a sitting position. The face staring back in the mirror made him grimace.

He dressed slowly, then went downstairs to get some breakfast. The crowd in the bar rose as one and gave him a standing ovation. Jack couldn't understand why a soundly beaten man would be reaping applause. He nodded in embarrassment and walked through to the kitchen.

"Good morning, Jack!" Tom O'Shea led him to a table. The cook and waitress eyed him respectfully. His favorite breakfast was in front of him in minutes. Tom O'Shea sat down next to him.

"Have you seen the morning paper, Jack?"

"No," Jack answered through swollen lips.

Tom laid it on the table in front of him. In bold type at the bottom of the front page the headline read: "Local Bartender Decks Future Champ."

Jack put down his fork. He started reading the article.

*Last night in our fair city the future heavyweight champion of the world was given a lesson in the gentlemanly art of boxing.*

*Jack Hannon, bartender at O'Shea's Tavern, invited heavyweight contender Otto Sollenburg out into Delaware Street. By lantern light the action was fast and furious as each of the combatants sparred for the advantage.*

*Blow after crushing blow was landed as each man probed for a weakness. After thirty minutes of combat under the stars, Hannon lured the heavyweight contender into a mistake and decked the German with a straight right hand.*

*To avoid further embarrassment, Sollenburg's manager hustled his fighter away into the night.*

"There's a picture for you. The champion reading of his exploits." Kevin stood in the doorway.

Jack threw down the paper. "Kevin Donavan, never have I read such a slanted piece of journalism. He beat me to a pulp. I landed one lucky punch. If his manager hadn't hustled him away, I would be a dead man."

Kevin walked over to the table. He grabbed a piece of bacon off Jack's plate. "A man in the heat of combat has a narrow view of the battle. It takes a reporter of my talents to sort out the drama and present it to the public."

"This article is not true!" Jack protested. "I can hardly wait for Otto Sollenburg to read this and come back for revenge."

"He boarded a steamboat this morning for Saint Louis."

"Before the paper came out, I assume?"

Kevin smiled.

"And what about the men who were watching this exercise in futility called a fight?"

"The fight will reside in the annals of Kansas City sports history the way I described it," Kevin said confidently.

In the weeks ahead, despite Jack's protests, Kevin proved himself right. Even those who witnessed the fight somehow convinced themselves to believe the newspaper account. For what reason, Jack hadn't the slightest idea.

Two weeks later, when Otto Sollenburg won the heavyweight championship of the world, Jack Hannon was on his way to becoming a Kansas City legend.

* * *

On a hot August night in the year 1872, Tom and Connie O'Shea called Jack into their office. "Have a seat, Jack." Tom had a look of serenity about him.

"What are you two plotting?" Jack asked.

The O'Sheas laughed.

"We have a favor to ask of you concerning the business."

"All you have to do is say it."

"Connie and I have done quite well in the tavern business," Tom said slowly. "We'd like to retire with some good years ahead of us."

"And you deserve to," Jack said. "I'll be glad to manage the place for you if that's your concern."

"No. It wouldn't work," Connie said. "If Tom owns the business he would never relax. We have to separate ourselves from O'Shea's tavern."

"Are you selling out?" Jack asked, surprised.

"Not exactly," Connie replied. She paused. "We would like for you to have the tavern."

"That is very kind of you, Connie, but I'm afraid that my savings would not dent the purchase price," Jack said quickly.

Tom laughed. "That's because you have it all loaned out."

"You have been like a son to us, Jack," Connie continued. "We have all the money we need. Tom and I want to give you the tavern."

"Give it to me?" Jack was stunned. "You're not serious?"

"Serious we are, Jack. We already have a nice home picked out in McGee's Addition."

"I'm flattered, but I cannot accept," Jack said.

"I told you this would happen, Tom." Connie folded her arms over her chest. "He is going to let that damn Irish pride stand in the way of our retirement."

"It would mean a lot to us Jack," Tom pleaded.

"You could sell this tavern for thousands," Jack said.

"Yes, Jack, but you would take care of O'Shea's tavern. That means more to us than money."

Jack studied the couple as he pondered. "There is only one way that I will accept your offer," he said finally.

"Let's have it," Tom said.

"I own the business. We split the profits fifty-fifty for the first five years. You get twenty-five percent for the next five. At the end of ten years the business becomes mine."

Tom looked at Connie. She nodded. Tom held out his hand. "It's a fair deal."

"There is one more thing," Jack continued. "The name O'Shea is respected for quality and service. You will have to grant me the continued use of it."

Tom O'Shea smiled. "You're a good man, Jack Hannon." They shook hands.

* * *

The celebration spilled out of the tavern into the street. Jack had invited half the town. He sat at the head table with the O'Sheas, Kevin Donavan, Red Farrel, and Adam Quint. The four men had become the best of friends. Jack had never forgotten the kind treatment afforded he and Kevin their first day in the city. Adam and Red were responsible for landing Kevin the job he had always wanted, so Jack would be forever in their debt. Adam and Kevin had also formed a friendship from their work at the newspaper. Adam found that beneath the surface of Kevin Donavan there was a man who took his newspaper work as seriously as Adam Quint did. Every Friday evening the two of them discussed the week's events over cold beers at O'Shea's.

Red liked to keep in touch with Adam, so he would ride in from the ranch to join them. When Jack discovered that Red was also an orphan, the bond between the four men was sealed. They all enjoyed a game of poker, so Jack moved the meeting into his back room office at O'Shea's.

They were as different as four men could be. Adam Quint was articulate and well educated. He combined his school-teaching duties with a part-time writing job at the *Kansas City Times*.

Kevin Donavan was a womanizer, a practical joker, and one of the best reporters in the city.

Jack Hannon was tavern owner, gambler, and brawler — a man who would do anything for a friend.

Red Farrel was quiet and introspective — a man who had seen much and was struggling to sort it all out. He was the best judge of horses in the territory.

Jack stood at the table.

"Quiet, please!" he shouted above the noise. The din subsided.

"I would like to propose a toast." he held up his beer mug. "To Tom and Connie O'Shea: My thanks for taking a penniless orphan off the street and making him one of their own. A finer couple never lived." Cheers resounded through the tavern. "May they have a long and happy retirement!" Toasts were made to the O'Sheas throughout the evening. The party broke up in the early hours and the O'Sheas were escorted to their new home in McGee's Addition.

Afterwards, Jack trudged through Market Square with his three friends. "Congratulations are in order," Adam said. "You have worked hard for this opportunity, Jack. If you will all be my guests tomorrow night, we will take in a play at the Coates Opera House and then have dinner at Gastone's Restaurant."

"That's a ways up town for the likes of us," Jack said.

Adam laughed. "You'll accept?"

"Of course we will, Adam," Jack replied.

* * *

Melissa Graham made a final stroke through her hair. She laid aside the silver-handled brush and surveyed her image in the mirror. Soft violet eyes stared back at her. She adjusted the coal black hair gathering at her shoulders.

Her cousin Sarah entered the room. "Melissa, you look beautiful."

"Thank you, Sarah. I need a boost of confidence to begin the evening."

"If Melissa Graham has self doubts, that bodes well for the rest of us."

Melissa laughed. "If you keep complimenting me you're going to have a permanent house guest on your hands."

"John Keeney would love that. He wouldn't have to drive his buckboard thirty miles to call on you. Has he proposed yet?"

"Oh, Sarah!"

"Well, has he?"

"Yes. Every month since last February."

Sarah let out a sigh of frustration. "John owns the most successful brick and lumberyard in the city, Melissa. He's handsome, well educated, and obviously in love with you. What are you waiting for?"

"Heart," Melissa answered.

"Heart?"

"Yes, the little muscle that goes pitter patter. It hasn't spoken to me yet."

"You don't love him?"

"I'm not sure."

"What if someone steals him away while you're making up your mind?"

Sarah teased.

"Then my destiny will be to linger on as your old-maid cousin."

Melissa's pale blue dress of grenadine twirled as she got up from the dressing table. White ruffles lined the cut of the dress across her shoulders. They matched the flowers caught in the ruffles at the bottom of the fluffy skirt.

Sarah's eyes widened at the knock on the downstairs door.

"They're here!" She pushed frantically at her hair.

"How do I look?"

"Lovely."

"How can you be so calm, Melissa?"

"You should come out to the ranch more often, Sarah. Living with horses and cows has a quieting effect."

The sound of Sarah's mother greeting the suitors drifted up the stairs. Sarah gave one last glance at the mirror. "It's time for our grand entrance."

"Shall I follow you or play the trumpet?" Melissa asked.

Sarah laughed, moving out the door. Melissa lifted her skirt off the floor and followed Sarah down the stairs.

* * *

The carriage crept slowly down the hill. Last rays from the evening sun glistened off the horses' flanks.

Lost in thought, Melissa half listened to the chatter going on around her.

A steamboat docking at the levee let loose an answering whistle to a train speeding across the Hannibal Bridge.

"You're rather pensive this evening, Melissa."

Melissa glanced at her escort. At thirty-three, John Keeney was ten years her senior. A slight graying at the temples gave a distinguished look to his youthful appearance. A string tie against his white lace shirt matched his tan jacket and top hat.

"I'm sorry, John. It's been a while since my last visit to the city. I can't believe the expansion."

"The city's growing, alright. Completion of the bridge kicked off the building boom. The smart money is going into real estate. Would you like to live in the city, Melissa?"

"I'm not sure Mother or I could leave the ranch, John."

"Kersey Coates is building some fine homes up on the hill."

"Yes. I saw them as we passed."

She glanced back at Sarah. Her cousin gave her a conspiratorial wink.

As the carriage made the turn onto Broadway, a shot was fired. John steadied the horses. A gang of rowdies rode down Broadway firing into the air, showing off in front of the crowd entering the opera house. John kept a wary eye on the ruffians as he guided the carriage along Broadway.

On their next run down the street, one of the men stopped his horse beside the carriage. Melissa flinched as spurs were driven into the horse. Blood dripped from the animal's flanks. The man laughed. He charged back up the street. The gang obviously had an early start on the bottle. On their next trip down the street, the man stopped. He spurred his horse again. The animal reared into the air. From out of the shadows of the boardwalk another man rushed into the street. He pulled the ruffian off the horse and into the middle of the street.

"This is one of my horses, Charlie!"

The man rose out of the dirt. He brushed himself off. "We were just having some fun, Red."

Red quieted the animal, inspecting the injury from the spurs. "We had a deal, Charlie. You failed to live up to it." Red removed the saddle from the horse and dropped it in the street. He reached into his pocket and took out some money. "Here's seventy dollars. Sixty you paid for the horse and ten for the bridle."

"What if I don't want to sell?"

"You got no choice."

Charlie's friends rode up and dismounted.

"Don't let him take your horse, Charlie."

Adam Quint, who had been watching from the sidewalk with Bonnie, stepped into the street. Jack and Kevin Donavan moved to follow but Adam motioned for them to stay. The two Irishmen watched as the mild-mannered schoolteacher walked over to Red's side.

"Why don't we give the horse back to the original owner, boys?" Adam said.

John Keeney tried to move the horses, but Melissa steadied his arm.

The men smiled at Adam.

"Now don't he look nice in his opera clothes," one of them said. Charlie, becoming more confident, laughed with his friends.

"Come on boys," Adam said. "You've had your fun. Let's quit this nonsense."

"Your friend here likes to poke his nose in other people's business. What's it to you, anyway?"

The man looked Adam up and down. He snickered. "You sure are the fancy dude."

"You may call me that, but I answer to Adam Quint."

"Adam Quint? The Adam Quint? You rode with . . ."

"That's right," Adam interrupted. "As did my friend here."

The man laughed nervously. "We were just having some fun, Mr. Quint."

The men backed away. They mounted their horses, Charlie mounted behind one of the riders. They rode off down the hill toward the levee.

Red breathed a sigh of relief. "Thanks, Adam."

Adam nodded. "Take care of your horse, Red. We'll meet you in the opera house."

Adam returned to his companions, apologizing to Bonnie.

Kevin was more than curious as to why the name of an unarmed schoolteacher would strike fear into a gang of young toughs.

With the handkerchief from his coat pocket, Red wiped down the flanks of the horse. He led the animal up the street toward the livery stable. His hands were sweating. It had been his first brush with violence since the war years. As he passed the opera house he glanced across the street and stopped suddenly. The horse, following close behind, nudged him in the back.

The angel face that had haunted his dreams for the last few years was watching him from in front of the opera house. Mesmerized, he led the horse across the street. He seemed locked into those violet eyes. He stopped next to the carriage.

Melissa flushed with embarrassment as he stared at her.

"It's you," he said.

"I beg your pardon?"

Red was transfixed by this apparition come to life. It was the same girl. He would never forget that face from the raid on Lawrence.

"You're very beautiful," he said.

Melissa flushed again.

"Now see here!" John Keeney stepped off the carriage.

"Sorry," Red apologized. "I didn't mean to be rude."

John appeared relieved at the apology.

"It was kind of you to stop the mistreatment of the horse," Melissa said. She was flustered by the young man, who continued to stare at her. "What did you mean by the man not living up to your agreement?"

"I have a horse ranch north of the river. When a man buys a horse from me he has to agree not to mistreat it. If he does, I have the right to buy it back."

"That's a unique business arrangement. How would you ever know?"

"They give me their word and I check on my horses wherever I go. The owners never know when I might show up."

Melissa smiled.

Red stepped closer. He took off his hat. "I'm Red Farrel."

"And I'm Melissa Graham."

"We had better go in, Melissa," John said, impatiently.

"Of course, John. It was nice meeting you, Mr. Farrel."

Red tipped his hat. "Miss Graham."

With Sarah at her side, Melissa entered the opera house. She walked up the stairs to the balcony. "You lost your composure, Miss Graham," Sarah whispered. Melissa raised her eyes at Sarah. They took their seats. Sarah scanned the opera house. "Isn't it beautiful, Melissa?"

"Yes, it is."

The Coates Opera House was said to be the finest such facility west of the Mississippi. A medieval scene was painted on a giant curtain hiding the stage, a beautiful backdrop against an auditorium carved in polished walnut. A square piano stood well out on the apron of the stage.

Sarah poked Melissa in the ribs. Down below, Red Farrel was following his companions into a row of seats in the mezzanine section.

A violinist entered, followed by a parade of dancers. After a brief performance a man walked onto the stage. He paid a glowing tribute to Kansas City's progress in general, and to Kersey Coate's vision in particular. An opera house on a muddy street in the middle of a cowtown was a risky venture at best.

The first half of Bulwar-Lytton's play, *Money*, was only a partial success, for the patrons seemed more interested in the shiny new opera house than in what was happening on stage.

At intermission the audience gathered downstairs for talk and refreshments before the curtain call for the second act.

"Sarah and I will be along in a moment, John," Melissa said.

Melissa grabbed Sarah by the arm. She led her over to where Red was standing with his friends.

"Excuse me, Mr. Farrel."

Red's cheeks flushed with pleasure as he bowed. "Miss Graham."

"My cousin, Sarah Davis," Melissa said. Sarah burned with embarrassment.

"Are you enjoying the play, Mr. Farrel?" Melissa asked.

"Yes. And you?"

"I live on a ranch out west of the city. I haven't convinced myself that I'm refined enough for the opera."

"That's refreshing, Miss Graham," Jack said, "but obviously untrue. However, we of the levee district harbor those same doubts."

Melissa smiled.

Jack glanced at Sarah. She was a much smaller woman than Melissa. The emeralds around her neck sparkled off snow white skin and accentuated the green of her eyes. Her hair was light brown and set in large curls at the top of her head.

Sarah realized Jack was staring at her. She met his gaze. Embarrassed, Jack looked away.

"Are you a cattle rancher, Miss Graham?" Red asked.

"Yes. Although we do raise a few horses. Are you familiar with the Morgan horse, Mr. Farrel?"

"Yes. Why?"

"We recently acquired two in a trade. I thought if you were ever out our way you might stop by and explain any difference in caring for the breed."

"I'd like that, Miss Graham."

"The ranch is located five miles west of Gardner."

Red looked into those violet eyes. "I'm sure I can find it, Miss Graham."

The final curtain call was announced.

"If you will excuse us," Melissa said. "It was nice meeting all of you." Melissa turned Sarah toward the balcony.

"You have more gall," Sarah hissed angrily.

Melissa smiled at her cousin. "I was just thinking of my horses, Sarah."

Sarah ran up the stairs in a huff.

* * *

After the opera, Red excused himself from the group. He headed north with the injured horse.

Adam insisted on taking Jack and Kevin to dinner.

At Gastone's restaurant they sipped their drinks, waiting for dinner to be served.

"You've been eyeing me all night, Kevin Donavan," Adam said. "Go ahead, ask."

"Sorry Adam. Always the reporter, you know. Why would the name of a schoolteacher back down a gang of young toughs?"

Adam finished his drink. "Off the record?"

Kevin nodded.

Adam told Kevin and Jack of his involvement in the border war, his meeting with Red Farrel, and the Civil War years.

"It's something I've put behind me. Red has tried, but I'm not sure how successfully. That brown stallion was a symbol of stability for him. I found him on the battlefield that day with his arms wrapped around the dead horse's neck. He was holding on to his last link with Texas and his youth. He's just beginning to get over those years. Most of us were fighting for a cause, but Red Farrel got caught up in all the horror of the war. It was a terrible price to pay just to be with his friends. The memories from the past are not pleasant. I'd like to keep them buried."

"I can certainly understand why," Kevin said as dinner was served.

* * *

At Westport, Red took the Santa Fe Trail to the southwest. This was his first ride into Kansas since the raid on Lawrence in 1863. Though it was a tranquil summer day, it gave him no pleasure. The sound of pounding hoofs and random gunshots seemed to echo out of the past.

He had made up his mind to tell Melissa about his part in the death of her father. He was still pondering how he would tell her when the Graham ranch came into view. The main house and barn rose out of the prairie as the memory of that night came into focus; clearer, sharper and not at all dulled by the passage of time.

Melissa walked outside onto the porch as Red rode up to the ranch house.

"Mr. Farrel. How nice you could come."

"Miss Graham." Red tipped his hat. As he dismounted he played the scene over again in his mind. Melissa standing on the porch, begging her father not to go. She was even more beautiful than he remembered. Melissa's black hair gathered neatly around her shoulders. Her lavender blouse matched the color of her eyes. Red could feel his heart pounding. He could barely speak. This was the woman he wanted. He had thought about her all during the war, but had never summoned enough courage to ride out and see her again. It was as if fate had placed her in his path. He planned on asking Melissa to dinner. But he had to be honest with her from the beginning about his part in the death of her father.

"Are you all right?" Melissa asked.

"Yes. Fine. Nice place you have here."

"Thank you." Melissa walked down the steps.

"What a beautiful horse!"

"I wanted you to see her. She's the only blue roan I have."

Melissa rubbed the mare's nose. "I would feel better if you would call me Red, Miss Graham."

"I'd like that, Red. Now, tell me how a man with brown hair acquired the name."

Red smiled. "A man named Jesse Farrel raised me. When I was a three-year-old youngster, he found me wanderin' lost in the Red River country. I guess he figured namin' me for the river was as good as anything else."

"Were you abandoned?"

"I don't know. Uncle Jesse seemed to think the Indians may have killed my parents, but it's only a guess."

"Where's your Uncle Jesse now?"

His eyes flickered with sadness. "After I left Texas I never saw him again. Where are those Morgan horses, Melissa?"

"Over here."

Red followed her into the barn. In jeans and riding boots, she looked as feminine as she had at the opera. "You seem to be at home here, Melissa."

"You're saying that I'm better suited to the barnyard than the opera house?"

Red flushed.

Melissa laughed. "Don't be embarrassed, Red. I'm sure you've figured out the Morgan horses are not the reason I asked you out here."

Flustered, Red walked over to the horses and started checking them over.

"What about the man you were with?" he asked. "Is it serious?"

She looked at him with those large violet eyes. "No," she answered.

Red smiled. "Your horses are in fine shape."

"Come inside the house, Red. I want you to meet my mother."

A hard life on the plains without a husband had taken its toll on Mrs. Graham. Though only in her fifties, she looked much older. Her brown hair and light complexion had been lost, in the transfer, to Melissa.

"I understand you raise horses, Red."

"Yes ma'am."

"My husband loved horses. He was killed during the border war. Did Melissa tell you?"

"No ma'am."

"I'll get some coffee, Mother." Melissa left the room.

"Melissa loved her father dearly. It was such a tragedy." Mrs. Graham stared out the window as if searching for visions of her departed husband.

Melissa returned with the coffee. "Careful, it's hot." She passed around the cups.

"I understand you met Melissa at the opera house."

"Yes ma'am."

"It's hard to believe that mudhole of a town is getting some culture. I remember when you had to wear hip boots to walk in the street."

Red laughed.

"Everyone thought Leavenworth would be the city of the future. I guess the Hannibal Bridge changed that."

"Yes ma'am. You have a nice place here. How do you manage to keep it up?"

"We have two full-time hands. When extra work has to be done there's always someone showing up to help out."

Red looked at Melissa. "I can understand why."

The women laughed.

Red stayed until late in the afternoon. After a tour of the ranch he said good-bye to Mrs. Graham. Melissa held the blue roan's bridle.

"Can I see you again?" Red asked.

"Of course. I'll be at my cousin Sarah's on Friday night. The address is 923 Penn Street."

"I'm already lookin forward to it, Melissa."

Red mounted his horse.

"Can I ask you something, Red?"

"Sure."

"The day we first met in front of the opera house, you said, 'It's you.' What did you mean?"

"Did I say that?"

"Yes."

He hesitated. "Sorry, I don't remember."

"I thought perhaps I reminded you of someone."

"No. I've never met anyone as beautiful as you."

Melissa smiled.

"I'll see you Friday night, Melissa." Red nudged the horse into a gallop. The war and everything connected with it was over. What would reviving it accomplish? Out on the open prairie he coaxed the blue roan into a run. Pounding hoofs purging unpleasant memories. The future was all that mattered, and it included Melissa Graham.

# 5

# MARY MCFARLAND

SEPTEMBER 17, 1872

"Donavan! Donavan!" Colonel Ellison, the squat, ill-tempered editor of the *Times,* walked down the hallway poking his head into each of the offices. He swore under his breath as he walked downstairs to the composing room.

"Donavan!"

Kevin slid off the desk of a lovely young secretary. He straightened his tie.

Colonel Ellison, chomping on a cigar, pulled Kevin into a vacant office.

"Could I ask you a question, Mr. Donavan?"

"Certainly."

"Do you think the people of this fair city are interested in your romantic pursuit of Miss Phillips?"

"Well . . ."

"Don't try my patience, Donavan."

"No sir."

"Do you think a holdup at the industrial exposition might interest them?"

"Yes sir."

"Then goddamn it! Get moving!"

Miss Phillips had her hand to her mouth in fright. As Donavan ran past, he gave her a wink.

The sunny September day was tainted by a stiff wind from the north. Outside the exposition building Kevin held on tightly to his notes. He listened to a nervous clerk recount the robbery. It was a familiar story. The city and surrounding area were fertile ground for bandits. The seeds of robbery and violence planted during the war years continued to grow. It was a way of life not easily terminated by the end of formal hostilities.

As he plodded back to the Times building, Kevin wondered at the sanity of people who still left their money lying around for outlaws to steal.

After filing the story, he made himself visible around the office for a few hours before sneaking downstairs. He stopped at Miss Phillips's desk.

"If he starts looking for me, tell him I'm doing a follow-up story on the robbery."

Miss Phillips gave him the thumbs-up sign as he went out the door.

He headed over to Christie's restaurant on West Sixth Street, a favorite hangout of elbow-bending journalists. As he walked along, his mind wandered between the imagined delights of Miss Phillips and the cold beer at Christie's. He had played the part of the understanding friend these past weeks. Miss Phillips had recently broken up with her fiancé.

Soon he would sample the charms of the beautiful young secretary.

Two reporters from the *Kansas City Journal* were at the bar. Kevin squeezed between them.

"Kevin lad! How are you?"

"Fine thanks. Bartender! A beer please."

"Any leads on who may have robbed the exposition, Kevin?"

"Take your pick, boys. The James gang, the Younger brothers, Charlie Pitts, Bill Chadwell. This town has the largest collection of gunmen and thieves in the civilized world."

"Did you say civilized?"

Kevin laughed. "Well, almost civilized."

One of the reporters shook his head in disgust.

"The law should start breaking up these gangs. They prowl like jackals outside the city, feeding whenever it strikes their fancy."

"The Marshall should ride out and bring them in," his friend agreed.

"There might be lawmen somewhere dumb enough to try that, but none of them live in Kansas City," Kevin said. "You can't fight everyone in the state of Missouri. The public still views these outlaws as heroes. It's a carryover from the war when the border gangs were the only protection a citizen had. Public outrage is the only thing that will bring the killing and robbing to a halt, and that isn't likely to happen anytime soon. Why are you two complaining? Reporters back east have to invent these stories. All we have to do is step outside and listen for gunshots."

"You're saying we should be thankful for crime?"

"Look, boys, I didn't make the world. I'm a reporter paid to chronicle events."

"And you would never think of twisting a story or adding a touch of sensationalism, hey, Donavan?"

Kevin took the last swig from his beer. He sat the empty on the bar.

"Can I help it if on occasion the world needs help to keep from being a dull place to live in?"

The two reporters laughed.

"Although I hate to leave good company, I'm off to O'Shea's for additional sustenance."

"Is Hannon still feeding you those free meals you're claiming on your expense account?"

"Gentlemen, how could you even entertain such a thought?" Kevin laughed as he went out the door.

* * *

Jack drove the rented buckboard slowly up Quality Hill.

Kevin sat next to him.

"I had no idea you were sweet on Miss Sarah Davis."

"You don't know everything about me, Kevin Donavan."

"Would you enlighten me on one point?"

"If I can."

"Why have I been dragged away from my evening beer to accompany you?"

"Moral support."

Kevin eyed the mansions as they drove along Penn Street. "Quality Hill may rise up in indignation and toss our Irish asses back down to the levee. Is it true that in the fall the leaves on the trees turn blue up here?"

Jack laughed. "Would you quit? I'm frightened enough as it is."

He guided the buggy around the turn on Ninth Street. He stopped the horses. An imposing red brick structure loomed above them.

Kevin's eyes traveled slowly up the walls of the mansion.

"Are you sure you want to go through with this?"

"I am." Jack straightened his tie.

Kevin jumped off the buggy. "You go ahead, Jack. I'm, going around to the back door with the rest of the Irish."

"Kevin, wait!"

Kevin quickly walked around the side of the house. He peered into the kitchen window. A maid was on her knees scrubbing the kitchen floor. He rapped on the back door. The maid wiped an arm across her brow as she rose to her feet. She was a wisp of a girl, not yet twenty. Brown strands of hair curled from beneath the cap she wore. As she opened the door, her hazel eyes searched the twilight.

Kevin stepped onto the porch.

She eyed him cautiously. "Beggin' your pardon, sir. Delivery time is over."

"I'm no deliveryman."

"Salesmen call on Mr. Davis at his office." Her voice was heavy with Irish brogue.

"I'm no salesman."

"Then why are you here?"

"You're right off the boat aren't you, lass?"

"And what business would that be of yours?"

"Might I have a cup of coffee?"

Kevin brushed past the surprised girl, into the kitchen. "My name's Kevin Donavan."

"Does that be given you the right to enter people's homes uninvited?"

"Pardon me, lass." Kevin made a slight bow. "I wrongly assumed we of Ireland are of one family." He turned to leave.

"Hold on there!" She went to the cupboard for a cup and poured hot coffee from the pot on the stove. "My name's Mary McFarland."

"I'm pleased to meet you, Mary."

"I heard the door a moment ago," she said. "Is your employer calling on Mr. Davis?"

"Sort of . . ."

Mary retrieved the scrubber from the bucket and dropped to her knees. She continued washing the floor.

"What are you doing, Mary?"

She brushed back a strand of hair that had fallen on her forehead. "President Grant is stopping by later on to escort me to the opera. I thought I might as well be scrubbing the floors until he arrives."

Kevin laughed.

"Your position as hired girl to the Davis family has not diminished your Irish spirit, Miss McFarland."

"Nor will it ever, Mr. Donavan."

"You may call me Kevin."

Mary eyed him coldly. She continued scrubbing.

"When did you arrive, Mary?"

"Last Saturday on the evening train."

"All the way from?"

"Kenmar in Kerry county."

"You came alone?"

She nodded.

"Don't you have a family?"

"Aye. My parents and eight brothers and sisters are back in Ireland."

"Why did you leave?"

"Because I . . . I . . ." Mary put her face in her hands. She began to sob.

"Oh damn!" Kevin said.

He put his coffee cup on the counter. He helped her off the floor.

Soapy water mixed with tears ran down her cheeks.

"Come on now. Don't cry." Mary laid her head on his shoulder. She cried harder. He stroked her shoulder until she gained her composure. Embarrassed, she pulled away from him, and wiped the tears from her eyes.

"You'll get used to it here, Mary. Have you seen any of the city yet?"

"Only the view from my room."

The outside door to the kitchen opened. An elderly man limped into the room. He stopped abruptly.

"I'm sorry, Mary. I didn't know you had company."

"It's all right, Carlos." Mary poured another cup of coffee. She handed it to the old man.

"Carlos is Mr. Davis's driver," Mary explained.

"I'm Kevin Donavan." They shook hands.

Carlos sipped his coffee thoughtfully. "Not Kevin Donavan of the *Times*?"

Kevin bowed. "The same."

"The story on the Hannon fight last year was a fine one."

"Thank you, Carlos."

"You're not a servant?" Mary asked, surprised. "You told me you were . . ."

"No, you assumed that I was."

"Of all the nerve! I may be fresh off the boat as you call it, but I'll not be made a fool of. If you're not a servant, than you'll be goin' to the front door and have coffee in the parlor."

"That's discrimination."

"Call it what you like." Mary grabbed a broom out of the corner.

"Okay, I'm going." Kevin went to the door.

"Do you have an evening off, Mary?"

"Are you writing an article on the hired girls of Quality Hill, Mr. Donavan?"

"She's off on Saturday evening, Mr. Donavan."

"Thanks, Carlos. It was nice meeting you. Good evening to you both."

* * *

Jack pulled at the stiff collar around his neck. A trickle of sweat ran down his back as he rapped the brass knocker on the door. No one answered. He rapped harder. Finally a butler came.

"May I help you, sir?"

"I would like to speak with Miss Sarah Davis. My name is Jack Hannon."

The butler stepped aside, motioning for Jack to enter, then escorted him into the parlor before he disappeared.

Jack looked around at the trap he had created for himself. The room was lavishly decorated in the renaissance style. Thick, draped curtains hung over the windows, blocking out the air and light. The furniture was stuffed to excess. A vase filled with wax flowers and peacock feathers sat on a round table that was draped to the floor with velvet cloth.

Miles Davis, Sarah's father, was a lawyer for several of the leading banking and investment firms. He had obviously done well over the years.

"Mr. Hannon?"

Jack rose quickly to his feet.

"I'm Helen Davis. Sarah's mother."

"It's a pleasure to meet you, ma'am."

Mrs. Davis was an attractive, youthful-looking woman.

"How may I help you, Mr. Hannon?"

"I've come to call on Sarah."

"Oh, how nice."

By the tone of her voice, Jack knew that it wasn't.

"Just a moment Mr. Hannon. I'll see if she's available."

"Thank you, ma'am."

Mrs. Davis retreated from the room. Jack listened to her skirts rustle up the staircase.

He was growing more uncomfortable with each passing minute.

The sound of voices raised in anger filtered down the stairs.

"I will not!" A door slammed.

"Sarah! Sarah!"

Jack felt the heat of embarrassment creep into his face.

Mrs. Davis was composed as she entered the parlor.

"I'm sorry, Mr. Hannon. Sarah's not feeling well today."

Jack accepted the lie graciously.

"Please tell her for me that I hope she soon feels better."

"Thank you, Mr. Hannon. I will."

"Good evening, Mrs. Davis."

Kevin was waiting on the buckboard. "What happened?"

Jack clamored up beside him. The big Irishman remained silent. He stared straight ahead. "She wouldn't see me," he finally said.

"She refused?"

"Yes. Her mother said she was ill."

"Maybe she was."

"No, she wasn't."

Carlos came limping around the side of the house.

"I'll prove it to you." Kevin said. "Carlos!"

Carlos walked over to the buckboard. "Yes, Mr. Donavan?"

"When did you last see Miss Sarah Davis?"

"Just now. She's in the kitchen."

"Is she ill?"

"She never looked better in her life. Why?"

"Just curious. Thanks, Carlos."

He walked away, scratching his head.

"The blue-nose bitch," Kevin muttered.

"Don't say that. It was my mistake to come up here." Jack picked up the reins. He moved the horses ahead. They turned in the buckboard at the livery stable.

Kevin tried to cheer up Jack as they walked along Delaware Street to O'Shea's. "It wasn't meant to be, Jack. You're better off having it turn out this way."

Jack walked somberly along the street.

"You are going to meet people in this world who don't like you, Jack. You've never been able to accept that."

They entered O'Shea's.

"Two beers, Harry!" Kevin called.

"There isn't a man alive who doesn't feel the sting of rejection, Kevin." Harry handed over the beers.

Kevin followed Jack outside. They sat in chairs lined up along the boardwalk.

"Don't take it personally, Jack. You were out of your element on Quality Hill. No one commands more respect in the bottoms and on the levee than Jack Hannon. Once a year those bluebloods roll some money down the hill and think they're doing their bit for mankind."

"There are some fine people up on the hill, Kevin."

"Is this a private conversation?" Adam Quint stopped on the boardwalk.

"Adam! Sit down." Kevin pulled over a chair.

"From the looks of you two, I thought my black coat and tie might be in order."

Kevin laughed. "It's not quite that bad." He recounted the afternoon's events.

Harry brought Adam a cold beer. He sipped it thoughtfully. "It's happened to me as well," he said.

The two Irishmen looked at him questioningly.

"A young lady from Independence," Adam explained. "Her family has roots deep in the catfish aristocracy. You were led to the parlor no doubt?"

Jack nodded.

"The curse of the nineteenth century," Adam continued. "A depository where a young man is left to be inspected. If for some reason he doesn't measure up, the belle of the family creates an excuse and ushers it downstairs with a chambermaid.

"The man is left to suffer this humiliation in front of everyone. Society dictates that we play this game politely and respectfully. Our friend Kevin has the right idea. A penchant for chamber maids and dance hall girls keep him out of these sticky situations."

"What you're saying, Adam, is that I should have stayed on the levee in the first place."

"Not at all, Jack. You made the effort. Just keep in mind that you had no control over the results."

"In any case, I've decided not to venture up on Quality Hill again," Jack said.

Adam looked up beyond Delaware Street. High on the bluffs, gas lights flickered in the dusk.

"I have a hunch, Jack Hannon, that one day Quality Hill may come down to you."

* * *

"Mary! Mary!"

Mary put down the sheet she was folding. She rushed down the stairs.

"Is something the matter, Mrs. Davis?"

"There's a telegram for you. You'll have to sign for it."

"For me? Who would be sendin' me a telegram?"

"I'm sure I wouldn't know."

Mary walked out on the porch. She signed the messenger's pad.

The messenger tipped his hat. "Thank you, Miss."

She carried the telegram past the curious eyes of Mrs. Davis. Carlos sat at the kitchen table drinking coffee. Mary held the telegram up to the light of the window. "What is it, Mary?" he asked.

"A telegram."

"Well, open it!"

She held the foreign object by thumb and forefinger. "It might be bad news."

"You'll have to open it some time."

"Oh, all right."

She delicately tore the side of the envelope and pulled out the telegram. Her eyes scanned the words. She looked up at Carlos and then read the telegram again. "He's daft!" she finally said.

"What does it say, for heaven's sake?"

"Will pick you up at seven p.m. Saturday night . . . stop . . . for dinner and the opera . . . stop . . . Will make scene in front of Davis house if refused . . . stop . . . You know I'll do it."

"Who's it from?"

"It's signed, Ulysses S. Grant."

"The president?"

"Nae. It's that newspaper reporter."

"Donavan?"

"Aye."

Carlos laughed.

"Would he make a scene, Carlos?"

"I wouldn't be surprised."

"It's blackmail. I should refuse."

"You won't," Carlos said.

"Why do you say that?"

"You like him too much."

Mary reddened.

"Well, don't you?"

Mary put the telegram back in the envelope. She stuffed it in her apron pocket.

"I haven't decided." She smiled slyly at Carlos. "Perhaps I should be goin' Saturday night to find out."

* * *

"Oh, Kevin, what a lovely evening it was," Mary sighed.

Kevin stopped the carriage in front of the Davis house.

"To have someone else do the cooking was a grand treat, and it was so thrilling when Adelina Patti sang 'Home Sweet Home'."

Kevin smiled.

"I'm glad you enjoyed yourself. Maybe now the city won't seem so foreign to you."

"Nae it won't. Thanks to you, I'm goin to quit feelin' sorry for myself and make a go of it."

"Good for you, Mary McFarland."

Kevin used the white collar of her dress for a guide in the moonlight. He leaned over and kissed her neck.

"Kevin, don't!"

Kevin put his arm around her. He pulled her close. He kissed her lips. "I've been wanting to kiss you all night."

She pulled out of his grasp and straightened her bonnet. "Kevin! Someone will see!"

He eyed the darkened mansion.

"No one's home."

"We have neighbors, you know."

Kevin helped her out of the carriage. They walked to the door. She held out her hand.

"Thank you, Kevin."

"Mary, if I could have but a cup of coffee before starting down the hill in the darkness. I'm not much of a horseman, you know."

She hesitated. "Oh, what's the harm. Come inside. I'll fix you a cup."

Kevin checked out the rooms as he followed her into the kitchen.

"Where's Carlos?"

"He sleeps above the livery across the street." Mary took off her bonnet. She put the coffee pot on the stove. Kevin looked around the kitchen. "The Davises have a beautiful home."

"Aye, they do." She agreed. "Sometimes when I'm here all alone I pretend it belongs to me. I fight hard not to be resentful when they come back."

"Mary McFarland, the queen of Quality Hill," Kevin said.

Mary laughed. She poured the coffee, handing Kevin a steaming cup.

He sipped the bitter liquid. He hated coffee.

She grabbed a dishcloth, nervously wiping the already spotless counter tops.

Kevin eyed her small waist and her firm breasts pushing against her dress. "Would you show me the rest of the house, Mary? Architecture is one of my hobbies."

"Aye, but let's be quick about it. We've been alone together long enough."

Half listening to her running commentary, Kevin followed her on a tour through the rooms. They ended up at the front door.

"That's about it, Kevin."

"I haven't seen where you sleep, Mary."

"Oh, I have but a small room off the kitchen. It's nothing to look at."

"May I see it?"

She hesitated.

"I can't say I've had the grand tour if you leave off a room, Mary McFarland."

"Oh, all right."

They walked through the kitchen and down a narrow hallway to the back of the house. She opened the door slowly, reluctant to share her private domain. Kevin peeked in over her shoulder. A brass bed took most of the space in the room. White curtains with blue flowers matched the blue and white comforter on the bed. A nightstand with an oil lantern sat next to the bed. A dressing table was tucked against the wall, and a gold rug on the hardwood floor completed the furnishings.

"It's a lovely room, Mary."

"The rug was in my room back home in Ireland," she said wistfully.

"The brass bed matches it nicely."

"Thank you, Kevin."

"Did you make the comforter yourself?" Kevin entered the room on the pretense of examining it.

"Nae. The Davises were kind enough to let me have it. Now you can say you had the grand tour, Mr. Donavan. It's time for you to be goin'."

Kevin closed the door. He leaned his back against it.

"You're a beautiful woman, Mary McFarland."

She felt the heat in her cheeks. She reached for the doorknob.

Kevin put his arms around her. She tried to avoid the kiss, but he held the back of her head. They were gliding back across the room. Her legs had no direction of their own. Somehow they were on the bed without interrupting the kiss. Mary pulled away. "Kevin, please stop!"

He kissed her neck and face. His hand started to explore beneath her dress.

"Kevin, please!" She tried to sit up. He pulled her back down on the bed. She could feel her resistance starting to ebb. Kevin was unfastening the front of her dress.

"Oh, Mary girl. It was meant to be. The two of us together like this."

She tried to push him away but her arms lacked the strength. She breathed hard against his neck, and tried to think. "Let me up, Kevin darlin'," she whispered. "I'll turn off the stove and get undressed."

"Oh Mary. Do you mean it?"

"Aye. Get undressed and lie on the rug."

"On the rug?"

"Aye. It has to be on the rug."

Kevin stood up. He slid out of his pants. Mary went to the kitchen. Kevin removed the rest of his clothes. In eager anticipation he lay down on the rug and waited.

Mary's footsteps sounded in the hallway.

"For God's sake, Mary! Hurry!"

She opened the door and threw a bucket of cold well water in the direction of Kevin's voice. The water hit him full force between the legs.

He screamed, raising a foot off the floor. In agony he managed to get to his feet. He started jumping up and down.

Mary came in. "And I thought you cared for me, Kevin Donavan! All you really wanted was to satisfy yourself!"

"I'll not be one of your levee dance-hall girls. If I were left with child and tossed into the street, what would you care?"

Kevin, half dressed, started limping for the front door. Mary followed close behind. She put her hand to her mouth to keep from laughing.

"Good night, Miss McFarland. Don't worry about me coming back. If the urge to venture onto Quality Hill ever strikes me again, I'll run down to the Missouri River, jump in, and quench it! Good night and good-bye!" Kevin slammed the door behind him.

Mary watched through the window as he limped down the steps and climbed on the buckboard. As she listened to the horse's hoofbeats fade down the hill, a terrible loneliness swept over her. She pictured the McFarland's whitewashed cottage tucked against rolling green hills under a deep blue Irish sky; and in turn she pictured the faces of her mother and father and each of her brothers and sisters. It was a ritual she practiced daily, afraid that if she missed a day she might not be able to remember what they looked like and they would be lost to her forever.

She sat down on the stairs, placed her elbows on her knees, and rested her face in the palm of her hands. Why had she been the oldest? Why had she had to leave? How tightly she had clung to her mother on the day of departure. "It will be a great adventure, Mary. America is the greatest land in the world."

For her mother's sake she had pretended to be excited. She knew that her parents could no longer afford to keep her.

She wiped a tear from her cheek, and remembered her words. "I'm going to stop feeling sorry for myself, Kevin."

She had finally found a friend after all these months and now she had lost him in one evening. She took a lace handkerchief from her sleeve and wiped her eyes. Still, she felt she had done the right thing tonight. She was a McFarland and the McFarlands were a resourceful clan.

She knew she was in love with Kevin Donavan. She would just have to find a way to get him back.

* * *

Kevin ignored the look from the desk clerk. He stormed upstairs to his room in the Coates House. He changed clothes, returned down stairs and headed for Delaware Street.

When he entered O'Shea's, Jack was behind the bar. "I do believe it's Mr. Donavan. Returned from a night on Quality Hill."

"Can't a man get a drink here without a lot of conversation?" Kevin muttered.

"Those aren't the words of a man fresh from conquest," Jack said.

"The night's young," Kevin replied as the men at the bar laughed.

"Tell us about your evening, Kevin lad."

He eyed Jack coldly as he sipped his beer. "Suffice it to say that if love were a two-strike game, you and I would both be out."

Jack threw back his head and laughed. "Was it painful, Kevin?"

"If you only knew how much."

Jack leaned over the bar. "Do you suppose we could find a couple of willing girls over at Bob Poteet's?"

"How easily you read my mind, Jack Hannon."

"Harry! Take over the bar!" Jack slipped out of his apron. "Come on, Kevin lad."

They left O'Shea's and walked through a deserted market square to main street. Music and laughter poured out of the saloons along the boardwalk. "Battle row" was warming up for the evening. Kevin put his arm out, pulling Jack to a halt. "What was that?"

**The Coates House**

Jack had heard the noise as well. They moved over close to an alley. A moan sounded in the darkness.

"This way!" Jack ducked into the alley. The sound was coming from some empty cartons stacked against a back door. They started throwing the cartons aside. A woman was propped against the building.

"Help me!"

"It's okay, Miss. Jack got down on one knee to examine her. "Strike a match, Kevin."

Kevin dug into his pocket. He struck a match on his shoe. He held it close to the woman. "My God! It's Sally!"

Sally's jaw was dislocated. One eye was swollen shut. Blood trickled from her lips and down her chin.

"Sally! It's Jack and Kevin. Can you hear me?"

She nodded.

"We've got to get her out of here and over to my place."

Sally moaned as Jack lifted her.

"Sorry, lass."

The big Irishman carried her back to Delaware Street. He hurried up the back stairs of O'Shea's.

"Kevin, go get Doc Meade."

Jack placed Sally gently on the bed. He went downstairs for some hot water. He was wiping blood from Sally's cheek when Doc Meade arrived. The doctor sat down on the bed.

"You boys go downstairs and get a beer. I'll call you when I'm finished."

Jack and Kevin went down to the bar. "Who could have done such a thing?" Jack asked, sipping his beer.

"Probably one of Curt Widell's men," Kevin speculated.

"For what reason?"

"Rumor has it that Curt is trying to organize the working ladies of the city. He offers them protection and cuts himself in on part of their earnings. If they refuse to cooperate, they meet with an accident."

"Sally?" Jack asked.

"I would say so, yes. Curt's had some large gambling losses at the House of Lords. A beating like this will warn the girls to keep the money flowing in his direction."

Doc Meade came down the stairs and motioned them over.

"She's had a severe beating. There's no concussion. I've taped her ribs and given her a sedative. She should be all right in a few days. Funny thing, though."

"What's that, Doc?"

"She had whip marks on her back. I couldn't get her to say who was responsible."

"Thanks, Doc."

Jack squeezed some money into the old man's hand.

"No, just take it off my tab, Hannon."

"You no longer have a tab. Goodnight, Doc."

"It was Curt, all right," Donavan said. "Have you seen those two French trappers that follow him everywhere?"

Jack nodded.

The one named LaBue is the fastest man on the river with a knife. The other one, Marceaux, carries a small riding whip."

Kevin followed Jack up the stairs. Sally was asleep. Jack tucked the covers around her shoulders. "Kevin, let's take a trip over to the House of Lords."

"You can't do it, Jack. You're no match for that bunch. We'll go over to market square and get the marshall."

"We have no proof, Kevin." Jack marched resolutely down the stairs and out of the saloon.

Kevin followed, arguing his case as they walked along the street.

Jack paid no attention. He walked through the swinging doors at the House of Lords. Kevin followed him to the bar.

The bartender came over.

"Good evening, Jack. So you've finally decided to drink in a decent establishment."

"Hello, Lou."

Jack scanned the room over the heads of the crowd. The patrons clapped along as a line of chorus girls in bright red dresses danced across the stage. The roulette wheel off to the side whirred along with the piano music.

Jack spotted Curt and the two Frenchmen back in the corner at a faro table.

"Lou!"

"Yeah, Jack?"

"Give me the biggest pitcher of beer in the house."

"Gonna tie one on, huh?"

The bartender grabbed a giant container from a lower shelf. "I keep this pitcher for smart ass trail drivers who ask for a Texas-size beer."

It took Lou several minutes to fill the two-gallon container. Jack grabbed the pitcher in his massive hands. He headed for Curt and the two Frenchmen. The crowd stepped aside, laughing and pointing at the pitcher. On his way to the table, Jack sized up the situation. LoBue sat on Curt's right. He was already watching Jack's approach. Marceux sat on Curt's left, watching the cards fall.

Jack bent over and whispered to the dealer. The man got up from his chair and scurried out of the way.

The two Frenchmen, instantly alert, pushed their chairs back, ready to spring.

Curt Widell leaned back, secure in his bodyguard.

"I don't believe I've had the pleasure, sir."

"I'm a friend of Sally's. She said I should buy you a beer."

Curt's eyes flicked back and forth at the Frenchmen.

Jack held the pitcher of beer over his head. He dropped it into the middle of the table. As the pitcher exploded, LaBue sprang from the chair, knife in hand. Anticipating the move, Jack blocked the thrust with the empty chair. He brought the chair down full force on LaBue's right shoulder. The Frenchman screamed in pain as his collarbone snapped.

Marceux's whip caught Jack on the side of the face. Warm blood flowed down his neck. Kevin hit Marceux above the eye with a straight right. Stunned, Marceux pulled the whip back to strike Kevin. Jack grabbed Marceux by the wrist. He pulled him around the table. Jack pushed the Frenchman's arm behind his back. He pushed upward until the bone snapped. Marceux's scream was muffled as Jack pushed him face first into the faro table. Marceux's nose burst in a spray of blood.

Curt backed into a corner. The two Frenchmen lay on the floor moaning in pain. The piano music and roulette wheel had sputtered to a halt.

"Let's go, Curt!" Jack stepped aside.

"Where are you taking me?"

"A steamboat leaves for St. Louis in half an hour. You and your friends are going to be on it."

Curt nodded. The two Frenchmen staggered to their feet. They followed Curt out the door.

Jack and the crowd at the saloon escorted them down to the levee. Everyone was glad to be rid of the trio that had terrorized the district for months. They watched the steamboat pull away from the dock and move out into the channel.

With Kevin at his side, Jack walked back up Main Street to pay for damages at the House of Lords.

* * *

Jack carried a bowl of vegetable soup into the room.

"You're looking better today, Sally."

"With the care I'm receiving, I should be. Kevin told me about your run-in with Curt. I want to thank you for getting rid of that bunch."

"You're welcome."

"Although it was a noble deed it won't do much good," Sally said.

"What do you mean?"

"Our profession attracts every bully in town who's looking for an easy way to make a living."

"I've given the matter some thought. You'll be up and around tomorrow. I want you and Wilma to round up the working girls of the levee and have them meet me here at noon."

"Whatever you say, Jack. Why don't you get under the covers and let me thank you for your kindness?"

"You behave yourself. In your condition that's the last thing you should have on your mind."

Sally laughed. "You'll make someone a good husband, Jack Hannon."

Jack went to the door. "You get a good night's sleep. I'm kicking you out in the morning."

Sally smiled at him from beneath the covers.

* * *

Jack walked out of his kitchen office into the dining room. Twenty of the levee's working girls lounged around the tables. "Good afternoon, ladies."

They eyed him suspiciously.

"I asked you here today to make you a proposition."

"So what's new?" one of the girls asked.

Jack laughed with everyone else. "You're correct. There's never anything new in the world's oldest profession. I wish merely to make a business proposal. We're all aware of what happened to Sally the other night. It could happen to any of you, and often does. What you ladies need is a place of your own. Let the public come to you in a controlled atmosphere."

"Sounds great," another girl said. "I'll sell the family jewels and buy us a place up on Quality Hill."

Jack lit up a cigar amidst the laughter. "I recently bought the Missouri Hotel down the street. It has only twenty-five rooms and it needs a lot of work, but here's my proposal. Take it or leave it. I'll refurbish the hotel. I will also provide protection for every working girl. You retain eighty percent of everything you make."

"What's in it for you?" another girl asked.

"Figure it out for yourself," Jack said. "Twenty percent of twenty salaries is not a bad day's work. Sally and Wilma will be in charge of all phases of the operation. They answer only to me. So there is no misunderstanding, if you fail to live up to our agreement, you will never work in this town again. You're aware that I deal fairly with everyone. If you question my motives, then I suggest you turn down my offer. Take your time and discuss the proposal. I'll be in my office when you have your decision."

"What's to decide?" One of the old pros got up from her chair. "I've worked enough towns to know we won't get a better deal. I say we take it."

The other girls murmured agreement.

"Is anyone in the negative?" Jack asked. No one replied. "Good. We'll open the hotel for business November lst." Jack turned at the sound of the swinging doors.

Kevin walked into the saloon. "Well, what have we here? All the lovely ladies of the city gathered in one location?"

Jack turned back to the girls. "The first rule of the house is that Mr. Kevin Donavan is not to be entertained on busy nights."

"And why is that?" a new girl in town asked.

Jack pondered for a moment. "Having followed Donavan into a room at a St. Joseph sporting house, a trail driver was heard to remark that he would have enjoyed the ride through the valley more if his arms had brushed the trees."

The girls roared with laughter.

Kevin had a puzzled expression on his face.

"We have gone into business together," Jack explained.

"You mean . . ."

"Yes, that's just what I mean. Good day, ladies, and thank you for coming."

Kevin followed Jack back to the office.

"You have actually banned your best friend from the premises?"

"Only on busy nights."

"My constitutional rights have been violated."

"I would love to read that passage. And besides, we're only extremely busy on the weekend. If you can afford it, you'll have four days of merriment."

Kevin smiled at his friend. "You know, Jack, I think I can live with that."

But it was a hollow boast. Try as he might he could not escape the searching hazel eyes of Mary McFarland. He tried to surpress them with hard work at the newspaper, but to no avail. Alcohol would not make them go away. He even tried frequent liaisons with other women, but Mary was always watching and afterwards he would somehow feel guilty and ashamed. It was his own fault. If he had only had the good sense to treat her with some respect, he would not be in this predicament.

She was nothing like the other women in his life and yet he had tried to get her into bed. Now he was suffering the consequences. She had wounded his pride and he was too embarrassed to call on her again. But as he went about his daily life he was defenseless against her. She was always lurking somewhere in his thoughts. And when he finished his day and headed home to the Coates House, he always looked longingly at the gas lights flickering up on Quality Hill.

# 6

# Xmas Wagon

October 12, 1872

Melissa fastened the corset around her waist. She pulled one of the petticoats over her head.

"And now for the difficult part. The man who designed this should have to wear it."

"Here, let me help you." Sarah arranged the horseshoe-shaped bars that made up the frame of the bustle. They pulled the overskirt over the birdcage bars.

"The designer must have been an admirer of women's hindquarters to come up with this contraption."

"Melissa, please!"

"Do I shock you, Sarah?"

"Sometimes you do, yes."

"Then you had better sit down."

"What do you mean?"

"I'm not coming home tonight."

Sarah's mouth dropped open. "How could he even suggest such a thing?"

"He hasn't."

"What will I tell mother?"

Melissa smiled.

"I'm sure you will think of something. We can't have my good name dragged through the mud."

"Please be serious, Melissa. Surely you'll get married?"

"That is up to Mr. Red Farrel, my dear cousin."

"You've only know him for two months," Sarah protested.

"Yes, the happiest two months of my life. Oh, Sarah be pleased for me!" Melissa hugged her cousin.

Mrs. Davis entered the room.

"Mr. Farrel is downstairs, Melissa."

Melissa smoothed her dress, then started down the stairs.

"What time will you be home, Melissa?"

"Sarah will explain everything, Aunt Clara, good-bye."

* * *

Red and Melissa were doubled over with laughter.

They had finished lunch and were taking a ride on the horse railway. The mule pulling the car along Fourth Street had decided to take a break on company time. To the delight of his only two passengers, the driver had tried everything to get the mule moving.

Melissa dried her eyes with a handkerchief.

"Surely your experience with animals could help the young man," she said.

"I'm afraid I don't know much about the Missouri mule."

The driver walked back to the open car. "Any suggestions? I have to get this car back to the barn or I'm in trouble."

Melissa smiled at Red. "It looks like you're on the spot."

"Sit down and rest a spell, my good friend."

The driver, haggard from pulling on the mule, plopped down on the seat.

"We'll have the ornery fella movin' in no time." Red jumped off the car.

"My, but you sound confident," Melissa said.

"You will have to close your eyes, Miss Graham. I can't give away trade secrets."

Melissa covered her eyes. "You don't want me to see you kick the poor beast."

Red laughed. He walked in front of the rail car. The mule flicked its ears as it watched him approach.

Red reached into his pocket and pulled out a sugar cube. He held the sugar enticingly in front of the mule's nose and walked ahead on the tracks.

As the car lurched ahead, Melissa opened her eyes.

The driver cheered. He jumped off the car and ran ahead.

Red discreetly passed him two sugar cubes. He walked back to the car.

"How did you do it?" Melissa asked.

"You have to be firm with these beasts."

"You couldn't be firm with a four-legged creature if your life depended on it."

Red smiled knowingly.

Melissa prodded him all the way to the barn on Seventeenth Street before he finally revealed the truth.

They took the next car back down to the levee.

"You've never invited me to see your home, Red. Why?"

Red shrugged. "I didn't think you would be interested."

"Well, I am. I want to see where you live."

"Now?"

"If you don't mind."

"I'm not sure we can make it back before dark."

"You're looking for excuses. You've probably got a wife and six kids you haven't told me about."

Red laughed. "Do you always get your way?"

"Only with you."

Red drove the rented carriage north across the Hannibal Bridge. The late afternoon sun was fighting a losing battle against the chill from the river.

Melissa fastened the top button of her short coat. With each tug of wind the trees along the road released their leaves. The orange and yellow foliage swirled around the carriage.

Red looked off to the west where dark clouds were building on the horizon. “It looks like a storm’s comin’. Maybe Jim will have a fire goin’ when we get there.”

“Jim?”

“My blacksmith. He’s an old Negro that lives on the place.”

“Did you hire him?”

“No. He’s always been there. The owner gave him deed to a couple of acres. I don’t know what I would do without him.”

“Who did you buy the ranch from?” Melissa asked.

“It was given to me by a friend. He was killed durin the war.”

“I’m sorry. He must have thought a lot of you.”

The buckboard moved up the lane to the white frame house. Jim met them in the yard. Red jumped off the carriage, then helped Melissa to the ground.

“Jim, I want you to meet Melissa Graham.”

“Miss Graham.”

Melissa held out her hand. “Please call me Melissa, Jim.”

Jim smiled as he shook her hand. “Yes, Ma’am, I will. I’ll put the carriage in the barn, Mr. Red. If you don’t need me, I’ll run on home before the rain hits.”

“You go ahead, Jim. That settles it, Melissa. We’re goin’ to have a storm.”

“Is Jim always right?”

“Yep, always.”

Red followed her up the steps into the house.

Melissa surveyed the rooms. “I must say I’m surprised. The house is lovely.”

“Would you like coffee?”

“Yes, thank you.”

Red took her coat. She followed him into the kitchen. “Can I help?”

“Nope.” He pulled out a chair for her.

“Have you seen much of your friends?” she asked.

“We get together every other weekend.”

“You’re fond of them, aren’t you?”

“Yes, I am.”

“I heard about what happened to Mr. Hannon when he called on Sarah. I’m sorry.”

“Why should you apologize?”

“Because we’re cousins. Somehow I feel responsible. Sarah has visions of grandeur concerning her place in local society.”

“It was her loss. She would have had the time of her life with Jack Hannon.”

Red poured the hot coffee. “Let’s go in by the fire.”

Melissa sat down. Through the window Red watched the dark clouds gathering over the house.

To brighten the fading light he lit an oil lantern. "I'll have to rig some canvas over the carriage to get you back tonight."

"Sit down and relax." Melissa patted the couch.

He sat down beside her.

"Your bein' here adds much to this humble house, Miss Graham."

"Why, thank you, sir. Is that an invitation to stay?"

Red felt the color in his face.

"I've shocked you again." Melissa teased him with her eyes.

He laughed. "Not really. I've pictured you here like this many times. Sometimes dreams do come true."

"What a lovely thing to say. Behind that quiet exterior is a true romantic."

"Only where you're concerned, Melissa," He said seriously.

"What do you intend to do about it, Red?"

He took the coffee cup from her hand and sat it on the table. Their lips met as he embraced her. She pulled away from him. Her eyes searched his face.

"Will you marry me, Melissa?"

"Of course I will."

"You will?"

"Yes."

Red kept staring at her. He could not believe this was happening. The only woman he had ever dreamed of having was here at this moment consenting to be his wife. He was actually going to marry the most beautiful woman in the territory! It was almost beyond belief. His heart was pounding and his mouth was dry.

He kissed her again. "When?" he asked.

"Christmas Eve. I've always wanted to be married on Christmas Eve."

"Then Christmas Eve it will be."

"Oh Red, I'm so happy." She wrapped her arms around his neck. She nestled her head into his shoulder. "Hold me tight."

A sheet of rain struck the house. Thunder rolled across the prairie.

In the excitement of wedding plans, time slipped away. Red moved off the couch. He looked out the window. "I have to get you home. I'll bring the carriage around."

"One more cup of coffee?" she asked.

He reluctantly agreed and went into the kitchen.

"Do you have a mirror where I can freshen up?" Melissa called.

"In the back bedroom. Take a lantern so you don't fall."

Melissa found her way. She sat the lantern on the table at the side of the bed. She swore at the bustle as she worked her way out of the dress and petticoats. Finally she freed herself from the corset and removed her undergarments. She studied herself in the mirror. Satisfied, she pulled the pins from her hair and slipped into bed.

"Hurry up! Your coffee's getting cold!" Red called.

Melissa sat up in bed. The covers fell away from her breasts.

Red walked back through the house to find her. He entered the room.

"Would you hurry . . ."

The light from the lantern glowed off Melissa's long black hair. Her breasts rose and fell with the pounding in her chest.

"You're surely the most beautiful creature alive," he said.

Melissa held out her arms.

* * *

Kevin poked his head into Adam Quint's office. "Adam, I want you to meet someone."

A heavy-set young man in his early twenties followed Kevin into the office. He was in a checked suit and vest and carried a bowler hat in his hand.

"This is Elvin Brewer."

"Pleased to meet you, Mr. Brewer." Adam shook hands.

"Elvin's been sent here to do some articles on our fair city."

"Sent from where, Elvin?"

"*The New York Times.*"

"Well, Kevin, our reputation must be growing."

Elvin smiled.

"If I may be of any help to you Mr. Brewer, don't hesitate to ask."

"Then let me do so, Mr. Quint. I have interviews lined up with Marshalls Hickok and Earp. Is there any way I might meet with some of the local outlaws?"

"I'm afraid you're out of my league, Mr. Brewer. I teach school when I'm not working for the newspaper."

Elvin nodded. "Nice meeting you, Mr. Quint." Elvin went out the door looking for more interesting quarry.

"Watch your step, Adam," Kevin said. "Elvin will question you to death if he finds out about your past."

"He does seem rather aggressive," Adam answered. "I'll try to stay out of his way."

"Red is going to make the big announcement tonight, Kevin. Try not to be late."

"I'll be there, Adam. This is my chance to rub shoulders with Quality Hill's finest. Do you think it would be all right if I invited Elvin? The Colonel has made me responsible for him."

"Bring him along. I'm sure Red won't mind."

"Thanks, Adam."

* * *

At five o'clock Kevin pushed back from his desk.

"Let's call it a day, Elvin. We'll go back to the hotel and freshen up for the party tonight."

Elvin stuffed his notes in a desk drawer and followed Kevin down the stairs. Miss Phillips was busy at her desk. The rest of the office staff had left early for the holiday. "I need to speak to you for a moment, Kevin," she said.

He walked over to her desk.

"My fiancé and I have reconciled our differences."

"Congratulations, Elizabeth. He's a lucky man."

Her brown eyes stared at him invitingly.

"Elvin! Go on over to the hotel. I'll be along shortly."

"Okay, Donavan." Elvin went out the door.

Kevin sat down on the corner of her desk.

"You've been such a good friend, Kevin."

Kevin looked around the office. "Is everyone gone?"

She nodded. Kevin moved around the desk. He reached for her.

"Not here, Kevin!"

"Where?"

"The Colonel's office. No one would dare go in there."

Kevin followed her upstairs to the editor's office. In a frenzy he searched for a place to consummate the deed. When he had furnished the office, the Colonel had obviously not prepared for this eventuality.

Elizabeth led him over to the Colonel's desk. She raised her skirt and petticoats.

Kevin noticed her lack of undergarments. Elizabeth had planned well. He kissed her face and neck. He pulled down his trousers and positioned her on the edge of the desk.

"Oh, Kevin!"

With his face tucked between Elizabeth's neck and shoulder, Kevin failed to notice the office door open. When he finally looked up, he was staring into the eyes of the astonished editor of the *Times*."

"Oh God!" he said.

"I know, Kevin," Elizabeth whispered.

"Oh God!" Kevin said again.

"Oh Kevin, Kevin," She repeated.

Colonel Ellison, Southern gentlemen that he was, backed out of the room. He quietly closed the door.

Kevin pressed on, willing to accept his fate another day.

* * *

To accommodate the crowd, the announcement party was held at Gastone's restaurant.

Elvin Brewer took the last bite off a leg of roast chicken. "New York's finest cannot compare with this feast," he said.

Kevin laughed as Elvin leaned back in his chair and moaned. "Wait until Gastone serves his famous chocolate cream pie."

Elvin moaned again.

Melissa and Red sat at the head of the table with Mrs. Graham and the

Davis family. Red and Melissa held hands under the table. Red was not comfortable being the object of so much attention, but he would put up with anything to have Melissa for his bride. Melissa acted as if this kind of thing happened every day. She was calm and gracious and always had a smile on her face. Her charm and self control were evident. She put everyone around her at ease, and Red was even feeling more confident with Melissa at his side.

After dinner, Red rose from his chair. He stood before the gathering. Adam Quint banged his spoon on a champagne glass to quiet the guests.

"I'm not much of a speech maker," Red began. "I am the happiest man alive. The loveliest woman in the territory has consented to be my wife." Everyone applauded. "Of course this is no secret. I've already told everyone within one hundred miles." Red continued amidst the laughter. "The wedding will take place at two o'clock in the afternoon of Christmas Eve day. Melissa and I would like all of you to come."

Jack rose to his feet, champagne glass in hand. "A toast to the future Mr. and Mrs. Farrel! May they be as happy every day of their lives as they are tonight."

Toasts were drunk around the tables. When everyone had finished, Red thanked the gathering. "Melissa and I will be in the side parlor to greet each of you personally. The bar will be open until midnight."

"Let's go to the bar," Jack suggested. He followed Adam, Kevin, and Elvin Brewer to a table.

"I hear you're running for the City Council, Adam." Kevin said.

Adam nodded. "I'm running on the democratic ticket representing the fifth ward."

"God knows we need help in government in this town," Kevin said. Absolutely nothing get's done. The last political reporter for the *Times* died of boredom."

"That's because there's no direction at city hall," Adam replied. "We have a group of businessmen running the city in their spare time."

"Do you really think you can make a dent in that mass of mediocrity, Adam?" Kevin asked.

Adam laughed. "At the very least I can pound away and see what happens. What this town needs is a coalition of strong ward leaders to get things moving. The squalor in the north end and the west bottoms is disgraceful. Open sewers run in the streets. People are packed into tinder box apartment houses. Children run ragged in the streets, and no one seems to give a damn."

"You'll never win the battle against apathy, Adam."

"Maybe not. But I will have a clear conscience having tried. The irony of the situation is that the squalor is located in the most populated areas. If these people had a direction, they could control their own destiny. With a strong ward leader, they could control city government."

"If you're waiting for the Messiah to rise out of the Missouri River and lead these gandy dancers to the promised land, you're in for a long wait," Kevin said.

"What's a gandy dancer?" Elvin asked.

"It used to apply to railroad workers who jumped up and down on an iron bar to loosen rails," Jack explained. "Now it refers to derelicts or anyone down on their luck."

"And that includes most everyone in the north end and the west bottoms," Kevin said.

"You seem to be advocating improved civic conditions, Mr. Quint. Isn't the spirit of the west every man for himself?" Elvin asked.

"No," Adam answered. "Every man should work to improve the lot of others."

We've failed miserably in that department. If I'm elected, my first priority is to find other civic-minded men to run for government office. The north end and west bottoms will be my top priority."

"I've only been in town a week, Mr. Quint," Elvin said. "Not enough time to really get the pulse of the city. But I have found out one thing. I've conducted dozens of interviews in the north end and west bottoms. From what the people tell me, your Messiah has already arrived."

Adam looked at Elvin questioningly.

"He's sitting next to you, Mr. Quint."

Adam looked at Jack. "My God! It's so obvious. Why didn't I think of it?"

Jack put his hands up. "Don't look at me like that, Adam. I'm no politician."

"No one is until they decide to make a contribution. Think of the good you could do, Jack."

"You overestimate my standing in the community. Sure, I have a lot of friends in the river wards, but they want elected officials who know something about government."

"That's the last thing they want," Adam said. "A friend they can count on to represent them in government is what they want. You could win in a landslide."

Jack laughed. "Kevin's constituents would have a field day. I can see the headlines now. 'Gambling and Prostitution King Elected to City Council'."

"The average working man doesn't care what you do for a living, Jack. He cares about what you are."

"Sorry, Adam, but I disagree."

"Then let me prove it to you."

Jack sipped his drink. "How could you possibly?"

"My campaign staff tells me I don't stand a chance in the first ward. There's no way I can win. We've written off the district altogether. From O'Shea's tavern you take up my banner."

"What would I have to do?"

"Nothing more than to tell your friends you're voting for me and would appreciate their support."

"That's all?"

"No. If I carry the first ward, you run for city council in the next election."

Kevin laughed.

"Adam was destined to be a politician, Jack. He has you out campaigning, and running for office all in the same night."

Jack smiled. "I haven't quite figured out how I got talked into this, but here's what I'll do, Adam. I will be glad to support you in the first ward. You will be a good friend to the working man. If you win we will seriously discuss the latter proposal. Fair enough?"

Adam raised his glass. "To victory in the first ward."

Kevin grabbed Elvin's arm. "Excuse us, gentlemen, we're going to seek more frivolous conversation."

Elvin followed Kevin to the bar. "By the way, Donavan," he said. "As I was leaving the Times building I ran into Colonel Ellison. He said to tell 'Oh Kevin Kevin' to be in his office on Monday morning. What did he mean?"

"Never mind the Colonel, Elvin. The man has visions of acquiring a sense of humor."

* * *

It was midnight when the party ended.

On his way out the door, Jack stopped by the bar.

"We're going to continue the party at O'Shea's, Kevin. Don't forget to pay your respects to Red and Melissa."

"Yes, sir," Kevin saluted drunkenly. The rendezvous with Miss Phillips and enormous quantities of alcohol had not erased his visions of Mary McFarland. "We're going to lose one of the gang to the old marriage vows," he said. "No more Delaware Street for Red Farrel."

"Isn't he awfully young to be getting married?" Elvin asked. "He seems no more than a boy."

"A boy!" Kevin replied indignantly. "Let me tell you something about that *boy*. When he was fourteen he was burned out of his home by renegade Indians. At fifteen he was chased out of Texas for robbing a bank. On his way to Kansas City he was ambushed by Jennison's redlegs. At seventeen he rode with Quantrill on Lawrence; and at nineteen he was seriously wounded at the battle of Westport. Some boy!"

"You don't mean it?"

"I swear by all that I hold holy." Kevin put his arm drunkenly in the air. "Come on, Elvin. Let's pay our respects and then head for O'Shea's. Kevin slid off the bar stool. Elvin followed him into a room off the main dining area.

Red and Melissa sat on a sofa holding hands.

"You two look very contented. Congratulations to the happy couple."

"Thank you, Kevin."

"This is Elvin Brewer, fresh from the *New York Times*."

Red shook hands.

"Thank you both for the invitation tonight," Elvin said. "The dinner was marvelous."

"You're welcome," Melissa replied. "Won't you come to the wedding, Mr. Brewer?"

"You're very kind, Miss Graham, but I'm returning to New York at the end of the week."

"Have a safe journey back."

"Thank you."

"And you, Kevin?"

"I will be in the front row, Melissa."

She laughed. "That's right. You are family, aren't you?"

Kevin grinned.

"I might not see you again, Mr. Farrel," Elvin said. "May I be so bold as to ask you a few questions?"

"This isn't the time, Elvin." Kevin grabbed Elvin's arm.

"It's all right, Kevin," Red assured him. "But Melissa will have to answer most of your questions concerning the wedding."

"It's not about the wedding. I'm writing a series of articles on the shaping of the West. I want to know what it was like when you rode on Lawrence with William Quantrill."

Red's eyes bored into Elvin Brewer. He felt Melissa's hand turn cold. She stood up, confronting Elvin.

"That's not true! You've mistaken Red for someone else!"

"I'm sorry if I upset you, Miss Graham, but I believe my source of information is accurate."

"Tell him it's not true, Red!"

Red stared straight ahead, afraid to look at her.

"Tell him, Red!"

"It's true, Melissa. I rode with Quantrill."

Dazed, she sank onto the sofa. A look of understanding suddenly crossed her face. "The day we first met at the opera, you recognized me. You remembered that night at the ranch," she said.

"I should have told you." Red reached for her. She shied away from his touch.

"Won't you let me explain, Melissa?"

She rose to her feet.

"No explanation is needed, Mr. Farrel. I remember every detail of that night quite clearly." Red stood up. "There's more to it than you real—. . ."

Melissa hit him hard across the cheek with her open palm. "How could you do this? How could . . ." Melissa suppressed a sob. She ran from the room. Kevin and Elvin Brewer watched, mystified. Red picked up his hat. He walked to the door.

"For God's sake, Red! What happened?" Kevin asked.

Red stared at the floor. He rubbed the brim of his hat. "Melissa didn't know I rode with Quantrill. The night of the raid on Lawrence we murdered her father."

"Jesus," Kevin whispered.

Red walked out of the room.

* * *

Adam Quint tied his horse to the hitching post in front of the Graham house. He knocked on the door. Mrs. Graham answered.

"May I see Melissa, Mrs. Graham?"

"Come in, Mr. Quint."

"I'll remain outside if you'll be more comfortable."

"No. Come inside."

"Thank you."

Melissa stood beside the fireplace in the living room. Her eyes were red and puffy from a sleepless night.

"Yes, Mr. Quint?"

"I have something to say to both of you."

She gave him a look of contempt. "It won't change anything."

"Let him have his say, Melissa," Mrs. Graham said. "Go ahead, Mr. Quint."

"I want to explain Red's part in what happened that night. He was just a young boy and was as horrified over what happened as you were."

"Then why did he participate?" Melissa asked.

"Let me tell you the story from the beginning."

Adam recounted the years during the war, the hatred on both sides, Red's trip out of Texas, and the deaths of Hester and Jake. "The raid on Lawrence was in retaliation for years of suffering the people of Missouri had endured at the hands of Kansas border gangs. Innocent bystanders were killed on both sides. I'm certainly not condoning what happened that night. I am begging you to try to understand. Red spent that day in Lawrence helping people save their possessions. He was just a boy. It was the only time he rode with the gang before joining the Confederate Army. I feel responsible. I let him go with us that night. The war had an effect on Red. He started to put those years behind him after he met you, Melissa. Don't ruin his life over something he had no control over. He loves you dearly."

"And I loved my father, Mr. Quint. As a little girl I used to follow him everywhere. He was my hero and my friend, as well as my parent. He cared nothing about politics or the war. All he wanted in life was to farm and raise a family. Do you know what I remember most about that night?"

Adam stared at her.

"Horses running in the night. To this day I have a recurring nightmare of pounding hoofs and masked riders milling about in the darkness. My father screaming at me to get back inside. It was the only time he had ever spoken harshly to me. The next day they brought him back in a wagon. He was covered with a blanket. The void in my life has never been filled. No, Mr. Quint. I couldn't live with Red Farrel. Every time I looked at him I would remember that night, reminded that I married a man who murdered my father."

"But he didn't, Melissa."

"You were all as guilty as the man who pulled the trigger. My father was shot by cold-blooded murderers. You and Red Farrel included. I would be grateful if you would not soil my father's memory by remaining on the premises, Mr. Quint."

"Venting your hatred on me is justifiable, Melissa. Venting it on past actions of a young boy is not."

"Do you think this has been easy for me? Losing the only two men I've ever loved? Twice in the last ten years I've had my world shattered. I don't have the words to describe how miserable I feel."

"Then leave the past buried, Melissa. I'm afraid of what might become of Red if you call off the wedding."

"There won't be a wedding, Mr. Quint. How could I wake up next to a man who helped murder my father? Red couldn't live with that, either. I'm sorry. Please convey my feelings to Red. I don't want him harboring any false hopes of changing my mind."

Adam rose to his feet. "Is that your final word?"

Melissa nodded.

"Red's life for your father's?"

"He will get over it, Mr. Quint."

"No, I'm afraid he won't. I've witnessed many of life's tragedies. Few have saddened me as much as this. Good day, ladies."

* * *

Melissa tucked her head against the wind. Snow flurries fell to the ground. They blew across the road in front of the horse. She pulled up the collar on her sheepskin coat. With her hair tucked under her Stetson, she looked like any other trail hand on the way to town.

It was Christmas Eve, the day she would have been married. The Thanksgiving party was the last she had heard of Red Farrel. The emotion and turmoil of the last thirty days had taken it's toll. Dark patches were visible under her eyes.

She tugged lightly on the reins, holding the horse to a walk. On the outskirts of the city people waved as they darted along the streets toward home. No one was a stranger on Christmas Eve.

Candles on the evergreen trees flickered out at her as she rode along in the gathering dusk. She studied the Christmas mottos on the archway of the houses. They were made of stiff paper and arbor vitae. The warmth and gaiety of the homes made the wind seem all the colder.

She rode the horse down Broadway. At the end of the bluff near the river she turned west, into the bottoms.

She stopped the horse in front of a one-story brick building and dismounted. The sound of lumber buzzing through saws played in the background. She tied the horse to a hitching ring and went inside the office of the Keeney lumber and brick yard.

John Keeney sat working at his desk. He glanced up. "Have a seat. I'll be with you in a minute." He had just received a large order that had to be delivered the day after Christmas.

Melissa took off her Stetson. She shook out her hair. "Hello, John."

"My God! It's you, Melissa! How good it is to see you!" He grabbed a chair and motioned for her to sit down. "You look tired, Melissa."

She rubbed the warmth of the office into her cheeks. "Yes, I suppose I do. How have you been, John?"

"Other than worrying about you, I've been okay. I'm genuinely sorry about what happened, Melissa."

"Thank you, John. I know you mean it."

"You shouldn't be out on a night like this. If you wanted to see me, why didn't you send word?"

"I wanted it to be this way."

"What do you mean?"

"I have something to say." She paused, taking a deep breath. "If you still want me to be your wife, I'll accept your proposal."

John stared at her, speechless.

"You have every right to throw me out of here, John." He hesitated. "Perhaps you're trying to punish Red Farrel at my expense, Melissa."

"No. I may not be capable of loving anyone that deeply again, but I will promise you a lifetime of friendship and devotion."

He stared at the floor.

Melissa got up from the chair. "I won't make a fool of myself any longer." She turned to leave.

"I should probably throw you out of here," John said. "Somehow having you outweighs the stigma of my being your second choice."

Melissa turned and faced him. "Before you commit to anything, John, there's something you have to know."

He stared at her questioningly.

"I'm two months pregnant."

John moved around the desk. He embraced her. "Will next week at the Presbyterian church be soon enough?" he asked.

Melissa rested her head on his shoulder. "Yes, John. That will be fine."

## FROM ADAM QUINT'S JOURNAL — DECEMBER 15, 1872

*Will repercussions from the war never end?*

*Just when Red was beginning to put the past behind him and get on with life, this has to happen. He loves Melissa deeply and I wonder what will become of him. Melissa is not only one of the most beautiful women in the country, but one of the most stubborn. I'm sure she will not change her mind about calling off the wedding.*

*Red is a fighter, but I'm not sure he can handle this. So many war veterans cannot achieve any stability in their lives. They end up as outcasts or outlaws on the run. Red will have to fight hard not to join their ranks.*

*Kevin Donavan and I rode out yesterday to inform Red of Melissa's decision. Red had not shaved for several days and he looked like he had not slept much. His home had the unkempt look of someone who had lost interest.*

*Red thanked us, and said that he did not blame us for what had happened. He said he was going to catch up on his work during the fall and then burrow in for a long winter. I could tell he had been drinking. Red only drinks on social occasions, so I know this must be hard on him. I will have to keep a close watch on him in the months ahead.*

*No matter how painful, a man must live with his decisions. If I had only resisted joining Quantrill's guerillas, this would not have happened. I was blinded by revenge and now Red must suffer for it. To be held accountable for one's mistakes is simple justice. To have your friends held accountable for them is a sorrow.*

* * *

Jack Hannon sat alone in his office at O'Shea's restaurant. He had sent the staff home early to be with their families on Christmas Eve. Through the window he watched snowflakes drift gently down onto a deserted Delaware Street.

Jack was content with his life. O'Shea's restaurant was a profitable business, and he required little in the way of material goods. He had friends in all the west bottom and north end neighborhoods — loyal friends he could count on.

Since his failed attempt at courtship with Sarah Miles, he had shied away from romance. When he needed companionship he would take one of the north end working girls out to dinner. He always treated them with respect and made sure they were compatible before any deal was struck. After his experience with Sarah he was apprehensive in his relationships with the opposite sex. He often thought about Sarah, and it was a puzzle to him how he could have felt so attracted to her and she could have felt nothing in return. Romance was a difficult emotional experience. Look what it was doing to Red Farrel. Jack would not run from love, but neither would he seek it out. It was a lot less wearing to just lay your money down, grab your hat, and say goodnight.

On this Christmas Eve night he had a lot to be thankful for. America was a generous land. Kansas City and it's people had been good to him and Kevin. He wished there were some way he could pay something back.

He heard a knock at the delivery door. Tossing his ledger into an open drawer, he opened the door.

A man in his mid-forties stood rigid against the cold. He was dressed in tattered clothes and wore crusted work boots. Flecks of snow clung to his black hair, and streaks of gray traced through his frozen beard.

"Hello, Frank."

"Am I too late to make a delivery, Mr. Hannon?"

"Of course not. Come in."

"Michael!" Frank called.

A young boy of no more than six years jumped off the wagon. He ran up to the door.

"This is Michael, my nephew, Mr. Hannon."

"Hello Michael." The boy nodded.

"He don't speak much English, Mr. Hannon." Frank grabbed a side of beef off of the wagon. He threw it on his shoulder. Michael ran ahead to open the storage room door.

"When did you start delivering meat, Frank?"

"This week, Mr. Hannon. I needed work until the market opens in the spring."

Jack watched as Michael inconspicuously worked his way toward the warmth of the coal stove.

"You have a fine lad here, Frank. Where does he live?"

"He's staying with me. His mother and father are still in Italy."

"Will they be over?" Jack asked.

"No. My sister-in-law is too poor to keep him. His father's in jail."

"He made the trip over alone?"

"Yes. He's a tough one, Mr. Hannon. He's only six years old, but the older boys in the neighborhood cross the street when they see him coming."

Frank slipped the side of beef off his shoulder onto one of the hooks in the storage room.

"If things don't get better, I may have to put him in the orphanage," Frank said. "Another mouth to feed in the winter is more than I counted on."

Jack nodded. Frank Pacini was but one of hundreds of Italians crammed into the squalor of the north end, where they eked out a meager living toiling in the stockyards or setting up stalls in market square to sell their produce.

"Sign here, Mr. Hannon."

Jack scratched his initials on the bill.

"Come on, Michael!" Michael opened the palms of his hands to the warmth of the coal stove. He reluctantly followed his uncle to the door.

"How many stops do you have left, Frank?"

"This is the last one, Mr. Hannon."

"Would you have a drink with me?"

Frank hesitated, not wanting to accept charity.

"You can't refuse a man on Christmas Eve."

Frank nodded in agreement. Michael followed them to the bar. Jack poured two whiskeys.

"I've got just the thing for young Michael. A glass of Christmas apple cider. Michael's brown eyes widened as Jack handed him the glass of cider. Jack went to the kitchen. He returned with a plate of pastries.

"It's too much, Mr. Hannon," Frank protested.

"We'll indulge him on Christmas Eve, Frank."

Frank tipped his glass and drank. He let out a slow sigh of satisfaction. "That does chase the cold, Mr. Hannon."

Jack poured him another. "You know, Frank, I came to this town with enough money in my pocket for two beers. As humble as it may be, I owe my success to the generosity of others. The people of the levee district have been good to me. The thought of those people going cold and hungry on Christmas Eve is a terrible one."

"You've earned what you have, Mr. Hannon."

"That I have, Frank. Tonight, with your help, we're going to distribute some of it."

"What do you mean?"

"I'm going to borrow your wagon and spread some of my good fortune around. Don't worry. I'll explain to your employer."

"Merry Christmas!" Kevin walked into the tavern.

"Hi, Frank. Who's your helper?" Kevin ruffled Michael's hair. Michael looked up at him, his mouth full of pastries.

"Grab a couple of bottles for your coat pockets, Kevin. We're going to make our Christmas Eve rounds."

"And what might that be?" Kevin asked.

"We're going to take food and coal to some folks. We'll call it the Christmas wagon. Will you help us, Frank?"

"Cold and hunger are no strangers to this district, Mr. Hannon. Are you sure you can afford it?"

"Yes. Let's get started." Jack grabbed a bottle of bourbon for his own coat pocket. He put one in Frank's. He went into the storage room and returned with a Chesterfield coat.

"This belonged to one of my Chinese cooks. He fashioned himself a gentleman before hopping a train to California. Jack helped Michael into the coat. The garment that was cut to fit above the knee hung all the way to the floor. The sleeves were a foot too long.

"Perfect fit, hey, Donavan?"

"It was made for him, Jack."

Michael proudly pulled back his shoulders. The three men laughed.

Jack poured some cider into a jar. He handed it to Michael.

"A gentlemen can't be without drink on a cold night. We're off!" Michael led them out the door. At the general store and the bakery they loaded baskets of food and bread onto the wagon. Jack hired a coal wagon to follow along behind.

"Michael will be our ambassador of goodwill," Jack said. "Can you teach him to say 'free food and coal,' Frank?"

Frank tutored his nephew as the wagon moved into the tenement district. The alcohol was beginning to take effect. As the English lesson progressed the three men chanted "free food and coal" along with Michael.

By the time they reached the first tenement, Michael was ready. The poor and down-trodden of the levee district could hardly believe that the elf-like creature in the Chesterfield coat was for real. They opened their doors to the chant of "free food and coal." Michael led them out to the wagon for Christmas provisions.

The three revelers and the coal wagon driver were drunk by the time the wagon arrived back at O'Shea's. Michael had taken over the reins from his uncle. He pulled the horses to a halt in front of O'Shea's.

"You got two baskets left, Mr. Hannon."

"They're yours, Frank. Have a very merry Christmas."

"I won't forget this, Mr. Hannon."

"I hope not. I'll expect you both here at the same time next year."

Frank spoke to Michael. Michael started to take off the coat. "That's his coat!" Jack almost fell getting off the wagon. "You tell him to keep the coat."

Michael smiled.

"I want Michael here the first day of the new year to go to work. A dollar a day wages to clean up around the restaurant."

"A dollar a day? For him?"

"Don't worry, Frank. I'll see that he earns it. Now go on home to your family. Merry Christmas to you both."

"Merry Christmas, Mr. Hannon."

As the horses started ahead, Michael turned around.

"Merry Christmas," he said. The wagon creaked slowly down Delaware Street.

Years later, when the Christmas wagon became a Christmas caravan, the poor children of the levee watched and waited for the boy in the Chesterfield coat.

* * *

Along with his two campaign aides, Adam sat in his small office at the Times building. He was preparing a note of concession to his Republican opponent. In the wards Adam felt he had to win, less than fifty votes separated him from the incumbent.

"Don't look so glum, my friends," Adam said. "We'll try again in the next election."

Kevin stopped at the office door. "Why the long faces?" he asked.

"My note of concession." Adam held up the paper. "We just received the results from the seventh and eighth wards."

"And?"

"Do we need to spell it out for you, Donavan?" an aide asked.

"Have you checked the river wards, Adam?" Kevin asked.

"We're dead in those wards," the other aide said.

"Before I embarrassed myself with a note of concession, I would check the river wards," Kevin insisted.

Adam studied him. "You know something?"

"The election results were coming in as I was having a pint of O'Shea's finest. The last I heard, a man named Adam Quint was winning in a landslide."

"Don't joke with me, Kevin."

"I would not joke about so serious a matter." Kevin held out his hand. "Congratulations, Adam."

"My God! Jack pulled it off!" Adam said excitedly. "Get your coat, Kevin. We're going to O'Shea's and celebrate."

# 7

# THE WEDDING

MARCH, 1873

Red rode the blue roan slowly up Delaware Street. The March winds blew incessantly, drying the mud-covered streets. This was his first trip to the city in four months. He had not seen his friends since before Christmas.

Kevin had ridden out with Adam Quint to tell him of Melissa's decision to call off the wedding. Kevin and Adam felt responsible. Red had tried to assure them that the story would have eventually unfolded.

Adam had been out to the ranch several times over the winter. Red had been polite, but he kept the visits as brief as possible. Adam was a good friend, but Red wanted to distance himself from everyone. Every time he got close to someone, something tragic seemed to happen.

He often wondered about his parents. What had happened to cause them to leave a three-year-old boy alone in some of the most rugged country in the West? Maybe destiny had cast him as a loner from the beginning. He thought of all the people he had cared about. Jesse Farrel, Hester and Jake Quint, Jason, Luke, and Ben. He could distinctly remember every inch of Catto, the best horse he had ever owned.

And now Melissa was gone. Losing her was the most devastating of all. You come to terms with the death of your friends; death leaves you few options. But the thought of Melissa going about her daily life with another man was almost more than he could bear. His plan had been to give her some time, and then ride out to the ranch and straighten things out between them.

The small column in the newspaper announcing her marriage to John Kenney had been a devastating blow for him. After the announcement, he had taken one day at a time. He had just tried to make it through the winter.

And then yesterday he had received the telegram from the War Department. His Uncle Jesse had served with Robert E. Lee's army of northern Virginia. Jesse's unit had been the 5th Texas, under the divisional command of General John B. Hood.

Stunned, Red had scanned the words over and over again. Corporal Jesse Farrel from Nacogdoches, Texas, had fallen, never to rise again, at the battle of Antietam Creek, near Sharpsburg in western Maryland.

Red could not imagine Jesse's death. Antietam had been the bloodiest battle of the war, but surely Jesse would have survived. Red had always seen

Jesse through the eyes of a little boy. Jesse Farrel was bigger than life. Red could not accept the fact that his Uncle Jesse was dead. The telegram had driven him into an even deeper depression.

The warm breezes from the south had done nothing to change his frame of mind. It was the same hostility he had felt when Hester and Jake were killed. He tied the blue roan to the hitching post in front of O'Shea's and went inside.

"Red! Good to see you!" Harry walked down to the end of the bar. He shook Red's hand.

"Thanks, Harry. Have you seen the boys?"

"Jack's down at City Hall. Adam and Kevin should be along any time. They never miss a Friday night."

"How about a beer, Harry?"

"Sure thing. The first one's on me."

Red was into his second beer when three men came into the tavern. They took a table in the center of the saloon. They were laughing and having a good time. O'Shea's was clearly not their first stop.

"Three beers, Bartender!"

Harry raised his eyebrows knowingly at Red.

Red smiled.

"Here's to you, boy!"

Red turned around. Two older men with beards held their beers aloft. A younger man sat between them.

"When that mountain lion flushed, you looked like greased lightning."

"I haven't seen anyone move that fast since General Price and his Rebs were hightailing it out of Westport."

"You were there?" The younger man asked.

"That we were. With Jim Lane and the Kansas militia. We had the Rebs runnin' so fast it was hard to get a bead on them. We chased those gray coats all the way to Arkansas."

Harry bent over the bar. "Don't pay no attention, Red. They're just some former redlegs over from Wyandotte looking for a good time."

Red nodded. He moved his beer on down the bar away from the men. The shadow of the war seemed to be with him lately. He listened to several more minutes of abuse directed at General Price and the Confederate Army.

In a burst of patriotism, the two bearded men rose to their feet. They held up their drinks. "A toast to General Lane and the Union Army!"

Avoiding trouble, Red kept his back turned to the pair. The patrons held their drinks aloft.

Harry raised his glass.

"How about your friend, bartender?"

Red ignored the man.

"You there! A toast to General Lane!"

Red turned around. "You talkin' to me?"

"Yeah."

"We're drinking a toast to General Lane."

"Then go ahead and drink it," Red replied.

"Ain't you gonna join us?"

Red stepped away from the bar. "No."

The man's eyes flicked over at his partner and then back at Red.

"Why not?" he asked.

"Because I don't toast jackasses or drink with redlegs."

Men at the surrounding tables scattered out of the way.

"Looks like we got us a Reb here, Tom."

The other redleg smiled.

"Ain't that right, Reb?"

"You boys ought to get your story straight. I lost a lot of friends at Westport, but I don't remember that anyone was shot in the back runnin' away."

The two men put their glasses on the table. Their younger friend stepped out of the way.

Red felt the initial tenseness drain away. He was in no mood to walk away from a fight.

"Now listen, Reb, we don't want no trouble."

The man went for his gun.

Red reacted swiftly. He pulled his Colt revolver, and ducked to the right. A shot exploded in his ear. He pulled the trigger on the Colt. The bullet caught the first redleg in the chest, throwing him backwards. Another bullet tore into the bar next to him. He fired two bullets into the second redleg's chest and stomach. The man pitched forward on his face. The younger man backed away.

"Don't try it." Red pointed the Colt.

"No, sir."

Jack was halfway up the block when he heard the shots. He ran the rest of the way to the tavern. He burst through the doors. He sized up the situation quickly.

"Harry! Run over to Market Square and get the marshall. What happened, Red?"

"These two found the fight they were lookin' for."

Jack knelt down. He felt for a pulse on each of the men.

By the time the marshall arrived Jack had taken statements from the witnesses and sent for the undertaker.

The marshall and his deputy bent over the bodies.

After completing the examination, they walked over to Red. "You'll have to come with us, Red," the marshall said.

"We've got witnesses that say it was a fair fight, Marshall," Jack said.

"They can have their say at the hearing."

"How long will that take?" Red asked.

"Several days," the marshall answered.

"Let's go!" The deputy grabbed Red roughly by the arm.

Red drew the Colt 45. He swung the barrel hard into the deputy's ribs. The man went down. The marshall reached for his gun.

Red put the Colt against the marshall's temple. He cocked the hammer. The marshall put his hands in the air. Red slid the gun from the lawman's holster.

"You're in a lot of trouble, Red."

Red backed toward the saloon doors. I'll leave your gun on the boardwalk, Marshall."

"I'll be after you, Red."

"You remember this, Marshall. When you cross the Hannibal Bridge you're in my territory, and your chasin' a man that don't much give a damn."

Red disappeared through the saloon doors.

* * *

From his position on the porch, Jim watched the dust from a fast-moving horse approach the house. He stood up and waited.

Red pulled the horse to a halt in front of the house.

Jim noticed lather on the blue roan's neck and shoulders.

"What's happened, Mr. Red?"

"Come inside, Jim."

Jim followed him into the house. As he shoved supplies into his saddlebags and made up a bedroll, Red related the events of the past few hours.

"You got nothin to worry about, Mr. Red. It was a fair fight. You got witnesses and friends to back you up."

"It's not the gunfight, Jim. It seems that every time I been ready to settle down, somethin's happened to ruin it."

Jim studied Red. "Your misery's still comin' from that woman, Mr. Red. I promise you it will get better if you give it time."

Red brushed past Jim and walked out of the house. He threw his saddlebags over the horse and tied his bedroll behind the saddle.

When Jim came over and stood beside him, Red put his hand on his shoulder. "With Melissa gone there don't seem to be any reason to life, Jim. Maybe some time on the run will help me sort things out." He mounted the horse. "I know you'll take good care of the ranch for me. Keep half the profits for yourself. Put my share back into the ranch."

Red reached his hand down and Jim shook it.

"Good-bye, old friend."

"Good-bye, Mr. Red."

Red turned the horse and rode away at a fast gallop.

* * *

Melissa walked into the dining room of her new home on Quality Hill. John was having his breakfast.

"Good morning, John," she smiled.

"Good morning, Melissa. Did you sleep well?"

"Yes, thank you."

"Would you like some breakfast?" John asked.

"No, not yet. I can't get accustomed to having someone wait on me. It makes me nervous."

John reached for her hand.

"I hate to be the one to have to tell you this . . ."

Melissa looked at him questioningly.

"Red Farrel killed two men in a gunfight yesterday."

John watched her expression of shock.

"Was it a fair fight?" she finally asked.

"Yes. When the marshall tried to take Red to jail, he pistol-whipped a deputy. Now he's on the run. Don't blame yourself, Melissa."

"I'm going to my room for awhile, John."

"I understand your feelings, Melissa, but please don't dwell on this. You have the baby to think about."

She squeezed his hand, then left the room.

* * *

Mary McFarland sat beside Carlos in the carriage. They drove down Broadway, turned east on Fifth, and headed for Delaware Street. She had waited months for Kevin to call on her. The newspaper had been her only link to him. She watched nervously from the kitchen every morning, waiting for Mr. Davis to finish the newspaper so she could devour every word of Kevin's column. She waited for his knock on the kitchen door through late summer and early fall. Though their encounter had been brief, she hoped that Kevin still cared for her, and she intended to find out.

Carlos stopped the carriage in front of O'Shea's place.

"Are you sure you want to go through with this, Mary?"

"Aye, Carlos."

He helped her off the carriage. She walked unsteadily into the saloon, feeling panic as the doors shuttered to a close behind her. Harry saw her standing self-consciously at the door. He motioned to one of the barmaids. The girl walked over to Mary. "Help you, Miss?"

"Could I see Mr. Hannon?"

The barmaid looked her over. Mary blushed. "It will be concerning a business matter," she said.

"That's what they all say, deary. Come this way."

Mary followed the girl back to the kitchen. The barmaid poked her head into Jack's office. "A 'lady' to see Mr. Hannon."

Mary gave the girl a dirty look as she walked past. Jack got up from his desk. "What may I do for you, Miss?"

"My name is Mary McFarland, Mr. Hannon. Could I be speakin' to you for a moment?"

"Have a seat, Miss McFarland. Just call me Jack. Mr. Hannon sounds awful stuffy."

Mary smiled. "Does my name mean anything to you, Jack?"

"No, I'm sorry."

"Kevin Donavan has never mentioned my name?"

Jack thought for a moment. "Not that I recall."

"I'm the hired girl at the Davis home on Quality Hill."

"Oh, Yes! Mary McFarland from a night at the opera."

She smiled. "I have not seen Kevin since that night." Embarrassed, Mary blushed and became silent.

Jack took the lead. "Would I be wrong in assuming that you wish to see Mr. Donavan again?"

"I know this is awful of me, but I would be knowin' no other way to go about it."

"I've often wondered what happened to Kevin that night. He came down from the bluffs looking like a whipped dog. Before committing myself to anything, Mary, I'll have to have the full story."

"Oh, I couldn't possibly be tellin' you everything."

Jack leaned back in his chair. "You'll have to be entirely honest with me, Mary, if we're to be friends. Now tell me what happened."

Mary succumbed to the Hannon magic. She instinctively knew the story would go no further. She sat on the edge of her chair and told Jack about her dinner and night at the opera with Kevin. She remembered every detail about her first night on the town.

Jack could hardly keep a straight face when she innocently described Kevin's ploys to lure her into the bedroom.

"He said he was a student of architecture?" Jack asked.

"Aye."

Jack bit down hard on his lip. "Go on, Mary."

She hesitated.

"The full story, Mary, if I'm to help you."

Mary sat up straight in her chair. She fidgeted nervously with the edge of the desk. "I didn't know what else to do. He being the most persistent man I've ever met."

"So you told him to get undressed and lie on the floor."

"Aye."

Jack's stomach was hurting from trying not to laugh.

"And?"

"I came back to the bedroom with a bucket of cold water. When I opened the door, Kevin urged me to hurry. I threw the water at 'im and it found its mark. He was angry."

Mary jumped back in her chair as Jack let go with a roar of laughter. The picture of Donavan being hit with the water was too much for him. He threw his head back and laughed until tears came to his eyes. He finally stopped laughing and wiped his eyes with a handkerchief.

"Ah, Mary girl, how could I not help you?"

"Will you be meaning it?"

"Yes. I think you just might be the girl to keep up with the likes of Kevin

Donavan. You will have to trust me and follow my instructions to the letter. Can you accept that?"

"Aye."

"I'll have to enlist some fellow conspirators in my plan. I want you here in my office Saturday night at six o'clock. Is that agreeable?"

"Aye. Thank you, Jack."

"Don't thank me yet. We've a ways to go. Good day, Mary."

She went to the door.

"Miss McFarland."

Mary turned around.

"I deeply regret having entered the wrong door of the Davis home on Quality Hill."

Mary smiled.

* * *

At seven-thirty on Saturday night Kevin walked into O'Shea's. He meandered up to the bar. Jack was helping Harry dispense drinks to the growing Saturday night crowd. He moved over to Kevin.

"Well, I see you finally made it."

Kevin looked at him indignantly. "I didn't realize I was on a schedule."

"There, you see what I mean, Harry? I try to do him a favor and what do I get? Sarcastic remarks."

"What favor?" Kevin asked.

"She's all yours, Major." The lecherous old man sitting beside Kevin got up from his stool. He finished his drink.

"Bless you, Hannon," he said as he departed.

"Where's that old pervert going?" Kevin asked.

"That's what I've been trying to tell you. I've hired a new girl to work at the hotel. A lovely creature she is, too. I tried to save her for you, but the major spied her. He's been going crazy ever since. Would you believe he paid ten times the going rate for the first crack at her?"

"My God! She must be something."

"You don't see many like her on the levee. Isn't that right, Harry?"

"One of the working girls told me she's a virgin," Harry whispered.

"You don't mean it?" Jack said.

Harry nodded.

"A pity to have that angel soiled by the old major," Harry continued. "She must need the money desperately."

"I don't think so," Jack said. "She was a hired girl to one of Quality Hill's finest."

"You never know," Kevin said. "Maybe she wants to spice up her life."

"I wouldn't have hired her if she hadn't been so insistent," Jack said, "her being an Irish lass and all." Jack scratched his head. "What was her name again, Harry?"

"Mary," Harry answered. "Mary McFarland."

Kevin choked on the beer that was halfway down his throat. He took off running through the kitchen and out the side door. He ran through the alley and down the street and burst through the front door of the hotel. He spotted Mary going up the stairs with the major.

"Stop!" He yelled.

Mary and the major turned around.

"And where do you think you're going, Mary McFarland?"

"Begging your pardon, sir?"

"You heard me. Where are you going?"

"And what business would that be of yours?"

Enraged, Kevin walked over to the stairs. "I'm making it my business."

Mary turned to the major.

"You'll have to be excusing this gentlemen, Major. It's someone I haven't seen for months."

Sally came out of a side room. "Kevin! You're disturbing my customers."

"I don't give a damn about your customers! Answer my question, Mary McFarland!"

Mary let out a sigh of frustration. "It took me a while Kevin Donavan, but I now realize that I can make more money lying on my back than scrubbing on my knees."

Kevin's eyes widened in indignation. He grabbed her by the arm. "You're coming with me."

"I am not!" She jerked free. Kevin reached for her. She hid behind the major.

"Damn you, Mary! You're going back to Quality Hill."

"Nae, I'm lonely up on the hill."

"I'll come and see you. I promise."

The old major was moving back and forth on the stairs between them.

"You're just saying that. I haven't seen you for three months."

"And whose fault is that?" Kevin yelled.

"Will you be holding a grudge forever?" Mary asked. She was two steps above the major, holding onto his shoulders.

"I thought you didn't want to see me again."

"You were wrong, but it's too late now. Come along, Major."

Kevin reached around the major. He pulled Mary, kicking and screaming, off the stairs. The three of them fell into a heap in the middle of the parlor.

Jack, Harry, and the rest of O'Shea's tavern were squeezed against the hotel windows laughing uproariously.

Mary got off the floor. She straightened her clothes. Kevin jumped to his feet. The Major brushed himself off. Jack chose that moment to rush through the hotel door.

"What's the meaning of this disturbance?" he demanded.

Kevin pointed his finger at Jack. "How could you be a party to this? Ruining a young girl fresh from the shores of Ireland. Is there no decency left in you?"

Jack searched the faces around the room. "Is this the Kevin Donavan I know? Worried about a woman's reputation?"

Kevin turned red in the face. "I'll settle with you later, Jack Hannon."

He turned on Mary. "If you try to resist I'll drag you out of here by the hair on your head."

Mary dropped her eyes. She followed him to the door, winking at Jack as she passed him.

Kevin marched her over to the livery stable on Main Street. The rented carriage creaked up Quality Hill. Kevin peered over at her occasionally, trying to figure out the reason for her downfall.

"Will they take you back?" he asked.

"Who?"

"The Davis family. You did quit your job?"

"Nae, I didn't."

Donavan stared at her in the twilight.

Mary took a deep breath. "If you cared enough to save me from a wicked life, why did you not care enough to come and see me?"

"I thought you were laughing at me."

"I would never be doing that. I kept waitin for you to come back."

"You did?"

"Of course."

"After what happened I thought I would be the laughingstock of Quality Hill."

"No one knows about that except Jack."

"Jack?"

"Aye. Let me explain about tonight. I won't be lettin' anything come between your friendship with that wonderful man."

Mary told Kevin about Jack's plan.

"Do you mean that I've been the victim of a put-up job?"

"Aye," she said softly.

"All those people were in on it. The major, Harry and . . ."

"Aye, everyone."

Kevin laughed. "I can picture how ridiculous I must have looked."

Mary giggled. "Only when you were lyin' on top of the major in the middle of the parlor."

They laughed together. Kevin turned to her, searching her eyes. "You went to a lot of trouble for the likes of me, Mary."

She moved over on the seat and curled her arm around his. "You're a fine man, Kevin Donavan."

Kevin pulled the carriage to a halt in front of the Davis home. He took Mary's hand in his. "I think we should get married in the spring, Miss McFarland."

Mary pulled her hand away. "Don't be teasin' me, Kevin."

"I was never more serious."

"But it's so quick!"

"Yes. But it's the way I do things. I have this all-consuming feeling that we were meant to be together."

"Oh, Kevin. So do I."

"Will you marry me?"

"You'll be needin' some time to think about it, Kevin."

"No. I decided the matter when we were struggling on the stairs."

Mary rested her head on his shoulder. "I love you, Kevin."

Kevin stroked her hair. "I assume that's a yes," he said.

"Aye," she answered happily.

## APRIL, 1873

Kevin sat beside Jack in the open carriage. The driver, dressed in a frock coat and top hat, moved the horses up Broadway. White blossoms on the dogwood trees decorated the green of the bluffs. Easter lilies and tulips basked in the sun along the way.

"Isn't it a fine day, Jack?"

"A lovely setting indeed, Kevin."

The town's residents applauded as the carriage moved past. The impending wedding had turned out to be the social event of spring, a victory celebration for the populace over the hardships of winter.

Cheated out of Red's wedding, Jack had seen to it that his best friend would be married in style. No expense had been too great. The wedding's participants rode in stylish carriages. Silver trappings adorned the harnesses of the horses as they pranced south along Broadway toward the Catholic Church.

Jack and Kevin were dressed in white silk shirts and black trousers. A white boutonniere decorated the lapel of their black waistcoats.

"Are you nervous, Kevin?"

"Yes. I had no idea you would invite the entire city."

"You're a popular fellow, Kevin Donavan."

Kevin laughed. "Maybe I should run for governor."

At Eleventh Street, Kevin spotted the crowd gathered around the church. The women were dressed in all the light colors of spring. Their bustles stuck out like strutting roosters.

He closed his eyes and inhaled the smell of fresh flowers. "I'm a happy man, Jack."

"You have every right to be. She's a fine woman."

Jack stopped the carriage in front of the church. The bells in the steeple were ringing with abandon. The sound echoed off the bluffs and down into the levee below.

Jack and Kevin went up the church steps together.

Jack noticed the look of concern on Kevin's face.

"What's the matter Kevin?"

"I was just thinking about Red. I wish he could be here."

"So do I," Jack said. "But he has too many dollars on his head to risk being in public."

"It would make great copy, though. 'Farrel Gang Attends Local Wedding.'"

Jack laughed. "Always the reporter. I'll be surprised if you don't do the story on your own wedding."

"As soon as I utter I do, I will."

They entered the church under a horseshoe arch of flowers.

* * *

"The most important dress you will ever wear and you leave it in the hands of a saloon keeper!"

Mrs. Davis paced back and forth nervously. Jack had insisted on buying the wedding dress. Mary had been going to the dressmaker for months for the fittings but had never seen the finished dress.

"The dress will be here," Mary assured Sarah and Mrs. Davis, who were helping her get ready.

"Do you even know what it looks like, Mary?'

"Nae, Mrs. Davis. I left everything to Jack."

"What does a man know about wedding dresses? I hope it isn't delivered in pieces."

"Please, Mother!" Sarah put her arm around Mary. "I'm sure the dress will be fine."

Mrs. Davis saw the strained look on Mary's face.

"Of course it will. I'm sorry, Mary. You girls go upstairs and start getting ready. I'll wait for the dress."

The marriage of a hired girl to a newspaper reporter was not a big event on Quality Hill. But the residents started to take notice when two white horses in silver trappings crested the hill. The landau carriage was the finest anywhere. Two coachmen in top hats directed the horses. The carriage pulled to a halt in front of the Davis house.

A coachman lifted a bulky garment out of the carriage. He carried it to the door. Mrs. Davis had been frantically watching through the window. She opened the door. "Do you have the dress?"

"Yes, ma'am."

"Thank God! Well, come along. Bring it upstairs."

The coachman followed behind Mrs. Davis. They entered a bedroom at the top of the stairs. He laid the garment on the bed.

"We'll be waiting downstairs for the bride," he said as he departed.

"Mary! Your dress is here!" Mrs. Davis called.

Mary and Sarah tore into the room.

"Oh, I'm afraid to look!" Mary cried.

"Let's try it on her, Sarah. We can make the last minute repairs and adjustments. Open the package, Mary!"

"Nae. I can't. Take it out for me, Sarah, please?"

"Oh, all right."

Sarah went to the bed. She started pulling up the bulky garment bag. Mary bit her thumb nervously as she watched.

"Oh, my goodness, Mother! Look at it."

Mary closed her eyes, sure that something was wrong.

Mrs. Davis went to the bed. She held up the dress.

It was made of white satin, with elaborate trimmings and frills. Yellow roses and lace banded the dress. The white tulle veil reached all the way to the floor. Sarah picked up the wreath made of yellow roses and green leaves.

"It must have cost thousands," Sarah said.

Mary opened her eyes. For a moment she was speechless. "There must be a mistake. That can't be mine."

"There's no mistake Mary," Mrs. Davis assured her.

Mary started to cry. "I've never seen a dress so beautiful."

"Come now," Mrs. Davis said kindly. "We can't have tears on the most beautiful bride the city has ever seen."

Mary wiped her eyes. "I'll be thankin' you, Mrs. Davis."

* * *

The bride's coach came to a halt in front of the church.

Jack was waiting for Mary at the foot of the steps.

She stepped down from the carriage. Two young girls held the train off the ground.

Jack took her arm, beaming proudly.

"How can I ever thank you, Jack Hannon?"

"Just make him happy, Mary."

"That I will, I promise you. You'll not be losing him, Jack. You'll be part of our family. If you're not at our house every Sunday for dinner, I'll be comin' down to the levee and drag you there."

"You have my word on it, Mary."

They entered the church. Adam Quint waited to escort Mary down the aisle. Jack took his place beside Kevin at the altar.

The church was overflowing with wedding guests. At the sound of Mendelssohn's Wedding March, they turned. There were gasps of astonishment as the crowd viewed the dress and the bride.

Kevin smiled happily as Jack leaned over and whispered to him, "The King of the Levee is dead. Long live the King."

After the wedding the Donavans walked down the church steps on a carpet of fresh flowers thrown by school children.

Jack had made the proper donations and all the church bells in town were ringing. The congregation, en masse, followed the newlyweds down to the levee. A large bridal bell hung over the entrance to O'Shea's tavern. Inside, a giant three-tiered wedding cake was presented to the bride by a local bakery. The cake was entwined with yellow roses and green shamrocks. Two love birds sitting between baskets of flowers festooned its top.

Kevin had invited Melissa and John Keeney to the wedding, but Melissa had sent a note saying they were going to be out of town. Kevin knew she had declined because she did not want to put a damper on the festivities. All of Red's friends would be there and they would be reminded of his engagement party at O'Shea's. In the note, Melissa said she would call on Mary after the honeymoon. Melissa and Mary had a lot in common: They were both strong willed, determined women, and they both had a streak of good humor. Kevin hoped they would become close friends.

Jack had tables lined along the walls of O'Shea's. They were piled high with turkey, chicken, beef, and ham. As a special treat he had ordered a railroad car of fruits and vegetables from California. O'Shea's was decorated with spring flowers from Connie O'Shea's flower garden, and violinists strolled through the tavern playing soft music.

There were hundreds of people in O'Shea's and hundreds more out on the boardwalk. Jack had sent an open-house invitation too all of his friends in the North End and the West Bottoms.

"Congratulations, Mary," colonel Ellison said. "It was a lovely ceremony and you are a beautiful bride."

Mary blushed with pleasure. "You're kind to say so, Colonel."

"I've had years of experience dealing with this rascal you married, so if you need any help with him just let me know," the colonel said.

Kevin laughed. "Now don't you and Mary team up on me, Colonel."

"I think Mary can handle him, Colonel," Adam Quint said. Adam had escorted Bonnie Morgan to the reception. Bonnie had the radiant look of the next bride to be. Adam had not yet proposed, but everyone knew it was just a matter of time. They were a hard-working couple. Bonnie ran her millinery shop, and Adam was on the city council, worked part time as a teacher, and still found time to write his weekly newspaper column for the *Times*.

"If you will excuse us," Bonnie said as she took Mary's hand. "I want Mary to meet some friends of mine." The two women moved across the room.

Colonel Ellison turned to Jack. "I must say you have put on quite a show. I'm a well-traveled man, but never have I seen a more elegant wedding and reception."

"Thank you, Colonel. Kevin is the only family I have, so I have to send him off in style."

"You're too good to that rascal," the colonel said affectionately.

"Adam tells me you may be running for the city council."

"In a few years, Colonel. I'm not a politician, but I did give Adam my word that I would run for office."

"And well you should," the colonel said. "Your kindness to the working people of the First Ward is well known around the city. I want you to know you have my support when you decide to run."

"Thank you, Colonel."

The colonel sipped his whiskey. "I can't help but think of Red Farrel on this grand occasion," he said. "Red is a true son of the South who was wronged by the war and is now on the run."

The colonel's philosophy, and that of his newspaper, *The Kansas City Times,* was rooted deep in the Confederacy. The newspaper staff thundered the views of an unrepentant South. The James brothers and other Missouri outlaws who had championed the Southern cause were editorialized as Robin Hoods of the West, men who had been wronged by the war and were forced into a life of crime. The colonel and most of his staff served with the Confederacy during the war. If someone opposed their point of view, the only recourse was to show up at the Times building with a pistol. If a man were so inclined to violence, there was usually someone at the newspaper to accomodate him.

"We all wish Red could be here Colonel," Kevin said.

The colonel realized he had injected a note of sadness on this happy occasion. He put his arm around Kevin. "I'm sure you, do my boy. Now, you have done an excellent job at the newspaper. To show my appreciation, and to honor you and your lovely bride, I'm raising your salary ten dollars a week."

"Ten dollars!" Kevin exclaimed. "Colonel, let me buy you another drink!"

The colonel laughed. "You have earned the increase and you will need a little extra to fund your new responsibilities."

"Thank you, Colonel," Kevin said, bowing with gratitude.

Bonnie and Mary stopped to get a glass of punch.

"Your wedding dress is absolutely stunning," Bonnie said.

"Thank you, Bonnie." Mary looked around the room in awe. "Have you ever seen anything so grand?" she asked. "I feel like I'm in a fairy tale, and I've been captured by the little people. Any time now they will be wakin' me up and takin' me back to my little room on Quality Hill."

Bonnie smiled. "It's not a dream, Mary. It's your special day, so enjoy every moment."

"Would you look at all the food," Mary said. "There's more here than in all of Ireland. Jack must have spent a fortune."

"The reception is far grander than anything I've seen," Bonnie agreed.

"Is it true that you own a business?" Mary asked.

"Yes. I have a dry goods and millinery store on Missouri Avenue."

"How exciting!"

"I don't know about that," Bonnie replied. "But it's comforting to know I can support myself."

"Aye," Mary said. "It's what worried me most when I left Ireland. Could I support myself in this world? It's a good feeling to know that I can."

"When you get back from your honeymoon I want you to come down to the store and have tea with me," Bonnie said.

"I would love to," Mary agreed, touched by her kindness.

"Have you and Kevin talked about having a family?" Bonnie asked shyly.

"Aye. We want to start on a large family right away. I miss havin' brothers and sisters around, and Kevin wants lots of children. I guess it comes from him bein' an orphan."

"That's wonderful," Bonnie said. "I wish you every happiness, Mary."

"Thank you, Bonnie. I can tell by the way Adam Quint looks at you that you'll soon be walkin' down the aisle."

Bonnie blushed as Kevin walked up. "Excuse me Bonnie, but it's time I took this beautiful lady on a honeymoon."

Mary beamed at him. She was so much in love, and the day had been so grand. It was as if her every wish had been granted. They went around the room thanking everyone and saying their good-byes.

Outside the tavern Jack escorted them to their carriage. Kevin gave Jack a hug. "Thank you, Jack. It has been the greatest day of my life."

Mary kissed him on the cheek. "You're a wonderful man, Jack Hannon."

"Go on, the two of you," Jack said modestly. "Enjoy your honeymoon."

The happy couple finally departed in a carriage showered with rice and slippers.

* * *

When the McFarland family of Kenmare in Kerry county received their letter, with pictures and newspaper clippings of the wedding, they thought their Mary must surely have been made Queen of the United States of America.

## FROM ADAM QUINT'S JOURNAL — OCTOBER 1874

*Bonnie Morgan has graciously consented to be my wife. We will be married in the spring. She is a wonderful woman, and I will do everything in my power to make her happy. She will continue to run her millinery business as we do not yet wish to start a family.*

*Red has been on the run for over a year. I have not heard from him directly, although rumor has it that he is riding with a group of outlaws down in the Oklahoma Territory. I was afraid this would happen to him.*

*Red is a strong individual, but a man can only take so many disappointments.*

*He knows he can count on me if he ever needs help. I don't think Red will change his way of life. Once a man is outside the law, it becomes very difficult to rejoin society. I only hope that he does not meet a violent death in some lonely place far away from his friends. Perhaps he will contact me sometime in the future and let me know where he is.*

*Two major factors have caused a large expansion in the growth of the city.*

*A man named Joseph McCoy came up with the idea of driving cattle from Texas to Abilene, Kansas, and then on to Kansas City for shipment to the east. The stockyards and processing plants are booming, and over 240,000 head of cattle passed through the city this year.*

*And a new drought-resistant variety of wheat, called "Turkey Red," has been introduced into Kansas by Russian immigrants. This wheat has revolutionized the wheat industry and it is estimated that over 400 million bushels will be processed in Kansas City in this year of 1874.*

*With these new growth industries the population has risen to over 50,000, and we are now the largest city between Saint Louis and San Francisco.*

# 8

# Goats & Rabbits

March, 1880

The two democratic factions in the first ward had been at odds for years. The Goats were led by John Mulroon, a moon-faced, ill-tempered Irishman who constantly chewed on a half-smoked cigar. John had a large, well-muscled frame that he used to good advantage in the political battles of the first ward. The Rabbits were led by Tim Clancy, a thin, hawk-faced man whose body had been emaciated by years of alcohol abuse. Tim used his wit and political savvy to maintain leadership of the militant Rabbits.

Years ago, in a political debate, Tim Clancy had called John Mulroon and his followers Goats. He was referring to Mulroon's neighborhood on the west bluff below Quality Hill. There, in an Irish working-class neighborhood, the Goats were allowed to roam freely with no respect for class distinction or property. John Mulroon was delighted to accept the goat as a symbol of his group's dedication to freedom and liberal views.

Tim Clancy's Irish neighborhood was over the hill in the southern part of town. Their homes were in a wooded area where small game abounded. Mulroon gave them the name Rabbits because he said they were deceptive, kept multiplying, and would run from the Goats in the next election. Tim Clancy embraced the name because he said Rabbits were quick and would always be way ahead of the Goats.

These two factions came to blows so often during an election year that the district became known as the Bloody First. In order to have a democratic candidate to oppose the Republicans, the Rabbits and Goats would usually reach some sort of compromise, but this was not one of those years.

From his saloon on Delaware Street, Jack Hannon had been a keen observer of the political process. He was careful to stay out of the fray and never took the side of either democratic faction. He let Clancy's Rabbits and Mulroon's Goats use his restaurant and hotel for meetings and political rallies. Jack had built his reputation on goodwill, so he had no enemies in either camp. He had also concluded that Adam Quint was right: To make a real contribution he had to get elected to public office.

This was democratic primary night, and if everything went according to Jack and Adam's plan, he would become the political leader of the First Ward.

"He is a man of compassion and will work hard for this district." John

Mulroon's booming voice carried through Jack's office door. The Goats were shoulder to shoulder in O'Shea's tavern, listening to their leader extol the virtues of Mulroon's candidate for office. Outside, Clancy's Rabbits were parading their candidate up and down Delaware Street.

Jack huddled in his office with Adam Quint and Frank Pacini.

"At the proper time Adam will step in and make a speech," Jack said. "Frank, if you will stay down in the crowd and say a few words in my behalf it will be appreciated."

"I'm no speech maker," Frank said. "But I will do it. I want you to be elected, Mr. Hannon."

Jack knew that Frank Pacini was well respected by the people of Little Italy. His help would be crucial in the hours ahead. Adam had stationed other men in the crowd who would give testimonials for Jack. These working men were from the West Bottoms and the North End. Their common goal was to elect Jack to public office.

In the next room Mulroon's voice was stirring his men into a fever pitch. With a loud roar the Goats stood en masse, and carried their candidate out the swinging doors of O'Shea's to be paraded through the streets behind a brass band. With a chorus of boos and insults they let the parade of the Rabbits go by. The noise was deafening as the two brass bands tried to drown out each other. A few punches were thrown, but for the moment the two groups seemed more intent on parading than fighting.

A bandstand for the dignitaries and speech makers had been constructed in the middle of market square. The Rabbits and Goats, with placards waving and bands playing, converged on the market area.

"We'd better get over to market square," Adam said. The three men hurried out of O'Shea's.

On the bandstand in front of the dignitaries, Tim Clancy was trying to quiet the crowd. The Goats were having no part of it. They continued shouting and waving their placards. Clancy waved his hands frantically for quiet. "Please! Please! we must have order," he pleaded. Mulroon stood up and motioned for his supporters to be quiet. Clancy gave him a nod of thanks.

"I would like to introduce the Rabbits' candidate for public office," Clancy said. "He is Clarence Miller, the owner of Miller's Mercantile Store."

A rousing cheer went up from the Rabbits as Clarence stood up and waved. He moved to the podium.

"He's a stooge for you, Clancy!" One of the Goats shouted.

"What does he know about government!" another yelled.

"Shut up and let him speak!" Clancy yelled back.

Clarence finished his short, uninspired speech to the sound of insults and catcalls from the Goats. Mulroon took center stage.

"Now that we have dispensed with the preliminaries, my friends, let me introduce Larry Neal, the next Alderman from the First Ward."

It was the Goats' turn to cheer. They struck up the band and waved their placards.

Mulroon quieted the crowd. "You all know Larry. He's a hard-working foreman at the stockyards."

Larry stood up. He had never faced a crowd and he was terrified. Mulroon grabbed him by the arm and led him to the podium.

"If you elect me I will do my best," Larry blurted out. With cheers from the Goats ringing in his ears, Larry raced back to his chair.

"You've got him in your pocket, Mulroon!" A Rabbit yelled.

"He's not qualified," another said.

The rage crept into Mulroon's face. "I chose Larry because he is the best man for the job!" he shouted.

"You chose him because he's a lot like you," a Rabbit yelled. "He smells like the stockyards and he's as ugly as grandmother Mulroon." The Rabbits howled with laughter.

"Who said that?" Mulroon was furious. "Get that man," he shouted. The Goats were converging on a man in the crowd. The Rabbits had formed a protective ring around one of their own. Mulroon threw off his jacket and rolled up his sleeves. Jack was standing next to Adam in the crowd. "It's time to move, Adam," Jack said. Adam hurried up to the bandstand.

Fists started flying through the air as the Goats and Rabbits converged on each other. With a roar, John Mulroon jumped off the bandstand and started flailing away with his fists. Tim Clancy followed close behind to join his men in the fray.

Adam Quint stood on the bandstand watching the Goats and Rabbits pummel each other. The two groups of men pounded each other back and forth across market square in waves, trading punches and insults. Adam waited until the two groups had pounded most of their frustrations out on each other. He reached under his coat and pulled out a Colt revolver. He put the gun in the air and fired three shots. The men instantly quieted. They looked toward the bandstand. Adam put his gun away.

"Tim Clancy and John Mulroon, come back up here!" Adam commanded. John and Tim brushed themselves off and headed back to the stage. Adam waited until the two men were seated. "My name is Adam Quint. You supported me in the last election. For that I am in your debt, so allow me to speak for a moment." The men moved closer to the stage. "What has happened here tonight should convince each of you that this ward is hopelessly divided, and that you have no chance of unifying against the Republicans in the coming election." Adam looked out at the working men of the district. There were no suits or silk shirts in the crowd. These were the hard-working, hard-drinking men of the North End and West Bottoms. "John Mulroon and Tim Clancy are fine men," Adam continued, "They have worked hard for this district, but they will forever be loyal to their own factional interests. It is time for you men to find a candidate who can unify the First Ward. The working men and women of this district deserve meaningful representation on the city council. How many times have you men passed a tenement house with scraggly children running unattended through the streets, or seen dead horses left to rot beside the road, or smelled raw sewage in a drainage canal, and not asked yourselves why things cannot be better in the First Ward?" The men were quiet, listening to Adam. "I am here to tell you that with a strong candidate you can control the future and the well-being of all the people in this district. The lawyers, bankers, and railroad owners who control the city council want to keep you divided. They can elect a Republican candidate who will support big business interests at the expense of civic improvements for the First Ward." A murmur of agreement swept through the crowd.

"You control the largest block of votes, so if you control the First Ward, you control the city. If you unite," Adam squeezed his hand into a fist, "you become the heart of the city, and your influence will flow into other districts. Tonight, I'm asking the Goats and Rabbits to come together behind a strong candidate for the good of the First Ward."

"And what candidate might that be?" someone in the crowd yelled.

"That's for you to decide," Adam answered. "But, I will tell you the qualifications the candidate must have. He should be a man of compassion who will help the poor. A man of strength who can stand up to the money interests, and a man of integrity who will work not for personal gain, but for the benefit of others. Do we know such a man?" Adam asked.

A man in oily overalls and wearing an engineer's cap waved his hand to be recognized. Adam pointed to him.

"When I first came to this town I had no money and no job. Jack Hannon loaned me money at no interest charge and he helped me get work on the railroad."

Frank Pacini spoke up. "At Christmas, Mr. Hannon gives free food and coal to the people in my neighborhood. He gave my nephew a job."

"He loaned me money," another man yelled.

"He got my sister a job," another said.

"He gave me money when I was sick and out of work," another said.

Adam had only four men stationed in the crowd, but as he had suspected, due to Jack's generosity, the testimonials went on and on.

"Who keeps his safe open to any man who truly needs help?" a man yelled. "Hannon!" the crowd answered.

"Who helps feed the poor?" another yelled. "Hannon!" The crowd had discovered their candidate. "Who will get you a job?" The crowd started chanting "Hannon, Hannon, Hannon."

Adam waved Tim Clancy and John Mulroon over to the podium. As the crowd cheered he spoke with the two political leaders.

"With your help, Jack wants to form the first democratic political club in the city. He needs your assistance in the coming election."

The two Irishmen looked at each other. They were too shrewd to be left off the bandwagon. "Shall we make it unanimous, John Mulroon?" Tim Clancy asked. Mulroon nodded agreement.

Adam quieted the crowd. Tim Clancy clasped John Mulroon's hand and put it in the air. "The Rabbits and the Goats are united behind Jack Hannon!" The crowd roared, and the chant began again. "Hannon! Hannon! Hannon!"

Jack walked up the steps of the bandstand and stood beside Adam, Tim Clancy, and John Mulroon. The crowd roared even louder when they saw him. Adam let the demonstration go on for several minutes before quieting the crowd.

"I give you the man who will lead the democrats to victory in the next election. A man of character, compassion, and goodwill. A friend to every working man in the First Ward. Your candidate for Alderman, Jack Hannon!"

For the first time in a decade the Rabbits and the Goats had a candidate they could unite behind. The roar from the crowd was deafening. Jack stood at the podium waving to the crowd. The two brass bands merged together and started playing "For He's A Jolly Good Fellow" as the Goats and Rabbits danced their placards back and forth across Market Square.

Jack did not want to dampen the mood of his flock with a long-winded speech. When the crowd finally quieted, he spoke. "I want to thank you for this nomination. You have put your trust in me and I will do my best for you and for the First Ward. With your support we will whip the Republicans in the April election." The crowd cheered. "And now, for a show of solidarity and for the good of the First Ward, I want every Rabbit out there to shake hands with a Goat."

Jack watched as the Rabbits grudgingly complied. "And tonight, for every Goat who walks into a First Ward saloon with a Rabbit at his side, the drinks are on me." The crowd roared its approval. "Now, let's go celebrate a new beginning for the First Ward!"

The Goats and Rabbits headed for their favorite watering holes. Jack shook hands with Adam, Tim Clancy, and John Mulroon. "Let's all get together Monday evening and make our plan for the April election," he said.

### FROM ADAM QUINT'S JOURNAL — APRIL 21, 1880

*The Goats and the Rabbits united behind Jack Hannon in the April election and he beat his opponent by a five to one margin. After the election Jack hired John Mulroon and Tim Clancy to be his assistants. It was a shrewd move as it will further unite the Goats and Rabbits, and Jack can be tutored by two veteran politicians.*

*Bonnie and I have purchased a home on Fourteenth Street in the new Reid's Addition. Kevin and Mary live on the same block, as do several other members of the press. Kevin dubbed the street Reporters' Row, and the name has caught on; although Bonnie says whenever she hears the connotation, it somehow brings to mind either birds or criminals.*

*I still have not heard anything from Red, although I keep up with his activities through news reports. It has been seven years since we last saw him. I still have hope that one day he will turn himself in, pay his debt to society, and have the opportunity to lead a decent life. The decades of lawlessness in the West are coming to an end, and men like Red will not survive the change.*

*It seems that a new generation of Americans has descended on the city. Everyone wants to make a dollar, and they are not afraid of risk or hard work. The West Bottoms and North End are booming with new industry, and every day it seems as if someone introduces a new service or product.*

*All of the new industry is in the First Ward, so Jack has most of the jobs and tax dollars in his district. The new saying around town is, "As Hannon goes, so goes the city."*

*Kevin says that Gully Town could not be in better hands, and I happen to agree with him.*

*After the cash crunch and slow economic growth of the seventies, there is a swell of optimism as we enter the 1880s. Thousands of people have taken up Horatio Alger's call to "Go West, Young Man," and most of them seem to be coming to Kansas City.*

## MARCH, 1882

Jack was savoring the election results at Democratic headquarters. He had been sent back to city hall for a second term as city alderman representing the First Ward. Adam Quint had won his first term as Missouri state senator.

For Jack, the victory was sweet. Due to a lack of representation on the city council, big business had invested heavily in the Republican candidates. They wanted control of the heavily populated river wards.

Not only had Jack won the election, but his candidates for office in three other wards had also won. Jack Hannon now had enough votes to control the city council.

The newspaper on his desk glared up at him. "Boss Hannon Still King of the First." The newspapers had sensationalized his interests in saloons, gambling, and prostitution. Jack threw the paper in the waste can. This boss business was created by journalists to sell newspapers. Coercing people or buying votes had never entered his mind. His political philosophy was simple: You do things to help people and at election time they will support you.

Rather than detract from his candidacy, the newspaper stories added to his mystique. His constituency knew there was more goodwill in O'Shea's tavern than in most of the city's churches. They had returned him to office with the largest majority in the city's history.

In an area consisting of hundreds of churchless blocks, Alderman Hannon was also the Father Confessor.

If a man showed up in town looking for work, his first stop was at O'Shea's tavern. A homeless family applied for assistance at ward headquarters. Runners wore a path from Jack's office to city hall. They obtained permits, paid fines, sought political favors — even asked for leniency in sentencing for those who had run astray of the law. No citizen in the world had better representation than the people of Hannon's river wards.

When Jack entered his office promptly at six each morning, people were lined up waiting to see him. A scribbled note on a piece of paper would usually solve the problem. Jack was careful never to promise anything he could not fulfill. His integrity meant everything. If Jack Hannon said it, it was as good as done.

Ward headquarters was the only place in this decidedly Southern city where a man could get a fair shake regardless of race or religion. Jack had caused a sensation some months back when he had posted bail for a Negro. This gesture was not lost on the black population at election time.

As Jack locked his office door at Democratic headquarters, he felt for the first time that he could control the direction of the city in the years ahead. He placed the key in his vest pocket and went out into the night.

* * *

Michael Pacini opened his eyes in the darkness. Outside the storage room something had interrupted the rhythmic chirping of the crickets.

A cat screeched and bounded away.

Michael closed his eyes. Years ago, when Frank Pacini was having hard times, Jack had given Michael the storage room to sleep in. Michael still used the room when he worked the late shift at the restaurant.

Footsteps sounded in the alley. Michael was instantly awake. He shifted noiselessly off the bed, crouched next to the window and looked outside. The gas lantern from the street illuminated part of the alley. Two men were visible in the shadows.

Michael slipped on his pants and crept back to the window. One of the men was snuffing out the gas lantern.

His partner kept looking around the corner of the building. "When he comes 'round the corner, you grab him around the neck. I'll take care of the rest," one of them said.

"Just do the job right. I don't want to return any of this railroad money."

Michael knew that the only man to use this alley at night was Jack Hannon. He tore into the kitchen. In the darkness he reached for, and found, the ice pick above the chopping block.

He slipped back to the storage room and quietly opened the outside door. He crept out into the moonless night, moving silently. No one knew the alleys of the levee district better than Michael Pacini. He could hear the two men breathing.

"Be ready! He's coming!" one of the men whispered.

Michael crouched low. He moved on the balls of his feet and crept closer, his eyes becoming accustomed to the darkness. He was ten feet away when he saw the flash of steel. The man was ready to strike.

Jack walked around the corner. He cried out as the bandit on the left grabbed him around the neck.

Michael held the ice pick tightly in the palm of his right hand. He took two steps forward and with all the force he could muster he plunged the ice pick downward into the bandit's back just below the man's shoulder blade. The assassin groaned and fell heavily into the street. Michael spun to his left.

Jack had freed himself from the other man. The man turned to run. He ran into Michael.

Taking a step forward, Michael drove the ice pick into the man's stomach. The bandit screamed. Michael pulled out the pick and plunged it in again. The man groaned in agony, then slumped to the ground.

"Who's there?" Jack called out.

Michael caught his breath. "It's Michael, Mr. Hannon."

"Michael?"

Jack went to the street light. He lifted the globe and struck a match. In the light, sweat glistened off Michael's olive skin. Jack bent over. He examined the two men.

"They're dead, Michael. What happened?"

"They were sent here to kill you, Mr. Hannon. I was in bed when I heard them in the alley."

Jack sat down on the boardwalk. With a handkerchief he wiped the sweat from his brow.

"Who sent them, Michael?"

"The railroad," Michael answered.

Jack nodded. "I'll get the police."

"Don't do that, Mr. Hannon."

"Why not?"

"Because whoever planned this knew they would get you either way. If you're not killed, you're involved in a scandal. The police will never find out who did it. The newspapers will twist the story. They will say the murder attempt had something to do with gambling or prostitution. They will say anything to make you look bad, Mr. Hannon."

Michael searched the pockets of the dead men. He found a wad of bills on each man and held up the money to Jack.

Jack contemplated for a moment. "What do you suggest, Michael?"

"Let me handle it. There won't be no publicity. And I promise, you won't be bothered again."

Jack realized he would be a dead man but for the quick actions of this sixteen-year-old boy.

"You handle it, Michael. I have every confidence in you."

The next morning, in two locations on Quality Hill, two railroad presidents were called into their yards.

A dead man was hanging on the wrought iron gates at each location. Both had ice picks stuck in their chests and their mouths were stuffed full of railroad money.

* * *

Kevin hurried past the Pacific House. The morning air was unseasonably warm for March. He crossed Third Street and headed straight for O'Shea's. He spotted his quarry sitting outside the tavern. The clomp-clomp of Kevin's shoes on the boardwalk shattered the Sunday morning solitude of Delaware Street.

Jack looked up from his newspaper.

"Kevin, lad! How are you?" Jack noticed the look of fire in Kevin's eyes.

"Don't you good morning me," Kevin said. Like a scolding father he pointed his finger at Jack.

"Just tell me if the rumors I've been hearing are true."

Jack raised his eyebrows questioningly.

"Don't play dumb with me, Jack Hannon."

Jack patted the chair next to him. "Sit down and calm yourself, Kevin."

"I don't want to sit down. Answer my question. Was their an attempt on your life during the March election?"

Jack looked back at his newspaper. "I wonder how these rumors get started," he said.

"Jack?"

Jack sighed. He dropped the newspaper into his lap. "If you must know, Kevin, the answer is yes."

Kevin sat down in the chair next to Jack.

"And Michael was involved?" he asked.

"Yes. Michael saved my life."

Kevin digested the words. "And you saw fit not to confide in me?" he asked.

"Only to spare myself the speech you are about to make."

Kevin pulled himself up onto the edge of the chair. "There are those in the political arena who wish you great harm, Jack. Surely you're convinced of that now."

"I've entertained the thought."

"Then why, may I ask, are you sitting out here all alone?"

Jack winked. "You're here to protect me."

Kevin slumped back in his chair, exasperated.

At the top of the hill at Eleventh Street, bells at the Catholic cathedral rang the call to Mass.

"If there are elements in the city desperate enough to try an assassination attempt, they must want you out of city government in the worst way," Kevin persisted. "I think you should oblige them. Why don't you forget politics and go back to running O'Shea's?"

A shaft of light from the rising sun streaked between the buildings across the street. Jack folded his newspaper against the glare.

"I appreciate your concern for my welfare, Kevin. But you know better than to suggest such a course. For the first time in the history of this city the working men and women will control the way government is run. Of course the money interests are desperate. They must lay their proposals out on the table for public scrutiny."

Kevin glanced over at the determined set of Jack's jaw.

"There are those uptown who say that Boss Hannon controls city government."

Jack's steel blue eyes flashed above his fashionable black Bismarck mustache. He turned and pointed behind him at O'Shea's. "My door is always open for those I represent. It is open every day for those who wish to express their views or hold me accountable for responsible representation."

Kevin held up his hands in mock defense. "I'm on your side, Jack."

Jack's expression softened. He leaned back in his chair.

"Do you think another attempt will be made to get you out of the way?" Kevin asked.

"Not an attempt on my life. I'm sure my enemies will change their strategy. Michael's calling cards were rather intimidating."

"Yes," Kevin agreed. "He has most of the city's populace scared to death of him. Michael won't always be around when you need him, Jack. Why don't you hire some bodyguards or a Pinkerton detective?"

"You are not listening, Kevin. My constituents would be as intimidated as my enemies. If I'm not approachable I become a politician, a boss," Jack said disdainfully. "I have been allowed to represent the working men and women of this district because they see me for what I am. I'm one of them. They laugh at these Boss Hannon and King Hannon headlines in the newspaper. And do you know why? Because I'm one of the family. And as a member of each family, I have an army of protectors."

That may be true in the North End and in the West Bottoms," Kevin countered. "But you do have to venture uptown on occasion."

Jack slowly shook his head in frustration.

"If it will ease your mind, Kevin, I will always have someone with me when I leave the district."

Kevin smiled.

A warm southerly breeze tunneled between the buildings, twirling pockets of dust along Delaware Street.

Jack looked out at the city mushrooming around O'Shea's. Buildings of every size and shape were under construction. He put his huge hand on Kevin's arm. "Can you believe that this is Gully Town, Kevin? It's been only thirteen years since we first crossed the Hannibal Bridge."

Kevin chuckled. "The other day, Mary remarked that you were not only leading a conspiracy to make this mountain of mud liveable, but to make it presentable in the process."

Jack laughed. "That's our Mary. How are she and the children?"

"They're fine. And they are eager for your Sunday visit today."

Kevin got up from his chair. "I have some work to catch up on at the office."

Jack walked with him to the edge of the boardwalk. "Has Adam received any new information on Red's whereabouts?"

"Nothing definite. Rumor has it that he is still in Oklahoma or Texas."

Kevin was startled as a burly-looking man appeared from around the corner of O'Shea's. The man was almost as big as Jack. A scar ran across his cheek, accentuating a jaw lopsided from brawling. He wore an old grey shirt and his brown knickers were held up with grey suspenders. His knee socks were grey and brown, and a brown billed cap adorned the top of his head. He was followed by another rough-looking man, and then another, until there were eight unsavory looking characters, all dressed in the colors of grey and brown, standing under the O'Shea tavern sign.

"Come on, Hannon! Out into the street!" Scarface commanded. "Let's get this over with."

Kevin stepped in front of Jack. He clinched his fists, ready for a fight.

From down the street a gangly scarecrow of a man stumbled to a halt in front of O'Shea's. He wore a fashionable suit and hat, and his black shoes glowed in the morning sunlight. On his shoulder he precariously balanced a tripod and camera.

From behind him, Kevin heard Jack suppress a laugh. He turned around and looked into Jack's smiling face.

"O'Shea's baseball team," Jack explained. "If you will kindly get out of my way, Mr. Donavan, we're going to have our picture taken."

* * *

Kevin chuckled to himself as he headed along Delaware Street to the Times building. Although he had made a fool of himself, he now felt reasonably satisfied that Jack was safe from harm. As he walked along in the sunshine, he inhaled a deep breath of air. Life was as sweet for him as the smell of spring flowers emanating from the bluffs above. Jack's rise from obscure poverty to the top of the political world was almost inconceivable, and his own success he could not have imagined. Even more remarkable was the change in his personal life. He had evolved from a roving, carefree bachelor to a man who could hardly wait to get home in the evening. Mary and his four little girls were a constant delight, and last year they had been blessed with a baby boy.

Kevin tipped his hat to three women passing on the street.

"Good morning, ladies."

Dressed in their Sunday best, the women smiled politely, and with a rustle of skirts proceeded on down the street.

As he entered the Times building, Kevin felt a twinge of guilt as he pictured Mary's struggles to get the children off to Mass, reminding him that his reformation was far from complete.

* * *

Mary Donavan eyed the four curly heads in front of her. The Donavan girls sat stiffly in dining room chairs facing away from their mother. Mary's mouth was stuffed with hair pins. She held a hair brush in one hand, and Margaret's hair in the other.

Margaret grimaced as Mary firmly stroked the brush through her hair. "Quit kicking your feet, Margaret," Mary mumbled through the hair pins. She slipped a hair pin neatly in Margaret's hair and moved on to Teresa.

With curly light brown hair and hazel eyes, the four girls were the image of their mother. Anna, the seven-year-old, was born in 1875, Teresa in 1876, and Margaret in 1877. The Donavans took a respite in 1878 and then Molly was born in 1879. The Donavans were blessed with their first boy in 1881. They named him Joe.

The Donavan girls suffered their grooming in silence. Their mother was a crusader for neatness, and dirt was her sworn enemy, so they knew better than to protest. Mary Donavan was determined that her home would be an oasis of cleanliness in a city composed of mud and grime.

Kevin and the four little girls risked a broom on the backside if they brought even a speck of dirt into the house. Every other evening, Mary scrubbed the girls in the bathtub, brushed their hair, and had them waiting for Kevin when he returned home in the evening.

As she stroked Molly's hair, she watched for Kevin through the parlor window. She loved Kevin and her children and wanted nothing more from life than to make a happy home for them. Kevin left the care of the children and all other domestic matters to her and even insisted that she take over the family finances. Mary Donavan would never stray from her roots. She was a poor Irish working girl and she knew the value of a dollar. Although she was miserly with herself, she made sure that Kevin had money for O'Shea's. Kevin's happiness was more important than worldly goods, but if he overspent his allowance, no amount of coercion would convince Mary to give him more. Mary Donavan's purse strings were as inpregnable as the Bank of England.

She set aside a monthly stipend for the Catholic church and without fail put money into a savings account at the bank. Mary had made a solemn vow that the Donavan children would never repeat her experience of having to leave home because of financial matters.

After ten years of living in the West, she had lost most of her Irish brogue, but as Kevin could testify after too many nights out drinking with the boys, she had lost none of her Irish temper.

She was also happy to play the primary role in raising the children because she came from a large family and she felt better equipped to do so. Kevin had not the faintest idea of how to bring up children. To say that he was a doting father would be an understatement. He was incapable of punishment for the girls, so all discipline was left to Mary.

"Here comes Father!" Teresa shouted. The girls jumped from their chairs and ran to the door to meet him. They surrounded him as he entered the house.

"Look at all these beautiful women," Kevin said as he bent over to receive warm kisses.

"Hello, dear," Kevin kissed Mary on the lips.

"I knew there was something missing in my day," he said.

"From the look of these well-scrubbed girls, I can tell you've been busy. How's the baby?"

"He's fine, and he's sleeping soundly." She smiled as Kevin tiptoed toward the nursery.

"Father, can we go out and play?" Margaret asked. Kevin turned around. With a finger to his lips he made a quieting gesture. He pointed to Mary, the final authority, then crept into the nursery.

"No, you may not, Margaret," Mary scolded. "You know the rules. No playing outside after your evening bath. Stop trying to use your father to get your way."

Margaret squinted her eyes at Mary in defiance. Mary ignored the look of rebellion. "You girls go upstairs and play until I call you for dinner," Mary ordered. The girls bounded away.

"Sound asleep," Kevin said as he reentered the room. "I do believe that he grows an inch every day. Can I help with dinner?" It was a question he always asked and Mary always refused.

"You look tired, Kevin Donavan. Come into the kitchen and tell me all about your day."

Kevin retrieved his bottle of scotch from the kitchen cupboard. He poured himself a drink. "What's for dinner?"

"Vegetable soup," Mary replied as she trimmed the top off a carrot.

"The rumors I've been hearing were true," Kevin said. "There was an attempt made on Jack's life."

"You're not serious!" Mary was shocked.

"I'm afraid so. If it were not for the quick actions of a young Italian boy who works for Jack, the assassins would have been successful."

"Did he chase them away?"

"No. He killed them."

"Oh my. Who was the boy?"

"Michael Pacini."

"He's the boy who rides on the Christmas wagon," Mary remembered.

"Yes. He and his Uncle Frank."

"Well thank God he was there when Jack needed him. How did a young boy overpower two assassins?" Mary asked.

"You would have to meet Michael to understand what I mean; he is no ordinary boy. He can take care of himself. I've seen him intimidate grown men who were causing a disturbance at O'Shea's. Not many men want to risk making Michael mad. He is well mannered and friendly, but he also keeps everyone at a distance. When he's not working for Jack he's the leader of a gang of hoodlums over in the North End tenement district. His reputation will spread after the killing of the two assassins. I like Michael, but I'm afraid he's headed for a life of crime."

"Surely Jack can handle him," Mary said.

"Jack has a blind spot where Michael is concerned. All he can see is the little orphan boy in the Chesterfield coat. He thinks Michael will grow out of his wild streak."

"And maybe he will," Mary encouraged.

"Regardless, Michael was there when Jack needed him. He saved Jack and that makes him my friend for life. I just wish there was some way to guide him in the right direction."

"Perhaps you can help influence the boy," Mary said.

Kevin pondered for a moment. "Michael's always hanging around the Friday night poker game. Maybe we could let him sit in on a few hands. An association with Adam Quint might do him some good. He can see how a real gentleman behaves." Pleased with the solution, Kevin sat his drink on the kitchen table. He put his arms around Mary and pressed against her back. "You're my inspiration, Mary Donavan." He started kissing her neck. "Kevin, stop that," Mary said unconvincingly. He nibbled on her neck. "You know that makes me weak," Mary said, forgetting about her vegetable soup.

"I want you weak," Kevin replied. "Do you see any reason why we can't retire early tonight?"

"Yes. Four of them are running around upstairs and one is in the nursery." Kevin chuckled as he continued kissing her neck.

"Father, they won't let me play," Molly came crying into the kitchen. She wrapped her arms around Kevin's leg.

"Who won't let you play?" Kevin asked as he pulled Molly up into his arms.

"Teresa and Margaret," Molly wiped at her tears.

"We will just see about that, Molly girl," Kevin said playfully. "Come on. The big bad wolf will take care of those girls." Molly had a vengeful smile on her face as Kevin went growling out of the kitchen. The girls heard him coming and started screaming and running through the upstairs. The baby cried out.

Mary sighed. She smiled and put her eyes to heaven before heading for the nursery.

## MONDAY — APRIL 3, 1882

Kevin had risen to general assignment reporter for the *Kansas City Times*. His primary love was sports, but there was little interest among the populace for sports news. The paper's editors usually hid his stories of sporting events somewhere in the back of the paper. The colonel thought sports were a waste of time, but he gave up the needed space to humor Kevin. Kevin Donavan was a news hound and the colonel did not want to lose him to a competing newspaper. If a story was developing, or needed inspiration to develop, Kevin was the man who could shape it into news.

Kevin learned early that a reporter's lifeblood was his sources of information. He had men and women stationed in every section of the city who would rush a message of fast-breaking news to him. He could not afford to pay them in dollars, so he always gave them credit by including their names in the story. With advance information from his sources, he was usually at a news scene long before any other reporter, and sometimes he was there as the news actually happened. His competitors at other newspapers jealously accused him of staging or creating news, but Kevin knew timely information was the key to his success.

Other reporters would spend days riding through the countryside with a posse to pick up information on the James Gang, the Younger Brothers, and other outlaws; but not Kevin Donavan. Colonel Ellison had served with all of these men during the war, and he still kept in contact with them. During one of the colonel's bouts with the bottle, he had mentioned to Kevin that Jesse and Frank James crossed the Hannibal Bridge every other Sunday to visit their uncle who lived near Market Square.

Kevin had garnered several exclusive interviews by meeting the outlaws on the bridge. He would say that Colonel Ellison sent his regards, and then walk with the James boys over to the market. The outlaws were not reluctant to talk because they knew the colonel would treat them fairly. Kevin did not view the James boys as romantic figures. He had been to the scene of several bank robberies and seen their handiwork, and he had interviewed several women whose husbands had been murdered by the outlaws.

Kevin also had easy access to the Younger Brothers, for one of them could usually be found somewhere in the market area on weekends. You just had to know where to look.

Jack Hannon filled him in on fast-breaking political news, which he in turn passed on to Colonel Ellison.

The colonel repaid him by giving him advance information on celebrity visits and newsworthy items he picked up at social functions and newspaper conferences.

The newsroom was in its usual Monday morning uproar. Two freshman reporters were on duty at the ticker tape. One of them relayed messages off the tape, and the other shouted the news through a megaphone to reporters scattered throughout the newsroom. The reporter at the tape spotted Kevin and frantically started pointing at the colonel's office.

Kevin acknowledged him, and headed for the colonel's door. He knocked.

"Come in," the colonel said.

Kevin entered the office and closed the door behind him. The colonel had his back to him. He was standing at the window looking down on the street below. He remained silent for several minutes.

"Is everything all right, Colonel?" Kevin asked.

The colonel turned around. Kevin read the pained expression on his face. The colonel sat down at his desk and rubbed his eyes.

"Kevin, this is a sad day for the state of Missouri," he said.

"Governor Crittenden's blood money caused this despicable act."

Kevin looked at the colonel questioningly.

"I just received the message. Jesse James was murdered an hour ago in Saint Joseph, Missouri."

Kevin's eyes widened. He glanced at the clock above the colonel's desk. The colonel was obviously upset, but he was also giving him a head start on the rest of the newsroom.

The Saint Joseph express was leaving Union Depot in twenty minutes. Kevin was already out of the colonel's office and running through the newsroom.

* * *

The train seemed to take forever to get to St. Joe. Kevin had hastily checked the other cars to see if he had a head start on his competitors. He breathed a sigh of relief when he found no other reporters on the train. Most of them would write the story off the ticker tape, and fact would mingle with fiction. Kevin was not above helping a minor news item become newsworthy, but he was a stickler for facts on major stories, and he knew the killing of Jesse James would be one of the major stories of the decade.

At St. Joe he jumped off the train while it was pulling into the depot and ran for the telegraph office. The telegraph operator was sure to have some information.

The station was buzzing with the news. A large crowd had gathered around the telegraph operator. Kevin did not have time to fight his way through the crowd.

"Where was Jesse James killed?" he asked a man standing next to him.

"In a house at Thirteenth and Lafayette," the man answered.

Kevin had not been in Saint Joseph since he and Jack had made a quick exit back in 1869, but he was familiar with the layout of the city.

On every street corner there were groups of people huddled together talking about the killing. Kevin made his way up the hill to Thirteenth and Lafayette. The one-story house was painted white with green shutters, and it had a large yard and stable. It looked more like the cottage of a retired schoolteacher than the home of a wanted criminal. It seemed a strange hideout for the nation's most wanted outlaw. You could see the house from several miles away as it sat on a bluff overlooking the Missouri River and a major portion of the city.

As he walked up to the house there was a man in the yard talking to a deputy sheriff. The man was writing on a note pad. Kevin walked up to the two men.

"Mind if I go inside?" Kevin asked the deputy.

"What's your business?"

"Newspaper. I work for the *Kansas City Times*."

"Ah, a compatriot," the man standing next to the deputy said.

"I'm Woodrow Wingate of the *St. Joe Daily News*. My friends call me Woody."

Woody was a big man. Kevin estimated he was six foot three and weighed about two hundred and forty pounds. Not as big as Jack Hannon, but a good-sized man. Woody had high cheekbones and one of those aristocratic noses that looked as though it belongs on a statue. He had large blue eyes that seemed to take in everything at a glance. Kevin guessed that Woody was also a big man with the ladies.

"I'm pleased to meet you. I'm Kevin Donavan."

The two men shook hands.

"Donavan, you say?" Woody inquired.

"Yes."

"Our paper has run several of your articles on the James Gang," Woody said.

"It's good of you to remember," Kevin said. "If you'll excuse me, I had best get to work."

"Hold on there," the deputy said. "You can't go in the house."

"Why not?" Kevin asked.

"Souvenir hunters are takin' everything that ain't nailed down," the deputy said.

Woody grabbed Kevin by the arm and moved him across the yard.

"Listen, Donavan," he said. "I usually work alone, but I can see we need each other. I can get you in the house, and I have all the information on the killing."

"So why do you need me?" Kevin asked.

"You've met Jesse James in person and you know what he looks like. I need a positive identification of the body. How about it?"

Kevin liked to work alone as well, but what Woody said made sense. He extended his hand. "Let's go in the house, partner," he said.

"Jesse was living here under the assumed name of Thomas Howard," Woodie explained as they entered the house.

"Who killed him?"

"A young man named Robert Ford. His brother Charles was an accomplice. They had both been living here with Jesse and Jesse's wife and children."

"How did it happen?" Kevin asked.

"Come over here," Woody said. "Jesse put his gunbelt on the bed over there," Woody pointed. "He got up on this chair and was dusting the picture on the wall. The Ford boys got between Jesse and his gunbelt. Robert Ford pointed his gun at the back of Jesse's head and pulled the trigger. The bullet entered the back of Jesse's head and came out over his left eye. He died in his wife's arms, right here." Woody showed Kevin the blood on the floor.

"It's hard to believe Jesse would have taken his gunbelt off and turned his back with two armed men in the house," Kevin said.

"We're thinking alike, Kevin Donavan. That's why I need you to identify the body."

"Where are the Ford boys?" Kevin asked.

"They're down at the Sheriff's office. They freely admit the killing, and even sent a telegram to Governor Crittenden claiming responsibility for the act."

Kevin knew that Colonel Ellison would be outraged. This murder was the result of the $50,000 dollar reward the Govenor had put on Jesse's head.

"What's the matter, Donavan?" Woody asked. "You look a little gloomy."

"I guess I expected something different," Kevin said. "I thought Jesse would be killed in a gunfight, or shot while robbing a bank. This was just premeditated murder. He was shot down in cold blood while he had his back turned."

"Get hold of yourself, Donavan," Woody said. "Noble deed or not, this will be headline news around the world, and right now we're still ahead of the hounds."

Kevin shook off his revulsion. "Of course you're right, Woody. Where did they take the body?"

"Sidenfaden's Funeral Home," Woody answered. "Shall we go?"

"I'll meet you out in the yard," Kevin said.

Kevin moved through the house taking everything in. He made a few notes, but as he usually did, he committed everything to memory. If he took his time and had no distractions, he had total recall when it was time to write his story.

He had always felt that reporting the news was a tricky business. You could only be opinionated in the editorial pages, and to a degree you had to set your personal feelings aside — but not enough for the story to become impersonal. Good writing came from the heart, and that left him vulnerable to the events he reported. He was always straddling the line between his duty as a reporter and his feelings as a man.

Woody stuck his head in the door. "Are you ready, Donavan?"

Kevin took one last look around and went out the door.

When they arrived, a crowd had gathered outside the funeral home. Woody managed to talk himself and Kevin by the deputy stationed outside the entrance.

"I have someone with me who can identify the body," he told the funeral director.

The man led them to a back room. The neatly-dressed body was laid out on a bare table. Woody and Kevin moved closer. The face had not been disfigured as Kevin expected, but there was a bullet hole above the left eye. Jesse now had a beard, and his hazel eyes were closed, but these were the same square cheekbones and prominent chin Kevin had remembered.

"Well?" Woody asked.

"This is Jesse James," Kevin said.

"You're sure you're not mistaken, Donavan? A man looks different with the life out of him," Woody said.

Kevin turned to the funeral director. "Jesse was missing the tip of his middle finger on his left hand," Kevin said.

The funeral director unfolded the hands and confirmed the missing tip.

"That's good enough for me, Donavan," Woody said.

"Let's go over to the marshall's office and interview the Ford boys."

* * *

The Ford brothers were holding court outside the marshall's office when Woody and Kevin walked up.

Bob Ford looked much younger than his twenty-one years, Kevin thought. He had brown hair, blue eyes, and he wore a nervous smile on his face. He was slight, with broad shoulders, and he had that gangly appearance of youth.

His brother Charlie had black hair and large brown eyes, and did not seem to have the brashness of his younger brother. He stayed in the background behind Bob and nervously watched the street.

"Did you kill him for the reward money?" a reporter asked.

"Yes," Bob freely admitted. "We struck a deal with the Govenor quite a while ago. We said we would bring him in and we did."

"Why did you shoot him in the back?" another reporter asked.

Bob Ford grinned. "I don't reckon it would be healthy to try and shoot Jesse James from the front," he said.

Some of the reporters laughed at Bob's attempt at humor.

"Where were Jesse's wife and kids when you shot him?" another reporter asked.

"In the kitchen," Bob said defensively. "We had no choice but to do it then, it was the only time I ever seen Jessie take his guns off."

"Do you think you'll live long enough to enjoy the reward money?" Kevin asked. "I don't think it will take Frank James long to get to St. Joe."

Charlie Ford stepped forward. He looked up and down the street, and then whispered something to the marshall. The marshall grabbed Bob by the arm and ushered both of the Ford boys back into the jailhouse.

"I'll be damned if you don't know how to break up a news interview, Donavan," Woody swore.

"Sorry, Woody," Kevin apologized. "But I couldn't resist."

"Come on, Donavan." Woody grabbed him by the arm. "Let's get over to the courthouse. The inquest will be held within the hour. Just remember that I will be the partner who asks all the questions."

At the inquest Jesse's grieving widow had confirmed the story told by the Ford boys. Woody Wingate's report of the killing had been accurate.

After the inquest, Kevin and Woody put away their note pads and retired to the nearest bar for refreshments. Then Woody had escorted Kevin back to Saint Joseph's Union Station. They stood on the platform together as the express to Kansas City pulled in.

"I'm sure you will mention my name as co-author when you write your story, Donavan," Woody said.

"We were good partners, Woody," Kevin said with a grin.

"But not that good." Woody laughed good naturedly. "I like you, Donavan. Even if you do know how to break up a news interview."

"It's been a pleasure, Woody. I appreciate all your help, and if I run across any interesting news, I'll put it on the wire and send it your way."

"You read my mind, Donavan," Woody said. "I'll be your eyes and ears in St. Joe and our partnership will remain intact."

The two men shook hands, and Kevin jumped aboard the train.

As it pulled away from the station, he took a seat in back of the coach away from the other passengers. He wanted privacy so he could go over the day's activities and formulate the story he would put on paper in the morning.

The inquest had been a sobering experience. Jesse's widow was a well-dressed, attractive woman. She carried herself well and looked as though she must have come from a good family. There was no doubt she had cared deeply for her husband. Jesse and his wife looked like any average American couple, but led vastly different lives. It would be interesting to interview the widow after all the hoopla died down, and find out what life was like for a family on the run. He made a mental note to do just that. In reality Jesse had died as violently as he lived. He had certainly not shown any mercy to some of his victims. He had shot Conductor Westfall from behind during the Winston train robbery, and some say he shot a man named Ed Miller while Ed slept, so maybe it had been simple justice.

Still, Kevin knew he would miss the excitement that surrounded the bandit. Jesse was a newsmaker and Kevin wondered if this would not be the end of an era in lawlessness: From now on, every bandit in the West would be nervously watching his back, wondering if he could trust his friends.

Kevin leaned his head back on the seat and listened to the clack, clack of the rails as the train sped along. Woody had been right about him today; he had let his own personal feeling interfere with the job he had to do. Perhaps it was because he had come face-to-face with his own mortality. He and Jesse James were about the same age. They both had young children and loving wives. He wondered how Mary would make it if something should happen to him. Life could be a short experience, especially if you lived west of the Mississippi.

But, as Woody had reminded him, he had a story to write, so he mentally put everything else aside and concentrated on the day's events.

An hour later the train was speeding across the Hannibal Bridge. Kevin looked out the left side of the coach at the lights of Kansas City. He thought of Jesse lying on the cold slab in the funeral home, and Jesse's wife crawling into a lonely bed. He was thankful he had Mary and the children to come home to. It had been a long day and he was tired, but it had all been worth the effort. He had his news story ready to go, and he would give his readers an eyewitness account of what had happened. While other reporters wrote down facts from the ticker tape, he would make sure his readers saw the slight smile of treachery on the face of Bob Ford. The nervous look on Charlie Ford that said, "I will never again sleep soundly with this on my conscience." The look of relief on the faces of all the law enforcement officers who were glad to see Jesse meet his fate. The forlorn, lonely look on the face of the Widow James, and the looks of bewilderment on her children. The feel of betrayal and murder in the white house on the hill.

He would let them see Jesse's blood on the bare wood floor, and he would show them the defiant set of Jesse's jaw that even in death said, "I will not be taken alive."

His readers had followed Jesse's life, and he would make sure they were there when Jesse died.

As the train chugged to a stop at Union Depot and he stepped out onto his own turf, he had regained the self-assurance he had lost during the day.

This story was one of his best, and as he headed home to his family, he had not the slightest doubt that he was still the best damn reporter in the city.

## LATE SUMMER, 1882

Red and his companions were camped on a ridge halfway up the mountain. They had found a stand of pine trees protected on all sides by large boulders that sheltered them from the wind.

Red lay back on his bedroll watching stars shine brightly out of a clear summer night. His three companions had turned in and he was left alone with his thoughts. A slight wind whistled through the pine trees above him, and made embers from the cooking fire glow in the darkness. This was his first trip back to Missouri in years. As he often did before drifting off to sleep at night, he thought about Melissa, and all of his friends in Kansas City. He had heard that Adam and Jack were still involved in politics, and he knew that Kevin still worked at the *Kansas City Times*. In Austin, Texas, he had bought a newspaper that had carried Kevin's article on the death of Jesse James. He wondered about Melissa, whether she had children, and what her life was like. The first few years he had worked hard at trying to forget her, but after a while he realized he could not. Even if they could never be together, she would always be a part of him, so he saved these moments before drifting off to sleep at night to think about her, and to ponder what might have been if things had worked out differently. It had been nine years since he had seen her, but he could still picture her clearly and remember everything about her.

Over the years life had taught him some hard lessons. He had learned never to plan too far ahead. Fate had a way of steppin' in and changin' things, so he just took every day as it came, and that way he suffered no surprises or disappointments. He thought back to the day nine years ago, and the gunfight at O'Shea's. He had only planned to spend a few weeks in Crackerneck before turning himself in to the marshall, but fate had other plans for him. He had a lot of friends in bandit country, so he had drifted through the area earning his keep by doctoring livestock.

He knew some of his friends were involved in unlawful activities, and they had heard about his gunfight with the two redlegs. An instant trust was established that let him roam freely through the area.

He had accepted the fact that he was going to have to live without Melissa. She was married to someone else, and there was nothing he could do to change that. He also knew there would never be another woman in his life. He cared too deeply for Melissa, and he vowed never to make himself that vulnerable again.

He had been working at the home of Tom and Betty Jenkins, a newlywed couple. As he filed the edges off a horseshoe, he watched an early April snow fall gently to the ground. Outside the barn, in the gathering dusk, Tom was filling the woodbin against the unexpected return of winter.

Red reached in his pocket. He struck a match on his boot and lifted the globe on a kerosene lantern. In the distance he heard the sound of hoofbeats moving fast through the thin cover of snow. He blew out the match and hung the lantern back on the post. He ran to the barn doors, pushed them shut, and then climbed the ladder to the loft. He peered through a crack in the wall as four men rode swiftly into the clearing.

Tom ran toward the house. One of the men fired a shot in front of him. Tom stopped running and put his hands in the air. The four men rode up to the cabin.

"Good evening, Reb," one of the men said.

Betty walked out of the cabin. She stood beside her husband.

"What do you want?" Tom asked.

"We want you, Reb. We've followed your tracks since sun up, from across the state line."

"We were just married," Tom said. "I haven't left home in three days."

Two of the men dismounted. They walked up to the porch and grabbed Tom. They threw him off the porch into the snow.

"Don't hurt him!" Betty screamed. "You have the wrong man!"

"That don't matter none, ma'am." The leader of the group was dressed in a sheepskin coat. A black beard flowed from beneath his worn black Stetson. Rolls of fat hung loosely from his neck. His horse was bowed from the weight of this huge man.

"We're here to teach a lesson." The fat man's neck quivered as he spoke. "A grieving bride will spread the word that it's not healthy to plunder the state of Kansas."

Red moved swiftly down the ladder. The gang of men had obviously lost the trail of a bandit, and with darkness falling, they were going to take their frustrations out on Tom. Red lifted the carbine from beside his saddle. He crept out of the barn. The snow muffled the sound of his boots.

One of the men was throwing a rope over the limb of a tree. "Don't hurt him!" Betty pleaded hysterically.

The fat man and one of his companions remained on horseback. The other two men tied Tom's hands behind his back.

Red crept up behind the men. He stopped ten yards away. He shifted the carbine to his left hand and lifted the Colt revolver from his holster. Red pulled the hammer back on the revolver. The four men spun around.

"Hold it!" Red pointed the Colt.

The men froze.

Red moved around to where he could face them with the cabin at his back.

"Untie his hands," Red commanded.

The two men looked at the fat man. He nodded his head.

Tom rubbed his wrists.

"Tom, take Betty into the cabin," Red ordered.

Red waited until he heard the bolt fall across the door.

He motioned for the two men on foot to mount their horses.

The man closest to Red leaned forward in the saddle. He peered through the gloom. "I do believe that we have stumbled on bigger game than we planned," he said. "You're Red Farrel!"

Red recognized the man as a regular at the House of Lords.

"The marshall in Kansas City would like to have a talk with you, Red."

Red moved the carbine.

"Turn those horses around real slow and move out of here," he commanded.

The men remained motionless.

Later, Red could remember every detail of the next few moments. He could still hear the owl that was mournfully hooting in the distance, and he could feel the flakes of snow that pushed against his face. He and the four men seemed locked in a time frame. The moment lasted until the man on Red's right turned his horse and went for his gun in the same motion.

The clearing exploded with the flash of gunfire. Rifle fire from the cabin blew two men out of their saddles. Red ducked down. The fat man was going for his gun. Red fired one shot from the Colt revolver. The fat man pitched forward. His horse reared in the air and tumbled the huge man backward into the snow.

The fourth man rode quickly away from the clearing. The hoofbeats of his horse faded in the distance.

Red walked over to where the men lay. The snow was crimson with blood. Two of the men had holes in their chests. Red was thankful that Tom and

Betty were good shots. He turned the fat man over with his boot. What he saw made him realize that his life would never be the same again. The man had taken a bullet above the eye, and beneath his coat gleamed the badge of a county sheriff.

* * *

After the killings, Red had instructed Tom and Betty to leave the area for a few months. He was almost certain they would not be blamed for the killings, but there were those who might want revenge.

Red stayed in Crackerneck until he saw the headline in a Kansas City newspaper: "Kansas Sheriff and Two Deputies Murdered." He only read the first sentence: Red Farrel, fugitive from the law, wanted for murder.

This latest incident confirmed to Red that he was destined for a life on the run. He joined a gang of men he had known during the border war. After several years he became the leader of the small band of outlaws. Red could identify with them, because like him, they didn't seem to fit in anywhere. After all the excitement of the border war and the Civil War, unless a man had a wife and family, it was hard to settle down and lead a normal life.

Six months after the incident in Crackerneck, Tom and Betty Jenkins had come forth and cleared his name in the murder of the sheriff. But Red had already helped rob several banks, and the revelation had only reduced the price on his head from thirty to twenty five thousand dollars.

Red turned over on his side and pulled his blanket over him. He had to get some rest. Tomorrow, in the valley below, they were going to rob the Hannibal & Saint Joseph express train.

* * *

From his vantage point halfway up the mountain, Red watched black smoke curl into the sky. A train whistle sounded in the distance. He moved his horse slowly through the scrub pines, working his way down into the valley below. In the oppressive heat, wisps of dust rose from the horse's hooves. Red watched as his three companions moved off to the left and disappeared around a ridge. An hour earlier they had cut timber and stacked it across the railroad tracks. The train engineer would earn his money trying to stop the train in time as it came out of a steep curve into the barrier. If the engineer succeeded, he would be looking down the barrel of a Colt revolver.

Red made it down to the valley floor. He stationed the horse behind a giant boulder next to the tracks and waited. He preferred robbing trains because there were no town people around, desperate to protect their savings. The robber barons who controlled the railroads had done nothing to endear themselves to the common man. They bled the public with unreasonable freight rates and tariffs. A man would fight to protect his money in a bank, but would not lift a finger to stop a train robbery. The railroads had resorted to hiring detectives to ride with valuable cargo.

The steady clack-clacking on the rails slowed as the train braked for the curve. Red pulled his bandana over his face, lifted his Colt revolver out of his holster, and steadied his horse.

The sound of metal tore against metal as wheels ground against the rails. The train screeched to a halt in front of the barrier. The engineer breathed a sigh of relief. He leaned out the window.

Red moved his horse out from behind the boulder. "Good afternoon, gentlemen."

"Damn!" the engineer swore. He put his hands in the air. The fireman standing behind him did the same.

"Now don't get testy, gentlemen," Red commanded. "We're only going to relieve the Hannibal and Saint Joseph of some excess capital." Red looked down the tracks. His three companions had opened the door of the mailcar. They disappeared inside.

Red kept his gun leveled on the two men until he received a signal from down the tracks.

His companions mounted up. They rode off at a gallop.

Red started to turn his horse. A slug tore into his shoulder an instant before the shot echoed through the valley.

The force of the bullet spun him around in the saddle. He held onto the saddle horn. A man was crouched down next to the tracks aiming a rifle at him. Red spurred his horse toward the shelter of trees in the distance. The next shot ricocheted off the boulder. It whined next to his ear.

The fireman reached down and grabbed a pistol. He fired at the retreating bandit.

Red felt the bullet rip away the flesh on his right side. He leaned low in the saddle.

When he entered the shade of the trees he pulled the horse to a halt. He dismounted. He fell to his knees and waited for the initial shock of the wounds to pass.

The men on the train wouldn't be foolish enough to follow a wounded outlaw into the timber. Red steadied himself against a tree. He rose to his feet. He pulled a shirt out of his saddlebag and threw it on the ground. Holding down the shirt with his foot, he tore it apart with his good arm. He folded the shirt into compresses and placed one against the wounded shoulder, the other against his side.

He gritted his teeth as he remounted the horse. If he was going to pass out he wanted to be in the saddle when it happened.

He headed the horse west.

He was on his own. After a robbery the gang always scattered to make tracking harder for the lawmen who were sure to follow. After several days they would meet up again at a prearranged location.

It was sunset by the time he crossed the Platte River.

The ranch was his only chance for survival. He turned the horse southwest until he came to the St. Joe road. He rode along in the darkness until he started to lose consciousness. He moved the horse off the road into a stand of trees and dense brush. The last thing he remembered was sliding from the saddle.

It was just before daybreak when he opened his eyes. The wounds were starting to seep fresh blood. The thought crossed his mind that he might die. He made several attempts to rise but was too weak.

The horse, reins down, remained at his side.

Several hours passed. The sun started its climb into the morning sky.

Using all the strength he could muster, he rose to his knees and pulled his rifle from the scabbard beside the saddle. Some people weren't charitable towards a man with twenty five thousand dollars on his head. He leaned back against a tree and lost consciousness again.

The sun was falling into the western sky when Red jerked awake. A man's voice could be heard in the distance. The sound was moving closer.

"Swing low, sweet chariot, comin' for to carry me home."

The singing grew louder as the creaking wagon moved along the road.

As it moved past, Red put the butt of the rifle on the ground. He pulled the trigger.

As the shot exploded in the brush, the driver fell backward into the wagon bed.

"Goddamn!" he screamed. He scrambled into a sitting position. He checked his arms and legs for a wound.

"Are you taking good care of those horses, Hemp Cotter?"

"Who's that?" Hemp yelled. "Is that you, Red?"

"It's me all right, you old codger. Answer my question."

"Yes, sir, Red!" Hemp came toward the brush.

"I check their feet every day just like you told me." Hemp pushed away a branch. He saw Red propped against a tree. The wounds had turned his shirt into a mass of blood.

"Goddamn!" Hemp said. "You're shot full of holes, Red Farrel! Have they killed you?"

"I'm not dead yet, Hemp. Could you pull your wagon over here and get me to the ranch?"

Hemp ran for the wagon. When he returned, Red had lost consciousness again. Hemp made a place between the empty vegetable baskets. He lifted Red into the wagon. He tied Red's horse to the back railing.

Hemp turned around to see if Red was watching. He put a whip to the horses.

At Red's place Jim greeted him in the yard. The old Negro climbed into the back of the wagon. He examined Red's wounds.

"We have to get him to a doctor."

Hemp cracked the whip. He drove at a furious pace.

Jim made Red as comfortable as he could.

Hemp drove across the Hannibal Bridge. He yelled at the first man he saw. "Where's a doctor?"

"Doc Meade, over at Second and Walnut," the man replied. "If he's not in his office he lives over on the Pearl Street Hill."

The doctor's office was locked up tight. Hemp turned the horses north on Walnut into the Pearl Street neighborhood.

They stopped a man on the street and he pointed to the doctor's house. Jim beat on the door. A maid answered.

"I got to see Doc Meade."

"He's not in."

"Where can I find him?"

"He's gone to a party up on the hill."

"What's the address?" Jim demanded.

The Negro maid looked him over.

"Don't get uppity with me, woman!"

The maid swallowed hard.

"Judge Braden's place. He lives at Tenth and Penn Street."

Without a word, Jim ran back to the wagon.

Night had fallen by the time the wagon crested the hill.

Music was pouring out of a house down the street. Hemp directed the horses toward the sound. He stopped the wagon in front of two Roman statues guarding the entryway. "We got to be careful about pulling the Doc out of a judge's house," Hemp said. "The place is probably swarmin' with lawmen."

Red moaned. He sat up in the wagon. "Where are we?"

"Don't move, Red. You'll bleed again," Hemp said.

"Who's that with you?"

"It's me, Mister Red. Lie still."

"Jim. How you been?"

"Real good, Mr. Red."

"Where are we?" Red asked again.

"Judge Braden's house. The doc's inside."

Jim jumped off the wagon. "I'll check around back." He returned moments later. "Come on. Let's take him around to the servants' quarters. They're all busy inside."

Red slid off the wagon. "I can walk."

Jim caught him as he started to fall.

"Put your good arm around my shoulder."

In the darkness they moved around the side of the mansion. They entered the servants' quarters, which were stationed about fifty yards in back of the mansion.

"Lay him on the bed, Hemp," Jim commanded.

Red sat down.

"I'll stay with him, Jim."

"Suit yourself. I'll get the doc." Hemp followed Jim out. "Guess I'd better move the wagon down the street a ways."

Melissa Graham was sipping a lemonade. She had just finished her third dance in a row. She was talking to Sarah and Sarah's husband when she saw Jim enter the room. He looked familiar but she couldn't place him. She followed him with her eyes as he moved about, searching the room. Jim asked one of the servants to point out Doc Meade. He pulled the doc away from a group of men and whispered something to him.

As Jim turned to leave, his eyes met Melissa's. There was a spark of recognition. He hurried from the room.

Suddenly she remembered. It was the blacksmith from Red's ranch.

"Excuse me for a moment." Melissa followed Jim into the kitchen, wondering if he was now working for Judge Braden.

The outside door to the kitchen closed as she entered.

She followed the man outside. He entered the servants' quarters.

Melissa walked across the lawn and knocked on the door.

When she pushed it open, Jim stood in the lantern light, a shocked look on his face. As the door closed behind her she heard the hammer on a gun pull back. She turned around. Red leaned against the door. He was covered with blood, and he was pointing a gun at her.

Jim put his hand over her mouth as she started to scream.

Red looked into her eyes. "My God! Melissa!" They stared at each other. "It's all right, Jim."

Jim took his hand away.

Melissa had turned white in the lantern's light and stood speechless.

Doc Meade entered the room. "Where's your sick wife?" he asked Jim.

Jim pointed. The doc turned around.

"Get him on the bed at once!" he commanded.

The doctor cut Red's shirt away and went to work. Hemp and Jim kept the hot water coming. Melissa stood by, watching. Red passed out as the doctor probed for the rifle bullet in his shoulder. When the doctor had finished, he rolled down his sleeves.

"We'll have to move him down to my office."

"Can't do that, Doc," Hemp said.

"Why not?"

"His name's Red Farrel."

"Red Farrel?"

Hemp nodded.

"We can't leave him here," Doc Meade said.

"I live two doors down the street," Melissa said. "Take him around to the guest house. I'll be waiting for you."

John was in Chicago at a lumbermans' convention. She would have to find a way to explain Red's presence to Beth and the housekeeper.

Minutes later they were carrying Red inside the cottage. Melissa had the covers on the bed pulled back.

"We'll get him undressed and into bed, Mrs. Keeney. I'll need some hot water and towels."

"Will he be all right, doctor?" Melissa asked.

"If there's no infection, he should pull through."

She nodded and went to the main house. Beth and the housekeeper were at the door.

"Who are those men, Mother?" Beth asked. Natty, the housekeeper, peered out the door.

"Someone's been hurt," Melissa explained. "A man I knew years ago. The doctor's with him now. He will have to stay here until he can be moved. I want nothing said about this to anyone, understand?"

Beth and the housekeeper nodded.

"Heat some water, Natty. I'll go upstairs and get some towels."

* * *

Melissa laid the morning paper on the table. Natty took away the half-eaten plate of pancakes.

Natty gave her a look of concern.

"I'm sorry Natty. I'm not hungry."

As Melissa sipped her coffee, she read the headlines again: "Armed Gang Robs Train." The article stated that one of the bandits had been badly wounded.

Last night had shocked her considerably. Nine years had passed since the Thanksgiving eve of their wedding announcement party. She had thought about Red often over the years. For her, Christmas Eve was the worst night of the year.

The events of last night had stirred up all the feelings and emotions she had suppressed over the years.

But she had done the best thing under the circumstances. Her marriage to John Keeney was a successful union. He was a wonderful father to Beth.

Melissa took a last sip of coffee. She put the empty cup in the china saucer.

"Are you going back to the guest house, mother?"

She looked across the table at her daughter. Beth had Red's light brown hair and gray eyes.

"Just for a little while, Beth."

"Can I come with you?"

"No, darling. Finish your breakfast." Melissa caressed her daughter's head as she walked past and went out the door.

Red was still asleep. He hadn't awakened since losing consciousness at Judge Braden's place. Perhaps it was just as well. She had mixed emotions about having to face him. She pulled the covers up around his shoulders and left the cottage.

Red blinked his eyes open. A woman was standing over him.

" 'Bout time you came around," she said.

Red tried to get his bearings. "Where am I?"

"You're in the guest house of the Keeney home."

Melissa's face hadn't been a dream.

"Who are you?"

"The housekeeper. You want something to eat?"

"Yes, ma'am."

Natty's expression softened. "I'll tell Mrs. Keeney you're awake."

In the kitchen, Natty fixed hot soup and coffee.

Melissa came in.

"He's awake, Mrs. Keeney."

She stared at the housekeeper.

"You want to take him his dinner, Mrs. Keeney?"

Melissa sat down. "No, Natty. You take it."

Natty put the food on a tray. "You're afraid of something, aren't you?"

"You know me too well, Natty. Just take the man his food. He hasn't eaten in three days."

Several hours later it was time for Red's medication. Melissa put the pills on a tray. She would have to face him sometime. She walked down to the guest house, opened the door and backed into the room. When she turned around, her heart sank. Red Farrel was gone.

* * *

Red kept to the shadows as he made his way down the bluffs to the levee. He made it into the alley behind O'Shea's just as the Friday night poker game was breaking up. He hid in the shadows. Adam, Jack and Kevin came out the back door for their customary nightcap at the House of Lords. They passed next to him. Red stepped in behind. He pulled back the hammer on his pistol. The three men froze.

"Hands in the air!" he commanded.

"You can have our money," Adam said.

"You're gettin' damn careless, Captain Quint."

Adam spun around.

"Red!"

"Hello, Adam."

Adam held out his hand.

"Sorry I can't shake, Adam. I've got a couple of holes in me."

Adam struck a match in the darkness.

"Doc Meade patched me up, but I think the wounds are open again."

Adam checked him over. "Come on, you damn fool. We have to get you over to my place."

Mrs. Quint tucked Red into bed. Adam sent for Doc Meade.

"A state senator harboring a wanted fugitive will make a hell of a story, Kevin."

"Correction, Red. A state senator and a city alderman."

"You ran for another term, Jack?"

"I'm afraid so, Red."

"Congratulations to you both."

"Who shot you?" Adam asked.

"Two of the Hannibal and St. Joseph's finest. They don't like the way I keep borrowin' money from the railroad."

"You're lucky to be alive," Adam said.

Red related the story of his stay at the Keeney home.

"Were you afraid she might turn you in?"

"No. I didn't want her or her family to get in trouble with the law. Gettin' you three in trouble seemed more sensible."

"Where have you been the last few years?" Kevin asked.

"Texas and Oklahoma. How many kids have you and Mary had since I saw you?"

"Two more."

"Five girls?" Red asked.

"No. The last one was a boy."

"Good for you, Kevin. Give Mary my best."

Doc Meade walked into the room. "You sure get around, for a wounded man."

"Sorry to keep botherin' you, Doc."

"We'll be outside, Red," Adam said.

The three men left the room. Jesse James's murder a month ago was fresh in Adam's mind.

"I'm going to the governor and try to strike a deal," he said. "It's Red's only chance of surviving. He would have to serve a short prison term, but he could walk away a free man. The people of Missouri still hold most of these outlaws in high regard. Men like Red helped protect the people and their property during the war, and the people have not forgotten. With the election drawing near, it would be political suicide for the governor to sentence Red to more than two years in prison."

"Red won't turn himself in," Jack said.

"Perhaps you're right. I have to try, however."

* * *

Adam knocked on the Keeney's front door. The housekeeper answered.

"Mrs. Keeney, please."

Melissa appeared moments later.

"I stopped by to thank you for taking care of Red. He's resting at my house."

Melissa let out a sigh of relief. "Come in, Adam."

"No. I . . ."

"Please. I insist."

Adam walked into the house. She motioned him to a chair.

"Why did he leave?" Melissa asked.

"He didn't want to involve your family with the authorities."

"I see. I thought perhaps he didn't trust me."

"I assure you that wasn't the case."

"Will he be all right?"

"Yes. Red will survive, this time."

"This time?"

"He can only come to one end. I'm going to the governor next week and try to strike a deal. If we can get him to turn himself in he would have to serve two years in prison at most."

"Will Red cooperate?"

"I doubt it. He has no real incentive to lead a normal life."

Melissa flushed. "You blame me for that, don't you, Adam?"

"You did what you felt was right. Red is a victim of the times. A lot of men couldn't adjust to the post-war years. Not many of them are still alive."

"When will Red be well enough to leave?"

"It will be two weeks, at least."

"Would you do me a favor, Adam?"

"Certainly."

"After you talk to the governor, drop me a note to let me know Red's decision."

"I'll be happy to. Thank you for receiving me."

"Thank you, Senator. Good day."

Melissa received the telegram two weeks later.

". . . stop . . . Governor agrees . . . stop . . . Red does not."

It was signed Adam Quint.

Melissa walked up the stairs to Beth's room. She had already made the decision. Beth was busy rearranging her bedroom.

"Hello, sweetheart."

"Hello, Mother."

"I have to go visit a friend. Would you like to come?"

Beth made a sour face. "I don't have anything to do while you talk over tea."

Melissa laughed. "This is a secret friend."

Beth's eyes flashed with interest. "The man who stayed at the guest house?"

Melissa walked over and hugged her daughter. "You figured it out so easily."

"What shall I wear, Mother?"

"Whatever you like, darling."

* * *

Bonnie Quint answered Melissa's knock at the door.

"Hello, Bonnie."

"Hello, Melissa. Please come in."

"Thank you. Is Red still a guest in your home?"

"Yes. I'm afraid I have to admit to being hostess at the Friday night poker game."

Melissa smiled.

"They're in the study, Melissa. Would you like for me to announce you?"

"No, thank you. May I go in?"

"Of course."

"You stay here with Mrs. Quint, Beth."

"Yes, Mother. Don't forget your promise."

"I won't, sweetheart."

Melissa walked down the hall. She hesitated before entering the study.

The four men rose to their feet.

"Mrs. Keeney. This is a surprise," Adam said.

Red stared at her. She was as beautiful as he had remembered.

"I came to talk to Red."

Adam escorted her to a chair. She sat down.

Red continued to stare. He wondered how his feelings could remain the same after all these years. How could he still love her after all that had happened?

"We'll wait outside," Jack said.

"No. I want all of you to stay. If Red trusts you with his life, I can trust you with what I have to say. Your friends went to a lot of trouble, Red. Why don't you accept the governor's offer?"

Red looked into her eyes. She turned away.

"None of us wants to see you killed or imprisoned for the rest of your life."

"Thanks for your concern. But my life is my own." Red stated matter-of-factly.

"Not entirely," Melissa answered. She looked away. This was going to be difficult. "When I married John Keeney nine years ago, I'm sure you all thought I did so out of bitterness. That wasn't the case. John is a good man. I didn't realize how good until today. I want you to meet someone, Red." Melissa walked to the open door.

"Beth! Would you come in here?"

Beth walked cautiously into the room.

"Gentlemen, this is my daughter, Beth."

She introduced each of the men by name.

Beth walked closer to Red. "Are you really Red Farrel?" she asked.

"Yes, I am."

"You don't look like an outlaw."

Red laughed. "How is an outlaw supposed to look?"

"Mean, I think."

The men laughed.

"Mother says that you have a horse ranch."

"That's right."

"I love horses. Mother said I could come visit you sometimes."

"She did?"

Beth nodded.

"Go out with Mrs. Quint now, Beth. I'll be right along."

"It was nice meeting you, gentlemen."

Melissa closed the door behind Beth. She took a lace handkerchief from her handbag. Tears ran down her cheeks. She turned to Red. "If you turn yourself in, you can see her whenever you like."

Red looked at her, puzzled.

"Don't you understand, Red? Can't you see it?"

Red stared at her.

"Beth is your daughter. I was two months pregnant when I married John Keeney." Melissa sat down in a chair. She began to cry.

Adam put his hand on her shoulder. "I admire your courage, Melissa," he said.

Red stared at her, speechless. "I don't know what to say."

"Don't say anything. Isn't she worth living for?" Melissa asked.

"Yes. Of course she is," Red managed to answer.

"Then accept the governor's offer."

"Does Beth know about this?"

"No. You can tell her, if and when you think she should know."

Red leaned back in his chair. He stared out the open window. "Adam. Tell the governor we've struck a bargain."

On September 1, 1882, Red Farrel entered the federal penitentiary at Fort Leavenworth.

# 9

# MICHAEL

AUGUST 10, 1885

With four members of his gang, Michael Pacini walked along the street. They stopped on the outskirts of the Toad-a-Loup district.

Located on the Kaw River at the state line, between Kansas and Missouri, the no-man's-land deep in Kansas City harbored cutthroats, thieves, and gamblers. The police and local citizenry refused to go into the district. Escaped convicts or criminals on the run were safe if they could make it into the Toad-a-Loup. Anyone foolish enough to go into the district did so at their own risk.

Michael picked up a rock. He threw it hard against the side of a ramshackle building. Upstairs a window opened. A young man peered out. He had his fingers to his lips. Michael waved for him to come down.

With his boots in hand, Willy Lavetti hurried down the back stairs. He looked back up at the window.

"The Union Pacific called the old man back to work last night. He'll skin me if I wake him up." Willy sat down in the alley. He pulled on his boots. At sixteen, the hairline on his head was already beginning to recede. Unlike Michael's other companions, Willy was not a tough guy. He got by on his rough-looking exterior and a keen sense of humor. On another occasion Willy had guided Michael through the Loop district and Michael had taken a liking to him.

"Where are we going?" Willy asked.

"My Uncle Frank needs help with a past-due account," Michael answered.

"Not in the Toad-a-Loup?"

Michael smiled.

Willy stood up. "I was afraid of that." He glanced at Michael's companions. None of the group was over the age of eighteen. Billy clubs were visible beneath their jackets.

"I don't feel good, Michael," Willy said. "It could be the bubonic plague." Michael pointed for Willy to lead the way. He made a gesture of futility. "Like I said. Why don't we go down into the Toad-a-Loup." Willy headed out of the alley.

Three blocks from the Kaw, the overwhelming smell of garbage and stagnating water permeated the air. Groups of ragged men huddled in alleys and doorways. Two prostitutes lounged seductively against a building. Heavy rouge covered their worn, haggard faces. They smiled at the young men as they passed on the street. Michael tipped his hat.

"You better go back, Willy," one of the gang said. "They look like your type."

They all laughed. Willy was too busy scanning the alleys to appreciate the humor.

They arrived at the heart of the Toad-a-Loup. "Form a wedge," Michael said.

Willy went to the back of the formation. Michael unbuttoned his coat.

An occasional catcall of "spaghetti-man" or "dago-bait" sounded from an alley as they passed, but so far, so good.

Halfway down the block, Michael went into a one-story building. The structure was unique to the district, for it still had glass in the front windows.

Michael's gang followed him into the dilapidated restaurant. Their hobnail boots beat heavily on the dusty wooden floor. The dingy restaurant reeked of grease. Only three of the twenty or so tables were occupied. Michael walked over to the counter. A man in a coffee-stained green vest looked him over.

"What do you want?" he asked through rotten teeth.

"You Mr. Biddel?"

"That's what it says on the window."

Michael took a paper out of his pocket. He laid it on the counter.

"I'm from Pacini's Produce Company. You owe us eighty dollars. You're six months past due."

Biddel studied him. "You work on the market, young fella?"

"I'm the collector."

"You're awful young to be out doin' a man's job."

Michael pushed the bill across the counter. "Eighty dollars," he said.

Biddel scratched his greasy beard. "I reckon I won't have it 'til next month. Times is hard." Biddel smiled at three men who were sitting at a table watching the exchange.

"My uncle took a chance on you, Biddel. You couldn't get credit anywhere else on the market. Why don't you pay your bill?"

Biddel waved Michael away. "Tell your uncle I'll pay when I can. Now get out of here!"

Biddel watched as Michael moved around the counter toward him. Biddel backed away.

Michael reached down and took a metal cash box off the shelf.

"You can't do that!"

Michael counted the money. "Thirty dollars. Where's the rest of it?"

"That's all I have. I swear it."

Michael reached in his jacket. He pulled out a small derringer and placed it at Biddel's temple.

"You have five seconds to come up with fifty dollars, Biddel."

One of the men sitting at a table slipped quietly out of the restaurant. "Don't shoot!" Biddel reached for his wallet. His hands shook as he counted out the money. Michael slipped the fifty into his pocket. With his companions he backed out of the restaurant. Out on the street he looked around. It was too quiet.

"Get ready," he said. His companions reached for their clubs.

"Don't run and don't let yourself get separated from the wedge."

They started down the block. Shadows were visible in alleys as they passed. Down the street a group of men materialized from out of an alley. They moved out into the street to meet the young intruders. Michael kept the wedge moving. The Toad-a-Loup men walked quickly along beside them. Two of the men lunged at the wedge.

"Go for the knees!" Michael yelled.

The thud of clubs smacked against flesh and bone. The two men went down screaming.

"Keep moving!" Michael directed. They quickened their pace. Angry voices sounded all around. Michael made a visual count. They were outnumbered at least three to one.

Two more blocks and they would be out of the heart of the Toad-a-Loup.

The mob of angry men rushed the wedge in an all-out assault. Clubs and fists went flying through the air. Michael and his gang were separated along the street. He clubbed a man across the back. He hit another in the rib cage. Willy was next to him fighting with his fists. There were too many Toad-a-Loup men. They were going to be overwhelmed.

Michael pulled out his derringer. He fired a shot into a man's leg. The man cried out and fell to the street. At the sound of gunfire the Toad-a-Loup men fell back.

Michael lifted Willy out of the street.

"Are you okay?"

Willy nodded.

Michael formed up his gang. Down the street more men were coming at them.

"Run!" Michael yelled. He fell to one knee and fired another shot. The angry mob scattered. Michael took off running after his companions. They didn't stop until they were out of the Toad-a-Loup.

Willy leaned against a building. His chest heaved as he gulped in air. "Everyone okay?" Michael asked. They all nodded. Willy started walking away.

"Where you going?" Michael asked.

Willy turned around. "Home, where it's safe."

"You weren't scared were you, Willy?"

"No. I always repeat the Twenty-third Psalm."

Michael laughed. He watched Willy disappear between the houses.

A caravan of watermelon wagons went by, headed out of the Kaw River Valley toward Market Square. Michael and his friends jumped aboard. They rode the wagons north through the West Bottoms and around the bluffs.

At Market Square Michael's gang jumped off the wagons and faded into the tenement district.

Michael whistled a tune as he walked east along Fifth Street. He felt secure back in the Italian section.

During his nine years of employment at O'Shea's, Michael had worked his way from sweeping floors and washing dishes to the assistant manager's position. His olive skin stretched tautly over a thin muscular frame, and his black hair and dark eyes made him the darling of the girls in Little Italy. The killing of the two men three years ago had created an aura of respect and mystery about him. He did nothing to dispel his image as a loner and street character. Not many eighteen-year-olds were taken as seriously as Michael Pacini.

He thought about what he would say to his uncle. Nothing seemed right.

Frank Pacini had moved his family out of Little Italy into a fashionable home on the east side.

The white frame house appeared from out of the night. He walked up the steps and went in.

"Is that you, Michael?"

"Yeah, Aunt Leah."

His aunt met him in the hall. She kissed his cheek. "Your dinner is on the stove, Michael."

"You saved me dinner?"

"Yes. Steak and potatoes."

"Umm, sounds good."

"Go sit down." Leah pushed her nephew gently toward the kitchen.

"Where's Uncle Frank?"

"He's out on the back porch, resting."

"Is he in a good mood?"

"Don't upset your uncle tonight, Michael."

"I just want to talk to him, Aunt Leah."

Leah raised her eyebrows knowingly.

The back door slammed. Frank Pacini walked down the hallway.

"Did Michael get ho —. . . Oh, hello, Michael."

"Hello, Uncle Frank."

Michael reached in his pocket. "Here's your Toad-a-Loup money." He handed the cash to his uncle.

"You went into the Toad-a-Loup? How did you know Biddel owed me money?"

"Your foreman eats at O'Shea's."

"I want you to stay out of the Toad-a-Loup, Michael."

"Okay, Uncle Frank. How was business today?"

Frank smacked his fist into his open palm. "I tell you, Michael, business gets better every day. I can't handle it all."

Here it comes, Michael thought.

"For years I scratched for any business I could find. Now I'm turning it away."

"That's great, Uncle Frank."

"Great? What's great about it?"

"You can hire more men, Uncle Frank."

"Sure. But will they care about the business? No! I need someone I can trust. Someone to carry on after I retire."

Michael put down his fork. "I have to talk to you, Uncle Frank."

"What about?"

"I've been offered a job at another restaurant."

"Where?"

"Tony Latta's place on south Main."

"What kind of position?"

"Tony wants me to manage the restaurant and buy in for twenty percent of the profits. The closer Tony gets to retirement the more I control. Someday I'll own the restaurant."

Anger welled in Frank Pacini's face. He slammed his fist on the table. Michael's fork flipped off the plate onto the floor.

"Twenty percent! You could go to work for me and make three times the money. I'll give you fifty percent ownership today."

"I don't want to run a produce stall on the market, Uncle Frank."

"Run a stall? Who's asking you to run a stall? My wagons deliver produce all over the city. I'm on the phone constantly: Buying, selling, meeting deadlines. The produce business is the fastest, most exciting in the world. If you would take time to stop by the market you would know what goes on!"

"I don't like the produce business, Uncle Frank."

"You don't like it? Do you hear that, Leah? He don't like the produce business!" Frank knew that Leah would be listening intently in the parlor. Frank pointed his finger at Michael.

"You would have starved if I'd had that attitude!"

"I always paid my own way, Uncle Frank."

Frank moved around the table. He faced his nephew.

"Not enough glamour in the produce business for you, Michael? You want to be a big shot. Walk around in your fancy clothes, impressing the girls. The wrong kind hang out at Latta's place!"

"Who are the wrong kind, Uncle Frank?" Michael's eyes flashed with anger. "People who don't smell like they're fresh out of the stockyards or Market Square?"

"There, you see?" Frank pointed his finger at Michael. "You don't care about the restaurant business, Michael. You want a position that will help you move up in society. You even talk like Quality Hill, not like an Italian."

Michael angrily pushed his uncle's hand away. "I talk like an American, Uncle Frank. Why don't you let me live my life?" Michael knew just how far to push his uncle. As a youngster he had watched Frank Pacini destroy two men with his bare hands who had tried to extort money from him.

"Because you're determined to make a mess of it!" Frank shouted.

"Then let me, Uncle Frank!"

Leah Pacini walked quietly into the room. She stood beside the kitchen table. Frank looked at her. He slumped wearily into a chair. Michael knew his aunt had heard enough. He sat down.

"Where are you going to get the money for your twenty percent?" Frank asked.

"I've saved part of it. I have to borrow the rest."

"And what does Mr. Hannon say after employing you all these years?"

"He hates to lose me, Uncle Frank, but he got started the same way."

"I suppose he's willing to loan you the money?"

"If you refuse."

Frank raised his hands in a gesture of futility.

"How much do you need?"

"I have a thousand. I need another."

Frank Pacini's shoulders sagged as he got up from the table.

"A check will be on the table in the morning." He left the room.

Michael stared at his food, afraid to look at his aunt.

The argument wasn't supposed to end this way. He had pictured himself shouting the last words and running from the house. He took a half-hearted bite of cold potatoes.

"Your uncle worships you, Michael. Why do you treat him this way?"

He put down his fork. "I'm sorry, Aunt Leah. He just don't understand how I feel."

"He has three daughters, Michael. Try to understand how *he* feels. He's worked his whole life to build something that you don't want any part of. You're rejecting him when you reject his work."

"I don't mean to, Aunt Leah. It seems every time we try to talk it turns into a fight."

"I know. You're too much alike."

Michael pushed away his plate. "I'm going outside and get some air."

He walked out on the porch. He looked up at the starless sky. His stomach was in knots from the argument.

A glowing ember moved along the street. Old man Ramponi failed to notice Michael as he passed in front of the house puffing on a cigar.

It was Thursday night and he was headed for the Sons of Italy meeting. Ramponi had recently married. He had agreed to take a bride from the old country to save her from a life of misery.

Michael imagined the old man's glee when he went to the train and found the luscious creature that was Maria Ramponi. She was forty years Ramponi's junior. The most stunning woman Michael had ever seen. When she ate at O'Shea's restaurant with her husband she would watch him with those black eyes until he met her gaze. Then she nonchalantly looked away.

Michael imagined her naked body in front of him. He looked up the street. Why not? Mr. Ramponi would be at the Sons of Italy meeting for three hours at least. Four, if he got drunk. Michael walked off the porch and headed up the street. He paced nervously back and forth watching the house. A shadow passed by the lamp in the window. He went up to the house and rapped on the door. Maria Ramponi answered. She stood in the doorway, a questioning look on her face.

Michael looked into her eyes. He let his gaze roam over her body. Maria tried to close the door. Michael smiled at her. He held the door open with his leg. He pushed his way into the house. Maria backed away. Her dark eyes glared at him. Dressed in a thin blue nightgown, she held a robe in front of her.

Michael grabbed the robe out of her hands. He tossed it aside. Maria reached for the door. Michael grabbed the back of her hair. He pulled her close to him and roughly kissed her on the lips. Maria fought free. Michael backed her into the dining room. She felt the edge of the table against her back. Michael watched as her breathing pressed the wide brown nipples of her breasts against the nightgown. He cupped her breast with his hands. Maria pursed her lips. She spit on him. Michael smacked her hard across the face. He cut her lip. Blood ran down her cheek. He grabbed the back of her hair and pulled her down on the table. Maria fought hard to push him away. The table was full of dinner dishes. A plate of leftover food went crashing to the floor. Michael grabbed the top of her nightgown. He ripped it away from her breasts. Maria tried to knee him in the groin. Michael pushed his knee between her legs and forced her back onto the table. He could vaguely hear plates and saucers crashing to the floor. He kissed her face and neck. Maria grabbed a knife. Michael squeezed her wrist until the knife dropped to the floor. He was conscious of her fists pounding against the side of his head. He ripped the rest of the nightgown from her body. Somehow he was out of his pants. Michael wasn't sure when she stopped fighting. Her love-making was as violent as her temper. They tore hungrily at each other.

He held back until he felt her spasms. She moaned against his neck. He let go.

The smell of leftover food reached his consciousness and he rose to his knees on the dining room table. He looked around. The room was a shambles. He pulled up his pants and slid off the table. He started picking the plates up off the floor. He gave Maria a look of apology.

She smiled as she got off the table.

Michael picked up her nightgown from the floor and handed it to her. She tossed it aside. She took his hand and led him upstairs to the bedroom.

Several hours later, Michael smiled as he headed home in the darkness. It had been quite a day. Not only was he part owner of a successful business, he now had his own mistress. He whistled softly as he turned for one last look at the light shining in the Ramponi's second story bedroom.

## FROM ADAM QUINT'S JOURNAL — SEPTEMBER 1, 1885

*Red has been out of prison for a year now. He keeps to himself, but he does seem to be adjusting well. He sees Beth at every opportunity, and he seems to come out of his shell when he's around her. All of us hoped he and Melissa might one day be friends, but that does not seem to be happening. Red does not speak of her or make any attempt to see her. Perhaps in the future he will feel confident enough to try a friendship. At any rate, it is good to have him back with us.*

*The doctor informed Bonnie and I last week that we will probably never have children. It was a blow for us, but something we will just have to accept. We are fortunate in that one or two of the Donavan girls always seem to be in the house. We love them dearly, and it's almost as if they belong to us. I'm certain that Kevin and Mary make a special effort to share them with us. The girls call Bonnie, Aunt Bonnie, and me, Uncle Adam. It is such a joy to have them around.*

*Bonnie and I rent a house in Jefferson City when the Missouri senate is in session. We don't like to be away from Kansas City for too long, so we come back as often as possible. Although I had to give up my teaching job, I still send my weekly column into the Times by courier. Over the years the column has acquired a life of its own, and it's always around whispering in my ear to be finished. Jack has been in control of the First Ward for five years now. His hand-picked men are winning elections in other districts of the city as well. He is the most powerful politician in the city and his influence is reaching across the state of Missouri. Jack is a people's politician, and he has turned out to be everything I had hoped. If his humanitarian brand of politics can spread across the city and the state, the common man will be all the better for it.*

*The city continues to grow. Speculators from the East have started a real estate boom by bidding up land prices. Most prices are inflated well above value, and there should be a correction soon.*

*We now have over 600 arc lights that are serviced by an electric power company, and cable cars have been introduced in the city.*

## MAY 11, 1886

Mary Donavan dried the last of the luncheon dishes. She placed them in the cupboard.

Thunder rumbled menacingly in the distance.

She tried to ignore the nervous quiver in her stomach.

She walked outside and looked at the sky. Thunderheads were building in the west. Lightning flashed through the bulging clouds, streaking the sky.

She had lived through one cyclone that had struck the area, huddled against the walls of the house with the girls pulled close to her. The experience had left her terrified of storms. The cyclone had missed them by a few blocks and devastated parts of the city.

No experiences in Ireland had prepared her for the storms of the Midwest. The city's residents went about their daily tasks watching skies that at any moment could sweep down and claim them as victims.

Mrs. Kratz, her neighbor, came out into the yard. "How's Joey, Mary?" "Fine, Mrs. Kratz."

"Are the girls at school?"

"Yes."

They watched the clouds move slowly across the sky. The thunderheads expanded up and out like giant mushrooms.

"I'm sure they'll release the children early, Mary."

She walked around to the side of the house. After the last cyclone she had insisted they have a storm cellar built. She opened the cellar door and climbed down. She lit a candle and brushed away the cobwebs. All her supplies were in place. She climbed the steps and closed the trap door.

She heard Joey talking as she entered the house. She went into his room. "Did you have a nice nap, sweetheart?"

He smiled up at her.

Joe Jack Donavan had been born on a cold night in January in 1881. He was a frail baby weighing four pounds, one ounce. His red fingers had constantly formed into miniature fists like a boxer flexing his knuckles. Even though it was her fifth delivery, Mary had checked every inch of him for defects.

"Why doesn't he cry, doctor?"

"I assure you he's perfectly all right, Mrs. Donavan."

"All babies cry, doctor."

"Perhaps he has no reason to cry."

"Is something the matter with his voice box?"

"Mrs. Donavan, your baby is in perfect health. I'm sure he will eventually do his share."

But he never did. He would sound an occasional outcry if he needed attention. The Donavan household came to a complete standstill when this occurred. Everyone rushing to the baby's crib to lend assistance.

The two older Donavan girls couldn't keep their hands off the bundle in the nursery. At least once a week, Kevin lectured the household about the danger of turning the boy into something less than a rough, tough Irishman.

When Joey was old enough to crawl, Anna, the oldest of the Donavan girls, would play patty-cake and tickle him under the chin until he lost his breath from laughing.

"Roll it and roll it and mark it with a T, and put it in the oven for Joey and me."

"His name is Joe, Anna!" Kevin always admonished her.

"Yes, Father." But to Anna the verse sounded out of rhyme. Joe Donavan became Joey to everyone but his father.

The five-year-old raised his arms to Mary as thunder shook the house. Mary walked outside holding Joey in her arms. The sky had turned a hazy green. Not a breath of air stirred. The clouds were starting to roll from the energy trapped inside them.

Mary could stand it no longer. She put Joey on the ground and took off her apron. She threw it in the kitchen door. She lifted Joey off the ground and took him over to Mrs. Kratz's house.

"I'm going to meet the girls, Mrs. Kratz."

"Joey will be safe with me, Mary."

She hurried out of the yard and started walking north on Wyandotte Street.

Why am I doing this? she thought. An hour from now the sun will be shining, the birds will be singing, and the girls will be safe at home. She started to run. Her foot caught in her skirt and she fell. She picked herself off the ground and brushed at her clothes. She glanced off to the west and saw a funnel spin out of the clouds. It dipped down for a moment as if searching the ground, then spun back into the clouds. Feeling panic, Mary held onto her skirts. She turned the corner on Eighth Street and headed west to May. The horizon was a splash of pinks and greens as lightning flashed about. It would be almost beautiful if I weren't so afraid, she thought. The clouds above seemed to be closing in on the ground, as if a giant vise were squeezing shut and would catch her in its grasp. Mary stopped running to catch her breath.

To the west, an enormous thunderhead started to roll. It turned faster and faster. Terrified, Mary watched as the mass of turbulence spun across the sky. It dipped down and reached the earth in a swirling, churning mass of destruction. The giant cyclone headed across the river into the heart of the city.

"No!" Mary screamed.

The Lathrop School had just been dismissed. The children were on their way out of the building when the cyclone slammed into the schoolyard.

A giant bell at the top of the school was torn loose by the violent wind. It came crashing down through the floors, crushing everything in its path.

Mary ran up to the school moments after the cyclone had passed.

Injured children were lying everywhere. She frantically searched for the girls. They were nowhere to be found. She spotted the principal.

"Where are the rest of the children?"

He looked at her in a daze. "The bell in the tower collapsed on the floors. Everything fell into the basement."

Her heart seemed to stop. She looked at the tons of stone.

She started lifting the debris and throwing it aside. The thought of her little girls crushed and bleeding was more than she could bear. She cried hysterically as she tore at the mass of stone. Her fingers were cracked and bleeding. She worked on until someone grabbed her roughly from behind. She fought to get away.

"Let me go! My babies are in there!"

Kevin turned her around. He smacked her hard across the face.

"Mary! Listen to me! The girls are safe. I got them out before the storm hit. Do you hear me, Mary?"

"Oh, Kevin." Mary collapsed, sobbing on his shoulder.

"I thought they were dead, Kevin."

He held her tight, stroking her hair. "It's all right, Mary. It's all right."

When she calmed down he wiped her face with his handkerchief.

"We have to help with the injured children, Kevin."

"I'll help. You go over to the office and take the girls home."

"Yes. I should do that." Mary walked away from the rubble.

When she arrived home with her girls, she hugged each of them tightly to her. She thanked God they were safe.

* * *

John Keeney's office door flew open. His foreman filled the space.

"Mr. Keeney! Big storm's comin'!"

John placed his pen back in the ink well and hurriedly shoved his papers in the top drawer of the desk. He rushed outside to supervise moving the lumber that was ready for delivery back under cover. Out in the lumber yard all was quiet. The air lay thick and heavy. John loosened his collar as sweat ran down his back. Suddenly, several stacks of lumber lifted into the air. The boards hung suspended in the air for a moment before settling back to earth. The lumber yard buildings expanded and contracted as if they had a life of their own. John moved further out into the lumber yard to observe the phenomena.

"Mr. Keeney!" John spun around, reacting to the terrified yell of his foreman.

"Oh my God!" he stared, mesmerized at the spinning black cloud. He tried to run, but he was already caught in the vacuum. His screams were lost in the violent winds.

* * *

"Uncle Jack! Uncle Jack! Look at my new dress!" Teresa, Kevin's ten-year-old daughter, spun around. Molly, the six-year-old, tugged at Jack's sleeve.

"Would you read us a story after supper, Uncle Jack?"

"Children, please!" Mary called. "Leave your Uncle Jack alone."

"It's all right, Mary. Your dress is lovely, Teresa. We'll have that story, Molly. But first you have to eat all your supper."

"Ugh." Molly made a sour face. "We're having cooked cabbage."

Jack chuckled. He loved Sunday afternoon at the Donavans'. It was his refuge from the business world and the problems of government. He could leave Boss Hannon out on the porch and become Uncle Jack for a few hours. The girls sat wide-eyed at the table, watching his every move.

"Did you see the cyclone, Uncle Jack?" Margaret, the nine-year-old, asked.

"No, Margaret. I heard it, but I didn't see it."

"Me neither," Margaret said dejectedly.

Anna, the oldest, tugged at her pigtail. "The paper said sixteen children were killed."

"That's correct, Anna," Jack answered.

"I feel so badly for the parents," Mary said.

"Yes, we all do."

"Can city government do anything to make the schools safer?" Kevin asked.

"We've ordered that all bells be taken down from school towers. In the future, at the first sign of a dangerous storm, we are going to have the schools dismissed."

"When will the services for John Keeney be held?" Kevin asked.

"Wednesday at the Presbyterian Church."

"How's Melissa holding up?"

"She's taking it hard. She and John had grown very close over the years."

"I went over to the West Bottoms yesterday to have a look at damage," Kevin said. "I'm surprised anyone survived. John was evidently standing in the lumber yard when the cyclone hit. It was like a thousand spears were thrown at him. After striking the bottoms, the cyclone skipped over the bluffs at Eighth Street and slammed into the school."

Mary looked at her children, thankful they were safe at the table. "We'll pay our respects to Melissa after supper," she said.

## OCTOBER, 1887

Melissa put down her pen. She closed the ledger. It had been seventeen months since John's death. She had decided to stop feeling sorry for herself and start running the lumber business John had worked so hard to build. Three months ago she had gone down to the West Bottoms and had taken over management of the company. Hard work had proven to be the antidote she needed.

Real estate transfers had risen from five million in 1880 to one hundred and ninety million in this year of 1887. People were buying property and building at a frantic pace. Speculators from the East were paying $2500 a front foot for property that previously had sold for $250 an acre. Like everyone else, Melissa was riding the boom. Demand for lumber was exceeding supply.

Day by day, with hard work and shrewd dealing, she was earning the respect of her employees. Last Wednesday she had shut down the lumber yard after two weeks of reported customer shortages. On the busiest day of the week she had demanded an inventory be taken. At the end of the day she fired a foreman and his entire crew for stealing.

Beth walked into the room.

"All ready to go?" Melissa asked.

"Yes, Mother." Beth went to the window. She pulled back the curtain. At fourteen, she was going through a rebellious stage in which she wanted to become anything but a young lady. Melissa did not push her, as she remembered those days of childhood when nothing seemed less important than frilly dresses and social graces.

"You seem even more excited than usual."

Beth smiled. "Uncle Red said he had a surprise for me."

Red had been released from prison in the fall of 1884. His first weekend out of jail he had shown up outside the Keeney home. He had sat in his carriage until John had gone out to talk with him. John had been comfortable with Red's visits. John had a good relationship with Beth, and he knew Red was too good a man to come between them. No amount of persuasion had convinced him to enter the house. Beth had packed her bag and gone to the ranch with him. When Beth arrived home on Monday, Melissa knew she had made the right decision. Beth was ecstatic about her weekend. Red had decorated a room for her and given her a horse. Every other weekend, Beth could hardly wait to leave.

"He's here!" Beth grabbed her bag off the stairs.

"Good-bye, Mother." Melissa hugged her daughter.

"Have fun, darling." Melissa moved to the window. She watched Beth bound down the steps to the carriage. How many times had she watched this scene the last three years! Red never looked toward the house or made any indication she even existed. At first she thought it was out of respect for John; but over the years she began to realize that any feelings he once had for her were gone. As the carriage pulled away, Melissa dropped the curtain. She went back to her desk.

Fourteen years was a long time to think about a decision made in anger. She had been so young, and so very right. Perhaps prison had hardened Red. It had been five full years since she had gone down to Senator Quint's house and asked Red to turn himself in. Five years since a word was spoken between them. Time had diminished the war, even visions of her father, but time had not diminished her love for Red. Perhaps if he had been willing these past few years, they could have reached some sort of compromise. But time had hardened Red. He would not even acknowledge her existence. She knew she was responsible for the way things had turned out, but that did not make them any easier to bear.

"Your dinner's ready, Mrs. Keeney." Natty poked her head around the corner.

"Thank you, Natty."

The weekends were hardest to bear. She had started going to the office

**Old Union Depot in the West Bottoms**

on Saturdays to get away from the house. She walked through the dining room to the side porch. Below her, lights from the West Bottoms glowed in the dusk.

The city was alive on this October night. Within an hour, Grover Cleveland and his beautiful young bride would be riding an express train across the Hannibal Bridge into the city. Down below, the crowd was already gathering at the Union Depot. She went back inside.

"You had better eat," Natty admonished her. "Mr. Compton will be here soon."

"Did you lay out my dress, Natty?"

"Yes. Now hurry along!"

* * *

Red pulled the carriage to a halt in front of Bullene, Moore and Emery.

"Why are we stopping here, Uncle Red?"

"We have to pick up a dress for you."

"A dress?" Beth made a face.

Red laughed. He pulled an envelope from his pocket. He handed it to Beth.

"What is it?" she asked.

"Read for yourself."

Beth pulled a white satin invitation from the envelope. She opened it and read the gold-embossed letters.

"I think I'm going to faint," she said.

"Don't do that. I'll be without an escort."

Red's fourteen-year-old daughter read the invitation again.

"Mr. Red Farrel. You and your guest are invited to the Coates House for dinner with the president and Mrs. Cleveland. Dancing after dinner." Like a lot of people in the East, the president had a fascination for the wild West. Elvin Brewer's books and articles had made Red a folk hero, and the president wanted to meet him.

"You'll be my guest, won't you?" Red asked.

"Uncle Red, I'll be so nervous!" Beth's hands shook as she held the envelope.

Red laughed again. "Won't we all," he agreed.

Beth took his hand. She jumped unceremoniously from the carriage into the middle of the street. She put her hand to her mouth and looked at Red. They went laughing into the clothing store.

Jack and Adam waited on the station platform with the rest of the dignitaries. The crowd bulged away from the station for a half mile in every direction. They had come to greet the first Democratic president elected since before the Civil War. Kevin stood behind the pair, pencil and paper in hand.

The city had prepared months in advance for the visit. The crowd was happy and ready to celebrate.

Mary had implored Kevin to remain sober. They both knew better.

The crowd cheered as the presidential train swept across the bridge and thundered into the station. The cheers resounded as the president and his lovely bride stepped onto the station platform.

"She's a beauty," Kevin said.

"That she is, Kevin," Jack replied.

"There are rumors that he beats her," a bystander said.

"If he does, I'd like to watch," Kevin said.

Jack chuckled. "You're absolutely perverted, Kevin Donavan."

The bride, dressed in brown silk with matching bonnet, spoke graciously to all the dignitaries.

The presidential party was loaded into a carriage pulled by six white horses. They were escorted to the Coates House by the swarming crowd.

Melissa stood in the receiving line with her escort, Fred Compton. She had been selected by the business community to accompany the presidential party. Fred owned a tannery in the West Bottoms. On those rare occasions when she ventured out, Fred was usually at her side.

She shook hands and made small talk with those passing in front of her. She looked down the line, shocked to see Red and Beth moving toward her.

"Are you all right, Melissa?" Fred asked.

"Yes, I'm fine." How would she face Red after all these years? She looked for an escape route. There wasn't any.

Beth stopped in front of her, grinning.

"Hello, Mother."

"Beth, darling, what a beautiful dress. So, this was your surprise?"

"Yes. Isn't it exciting?" Beth whispered. She moved on down the line.

Red took Melissa's hand. He held it briefly without looking at her. He continued down the line behind Beth. Melissa watched him until he finished the receiving line. He never once glanced in her direction.

After dinner the president moved to the podium for a short speech. With his sturdy frame and walrus mustache, he looked more the president of a local union than chief executive of the country.

Red and Beth were introduced to the president as they entered the ballroom.

"This is a pleasure, Mr. Farrel."

"Pleasure's mine, Mr. President."

The president grinned. "And who is this lovely young lady?"

"My number-one trail hand, Mr. President. Her name is Beth Keeney."

The president laughed. "If only all trail hands were so beautiful."

Beth flushed. "Thank you, Mr. President."

Red leaned close to the president and his bride.

"The newspapers were right. If you want anyone's undivided attention, Mr. President, you're gonna have to leave your wife at home."

The president and Mrs. Cleveland laughed. "That comment just earned you the first dance of the evening, Mr. Farrel," Mrs. Cleveland said.

All the invited guests had entered the ballroom. The president and his wife walked through the crowd to where Beth and Red were standing. Everyone applauded as Mrs. Cleveland took Red's arm and led him onto the dance floor. The president and Beth followed. The orchestra struck up the "Missouri Waltz." The couples began twirling to the music.

At O'Shea's, Kevin lay passed out on a table.

The presidential train had long since pulled out of Union Depot and away from the exhausted city.

Jack said good-bye to the last of the merrymakers as they staggered out the door. He lifted Kevin off the table, put him over his shoulder and carried him out the door. Mary was still awake when he pushed open the Donavans' front door. She pointed to the stairs. Jack carried Kevin up and deposited him on the bed.

"Did he get his story filed?" Mary asked.

Jack patted his coat pocket. "I have it here."

Joey walked into the bedroom dressed in his nightgown.

"Is Daddy drunk?" he asked.

"What are you doing up, young man?" Mary lifted him into her arms.

"Daddy overdid," Joey said.

Jack chuckled.

"He certainly did," Mary agreed.

"Does he hurt?" Joey asked.

Mary smiled. "No, dear. He won't hurt until tomorrow. Now let's get you to bed."

"Good night, Uncle Jack."

"Good night, Joey."

Jack started undressing Kevin. Mary came back and they managed to get him under the covers.

"When he revives, tell him I've filed the story," Jack said. "I'll explain his absence to the editor."

"Come downstairs," Mary commanded. "You're going to have some coffee before I turn you loose on the streets."

"Good idea." Jack followed her down the stairs. Mary put a pot of coffee on the stove. She sat down.

"Was she as beautiful as they say, Jack?"

Jack laughed. "Poor Grover Cleveland. No one's paid much attention to him since he married that beauty."

"Tell me all about it."

Jack reached into his pocket. He handed Mary the story Kevin had written.

"The presidential visit, described by an expert. I'll pour the coffee."

When Mary finished she handed Jack the story. "He's a good reporter."

"The best there is," Jack agreed. "You won't be too hard on him will you, Mary?"

"You two," Mary said, shaking her head. "After all these years you're still protecting each other."

"Kevin worships you, Mary. Drink is his only vice."

Mary nodded. "I've always thought so."

Jack sipped his coffee. "We don't get much chance to talk, Mary. Don't think me bold, but I've wondered about your finances."

"We're doing fine," Mary replied. "We're living better than I ever thought possible."

"You won't hesitate to ask if you're in need? I like to think of these little ones as part mine, you know."

Mary took his hand. "You're as much a part of this family as any member. Of course we will come to you."

Mary put down her cup. She leaned back in the chair.

"What about marriage?" she asked.

"For me?"

Mary nodded. "Don't you need a refuge from the frantic pace of government?"

Jack mulled over the question.

"I went through a period when I yearned for a companion. Over the years it's become less and less important."

"But it isn't too late!" Mary said. "You're only thirty-seven years old."

Jack laughed.

"Don't you want a family of your own, Jack?"

"I have more families than anyone, Mary. Go down to the North End or the Bottoms and ask anyone who his father is. If he doesn't reply Boss Hannon, you get his name and address."

Mary chuckled. "In this town, the departed Grover Cleveland pales in your presence."

They laughed together.

Mary sipped her coffee. "Kevin is worried about you, Jack."

Surprised, Jack looked up from his coffee. "Why, for heaven's sake?"

"He says that having too much power can be dangerous. You do have your enemies."

"No, Mary. I have adversaries. There's a difference. Put Kevin's fears to rest. I have most of the town looking out for my welfare." Jack finished his coffee. "We should do this more often. You're a good friend, Mary Donavan." Jack kissed her hand.

"Tell Kevin his hangover remedy will be ready when he arrives at O'Shea's."

"I'll tell him." She walked over to the door. "Good night, Jack. Thank you for bringing him home."

"Good night, Mary."

* * *

Guided by gas lights along the street, Red drove the carriage along Penn Street. He held onto his hat as a gust of wind blew across the bluffs.

"A storm's coming, Uncle Red," Beth said from the seat next to him.

"Looks like it," Red agreed.

In the distance, lightning flashed through the clouds, illuminating the darkness.

"You had better stay with us," Beth said. "You can't ride home in this storm."

"That's mighty kind of you, but I think I'll wait it out at O'Shea's."

Beth put her arm in his.

"I'm not a kid anymore, you know."

Red looked at her. "What has that got to do with anything?"

Beth turned away. She looked straight ahead. "You're afraid to face my mother," she said.

Startled, Red searched for words.

"At first I thought you were just shy," Beth continued. "But it's more than that."

"And what makes you think so, young lady?"

"It's just a feeling I have. I've seen the way Mother watches you from the window. At the Presidential Ball you went out of your way to avoid her."

The first sprinkles of rain touched the ground. Red moved the horses briskly down the street. He pulled them to a halt in front of the house. The rain started falling harder. "See you in two weeks, Beth!"

"Thanks for a fun weekend, Uncle Red." She kissed his cheek and ran for the house.

As the rain started to fall in torrents, Red moved the horses across the street into the open carriage shed. He unhitched the horses and wiped them down with a blanket.

The rain slammed hard against the shed. After pouring some oats for the horses he sat down and propped himself against a support post to wait out the storm.

An oak leaf blew through the door. It came to rest at his feet. He picked up the leaf and spun the stem in his fingers. The leaf reminded him of the storm fourteen years ago. The day of Melissa's visit to the ranch.

Through the open door he watched the torrents of rain. Lights were visible in the Keeney home across the street. Red closed his eyes and dozed off.

A bolt of lightning struck close by. He opened his eyes. Across the street a single light was still visible in the darkness. He started to get to his feet when he saw Melissa move in front of the light.

Through the falling rain he watched as she took the pins from her hair. He looked down. The oak leaf was still in his lap. When he looked up Melissa was gone from the window.

How many seasons had passed. The weeks turning to months, the months to years. Five years without a word spoken between them. Time had done nothing to diminish his feelings for her. Beth was right. He was afraid to face her. For a long time he sat there, thinking. Then he walked out of the shed into the pouring rain and crossed the street. A step creaked as he walked onto the porch. He turned the knob on the front door, and pushed it open, then walked inside and moved toward the light shining from the bedroom. From the shadows of the hallway he watched her. She was in bed. Her eyes were down, reading a book. He walked into the light and leaned against the doorjamb.

Melissa's body went rigid. Her eyes rose slowly from the book and locked into his.

"I'm sorry if I scared you," he said.

Melissa was too startled to speak. She stared at him.

"Beth said I was afraid to face you."

"She did?"

Red nodded.

"Five years, Red. Do you hate me so much?"

He walked over and sat down on the edge of the bed. He handed her the oak leaf. "For the first time in my life I feel the seasons are movin' too fast."

"Yes, I know," she said.

"No, Melissa. I could never hate you. My feelin's haven't changed since that day I first saw you in front of the opera house. The only way I could go on was to block you out. If it was revenge for your father's death you wanted, you've had fourteen years of it."

She took his hand in hers. "I was young and very idealistic."

"The right or wrong of it don't matter anymore. I came here to ask if you think it's worth another try."

A tear ran down her cheek. "I'd like to spend the next weekend with you and Beth. Would you mind?"

Red squeezed her hand. "No, I wouldn't mind at all," he said.

## October, 1888

Red and Melissa spent the next year getting to know each other again. There was no talk of marriage, just a conscious effort on both their parts to be good friends and build a solid relationship. Even though she had the lumber business to run, and he was busy with the ranch, they always put each other first, and they included Beth in everything they did.

One Sunday evening Red had brought Melissa and Beth back to the house on Quality Hill after a day at the ranch. Beth was in the house getting cleaned up for the dinner Natty was preparing in the kitchen. Red and Melissa sat on the top step of the side porch watching the sun set over the West Bottoms.

"We had better get out of these dusty riding clothes, or Natty will refuse to serve us dinner," Melissa said.

Red reached over and took her hand in his.

"Do you know what next Sunday is?" he asked.

She looked at him questioningly.

"It will be exactly one year since I walked into your bedroom that rainy October night and we started over again. I never said anything, but I figured it would take a year for things to settle down, and for Beth to get used to us bein' together. I want you to know it's been a long, hard wait. I've loved you since I first set eyes on you, and I want to know if you will marry me."

Melissa looked out at the western sky. The time had gone so fast. During the past year she had never known such peace and contentment. She could not imagine the future without Red at her side. "Yes, I will marry you. I've waited a lifetime to be your wife, and nothing would please me more."

Red put his arms around her and gave her a long, lingering kiss. "Is next Sunday okay?" he asked.

"Next Sunday? She pulled away in astonishment. "We haven't discussed any of our future plans, where we will live, or . . ."

Red put his finger on her lips. "Next Sunday," he said. "My future is you. We can work everything out after we're married."

"Let's have a small ceremony," she said. "Just family and a few close friends."

"I think that would be best," he said.

"Beth will be pleased."

"Yes," Red agreed. She's worked hard at pushin' us together the past year."

Melissa smiled. "Let's go in and tell her the good news."

* * *

Melissa stood next to Red at the church altar. She savored every word of the wedding ceremony, but in a way, the vows were meaningless. Their relationship had already been tested by sickness, death, and sorrow. Time had been the greatest test of all, and fourteen long years apart had not diminished their love for each other.

Red kept staring at her. He could hardly believe the moment he had waited for all these years was actually at hand. He managed to say "I do" at the appropriate moment, and then he was slipping the ring on Melissa's finger.

"I now pronounce you man and wife," the minister said. "You may kiss the bride."

Red pulled up Melissa's veil and kissed her tenderly on the lips.

The assembled guests broke into applause.

Beth, the maid of honor, gave her mother a hug. "I'm very happy for you, Mother."

"Thank you, sweetheart," Melissa said, as tears ran down her cheeks.

Adam Quint, the best man, shook Red's hand. "I don't think I have had a happier day," he said.

Mary and Kevin Donavan offered their congratulations, as did Bonnie Quint and Jack Hannon. It was so satisfying to all of them that these two people who were so right for each other could at last be united in marriage.

"You did it, Uncle Red," Beth said as she kissed his cheek. "Is it all right if I keep calling you Uncle Red?"

"Yes. We've both gotten used to Uncle Red, and I kinda like it."

Beth smiled.

Everyone followed the bride and groom out of the church.

* * *

Melissa Farrel sat next to her husband at the breakfast table. After their wedding three days ago, and a brief reception at O'Shea's tavern, they had boarded a train at Union Depot. They had decided not to travel far on their honeymoon, so they had taken the train about twenty five miles northeast of Kansas City to the Elms Resort Hotel in Excelsior Springs, Missouri. The small community, located in a valley on the east fork of the Fishing River, was becoming world famous for the health and healing properties of its mineral waters.

The Elms Hotel was a new, three-story wood-frame hotel with large, shady verandas and two hundred guest rooms. The grounds covered a thousand acres of parks and paths that were shaded by giant oak, elm, and hickory trees. There were four tennis courts, miles of riding trails, a 1200-seat music hall, a bowling alley, and a swimming pool. The main attraction, however, was the water and the baths. There were hot and cold baths, Turkish baths, and Russian baths. The baths were located in the hotel and each had an attendant and a supervising physician.

The ornate, curly pine walls of the dining room hummed with the sound of couples making their plans for the day.

"Would you like to take a walk after breakfast?" Red asked.

"We probably should," Melissa answered. "We have not left the room for three days except for food and water. The other guests are beginning to whisper and point in our direction."

Red smiled. "Have we been here three days?"

"Yes. And I believe it's time we went outside for some fresh air."

"I'm to blame, Mrs. Farrel. I can't seem to get enough of you."

"The feeling is mutual, Mr. Farrel. Our years apart have made this reunion all the sweeter."

"Yes," Red agreed. "I can't believe we are finally together. I keep waitin' for someone to tap me on the shoulder and tell me I'm not supposed to be here."

"We were both on edge during the wedding ceremony," Melissa said. "I kept wanting to speed up the minister before something happened to spoil everything."

"Yes," Red agreed. "The ceremony did seem to last forever."

Melissa reached over and held his hand. "I'm determined that nothing will ever come between us again."

Melissa sipped her coffee. "We've spent the last year getting to know each other again, Red. We haven't discussed any of our future plans."

"A few more weeks of this and I'll be ready," Red answered.

Melissa smiled. She leaned back in her chair and studied her husband. "I guess we'll live at the ranch?" she questioned.

Red shook his head. "I've been thinkin' about it. You will need to be close to your business, and you and Beth are comfortable on Quality Hill. It will be easier for me to make the move."

"That's more than considerate of you. Are you sure you don't mind if I keep working?"

"I know how hard it is to let go of somethin' you worked so hard to build. I won't ask you to give it up."

"You seem to be doing all the compromising," Melissa said.

"I'm just tryin' to be sensible. I've spent most of my life on a horse, so ridin' out to the ranch won't be a problem."

Melissa smiled. "Somehow I can't picture you living on Quality Hill," she said.

"It just goes to show what love will do to a man," Red kidded.

"What about Beth?"

Red looked at her questioningly.

"When will you tell her you're her father?"

"I don't plan to. It might satisfy me, but what good would come of it? Beth always thought that John Keeney was her father. Let's just leave it alone."

Melissa squeezed his hand. "Beth loves you very much."

Red looked away. "She's quite a young lady. You did a good job with her."

"Thank you. With Beth around I was always reminded of you. She has your temperament and you look so much alike. I don't see a lot of myself in her."

"That's because you're to close to her to see it. Beth is a gentle person, but deep down she is just as strong-willed and determined as her mother. She has what it takes to get through hard times."

"She certainly has enjoyed her time with you at the ranch," Melissa continued. "You made me realize I was trying to shelter her with a genteel, Quality Hill upbringing. I was sending her to the best schools and preparing her for a place in society. After a few trips out to your ranch she began to blossom, and I realized how wrong I was. After mother died, I sold the ranch and settled in for a life on Quality Hill. I had forgotten what a wonderful experience it was to be raised on a ranch. We are so fortunate that we can have a home in the city and one in the country."

"Would you feel more comfortable if we lived somewhere else?" Red asked.

"What do you mean?"

"It's not every day a former outlaw moves to Quality Hill. Your neighbors might not like it."

"I'm past caring what people think," she answered. "All I care about is our happiness. The question is, how will you feel about it?"

"It's somethin' I'll have to get used to. If the city starts closin' in on me, I'll just ride out to the ranch."

"Come on. Let's take a walk outside," Melissa said.

Autumn had splashed the surrounding hills in the colors of red, orange, and gold. The sun had risen just above the trees and was shining out of a cloudless sky.

"Oh, Red. What an absolutely beautiful day," Melissa said as she took a deep breath of fresh air. "Autumn is my favorite time of year. Don't you just love October?"

"To tell you the truth, this is the first time in my life I've enjoyed bein' indoors."

Melissa hooked her arm in his. She gave him a look of intimacy shared only by lovers, and they started walking through the hotel grounds.

"Do you remember that October day fifteen years ago when you first took me out to your ranch?" she asked.

"Yes. It was a day like this, only windy and a little colder."

"And we had that terrible rain storm," Melissa added.

"The memories of that night with you helped get me through some rough times," Red said. "It was all I had to keep me goin'."

Melissa stopped walking. She laid her head on his shoulder. "I am so sorry about all the pain I caused you. Can you ever forgive me?"

"There's nothin' to forgive. You stood up for what you believed in, and that's all a person can do. Let's not speak of it again."

"Do you think Adam Quint will accept me as a friend after all that's happened?"

"I'm sure of it. He knows you made a sacrifice out of loyalty to your family. Adam likes you very much."

"I hope so. Through the years the Donavans and Jack Hannon have been such good friends. I'm so glad they didn't reject me after what happened to us."

Red agreed. "I missed their friendship when I was on the run."

"I so admire Mary Donavan," Melissa continued. "She is the most strong-willed, competent woman I have ever met. I'm sure Kevin doesn't make a lot of money at the newspaper, and yet her home and children are alway immaculate. She makes the most of what she has."

"And she can keep Kevin in line," Red added.

"That too," Melissa agreed. "She gives Kevin a lot of support, but she can also show him that fiery Irish temper. And Jack Hannon is such a special person. You usually don't find such a kind and gentle man in politics. I've never heard of him turning anyone in need away from his door."

"He is quite a man," Red agreed. "I remember when I first met Jack and Kevin back in '69. They were wilder than a pair of mustangs. Who would have guessed that Jack would become the top man in Kansas City. Adam tells me all the city's major business is handled at O'Shea's Tavern."

"Well, it could not be in better hands." Melissa said. "He's fast becoming a father figure for several generations of Kansas Citians."

"That's true. Kevin often accuses him of actin' like he gave birth to the city. But Kevin and everyone else know that Jack's arrival in the city was just as important as the arrival of the railroads. He has done more for the city than all the banks and railroads put together."

"I often wonder why he has never married," Melissa said. "I hope it has nothing to do with my cousin Sarah rejecting him. I think he really cared about her. I'm sure he has plenty of women friends, but he never seems to get romantically involved."

"I don't know, Melissa. Maybe he's just waitin' for the right woman to come along."

"Possibly. I just hate to think of him spending his whole life without a companion. We both know what it's like to be lonely."

They continued walking arm-in-arm in the warm sunshine. "I thought you might be interested in helping me run the lumber yard," Melissa said.

"It's good of you to offer, but a man has to do what he knows best. I know horses and cattle. Lumber has always been a man's business, but you showed everyone you could handle the job. I admire you for goin' ahead with the business after John died. It took a lot of courage."

Melissa flushed with pride. "Thank you, Red. I'm so glad I have your support."

They came to a bridge south of the hotel that led across Fishing River to Regent's Spring, one of the natural springs the area was famous for. A round, wooden pavilion with a peaked roof was built around the spring. The pavilion was shaded by a stand of oak trees, and benches were built against the walls so guests could relax and enjoy the waters.

"Let's cross the river and get a drink," Melissa suggested.

"Good idea," Red agreed.

Melissa stopped walking half way across the bridge. She turned and faced him. "I wish I had the words to explain how happy I am," she said.

"There's no need to explain," Red answered. "I feel so good I'm about to bust." Melissa put her arms around his neck. She gave him a long lingering kiss. Around them leaves of red and gold rode a gentle breeze to the ground. Melissa finally released him from the kiss. They continued across the bridge to the spring and entered the pavilion. A young lady who was the attendant was the only one around. "If you would like to sit down and rest, I'll be glad to get you some water," she said.

"Thank you, that would be nice," Melissa answered.

The girl drew water from the spring and brought it to them in cool iron cups.

"Oh, that is so good," Melissa said as she sipped the water.

"What kind of water is it?"

"Iron manganese," the girl answered.

There were wells and springs located all over town. Each of the waters had different properties and healing powers. There was sulpho saline, salt sulpher, salt sea, excelsior saline, Lithia, soda, and salt-water crystals. Each well or spring had its own pavilion for guests to sample the waters.

"Legend has it that Indians used to bring their wounded here to soak in the waters," Red explained. "They swore by the healing power in the springs."

"Do you think the waters really work?" Melissa asked.

"I don't know. I'm sure the minerals help in some way, but I doubt if they cure kidney disease and rheumatism like they claim. When people come here they get to rest and relax, and that helps their illness as much as anything."

Melissa leaned her head back against the wall of the pavilion. "You're right. I didn't realize how fast my life was going until I had this chance to slow down. I'm so relaxed, you may have to carry me back to Kansas City."

Red laughed. "I know what you mean. I feel like the baths have soaked away all my get-up-and-go."

She squeezed his hand. "Let's head back to the hotel."

"Thanks for the water," Red called to the attendant.

"You're welcome, Mr. Farrel. Come back again."

Red looked puzzled as he escorted Melissa back onto the bridge. "I wonder how she knew my name?"

Melissa put her arm in his. “You don’t pay any attention to such things, but word of the presence of the notorious Red Farrel spread through the hotel five minutes after you signed the guest register.”

Red smiled. He put his arm around her waist, and they quickened their pace back to the hotel.

After dinner that evening, they were sitting on the south veranda. The other guests were at a concert at the music hall, so they had the veranda to themselves.

The sun had dropped below the trees, casting a reddish-blue glow on the western skyline. Arc lights lining the winding walkways blinked on against the gathering darkness. In the distance, a pair of mourning doves sounded their last calls of the day. The faint sound of music could be heard from the music hall.

“Oh, Red, what a beautiful setting this is,” Melissa said.

Red looked over at her. Her long, flowing black hair glowed in the gathering darkness. She did not tie it up in fashionable knots as some women did. She was dressed in a dark blue skirt, a white blouse, and she wore a lavender ribbon around her neck. She never wore a hat or a bonnet, or carried a sunshade. He could tell she dressed for comfort more than fashion, and yet she looked more elegant than women who dressed for style.

They sat in silence for a while, watching the sky and listening to the music from the concert.

“Do you ever think about how fast the world is changing?” she asked. “Just a few short years ago we were living in the discomforts of the wild, wild, West and now we’re at a resort that has tennis, bowling, hot baths, and attendants to look after our every need; we are looking out on electric lights, and listening to concert music. Sometimes I can’t believe all the changes.”

“It all seems strange to me. After spending most of my life on the prairie I can’t seem to get comfortable when I’m comfortable. Does that make sense?”

“Yes. It makes perfect sense. You feel guilty when you’re away from the land, and you feel creature comforts are for men who live in the city. You have to feel you have put in a full day’s work, or at least been cold, exhausted, or hungry. And you’re afraid that if you submit to the easy life you’ll become less than the man you are.”

Red smiled. “I guess there won’t be much use in tryin’ to hide anything from you if you can read me that easily.”

Melissa leaned over and kissed his cheek. “You have to learn to enjoy some of the rewards you earned for working hard all your life.”

Red watched the last faint glow on the horizon disappear into darkness.

“You’re so good and kind, Red. I sometimes feel guilty about all those wasted years. We could have been so happy together. Maybe even had more children.”

“That’s over and done with,” he replied. “We got a second chance, and that's what matters. I wouldn't trade an instant of the past few days for all of the past."

"Nor would I," she agreed. "I love you with all my heart, Red Farrel."

In the soft glow of electric lights they sat hand-in-hand on the veranda enjoying each other's company, and listening to music filter up from the music hall.

* * *

Miles Davis entered the Broadway entrance to the Coates House. He walked through the lobby and down a hallway to the back of the hotel, where he opened the door to the exclusive Missouri River Club and went inside.

He searched the room of the upper-crust organization, which catered to lawyers, bankers and railroad executives. A gloved hand waved in his direction. Miles walked over. "Hello, Lawrence. Sorry I'm late. An unexpected client."

Lawrence Dubois, the rotund lawyer for the railroad consortium, waved away the apology. "Never mind, Miles. You've given me more time to enjoy the serenity of alcoholic beverage."

Miles accepted a whiskey sour from the waiter.

"Ah, the antidote for a hard day." Miles sipped the whiskey.

"What's on your mind, Lawrence?"

He scanned the room. "A delicate matter, to say the least."

"No doubt concerning the upcoming election," Miles said.

Lawrence smiled. "Yes."

"I was under the impression your employers had given up the local political scene. Corpses decorating one's mansion does tend to weaken the resolve."

Lawrence leaned forward in his chair. "My employers feel a change of tactics are in order."

Miles drained his glass. He sat it on the table. "I'm listening."

"Then I assume the banking consortium is still interested in pursuing the matter."

"If the plan is worthwhile, yes."

"Not only worthwhile, Miles, foolproof."

"A creation of your own, no doubt."

"Yes. But it won't succeed without your cooperation."

"Go on," Miles said.

"What's the downtown real estate market doing, Miles?"

"Going through the roof, as you well know."

Lawrence nodded. "I've done a thorough investigation of Hannon's finances. All of his assets are in real estate. Six months ago he mortgaged O'Shea's tavern to buy property on Main Street. All his worldly goods are on paper."

"And?" Miles asked.

"My employers feel the real estate market is due for a tumble."

"In other words, the railroads are ready to puncture the inflated balloon."

"Exactly. We've recouped our original investments ten times over. Here's our proposal. We give you a month to alert your preferred clients and to pull out of the market. At the end of the thirty-day period we're going to dump our downtown real estate to eastern concerns at a bargain rate."

"How much of a bargain?" Miles asked.

"Half price."

Miles whistled. "Someone wants Hannon awfully bad. You're going to ruin a lot of people."

"Hopefully the right ones, Miles."

"Any chance Hannon could come up with the money before foreclosure?"

"None."

Miles rose to his feet. "I congratulate you, Lawrence."

Lawrence smiled. "Then we have the cooperation of the banks?"

Miles held out his hand. "You have it."

The fat man shook Miles's hand.

"Tell your clients to be discreet, Miles."

"We shall, Lawrence. We shall indeed."

* * *

Jack placed the telephone on the hook. He reached in the desk drawer for a bottle of whiskey. The last possible buyer for his real estate had laughed in his ear.

He took several gulps from the bottle. Eighteen years of hard work. He looked around the office.

Thank God Tom and Connie O'Shea had passed on and were not around to see the end. How could he have mortgaged the shrine that was O'Shea's? He took another drink.

A knock sounded at the door.

"Go away!"

Kevin opened the door and walked into the office. He was followed by Red and Adam. They sat in chairs that fronted Jack's desk.

Kevin eyed the bottle.

"I've never known you to cancel the Friday night poker game, Jack."

With the deft touch of an experienced bartender Jack reached for three whiskey glasses. He poured each of them a drink.

"I propose a toast." Jack lifted the bottle. "To good friends, and to O'Shea's and all she's stood for."

They drank the toast.

"If I'm not mistaken, you just spoke in the past tense," Adam said.

Jack nodded grimly. "I'm ashamed to say it, but I lost everything in the real estate crash."

"But the tavern was paid for," Kevin said.

"I mortgaged her for a quick killing on the market. I've been buying property every six months and reselling to eastern speculators at a profit.

The market has fallen out from under me."

"What about the profit on your other deals?" Adam asked.

"Gone. I've had several lean months at the race track."

"When are your notes due?" Red asked.

"Monday, I'm afraid."

"Won't the bank give you more time?"

"No. I've done some checking. The railroad's dropped a huge chunk of real estate on the market at a bargain price. If I'm correct, the bankers are waiting to call in the loans on Monday."

"You think it was a set-up job?" Kevin asked.

"I'm sure of it. I should have been alert enough to see it coming."

"Would the railroads drop that kind of money to get you out of the way?" Red asked.

"They would," Adam answered. "With control of the river wards they would recoup their investment, and more."

"How much are your loans, Jack?" Red asked.

"One hundred and fifty thousand," Jack answered. "When my good friend, Bob Poteet, went broke he put on his silk hat and walked calmly into the waters of the mighty Missouri. I now know how he must have felt."

Jack took another swallow of whiskey. "I've spent the day searching for a way out of the dilemma. I've concluded there isn't any. Monday morning I'll walk in and present my holdings to Mr. Miles Davis. He'll be waiting in eager anticipation. Until then . . ." Jack started clearing off his desk. "Let's play some poker."

The game ended at midnight. Jack escorted his friends to the backdoor of O'Shea's.

"I bid you good night, and good-bye from O'Shea's," he said.

"Could you gentlemen meet me here at daybreak?" Red asked.

They looked at him questioningly.

"There's a chance I might save Jack a walk into the Missouri. Bring a buckboard and a driver you can trust, Jack. Adam, wear your gunbelt."

Red walked out the door.

"What was that all about?" Jack asked.

"I don't know," Kevin answered. "But I'm going to be here at daybreak to find out."

* * *

With Jack and Kevin at his side, Michael Pacini drove the buckboard along the trail. Red and Adam were up ahead on horseback.

They had crossed the Hannibal Bridge at daybreak and followed the Missouri River upstream toward Saint Joseph.

Red brought the procession to a halt. They were on a ridge a hundred feet above the river. "We'll have to leave the buckboard and horses here."

From his scabbard beside the saddle Red took out a Remington double-barreled shotgun. He handed it to Michael.

"Stay out of sight back in the woods, Michael. Fire two shots if you're in trouble. One if you see anyone approaching."

Michael nodded. He disappeared into the trees.

The four men worked their way down and around the ridge line. Fifty feet above the river, a rock ledge jutted out from the face of the embankment.

Red kept his back to the wall as he crept slowly along the cliff. "Come on!" he called.

Jack and Kevin looked dubious.

"Come on! It's not far!"

The two Irishmen stepped onto the ledge. They crept along, afraid to look down. When they turned the corner, the ledge fed them into a crevice. The slice between the ridges ran from the top of the ridge line down to the river. The precarious walk along the lip of the ridge was the only passage to the crevice.

They followed Red up the slit in the mountain until they were almost back to the summit.

Red stopped in front of a boulder.

"It will take all of us to move it. Jack, put your back against the rock and push with your feet."

The four men moved into position.

"Ready now. Heave!"

The boulder moved off the ground.

"One more time. Heave!"

The rock turned over. With one last effort, the rock started to roll. They watched as it picked up momentum down the crevice. Down below, the giant boulder ricocheted off the rocks. It was in flight for a moment before being swallowed by the river.

Red lit a torch. He led them into the cave. Jack squeezed his way into the opening. He followed the light from the torch. The narrow passageway led into a large room. In the lantern light, water dripped from the stalactites hanging from the ceiling of the cave. The hollow sound of water on rocks sounded in the cavern.

"Over here!" Red called.

They followed him into a side room of the cave. Red made a thorough search of the room with the torch.

"No one's been here," he said. Red placed the torch on a ledge. He started clearing rocks that were stacked against one side of the room. His companions helped. The last of the rocks uncovered a strong box.

Taking out his Colt revolver, Red stepped back and shot off the lock.

The roar was deafening.

Adam pulled up the lid. Red reached in and pulled out one of the bags. He poured the contents onto a rock shelf. Gold coins clattered on the rocks. They glittered in the light.

"My God! It's a fortune," Kevin said.

"How much do you have, Red?" Adam asked.

"At last count, $175,000. We spent the currency and stored the gold here. It will be more than enough to pay Jack's debts."

Jack stared at the full box of money.

"What about your compatriots?" Adam asked.

"When I entered prison, Roy Canfield was the only one left alive. Last year he was killed by a posse down in Arkansas."

"I can't take your money, Red," Jack said.

"It's not my money, Jack. It belongs to the railroad. You can return the money to them and pick up your notes in the process. I've never really understood it."

"What?" Kevin asked.

"I served my time, but no one ever asked me to return the money."

They all laughed.

"After Jack pays his debts we'll bank the excess money and give it away to charitable causes."

Jack looked at Red. "I don't know what to say."

"Don't say anything. You can do me one favor, though."

"Anything," Jack said.

"Leave the money in the railroad bags when you pay your debts."

Jack smiled. "It will be a pleasure, Mr. Farrel."

FROM ADAM QUINT'S JOURNAL — OCTOBER 12, 1889

*With Red's help, Jack managed to survive the real estate collapse. He paid off all his debts and was able to keep O'Shea's. If he had gone under financially, it would have ruined his political career, so we are all greatly relieved.*

*Red and Melissa have been married for a year now. It is a joy for me to see them so happy. Red is more outgoing and self-assured, and for the first time, I think he is really enjoying life. Beth has grown up to be a beautiful young lady. She has dark gray eyes, and light brown hair like her father; and she has Melissa's curvaceous figure. She will be quite a catch for some lucky young man. Melissa's lumber business also managed to survive the real estate crash, and now she is doing as much business as ever. It is not a popular notion, but having watched Bonnie and Melissa over the years, I sometimes think women are more suited to running a business; they are tenacious competitors and they don't ever let their egos get in the way of business judgments.*

*The decade of the eighties has brought an unbelievable amount of progress and change. The city boundaries now run south all the way to Forty-ninth Street. Almost all of the cable cars are electrified, and the telephone has been introduced in the city. A park system is in place, and six- and ten-story buildings now dot the skyline. It is amazing that we have come so far in twenty years. However, I hope the city never loses the unique western flavor that made her great in the first place.*

*There is so much happening for the betterment of mankind that I look forward with great anticipation to the decade of the nineties.*

# 10

# Front Street Massacre

June 5, 1891

Michael's secretary poked her head into his office.

"Telephone, Mr. Pacini."

"Who is it, Betty?"

"The mayor. He says it's urgent."

Michael walked out to Betty's desk. He picked up the phone.

"Hello, Lloyd. What can I do for you?"

"I need your help, Michael." The mayor sounded frantic.

"You name it," Michael said.

"Be in my office in fifteen minutes!" The phone clicked in Michael's ear.

Michael hurried along Fourth Street toward city hall. Handsome, charming, and a flashy dresser, he was easily the most recognizable figure in the city. When Tony Latta retired, Michael had taken over management of the restaurant. With that responsibility came control of liquor sales and gambling in the North End. When he joined the organization, Michael had known the restaurant business was a front for more lucrative pursuits. He had broadened his sphere of influence out of the North End into city hall. His rise to the top was much easier than he had anticipated. Tony Latta's associates were getting on in years and wanted no part of a power struggle. The newspapers had assisted his ascension, with investigative reporters clamoring that he was heir-apparent to the Kansas City underworld.

Michael had great respect for the written word. The newspapers had put him where he wanted to be without a shot fired or an angry word spoken. The press and city hall were well aware of the low crime rates in the districts Michael controlled. A murder or rape was unheard of. The organization was known to deal swiftly with criminals who attacked the innocent. Unsavory types quickly learned to stay out of districts controlled by the organization. In this fashion Michael created a vigilante force that was much more effective than the local police. For the service of his organization, Michael had a silent agreement with city government. He would be left alone to conduct his business. Years of observing Jack Hannon had not been wasted. At every opportunity, Michael poured money back into the community. He sponsored youth baseball leagues, bailed out financially pressed business concerns, even gave money to destitute families in the North End. Unlike Jack Hannon, however, when Michael offered his help, it was for a price. If Michael needed you, you had better deliver.

Michael nodded to the fireman washing down a fire truck at the Fourth and Main fire station.

Further on, the three-story city hall building, constructed in the Romanesque style, loomed above him. He knew something important had happened the moment he walked into city hall. Uniformed policemen were everywhere. Two of them converged on him, ushering him into the mayor's office.

The mayor sat on the edge of his desk, nervously puffing on a cigar. He was surrounded by the police commissioner and members of the police force.

"What's going on, Lloyd?" Michael asked.

The mayor sprang from his desk. "It's my daughter, Michael. They've kidnapped my daughter!" The mayor was close to tears. He wiped his forehead. "Now goddamn it, Pacini! You listen to me! I want my daughter back! I want her back today!"

"Why are you yelling at me, Lloyd?"

"You know everything that happens in this town, Michael."

Michael's eyes narrowed. "You're not suggesting that any of my people are mixed up in this?"

The Mayor walked away holding his head.

"No, no, Michael. I'm sorry. This thing has me going to pieces."

"What have you got, commissioner?" Michael asked.

"Her name is Nancy Baker. She's seventeen years old. She was grabbed off the street on her way home from school. The kidnappers left a note in the mayor's mailbox. They're demanding ten thousand dollars."

"Any suspects?"

"None."

"It has to be someone from out of town," Michael said. "None of the locals would pull such a grandstand stunt."

"I agree, Michael."

"What do you want me to do, Commissioner?"

"Find my daughter, that's what!" the mayor cried. "Please, Michael," he pleaded.

"I'll do my best, Lloyd. Commissioner, I'll keep you informed." The police commissioner nodded. Michael walked out of the room.

* * *

Two of his lieutenants followed Michael through his office door. "The Mayor's daughter has been kidnapped. I want every neighborhood covered. Saturate a five-mile area around the city. We want to know about any strangers our people come in contact with. One thousand dollars to the person who gives us a reasonable lead."

"Okay, Michael." The two men left the room.

Michael stayed close to the phone through the day. It rang constantly. Countless leads were checked without results. He slept at the office. The next morning at ten a.m. the phone rang. Michael picked up the receiver. "Hello."

"Mr. Pacini?"

"Yes."

"This is Tommy Anna. I own a tavern here at the stockyards."

"And?"

"A man came in an hour ago. He bought a sack full of whiskey. I never seen the guy before."

"I'll send some . . ."

"No, no! Listen to me," Tommy said quickly. "I didn't want to waste your time so I had the wife watch the place. I followed the guy over to a rooming house on Gennesse Street. It used to be the Oaks Hotel. Do you know it?"

"I know it."

"Anyway," Tommy continued, "Me and the desk clerk are good friends. I been there a few times on the sly." Tommy laughed into the phone. "This guy, he checked in yesterday afternoon. He had a girl and two other men with him. He told the desk clerk the girl was his daughter. My friend didn't buy the story. He figured they were going to have some fun with the girl."

"What makes you think it's more than that, Tommy?"

"Because the clerk gave me the key to a vacant room next to theirs. I listened. It's the kidnappers, all right."

"What's the room number, Tommy?"

"Have I got the thousand?"

"I'll deliver it personally."

"Room 115, Mr. Pacini."

"Thanks, Tommy."

"Mr. Pacini?"

"Yes, Tommy?"

"Watch yourself. These guys is real amateurs. I want to collect my thousand."

Michael hung up the phone.

* * *

From his command post across the street, Michael sized up the Oaks Hotel. Built in the early sixties, the four-story brick building looked as tired and weatherbeaten as the ground it sat on.

The door of his room opened.

"How's it look, Willy?"

"Not so good, Michael. One-fifteen is at the end of the hall. A small window opens into the alley. The only way to get at them is through the door."

"Too risky," Michael said. "They might use the girl for a shield. We've got to flush them out of that room."

Willy sat down to wait for further instructions as Michael paced the floor. The situation was a touchy one. If the girl was harmed in the rescue, he knew his future in Kansas City would be nonexistent. Out of the window he watched as a wagon-load of hogs pulled up to the stockyard pens. On occasion, drunken cowboys would open the pens. The animals due for slaughter would have one last run at freedom before the police and fire departments were called out to round them up.

"That's it!" Michael said suddenly. Willy jumped to his feet. "Take two men, Willy. Get the driver of that hog wagon over here."

Moments later Willy was back with a boy who appeared to be in his late teens. The boy was wide-eyed with fright.

"Would you like to make fifty dollars?" Michael asked.

"Doing what?" the boy asked suspiciously.

"I'm playing a practical joke on a friend. He's the clerk in the hotel next door. Are you a good actor?"

"For fifty dollars, I'll sure try."

Michael explained the plan and the boy left to get the wagon.

"Willy! Get the rest of the men! Bring one of those portable animal chutes over to the hotel door!"

"Okay, Michael."

The boy moved the wagon up to the hotel and the men set the chute against the hotel door. The boy jumped off the wagon and fixed the ramp. He climbed up and started prodding the squealing hogs into the chute. Michael opened the hotel door. The pigs burst into the lobby. Michael followed close behind.

The hotel clerk stood speechless behind the desk.

Pigs snorted and crowded down the hallways.

"This is outrageous!" the clerk shouted.

The hotel's residents peeked cautiously out of their rooms at the milling animals. They tried to shoo the pigs away.

Michael looked down the hall. He could see a man's head peering around the door.

Willy walked up to the desk.

"This is disgusting!" he bellowed. "If these pigs are not out of here in ten minutes, I'm calling the police and the health authorities."

"But, sir," the clerk pleaded. "It's not my fault."

Two men came out of room 115. They started helping the other residents shove hogs down the hallway. They had left the door to room 115 cracked.

Michael gave the signal.

The two men came around the corner pushing hogs. Michael's men put guns to their heads and forced them face-down onto the floor.

Michael bounded down the hallway. He picked one of the smaller hogs off the floor. The squealing animal fought to get out of his grasp. Michael threw the pig into room 115.

"Get that pig!" he shouted.

The man in the room instinctively dove for the animal. The pig eluded him. He went sprawling on the floor.

Michael pulled out his gun and placed it at the back of the kidnapper's head. The man pounded his fist on the floor in frustration.

Willy picked the man off the floor and shoved him roughly through the door. Michael went into the bedroom. A young girl was tied to the bedpost. "Nancy?"

"Who are you?" The girl was terrified.

Michael walked over. He started untying her. "It's all over, Nancy. Your father sent me."

The girl went limp with relief and started weeping as Michael picked her up and carried her out of the hotel.

* * *

At Anna's Tavern, Michael handed over the thousand to a grinning Tommy Anna.

"I knew you was good for it, Mr. Pacini."

"Can I use your phone, Tommy?"

"Sure thing." Tommy walked away counting his money.

Kevin picked up the phone on the first ring.

"Mr. Donavan, it's Michael Pacini."

"Michael! How have you been?"

"Fine, thanks. Mr. Hannon tells me you have stiff competition for the sports editor's job."

Kevin laughed. "I'm afraid he's right."

"Get out your pencil, Mr. Donavan. We're going to put you ahead down the stretch."

"How's that, Michael?"

"I got the mayor's daughter in my car."

"Damn!" Kevin said excitedly. Michael heard him shouting orders on the other end.

"Go ahead, Michael."

He relayed the story. "I'll be at City Hall in fifteen minutes, Mr. Donavan."

"Michael, I owe you for this one."

"That's true, Mr. Donavan. Have a photographer waiting on the steps at City Hall when I arrive."

Kevin laughed. "He'll be waiting."

Michael hung up the phone. "You were right about one thing, Tommy."

"What's that, Mr. Pacini?"

"They were amateurs, Tommy. Real amateurs."

## JULY 10TH, 1891

"Eighteen years old. How can she be eighteen years old, Melissa?" Red asked.

Beth laughed. "No matter how much you try, Uncle Red, you can't keep me fourteen and in pigtails."

"Where would you like to celebrate your birthday?" Melissa asked.

"I'm craving Italian food. Where's the best Italian food, Uncle Red?"

"Latta's Restaurant."

"Then it's decided." Beth led them to the door.

At the restaurant they were greeted warmly and led to a table overlooking Main Street.

Rather than diminish with time, the legend of Red Farrel continued to grow with the years. His name always commanded the best table in the house. The curious stares made Melissa nervous, but Red had learned to ignore them.

He studied the menu, half listening as Beth and Melissa commented on the fashions worn by the women passing on the street below. He put the menu beside his plate and looked at the scene on Main Street.

Trolley cars moved back and forth. They collected and deposited the populace swarming over the steel rails. Tall buildings now dominated the corridor that was Main Street.

"Excuse me."

Red turned around.

"Mr. Farrel, it's so nice to see you again."

Red rose from his chair. "Hello, Michael." The two men shook hands.

"How's your Uncle Frank, Michael?"

"He's doing fine. He'll be pleased you asked."

"I believe you know my wife."

Michael bowed.

"It's nice to see you again, Mrs. Farrel."

"Hello, Michael."

"Beth, this is Michael Pacini. Our daughter, Beth Keeney."

"Yes," Beth said. "I recognize Mr. Pacini from his picture in the newspaper."

"Do I detect a note of disapproval, Miss Keeney?" Michael asked.

Beth flushed. "Are you seeking approval, Mr. Pacini?"

"And if I were?"

"I find you an enigma, Mr. Pacini. One day the newspapers tell us you're a hero, and the next you're Public Enemy Number One."

"Beth, please!" Melissa said.

Michael laughed. "That's quite all right, Mrs. Farrel. Do I look the part of the villain, Miss Keeney?"

"No more than my Uncle Red, Mr. Pacini."

Grinning, Michael bowed. "If I can be of further service, just tell the waiter. Enjoy your dinner with us tonight."

Beth watched Michael depart. The palms of her hands were wet.

"I didn't know you knew Michael Pacini, Uncle Red."

"I've known him a long time. He started working at O'Shea's as a youngster."

"Are the stories about him true?"

"I don't know, Beth. From my own experience I would say that most reputations are exaggerated."

"He's an attractive man," Melissa commented.

Beth flushed. Her mother could read her so easily.

The lasagna that had sounded so appetizing earlier would have to work its way through the knot in her stomach.

* * *

A knock sounded at the front door. Beth bounded down the stairway. "I'll get it, Natty!" She opened the door.

Michael Pacini leaned against the house. Beth stared at him. He smiled. "Is it frightening to have Public Enemy Number One show up on your doorstep?"

Beth flushed. "My uncle isn't in, Mr. Pacini."

"I didn't come here to see your uncle. And please, call me Michael."

She stepped aside. "Won't you come in?"

"No, thank you. I might become violent."

Beth bit her lip. "All right," she said. "I owe you an apology."

Michael bowed. "I accept your apology. What are your plans for the day?"

"Well, I . . ."

"Good, you don't have any. Why don't you join me for a ride in the country? My two-seater is on the street."

Beth laughed. "Your bicycle? Somehow I pictured you getting out of a fancy carriage surrounded by men in black."

Michael shook his head. "Already condemned. I at least deserve a word in my own defense."

Beth met his stare. "Yes, I think you do. Let me get my hat."

* * *

Beth sat at the Sunday dinner table with Melissa and Red.

"We've missed you at the ranch the past month, Beth."

"I've been busy, Uncle Red." Beth glanced at her mother.

"I'm afraid the ranch has some competition, Red," Melissa said slowly.

"Oh?"

"Michael Pacini has been calling on Beth."

Beth watched Red's expression. "You don't approve, do you, Uncle Red?"

"I don't know. I guess I've always pictured you with someone your own age."

"Michael's only six years older."

"Yes, but . . ."

"You're saying he's much more mature."

Red put down his fork. "Let me explain what I'm sayin'. Michael has been on his own since he was a kid. He worked his way up through the local street gangs. In his teens he became the number one man in Little Italy. You have to be tough to do that."

"In a nice way you're saying that he's a criminal."

Red wiped his hands with a napkin. "Tony Latta picked Michael to be his right-hand man because Michael can do what's necessary to carry on business. Look, Beth, I can speak to you this way because I haven't led a pure life myself. I also owe Michael a debt for savin' Jack Hannon's life. I won't judge you, but I don't want to see you hurt."

"You and Mother should realize that I'm no longer a school girl," Beth said. "I don't need your approval for everything I do."

"Beth!" Melissa said.

"You're right, Beth," Red continued. "You're old enough to decide for yourself. I just want you to know what you're gettin' into."

"I'm sorry, Uncle Red. Anyway, we're getting way ahead of ourselves. Michael and I are just good friends." Beth kept her head down. She was afraid to look at her mother.

Melissa did not want this to become an issue that would divide her family. "I'm glad the three of us are close enough that we can discuss these things openly," she said. "Now let's talk about something else." Beth was thankful for the reprieve.

"How's Jim doing, Uncle Red?" She asked.

"Just fine. We're havin' his eighty-fifth birthday next weekend. He won't like it if you don't come."

"I'll be there. Where will you two celebrate your third wedding anniversary?"

"We've talked about Colorado," Red answered. "Melissa has to wait and see if she can leave the business."

"Doesn't it bother you that mother is so independent, Uncle Red?"

"Nope. I have the ranch to run. Your mother enjoys the lumber business. Why should she give it up?"

"Some men would feel threatened to have a wife who is successful in business."

"Well, I'm not one of them."

"What would you have me do?" Melissa asked. "Stay home and do tatting or crochet? Unlike most American husbands, Red doesn't want to lock me away like an Oriental."

Beth smiled.

"What's so funny?" Melissa asked.

"I just had a picture of you shuffling along behind Uncle Red."

They all laughed.

"Now, why all this talk of independence?" Melissa asked.

Beth wiped her mouth with the napkin. "I've accepted a teaching position at the Webster school on Seventeenth Street."

"That's wonderful, Beth!"

Red held up his wine glass.

"Congratulations, Beth."

"You two are making this very difficult," Beth continued. "I'm considering moving into a place of my own."

"Why?" Red asked. "This is your home."

"I know. But here I'm also the dutiful daughter. Out there, I'm a working, independent woman."

She looked at her mother for support.

"You set me up beautifully for this one," Melissa said. "Do you have a place in mind?"

"Yes. Mrs. Dickinson's rooming house for young women."

"What's goin' on?" Red asked. "We have two homes and she has to live in a roomin' house?"

"She wants a place of her own, Red."

"Beth, you can have the deed to the ranch."

"No, Uncle Red. You earned the ranch. Now I have to earn my way."

"You sound like your mind's made up."

"It is. But, I won't feel comfortable moving without your approval."

"You'll give us some time to get used to the idea?" Red asked.

"Of course, Uncle Red."

* * *

"I can't look, Michael!" Beth covered her face with her hands.

Michael laughed. He pulled her hands down. The cable car moved down Ninth Street toward the incline.

The steep rate of descent off the bluff that ended at Union Depot in the West Bottoms below was thrill enough even for the most adventuresome spirit.

The cable car reached the end of the bluff.

Beth looked down at the West Bottoms. "Let's get off, Michael!"

"It's too late now!" The cable car went over the edge. Beth reached for the hollow pit in her stomach. She buried her face in Michael's shoulder. The car sped down the incline. It came to a halt near the Union Depot.

"Now that wasn't so bad, was it?" Michael asked.

Beth rolled her eyes as he laughed.

* * *

At the restaurant, Beth picked at her food.

"No appetite?" Michael asked.

"No."

"I guess it was poor planning to suggest the incline before dinner."

"The ride was worth it. Overcoming fear breeds confidence."

"Oh? I hadn't detected a lack of confidence."

"I hide it well."

Several moments of silence passed.

"Something's the matter, Beth. Do you want to talk about it?"

Ninth Street Incline

"Yes. I just don't know how to begin."

"After six months am I that hard to talk to?"

"In a way you are, Michael. You only show people what you want them to see. I don't think we've discussed one serious subject since we met."

Michael refilled the wine glasses. "When I'm with you, I don't have to be serious. It's one of the nice things about our relationship."

"What I'm trying to say, Michael, is that I don't know you very well. When I think I've got a door open, you close it."

"What is it you're looking for, Beth?"

"I'm looking for the real Michael Pacini."

Michael sipped his wine. "How's the teaching job coming along?" he asked.

Beth's eyes flashed with anger. "Why are you seeing me, Michael?"

"I like your company."

"Isn't Maria Ramponi company enough?"

Michael's eyes bored into her.

"That's it, Michael, get mad! Let me see the real man just once!"

Michael signaled for the waiter.

"Was everything all right, Mr. Pacini?"

"Yes, thank you. We have an early engagement."

Beth threw her napkin down on the table in disgust. "I want to go home, Michael."

Michael grabbed her by the arm. "I'm afraid not, Beth." He escorted her from the restaurant.

Michael's house loomed out of the darkness. Beth sat rigidly in the carriage as it passed through the gates. He helped her out of the carriage and escorted her inside.

Beth scanned the house. "Very impressive. Does the typical female guest run to the bedroom and tear off her clothes? I want to play the seduction scene to perfection."

"Would you like a glass of brandy?" Michael asked.

"Yes, my lord, if you would be so kind."

Michael remained unperturbed.

Beth took her brandy to the couch. She sat down.

A servant entered the room. He lit the fireplace. Beth watched his departure. "I can hardly wait for the violinists to stroll into the room," she said.

Michael ignored her. He stared at the flames darting around the fireplace.

Beth was beginning to feel the effects of the alcohol.

"You have a problem, Miss Keeney."

Beth looked at him.

"You no longer want a friendship, you want a relationship."

Beth gulped the last of the brandy. She turned away.

Michael refilled her glass.

"You're mad at me because you're fighting with yourself," he said. "I'm going to make it easy for you, Beth. My bedroom is at the top of the stairs. You're free to come up. If you want to go home, just call for the butler. Goodnight, Miss Keeney."

Beth listened to his footsteps go up the stairs. She finished her brandy and poured another. She stared at the fire until the flames were barely flickering. Her glass was empty. She threw it angrily against the fireplace. It shattered the stillness of the room. She got off the couch and walked to the stairs.

"How can I be doing this?" she wondered wildly. She walked slowly to the top of the stairs, unfastened the back of her dress and went into Michael's room. Finally she slipped out of her undergarments and crawled into bed.

Michael reached for her, taking her hand.

"I love you, Beth. I know I'm not what you want me to be, but if you'll marry me, I'll do the best I can."

"Oh, Michael." She kissed his hand. "That's all I've ever wanted to hear you say."

## SEPTEMBER, 1892

Mary herded her four teenage girls down Main Street. She had to keep them moving or she would lose the entire day. They had stopped and debated the latest fashions at every window display. They turned the corner on Main and headed east on Eleventh Street or Petticoat Lane, as the street was called by the locals, so named because strong winds that tunneled between the buildings would sometimes reveal petticoats and ankles of the women who scurried in and out of the stores.

"Oh, Mother, look at this dress," Anna said. Anna was seventeen and she had just started her last year of school. She had a thin frame and was several inches taller than the other Donavan girls. She was quiet, introspective, and an excellent student. She was also at that vulnerable age where she desperately wanted to put her childhood behind her and become a woman.

Mary stopped and looked at the princess-style evening dress. The neckline was heart shaped and lined with lace.

"Do you like it, Anna?" Mary asked.

"Yes Mother. It's beautiful!" Anna answered.

When it came to saving money on fashions, Mary had a photographic memory. She could study a dress for a few moments, buy some material, and when she returned home in the evening, turn out an exact replica of the dress she had seen.

"That dress is not for you, Anna," Margaret stated. Margaret was fifteen and Mary was convinced that she had inherited all the devilment in her father. With her thick, curly hair and narrow face, she even looked more like Kevin than the other girls.

Anna looked at Margaret questioningly.

"Because your . . ." Margaret discreetly looked at Anna's chest. "You aren't big enough," she whispered.

Anna giggled along with her three sisters. "You may be right, Mother will have to make this one for Teresa."

Teresa was the beauty in the family. She had large hazel eyes, auburn hair, and an ample figure. She was also unpretentious, and in the few disputes between her sisters, she was the peacemaker.

"Yes," Margaret agreed. "Teresa may end up looking like Mrs. Reese." Mrs. Reese was a teacher at the school the girls attended. She had large breasts that appeared to weigh her down when she walked. Margaret stooped her shoulders as though her breasts were pulling her over and started lumbering down the street.

Teresa burst out laughing with her sisters.

Mary bit the inside of her lip and tried to keep a straight face.

"Margaret, would you please behave yourself," Mary scolded half-heartedly. "We are in public."

"Yes, ma'am," Margaret replied.

**Petticoat Lane — 1908**

"Do you like the dress, Teresa?" Mary asked.

"Yes Mother. Although the neckline is a bit revealing."

"A full figure is nothing to be ashamed of, Teresa," Mary continued. "You would look stunning in this dress."

"Thank you, Mother. If you make the dress for me, I promise Margaret that I will keep my shoulders back, and tread lightly."

"You will not," Margaret scolded good-naturedly. You'll flaunt yourself in front of your three envious sisters."

"And your envious mother," Mary added, grinning.

Molly grabbed her hat as a gust of wind whipped down Petticoat Lane. At thirteen she was the youngest and smallest of the Donavan girls. Her light brown hair was thick with curls and she still carried the weight she would lose in adolescence.

"Hold onto your skirts, ladies," Margaret said. "A show of ankle and our reputations will surely be ruined. A scandalous affair," she said seductively as she rapidly blinked her eyelashes.

Mary shook her head hopelessly as the girls laughed at Margaret.

Mary stopped at a display window and studied a silver gray dress. "This is more what I had in mind for you, Anna," she said.

Anna eyed the dress. "It's lovely, Mother."

Mary calculated the amount of material she would need to make the bell-shaped skirt. She was convinced that designers and manufacturers of fashion material were plotting against her. Just when she thought she would save money on material for bustles, which were no longer in fashion, the designers came out with the bell-shaped skirt, which sometimes measured nine yards around the bottom. Leg-of-mutton sleeves were also back in vogue, each requiring another two yards of material.

She could make the dress out of wool and line it with mohair braid and velvet to protect against wear.

She would also have to pleat the skirt from knee to hem and make ruffles beneath the bottom of the skirt to make it rustle. Anna would also require a large hat and pompadour to balance the figure.

"She's borrowing another designer's work," Teresa said. "I can see that look in her eye."

"Mother's dresses put most designers to shame," Anna said. "They look more stylish and last longer than store-bought clothes."

"I don't know about that, but thank you, Anna," Mary said.

"I'll take a Donavan label over a Worth anytime," Margaret agreed, referring to the most fashionable designer of the day.

"I'm thirsty, Mother," Molly said. "Can we stop for a lemonade?"

"Yes, dear." Mary put her arm around Molly. "I think we can all use some refreshment. Come along, girls."

On the watch for speeding carriages, Mary followed the girls across Eleventh Street to Bullene Moore and Emery. The city's largest retail store now took up the entire block between Grand Avenue and Walnut Street. As the girls filed into the Eleventh Street entrance, Mary felt a surge of pride. They had grown into fine young women. All that she and Kevin could have hoped for. If only she could slow the passage of time and hold onto them a little longer.

But she knew she could not. There were too many young men at the Donavan's door seeking permission to call on one of the girls. The time was near when walks and picnics would not suffice, and one by one, she would have to give them up.

She reached in her purse and gave Anna some money. "If you will order us all a lemonade, Anna, I will be along in a moment. I want to buy some French Broadcloth on sale in the dress goods department for 95 cents a yard."

"Have you ever purchased anything that was not on sale, Mother?" Margaret asked.

"Don't be foolish, Margaret," Mary answered. "No one in their right mind would do such a thing. After we finish our refreshments, we have to stop at J. B. Barnaby's on Main Street to pick up some undershirts for your father. And I want to buy a hat for Anna at Bonnie Quint's Millinery shop."

"We're in for a long day of it, girls," Margaret sighed. "I'm sure mother intends to hire a carriage for our shopping convenience and for transportation home."

"How did you know, Margaret?" Mary asked, amazed. She reached over and gently pinched Margaret's cheek. "Lady Astor and J. P. Morgan are outside in the carriage waiting for us at this very moment. If they ask for me, tell them I won't be long."

The girls laughed as Mary put her nose snobbishly in the air and marched off to the dress goods department.

* * *

Kevin was busy putting the finishing touches on his newspaper column when Mary and the girls arrived home from shopping. The girls trudged into the house and collapsed into the living room chairs. They dropped their packages at their feet like contraband, and moaned and groaned like a troop of weary soldiers.

Mary took off her hat and walked over to Kevin. She hummed a tune, and she looked as if the shopping trip had revitalized her. She bent over and kissed his cheek.

"What happened to these girls, Mary? Did they get run over by a team of horses?"

"No Father," Margaret complained as she fanned herself with her hat. "Did you know that walking in the hot sun builds character and toughens the resolve?"

"Sounds strangely familiar, Margaret," Kevin answered. "From verse one, chapter two of the book of Mary Donavan."

"The same," Margaret replied.

Kevin smiled. He looked at the packages on the floor. "I'd say your Mother put a good size dent in Petticoat Lane."

"This is Anna's last year at school," Mary reminded him. "She will need clothes for parties and a graduation dress. Where's Joey?" she asked.

"He's gone down to the mission with Father Devin."

"Did you finish your column?"

"Yes, though I find it difficult to work in peace and quiet. I've written for too many years with screaming and yelling in the background."

Mary grabbed a package off the floor and handed it to Kevin. "Your undershirts," she said.

"My thanks to you and your weary helpers."

"Did anyone come by, Father?" Teresa asked.

"By anyone, she means Bill Jensen," Molly teased.

Teresa blushed.

"Bill stopped by earlier. I told him you did not wish to see him again."

"Father!" Teresa was exasperated.

"Well, that's what you said when you came charging into the house the other night."

"But that was the other night. We had a disagreement. We . . ."

Teresa looked at Kevin's smiling face. "Oh Father, you're teasing me again."

Kevin laughed. "Bill said he would stop by again this evening. And Anna had a caller as well."

Anna looked questioningly at her father. Most male callers at the Donavan's door were attracted by Teresa's beauty or Margaret's vivacious personality. Anna was shy and she seldom had anything to do with boys.

"A nice-looking fellow," Kevin continued. "He said his name was Scott Woodson."

"Scott Woodson!" The girls said in unison. They sat up in their chairs and stared open-mouthed at Kevin.

Kevin looked at Mary. "I've never seen four girls come back from the dead so quickly. To what do we owe this transformation?"

"Scott Woodson is only the best-looking boy in school, Father," Molly said, as if this were something Kevin should know.

"Yes," Margaret agreed. "I've thrown myself at him several times in the halls, but for some reason he failed to notice."

Anna looked disapprovingly at Kevin. "Father's teasing us again," she said. "Aren't you Father?"

"Now how could I come up with the name Scott Woodson unless the young man had been here?" Kevin asked.

The girls looked at each other, wide-eyed.

"And furthermore, Anna . . ." Kevin looked at the clock on the wall. "It is now five p.m. Mr. Scott Woodson will be back at my door at seven, because I gave him permission to call on you."

"Oh Father, you didn't!" Anna put her hands to her cheeks in shock. "Mother, look at me, how can I possibly be ready!"

"Now dear," Mary said. "You have plenty of time."

"But look at me," Anna protested. "I'm dirty, I'm tired, and I have nothing to wear."

"She's starting to crack," Margaret said. "The mere mention of the name Scott Woodson and women go aquiver."

Teresa put her arm around Anna. "Now don't be nervous," she said. "Mother will have you fresh and ready to go in less than an hour."

Anna looked pleadingly at her mother. "Come along, dear," Mary said. "We have work to do."

Teresa followed the two of them out of the room and up the stairs.

"Is Robert coming by this evening, Margaret?" Kevin asked.

"No Father. He left for the weekend with his parents. I thought it was going to be a dull Saturday night until I heard the name Scott Woodson!"

Margaret gave Molly a conspiratorial smile.

"I want the two of you to leave Anna and her caller alone tonight," Kevin said. "Between you, she would not get a word in edgewise."

Margaret feigned surprise. "Two quiet, unassuming wallflowers like us? Father, I am shocked beyond belief."

"I'm sure you are. Just remember that Anna will be nervous tonight and she will need your support."

"All right, Father," Margaret sighed. "We promise not to interfere. If we must worship the Greek god from afar, then so be it."

Kevin laughed. "There is no end to your suffering," he said.

* * *

Scott Woodson arrived promptly at seven. Kevin escorted him into the parlor. Scott was impeccably dressed in white flannel pants and a grey summer sports coat. He carried a low-crowned straw hat in his hand. He was square of jaw and shoulder and he had the bronzed look of an athlete.

Anna greeted him wearing a light blue visiting dress made of poplin. Mary had combed her hair back from her forehead into a flat knot at the back. Anna had never looked more beautiful.

"Hello, Scott. How nice of you to call," Anna said nervously.

"Hello Anna. Thank you for receiving me on such short notice." Anna smiled sweetly. "Scott, this is my mother, Mary."

"Mrs. Donavan," Scott bowed.

"You have already met father and I believe you know everyone else."

"Ladies," Scott nodded in the direction of the girls.

"It's a beautiful evening, Anna. With your parents' permission, I thought we might take a stroll before dark," Scott said.

"Father?" Anna asked hopefully. She knew that Teresa and Bill had already captured the porch swing.

"Yes. You have our permission, Scott," Kevin said.

"We'll be back before dark," Scott promised as he escorted Anna out the front door.

"Was that shy, demure creature the same woman who was running around here screaming and pulling at her hair?" Kevin asked.

Mary smiled. "That's just nervous energy. We women are always calm when it counts."

"I have this all-consuming urge to be outdoors," Margaret said. "Would you like to join me, Molly?"

"Yes, I would love to."

"Oh, no you don't," Mary said. "Where was your all-consuming urge to be outdoors when I needed help in the yard this morning? Teresa and Anna are to be left alone this evening."

"You're surely not suggesting that we would spy on them!" Margaret said innocently.

"Oh, but I am," Mary answered. "And I distinctly hear the dishes calling you from the kitchen."

Margaret sighed. She looked at Molly. "There are tragic figures in every family," she said.

"While our sisters are escorted about town in their finery, we are but slaves in our own home. When I grow up to be a famous novelist, I will write this sad story."

"Until that day arrives, go do the dishes," Mary said calmly.

"Come along, little sister," Margaret said. "Where there is drudgery, you will find the two of us." The two girls left the room.

Mary slowly shook her head. "She gets more like you every day, Kevin."

"Don't blame me. As I recall, we were both involved in the manufacturing process."

Mary walked over and put her arms around his neck. She laid her head on his shoulder. He sensed that she was about to cry. "What is it, Mary?"

Mary let the tears come. She pulled away and took a lace handkerchief from her sleeve. "We are so fortunate to have such a wonderful family, Kevin."

"Yes we are," Kevin agreed.

Mary wiped at her eyes. "When we were shopping today, I realized how grown up they are."

Kevin reached out and pulled her close. "So that's what this is all about. Children leaving the nest."

"I guess so."

"Shall I go get Joey's baseball bat and chase those boys away?" he asked.

Mary laughed through her tears. Kevin hugged her tight. "Things will change, Mary Donavan. We can't stop the passage of time, but we will always have our children."

"Is that a promise?"

"Yes. That's a promise."

## MAY, 1893

Beth sat at her desk looking out at the rows of happy, eager faces waiting to be dismissed for summer vacation. She had mixed emotions about the school year ending. She needed a rest, but she wondered if she would ever teach again. After her marriage to Michael last August, he had wanted her to stay at home. At first she had refused, but when she became pregnant in January, and later felt the first stirrings of life within her, she knew it was the right thing to do.

Although her mother and Uncle Red had not been in favor of her marriage to Michael, when they realized it was what she wanted, they had come forward and helped in every possible way. She knew they were genuinely delighted about her pregnancy.

Beth glanced at the clock on the wall. She got up from her desk and stood in front of her fourth-grade class.

"I want to thank all of you for a wonderful school year," she said. "It has been a pleasure having you and I hope you enjoy your summer vacation." She smiled as her words fell on deaf ears. The children's eyes were on the clock. They were ready to spring to their feet at the sound of the bell. When it rang, the room erupted.

"Go slowly now," Beth commanded.

"Good-bye, Mrs. Pacini," the children called as they filed out the door.

"Good-bye children."

Mrs. Pacini. The name still sounded foreign to her.

The children poured into the school yard. Their excited voices slowly faded in the distance.

Beth wiped the blackboard clean before taking one last look around the empty, silent room.

She had vowed not to cry, but as she moved her fingers back and forth across the smooth oak surface of her desk, the tears began to flow. She took out a handkerchief and wiped her eyes. For the past few months she could not seem to get control of herself. This pregnancy kept churning her emotions. She was either extremely happy or extremely depressed. She admired her mother more than any other person in the world. Not even chastising herself that she was the daughter of the strong-willed Melissa Graham and should act accordingly could bring her out of her crying jags. Maybe it was just a natural physical change; Mother Nature turning her inside out and purging the path to motherhood. She was not sure what it was, only that it was painful. She retrieved her parasol from the closet and walked slowly from the room.

As she arrived home, the wind tugged at her hat and thunder rolled in the distance. The maid met her at the door.

"Good evening, Mrs. Pacini. You just made it home ahead of the rain."

"Good evening, Rita. Yes, although it looks like one of those gentle spring rains that I love to walk in."

Rita smiled as she took Beth's hat and parasol.

Beth felt pangs of hunger as exotic smells emanated from the kitchen. She tested the air with her nose and looked questioningly at Rita. Rita raised her eyebrows and shook her head, pleading ignorance. The cook had been trained at Latta's Restaurant. She was an older Italian woman named Mrs. Dalporto and she kept the kitchen off limits to the rest of the household staff. Beth was even intimidated by her. The apex of Mrs. Dalporto's existence was to place another culinary delight in front of Michael when he returned home in the evening.

Beth headed up the stairs to her study. She had to admit that she enjoyed having a household staff. It was also one of the reasons she loved teaching. At the Webster School she could not dole out her responsibilities to someone else. She had to be self sufficient, and creative, and each day give something of herself. She was apprehensive about motherhood and she hoped that life away from teaching did not breed stagnation.

Beth worked in her study until she heard Michael enter the house. She hurried downstairs. "Hello, darling," she smiled.

He kissed her cheek. "How was your last day at school?" he asked.

"Bittersweet." she answered. He followed her into the living room and sat down while she fixed him a drink.

"I'm sure it was difficult for you."

She smiled as she handed him a bourbon and water. Michael always said the right thing. He was impeccably dressed and even though he had been raised in Little Italy, he had not the slightest Italian accent or voice inflection. He was comfortable in the company of bankers, lawyers and statesmen, and he was easily the most handsome man she had ever known.

"How was your day?" she asked out of politeness. Michael never talked about his business. It was one of their areas of conflict. She tried not to make an issue of it, but when Willy Lavetti showed up at all hours of the day or night to drag him away, her resentment would overflow. She loved Michael and she wanted to be a full partner in his life. She would not sit at home like a good wife and keep her mouth shut. She wanted to know where he was going and why. Maybe she was being naive, but if she had not felt she could change Michael, she would not have married him. All she asked was that he trust and confide in her.

"Just fine," he answered. "Have you been feeling okay?"

"A little shaky. Motherhood is unknown territory and I'm still trying to find my way. I wonder and worry about every pang."

Michael gave her a look of sympathy. "When do you see the doctor again?"

"Next week. I'm sure everything is okay. I just need him to bolster my confidence."

A gentle rain began to patter on the roof top. The smell of damp earth and spring flowers filtered through the open window. It had been a rough day for her. She felt safe and cozy in her home, and she hoped that Willy would not show up tonight.

Rita came in to announce dinner. When they had eaten, Michael retreated to the library with his newspaper. William Rockhill Nelson, the reform owner of the *Evening Star,* was on the rampage again. Nelson had spent years battling Tammany Hall and the Boss Tweed ring in New York. He was convinced that Kansas City politics were just as corrupt and he had vowed to change the system. Because of his vast real estate holdings, he was tagged with the name Baron Billy by his enemies.

Michael read the headlines: "Brewery-Saloon Monopoly Must End." Nelson wanted to end the collusion between the breweries and saloons that discouraged competition and promoted price fixing. The saloon interest had also become a powerful political force in the city. In his editorials the Baron was constantly accusing Jack Hannon of political patronage and collusion. Jack would just smile at the investigative reporters and say, "My friends help me and I help my friends. What's wrong with that?" Jack felt no ill will toward the Baron and even championed most of Nelson's civic improvements. Michael made a mental note to keep his own liquor interests at a low profile during the coming months.

Rita entered the room. "Sir, Mr. Lavetti is here."

Michael put down his paper. He conferred with Willy in the hallway and then followed him to the door.

"Rita. Tell Mrs. Pacini I'll be back in a few hours."

Through the streaks of rain on her upstairs window Beth watched Michael leave the house and get in his carriage. She felt a hollow sensation in the pit of her stomach. She could deal with the fears of marriage, and motherhood, and even the loss of her career, but she could not deal with her greatest fear of all — the fear that Michael was still seeing Maria Ramponi. As his carriage disappeared from view, she continued to stare into the night and listen to the raindrops beating gently on the roof.

* * *

Blocks away Michael was thinking about his wife. She was gentle, refined, and well educated; everything that he had wanted in a companion. Still, he could not give up Maria. She stirred a passion in him that he could not control. Tonight he had felt a twinge of guilt when he and Willy had played out the latest charade to get him away from the house.

Willy stopped the carriage in front of Maria's house. "Come back in a couple of hours, Willy," Michael said.

"Okay, Michael," Willy drove off in the rain.

Maria had been expecting him. She opened the door. She was dressed in a white robe that accentuated her black hair and dark skin. Michael grabbed her by the wrist and headed for the bedroom.

"No." Maria pulled her arm away. Her dark eyes flashed. Michael stared at her. "What's the matter, Maria?"

Maria turned away. She pulled her robe tight against her. "Why you never talk to me?" she asked with a pouting look.

"Talk about what, Maria?"

"Anything," Maria said gesturing with her hands. "I live alone. I don't speak good like you, Michael. You never talk with me."

Michael put his hand on her shoulder.

"You're learning to speak English better every day," he said, trying to pacify her.

"Come on," he tugged at her shoulder. "We'll talk in the bedroom."

"You no talk to me. You talk love in my ear. Not the same," Maria protested.

Michael had not seen her for several days. She looked beautiful and alluring, and he was in no mood to be the patient suitor. He put his hands tightly around her wrists and slowly pulled her toward the bedroom.

"No, Michael," she protested, but he was too strong and she was in the bedroom up against the wall. He grabbed the back of her head with his hands and started kissing her neck. It always ended this way. She could protest, but her desire for him was too great. He untied her robe and moved his hands over her body. They were too much alike. He knew how to exploit her passions. She kissed him and started tugging at his shirt. Michael removed his clothes and carried her to the bed. They moved together in a feverish embrace. He melted into her.

She had been mad about something . . . what was it . . . she tried to remember, but the reason was buried under a persistent ache that began deep within her, an ache that would not be denied. She moved against Michael with all her strength until the ache was all that mattered. She squeezed his back with all her might and cried out as everything ended in a rush of pleasure.

Later on, Michael was in front of the full length-closet mirror straightening his clothes. Maria stood next to him. He studied her thoughtful reflection.

"What is it, Maria?"

Maria turned away from his gaze. "Why you marry her instead of me, Michael?" she asked.

Michael remained silent, straightening his tie.

"You love her?" Maria asked.

"Don't ask me questions about my family, Maria," Michael said irritably.

"You love her, you make love with me," Maria persisted.

"Leave it alone, Maria," Michael commanded.

Maria was in no mood to be shunted away. She circled Michael like a wary cat.

"You have family. I have no one," Maria said.

"You have me," Michael countered.

"Only when you want love," Maria hissed. "I want more."

Michael turned and headed for the door. Maria would not be denied. She moved in front of him and blocked the doorway. Her dark eyes flashed angrily.

"Your wife Quality Hill and I your whore, huh?" Maria asked disdainfully. "How about I go see your wife?"

Maria watched his face harden and his eyes grow cold. Maria had never seen the look before.

"Get out of my way, Maria," Michael said firmly.

She stepped aside, a look of repentance on her face.

She was afraid to look at him. He moved past her and gently closed the door behind him.

A cold chill went up Maria's spine. She pulled her robe tight against her. Michael lived by his own rules. She had known men like him in the old country. She would have to be careful and not be blinded by love. She now knew for certain that he would kill her if she ever went near his family.

## FRIDAY EVENING — MARCH 7, 1894

John Mulroon sat in Jack's office discussing the March election. It was predicted the Republicans would finally overcome the Democratic machine and win election in most districts of the city. The First Ward was the only district in doubt.

"I never thought I would live to see the day when the First Ward would be the last Democratic stronghold in the city," John said.

"Yes, things have certainly changed," Jack agreed. "If the First Ward falls, the common man will no longer have a voice in city government; everything will be controlled by the big business boys up on the hill. If the Democratic party is to survive, we must win the First Ward."

"We're doing our best," John said. "We have made a block-by-block coverage of the ward to make sure everyone is registered to vote. Tim Clancy has been signing up all newcomers to the district, and he's been trying to persuade those Republicans still on the fence to cross over and join the Democratic cause. Some of the voters in the ward have been intimidated by the American Protective Association. They have joined forces with the Republicans, and their scare tactics may cost us some votes."

"I'm surprised the Republicans would have anything to do with the A.P.A.," Jack said. "They are a racist, mean-spirited group of troublemakers."

"We're keeping a close watch on them," John said. "Most of the A.P.A. men are armed, so I've told our people not to carry weapons. We don't want anyone getting themselves killed."

"All the boys have worked hard, John. I want you and Tim to know that I appreciate it. This is going to be our toughest fight ever. The Republicans have used Jeremy Wakefield as a spearhead of righteousness in their crusade of half-truths and innuendo. Jeremy has most of the city believing the First Ward is nothing more than a harbor for thieves, prostitutes, and gamblers. He's never spent one day of his life north of Thirteenth Street, and yet he thinks he knows what is best for the First Ward."

Jeremy Wakefield was the new police commissioner. He was a former minister, and he and his followers were religious zealots. They had vowed to clean up the saloons, gambling, and houses of prostitution in the First Ward. Twelfth Street was the southern boundary of the ward and was the street of revelry in Kansas City. One block on the street had the reputation of being the wettest block in the world; there were twenty four buildings on the block, and twenty three of them were saloons. To Jeremy Wakefield the street mirrored everything that was socially evil about Kansas City, and everything that was socially evil seemed to be in the First Ward. Jeremy felt that Twelfth Street was a disgrace to the God-fearing men and women of the city who had to walk past it every day. If the Republicans won the election, Jeremy would have enough support on the city council to shut down the street.

"I could handle the old-time preachers who spouted their Bible-thumping philosophies," Jack continued. "They believed what they were preaching. It's these new age, ivy league ministers who hide their bigotry behind the pulpit and public office that scare me. Jeremy feels that he has to save the poor Irish, Italian, Jew, and Negro from a wicked life in the First Ward. He and his followers judge us all by the red light district. Never mind that we have some of the best schools, neighborhoods, and social programs in the city. He wants to close down Twelfth Street so the boys will have no place to go and have fun after a hard day's work. I have nothing against reformers; Baron Billy Nelson and his newspaper have done some fine things for the working people of the city. What I dislike about Jeremy Wakefield is that he thinks he's better than the rest of us. We must find a way to win this election by a large margin. If Jeremy and his followers spot a weakness, they will concentrate all their efforts into winning the First Ward in the years ahead."

Jack was startled as his office door banged open. A man stumbled into the room. He had an ugly gash in his head, and blood flowed down his face. "What happened to you, Ed?" Jack sprang from his chair.

"It's Tim," Ed sputtered, trying to get his breath. "You got to save Tim."

John Mulroon grabbed a towel from the washroom and pressed it tightly to Ed's head.

"Now slow down and tell us what happened. What's this about Tim?" Jack asked as he helped Ed to a chair.

"They took Tim," Ed said. "We was tryin' to get this German immigrant registered to vote and the next thing I knew the A.P.A. was on us. They said the man was a good Republican and we were tryin' to force him to be a Democrat against his will. They hit me on the head, and they dragged Tim away."

"Which way were they headed?" Jack asked.

"Down Delaware Street to the river," Ed answered.

"Go get the boys, John," Jack ordered. "We have to go after Tim before they harm him." Jack pictured the frail frame of Tim Clancy. The former Rabbit leader was a veteran of political infighting. Jack owed his political career to Tim Clancy and John Mulroon. Through the years the two men had patiently coached him in all aspects of local politics. All the energy they had previously used fighting each other for control of the First Ward was put into making Jack a first-rate politician. Tim was also the grandfather figure for many of the Irish in the First Ward. The A.P.A. had picked the wrong man to beat up on; the Irish community would be outraged if Tim was harmed. Tim was older and frail, but there was not a tougher Irishman in the district. Jack was worried because the only thing Tim hated worse than the Republicans were the men of the A.P.A. He would not be intimidated by violence, and he would probably fight back and get himself killed.

Jack walked outside of O'Shea's into the middle of Delaware Street. John had sent runners to spread the word of Tim's abduction. There were men converging on O'Shea's from all over the market area. The sun had set and a sliver of moon shone on the horizon. A southerly wind pushed clouds across the sky with a promise of rain before morning.

John Mulroon emerged out of the crowd of men. "We're ready, Jack." With John at his side, Jack led about forty angry men quickly down Delaware Street.

A block from the river, one of the men John Mulroon had sent ahead to scout came running around the corner.

"They have Tim at a warehouse on Front Street," he yelled.

"Have they harmed him?" Jack asked.

"He's beat up pretty bad," the man answered.

"Let's go," Jack commanded.

"Wait!" the scout said. "They been passin' the whiskey bottle around and they're gettin' drunk. I heard them say they were goin' to take Tim over and hang him from the Hannibal Bridge."

Jack pondered for a moment. "They will have to come this way," he said. "We'll jump them when they come past Delaware Street."

He motioned for his men to step back in the shadows. Jack could hardly control his anger. If there was ever a man who championed the Democratic cause, it was Tim Clancy. He was Jack's mentor and the wise old owl of First Ward politics. Tim had worked hard for the betterment of the city and he deserved the respect of the Democrats and Republicans alike.

In the distance, shouting and cursing could be heard as the A.P.A.-led Republicans moved west along Front Street.

"All right men," Jack said. "Get ready. John and I will lead the way."

The mob of men came in sight. They were pushing Tim ahead of them. As they came abreast of Delaware Street Jack could see Tim's bloody face illuminated by lanterns carried by some of the Republicans. Tim fell to his knees. Two men ran up and started kicking him. They pulled him to his feet and shoved him ahead.

"Those bastards," Jack whispered menacingly. The mob of Republicans started across Delaware Street. As one, Jack and John Mulroon let out a roar and charged into the flank of the Republicans. They lowered their shoulders and rammed into the mob. A dozen men went down like bowling pins. Jack's men followed him into the fray and started pounding away with their fists. Jack took a blow to the head. He shook it off and punished the man who had hit him with a wicked right cross. The punch broke the man's jaw. He hit another man with a straight left and the man fell into the street. Jack and John Mulroon were back to back, punching away. Jack took several more punches to his face and body, but he was throwing punches too fast to notice. He pounded so many heads that his knuckles were swollen and bleeding. The Republicans started to fall back. They were no match for the two huge Irishmen or the brawling Democrats of the First Ward.

"Where's Tim?" Jack shouted.

"Over here," Tim called. He was throwing punches at several men who were trying to get away from him.

Jack moved over to him as the A.P.A.-led Republicans retreated down Delaware Street.

"Look at the scum run," Tim shouted gleefully. He shook his fist at the Republicans as they stopped a half-block away and gathered their forces.

Tim wiped the blood off his face. "I'll be thankin' you and the men for this, Jack Hannon. You saved my life."

"Are you all right, Tim?" Jack asked. "You look terrible."

Tim squinted through his swollen eyes. "You don't look so good yourself," he said.

Jack started to reply, but his answer was drowned in the crack of pistol fire. He watched as several of his men fell wounded into the street.

"Fall back!" He shouted. Another round of pistol fire crashed into his men.

"Get down!" Jack watched as more of his men fell, wounded. He could not believe the Republicans were firing on his unarmed men. Using weapons in a political battle was unheard of in Kansas City. The Republicans fired one more harmless volley and then scattered into the night.

Jack and John Mulroon moved among the men, checking the wounded. There were five men lying on the ground moaning in pain. Jack examined the men and determined that none of the wounds were life-threatening. John Mulroon sent a runner back up Delaware Street to get a wagon to transport the wounded to the hospital.

"Over here!" Tim shouted from across the street.

Jack and John ran over to a produce warehouse. Tim held a lantern in his hand. He was examining a man propped against the door of the warehouse. The man gripped a wine bottle tightly in his hand, and he bled from a small hole in his forehead.

Jack bent over and felt for a pulse in the man's neck.

"He's dead," Jack said.

They all stared at the lifeless, open eyes of the dead man.

"I don't know him," Jack said. "Who is he?"

John and Tim shook their heads. "Never seen him before," Tim said.

"Me neither," John concurred.

Jack called all of the men over to have a look, but no one recognized the dead man.

"I bet he's one of Father Devin's flock from the mission," Tim said. "He was sittin' here havin' a drink and mindin' his own business and caught a stray bullet. Poor soul." He shook his head at the injustice of it all.

"Lannie!" Tim called.

A young man ran up to Tim.

"Run over to the mission and get Father Devin."

"Yes sir." Lannie rushed off into the night.

Jack pulled a cigar from his vest pocket and bit off the end. He stared at the dead man as he struck a match and lit the cigar. Lost in thought, he took several puffs and blew smoke in the air.

"I've seen that glint in your eyes before, Jack Hannon. What is it your thinkin'?" Tim asked.

"A terrible thing has happened here tonight," Jack said. "We can't change the fact that a man has lost his life. We can see that his life was not in vain."

"And how might we do that?" Tim asked.

"We make him the political saviour of the First Ward," Jack answered.

Tim stared at Jack. His body ached from the pounding he had taken from the A.P.A. He was either getting older or politics was getting tougher. He longed for the good old days and the competition between the Goats and Rabbits. There had always been friendly fist fights, but no one had ever been killed in a First Ward political fight. He loved politics, but there were days like today when he thought a lot about retirement. If it were not for Jack Hannon he would probably get out of politics. Jack had unified the Goats and Rabbits and given the First Ward a direction. Tim had the brains to run the Ward, but not the charisma. And John Mulroon was his opposite. To the detriment of the First Ward, he and John always would have been brawling with each other. Jack Hannon had all the qualities of the consummate politician. He was shrewd, charming, and tough when he had to be. He had needed nothing more than a little coaching in the finer points of the political game. Jack was successful because he administered his political office from the heart. Unlike a lot of politicians, he did nothing for personal gain. Years ago, he had unknowingly laid the groundwork for his success when he had opened his safe at O'Shea's for those in need. A man never forgot a kindness when he was down on his luck. Jack had started the Christmas wagon so no one in the district would go hungry on Christmas Day. He had asked nothing in return for this kindness, but people would remember a meal from the Christmas wagon when they went to the polls on election day. He made sure the Democratic coffers always had enough money to give to victims of fires, floods, and tornados. Before entering politics Jack was called a humanitarian for helping people get jobs. Now Jeremy Wakefield and the newspapers were calling it political patronage. They were saying Jack was giving out jobs to buy votes. That was laughable to anyone who knew Jack Hannon. Jack never exacted a price from anyone he helped. Tim had been on the political scene for a long time before Jack came along, but Jack had taught him that politics need not be a dirty business. Jack had no political strategy. He had just started running the First Ward like everyone was part of a large family, and to Tim's surprise it had turned out to be the best strategy of all. Jack was the best thing that had ever happened to Kansas City, and Tim was going to see that he was reelected. Jeremy Wakefield and the newspapers had ganged up on Jack this year because they could not see past the red light district on Twelfth Street. They wanted the street shut down; all the positive aspects of the First Ward were forgotten. The Republicans had moved voters into the ward for the election, and Tim was sure they were padding voter registration rolls. Tim also knew that some people would be swayed by the religious fervor spewing from the Republicans, and some would be intimidated by the A.P.A., but he was confident the majority of people would go to the polls and vote from the heart, and that meant Jack Hannon would be reelected. Tim had been waiting for something to happen that might guarantee a Democratic victory on election day, and from the look on Jack's face, that something might have happened.

"Out with it, Jack Hannon," Tim said. "How can we make this poor soul the Democratic saviour of the First Ward?"

"What's going on, Tim?" Father Devin asked as Lannie led him into the lantern's light.

"Hello, Father," Tim said. Jack and John Mulroon shook hands with Father Devin.

Father Devin was a short, stocky man. He was bald except for a thin line of blond hair above his ears, and he peered over glasses that he wore on the tip of his broad, flat nose. He was the right man to administer religion to the First Ward. He was compassionate and good-natured, but he was also a former boxer, and if all else failed, Father Devin was not above throwing a punch for the Lord.

Tim put the light of the lantern on the dead man. Father Devin dropped to his knees. The men took off their hats as Father Devin administered the Last Rites.

When he was finished, Jack helped Father Devin to his feet.

"Who was he, Father?" Jack asked.

"His name was Cobb," Father Devin answered. "He drifted into town a couple of weeks ago from somewhere down in Oklahoma."

"Any family?" Jack asked.

"Not that he mentioned."

"Was Cobb his first or last name?" Jack asked.

"He didn't say. Cobb was a street person; one of God's lost souls who lived from one bottle to the next. We will have to give him a decent burial," Father Devin said.

"Please leave everything to us, Father," Jack said. "Cobb was killed in a First Ward political battle and we feel responsible. We will take care of the funeral and the burial."

"That's decent of you, Jack," Father Devin said.

"Lannie, please escort Father Devin back to the mission," Tim said.

Tim waited until Lannie led Father Devin away into the night. "Now, Jack Hannon, what is it you're thinkin'?" Tim asked.

"Can you imagine the outrage when the public learns that an unarmed, loyal Democrat has been murdered by the Republicans?" Jack said.

Tim Clancy stared at Jack. He mulled over the possibilities and a sly smile slowly creased his face.

"He's not a loyal Democrat," John Mulroon said, "He's a bum."

Tim Clancy sprang into action. "Give me your political badges," he said to the men around him. "Quickly now," he ordered. "The press will be here soon."

Tim took three of the badges and pinned them on Cobb's shirt front. One of the badges read "Save The First Ward," another read "Reelect Jack Hannon," and the third, "Vote Democratic."

"We will call him Moses Cobb," Jack said. "Because he has led us out of the political wilderness."

Tim Clancy smiled. Jack's idea was brilliant, but it would be up to Tim to pull it off.

Kevin had stopped at O'Shea's for his evening beer. When he heard about the trouble he raced down Delaware to Front Street. He saw the light of the lantern at the produce warehouse and went over to investigate. When he arrived on the scene, he looked at the bloody faces of the combatants and the body of Moses Cobb.

"What happened, Jack?" he asked.

"Tim Clancy was kidnapped by the Republicans," Jack said. "We had to fight to get him back."

Kevin looked at the body propped against the door of the building.

"A loyal son of the Democratic party," Tim explained.

"They used firearms against you?" Kevin asked.

"They did," Tim said. "As cowardly an act as I've ever witnessed. We were unarmed and havin' a fair fight when they shot our boys down in the street."

Kevin reached for his pen and paper. "How many men were hurt?" he asked.

"Five wounded and one killed," John Mulroon answered.

Kevin bent over to examine the body of Moses Cobb. He noticed the political badges on Moses' shirt front.

"Who is he?" Kevin asked.

"His name's Moses Cobb," Tim answered.

"Is he a party member?" Kevin asked.

"He joined last week," Tim replied.

"And I assume he is a registered voter."

"I signed him up myself," Tim said.

Kevin knew in an instant what Tim Clancy was up to. The crafty old politician was going to make Moses Cobb a Democratic martyr and in the process win the election for Jack.

Kevin gave Tim a look of disgust. "Do you think I just fell off the potato wagon, Tim Clancy? This man is a derelict."

Tim looked offended. "How could you say such a thing, Kevin Donavan? Moses may have been down on his luck, but he was a loyal member of the Democratic party. If you don't choose to believe a fellow Irishman, you can check the voter registration rolls on Monday."

"We all know you can make those registration rolls sing and dance if you want to, Tim Clancy," Kevin replied.

Tim sighed at his continuing bad luck. Why had Kevin Donavan been the first reporter on the scene? Tim could easily have fooled anyone else. He knew that Kevin would not compromise his journalistic integrity for Jack or anyone else. Tim needed time to think. "Let's all walk back up to O'Shea's, where we can repair our wounds, have a whiskey, and discuss this like gentlemen," he said.

"What about Moses Cobb?" John asked.

"Bring him along," Tim said. "Have the boys carry him into the back room at O'Shea's."

Tim and Jack led Kevin and the Democrats back up Delaware Street to O'Shea's.

Tim walked up to the bar.

"My God, Tim, what have they done to you?" Harry asked.

"Just a few cuts and bruises, Harry. Would you give me a towel and a bottle of whiskey?" Tim turned to Kevin. "John Mulroon and I would like to talk to you in the back room."

"After you," Kevin replied.

Jack went upstairs to get cleaned up.

Tim and John Mulroon sat across the table from Kevin. The body of Moses Cobb was stretched out on the floor in a corner of the room.

"Now, Kevin," Tim began. "We don't want you to compromise yourself as a journalist, but we have to think about your duty to the people of the city. If Jack loses this election, we will all be the poorer for it. All these years, he has been the buffer for the working man against big business. Can you imagine what life will be like if Jeremy Wakefield and his righteous crusaders get control of the First Ward? They mean to take all the fun out of the city. Of course, I would never take advantage of your friendship with Jack and mention all that he has done for you."

"Of course you wouldn't," Kevin said.

"Or mention that we are all brothers of Ireland," Tim continued.

"You would never do that," Kevin agreed.

Tim poured them all another drink.

"Will you do the story?" Tim asked.

John Mulroon scrutinized Kevin.

"Tell me the truth," Kevin said. "Was Moses Cobb a registered Democrat?"

Tim and John looked at each other.

Tim shook his head in the negative.

Kevin downed his whiskey. He looked over at the body of Moses Cobb. "You're right, Tim. I do owe Jack a lot. We might be bending the truth a little, but if Jack is reelected, it will benefit the common good. If I write a factual story, the killers will go free and Moses Cobb will go to a pauper's grave."

Tim Clancy poured them all another drink. "And what would be the harm in stretchin' the truth?" he asked. "The purpose of most editorials is to stir people up so they will work for the betterment of their fellow man."

"You make a good case, Tim, but the fact remains that I will still have to write a major story that is not exactly true. Because of my relationship with Jack, I have never written about politics."

"Kevin, lad. This is not about politics," Tim argued. "This is about simple justice. The Republicans and the A.P.A. went too far when they shot unarmed men and murdered Moses Cobb. This election is in your hands. Could you live with yourself if those responsible went free?"

Kevin looked over at the body of Moses Cobb. The man could have been anyone; rich or poor, Republican or Democrat. To Kevin, he represented the common man, and he cried out to be avenged.

"I'll have to go home and wrestle with my conscience over this one, Tim." Kevin held out his empty glass. Tim Clancy poured everyone another drink.

Kevin held up his glass. "To Moses Cobb," he said.

"To Moses Cobb," said Tim Clancy and John Mulroon.

* * *

At O'Shea's tavern Tim Clancy picked up the Sunday edition of the *Times*. A picture of Moses Cobb was displayed beneath the headline of Kevin's story. Moses was decked out in a suit and his chest was covered with democratic badges.

Tim read the headline: "Democrat Killed in Front Street Massacre." He began to read the story:

*Moses Cobb, a man who recently made Kansas City his home, was gunned down in the street by members of the American Protective Association, and members of the Republican party. His life was snuffed out on the very day he had exercised his constitutional right and registered to vote with the Democratic party, his party of choice.*

*In a confrontation at Front Street and Delaware over voter registration, the A.P.A.-led Republicans were losing a fist fight to the Democrats when the Republicans retreated down Delaware Street and opened fire with revolvers on unarmed members of the Democratic party. Five Democrats were wounded and Moses Cobb was killed.*

*The scene was reminiscent of political wars in foreign countries where votes are garnered by violence and intimidation. Around the city, Republicans and Democrats alike are saddened by this tragedy because Moses Cobb's death goes beyond party affiliation. Like any good American, he was only fighting for what he believed in. His death should make those in charge of the electoral process take a long, hard look at the strong-arm tactics used by certain political groups. The days are long past when important public issues are settled by gunfire in the streets of Kansas City. We are living in a civilized society and those responsible for the death of Moses Cobb should be brought to a swift and certain justice.*

*As citizens, our best weapon against this sort of intimidation is the vote, so in memory of Moses Cobb, vote your party of choice in the Tuesday election.*

*Some might say that Moses Cobb was the most common of men, but we are all common men and women; in a way Moses Cobb represents all of us. We will long remember his contribution to freedom of choice.*

*Father Devin will conduct a service for Moses on Monday at the Catholic Mission on Second Street.*

At the Union Mission on Monday afternoon, Jack sat between Tim Clancy and John Mulroon. The small chapel could not hold all of the mourners for Moses Cobb. Hundreds of people stood in the street outside the Mission. As Jack had predicted, there was public outrage that an unarmed man had been murdered in a political battle.

In the pew across from Jack, Jeremy Wakefield sat with his lawyer, Lawrence Dubois, and several members of the city council. All the public officials and those running for office were out in force to show the public their concern for Moses Cobb.

Jack knew it was just another ploy for votes. A last effort to salvage public sentiment for the Republican party and win the election. He also knew it was too late for the Republicans. The people were angry and they would express their anger on election day by voting Democratic.

After Father Devin's eulogy, the service was concluded. Jack walked outside with Tim and John. Jeremy Wakefield and his entourage walked by. Jeremy saw Jack and walked over to him.

"I just wanted you to know that I have learned a valuable lesson from this experience, Hannon."

Jack looked at him questioningly.

"It helps to have a member of the press on your payroll," Jeremy said. "You made Moses Cobb into a saint, when in reality he was nothing more than a drunken bum."

Jack gave Jeremy a look of contempt. "You just stated why you will never win an election in this district, Wakefield."

"And why is that?" Jeremy asked.

"Because where you see drunken bums, I see men down on their luck," Jack said. "Now if you value your health, I suggest you and your men get out of the First Ward."

Tim Clancy smiled at Jeremy Wakefield. Jeremy turned angrily away and walked to his carriage.

Father Devin walked out of the Mission with Kevin.

Jack tipped his cap. "It was a fine service, Father."

"Thank you, Jack."

Jack turned to Kevin. "The story on Moses Cobb was one of your best. The part about Moses representing all of us was true. I could tell you were touched by the death of this man, and I want you to know that we are going to name the new park on Front Street for Moses Cobb. Tim and I have some things to take care of before tomorrow's election. If you have time, stop by O'Shea's for a drink. Good day to you, Father." Jack and Tim walked away.

"Did you read the story, Father?" Kevin asked.

"Yes, I did."

"I fear I may have stretched the truth a bit."

"Perhaps a bit," Father Devin said. "But Jack will be elected again and that is the most important thing."

Kevin looked questioningly at Father Devin.

"I thought most of the city's churches were for Jeremy Wakefield."

"Not at all. Unlike some of my contemporaries, I realize Jack is the best man for the First Ward. The main difference between Jack and Jeremy is that Jeremy would want the people to come to him for help. Jack will always take help to the people. Perhaps in a way God used you to show us that Moses Cobb, who was one of the most common of men, is the most important man of all."

"I never looked at it that way before, Father. You and I should talk more often."

"Does that mean you will be coming to church more often with Mary and the children?"

Kevin cleared his throat. "I'll try Father," he said. Kevin backed away and headed down the steps.

Father Devin smiled at Kevin's discomfort. He turned and went back in the Mission.

Kevin felt much better as he headed up the street to O'Shea's. Father Devin had helped to clear his conscience, and an ice cold beer would be waiting for him at O'Shea's.

## JUNE, 1896

Mary Donavan and her four girls were in a side room of the Catholic church. It was Margaret's wedding day and they were all helping her get dressed for the grand occasion. This was Mary and Kevin's fourth June wedding in four years. Anna had married Scott Woodson in 1893; Teresa had married Bill Jensen in 1894; Molly had married in 1895; and now Margaret was getting married to Robert Hogan, the young man she had gone with for so many years. At least, the plan was for Margaret to marry Robert. An hour ago she had had a change of heart and decided she wanted no part of marriage.

"I'm sorry Mother, but I just can't go through with the wedding," Margaret said. "I've decided marriage is not what I want."

"Now dear," Mary said. "Every bride has her moment of doubt. You will be just fine."

"You don't understand," Margaret said. "I just can't do it. I don't know why I agreed to marry Robert in the first place. We have nothing in common."

Anna put her arm comfortingly around Margaret. "You and Robert have gone together for six years. You have everything in common. Why do you think Robert wants to marry you?"

"Because he wants the convenience of a woman to sleep with and marriage is the price he has to pay for it," Margaret answered matter-of-factly.

"I'm just another piece of merchandise to be bought and put on the shelf," she said derisively, referring to the Hogan family hardware business.

"That's a terrible thing to say," Teresa scolded her. "Robert loves you dearly, and you are lucky to have him."

"Oh sure," Margaret countered. "What he has in mind is to get me pregnant and stash me behind a picket fence while he's out doing whatever it is that men do."

Mary rubbed her eyes and shook her head with weariness. She knew her daughters, and she had finally realized that Margaret was serious about not marrying Robert. She thought of all the months of hard work and preparation that had gone into Margaret's wedding. Outside the door she could hear talking and laughter as the church began to fill with friends and family.

"Did you not think of this while we were planning a huge wedding and inviting half the people in the city?" Mary asked.

"If you find out you're making a huge mistake," Margaret said defiantly, "you don't go ahead with it just because of a little inconvenience to others."

"A *little* inconvenience to others, is it?" Mary's Irish temper started to flare, but she checked herself. Margaret had always been the most stubborn of the Donavan children and if you tried to force her against her will, she would only become more defiant. Mary took a deep breath and composed herself. "Whatever you decide to do is all right with us, dear," she said. Mary rolled her eyes pleadingly at Molly. Molly had always been Margaret's confidant. Molly sat down next to Margaret. She took her hand. "Margaret, you are too strong-willed to let Robert or any man control you," Molly said. "And, besides, that's not Robert's nature."

Margaret got up and started pacing the room. "Oh, it's not just Robert," she said. "Once I'm married I'll be expected to cook, clean, and make babies."

"Do the four of us look so miserable?" Mary asked.

"No, of course not," Margaret said. "You all seem very happy. But you must admit that I'm less suited for marriage than anyone in the family. I've always hated the domestic life."

"Marriage is a lot more than keeping house," Mary said. "You will be a partner in everything Robert does. You won't be giving up your life, you will be sharing his."

"From what I've seen, 'sharing' is letting men have all the fun while we do all the work," Margaret countered. "I wish I were more like you, Mother," she added dejectedly. "You are so unselfish. All you ever wanted was to take care of Father and raise a family."

Mary put her arms around Margaret. "Sometimes I wish I were more like you," she said.

"You do?" Margaret was surprised.

"Yes. Although I've always been happy with my life, I've often wondered if I could not have done something more."

"Then you won't be terribly disappointed if I don't marry Robert?"

Mary kissed Margaret on the cheek. "Of course not," she said.

"But you've worked so hard on the wedding. You made this lovely dress, and all the money you and Father have spent."

"It means little if you are not happy," Mary said.

A knock sounded at the door. Mary went over and opened it.

Father Devin stood in the doorway, giving Mary a questioning look from over his spectacles.

"We have a problem, Father," Mary whispered. "Margaret is getting cold feet. Can you stall for time?"

Father Devin chuckled. "I'll see what I can do, Mary."

Mary turned to Margaret. "The girls and I are going to leave you alone for a few minutes so you can gather your thoughts," she said. "Come along girls." They went out into the hallway and closed the door.

Molly walked down the hallway and peeked around the corner.

She came hurrying back. "The church is full, Mother. What are we going to do?" she asked frantically.

Mary saw Kevin standing in the lobby talking to Jack.

"We'll think of something, girls," she said. "Now stay here together in case I need you. I'm going to go talk to your father."

As Mary approached, Kevin pulled his watch out of his vest pocket and read the time. "We're running late, Mary. What's going on?"

"She's going to back out," Mary said.

"She's going to what?"

"Margaret is not going to go through with the wedding."

Kevin glanced at the throng of people gathered in the church. He laughed, not wanting to believe what he had just heard. "She's just nervous," he said.

"No, I think she means it."

Kevin took a deep breath and let it out. "Oh, God," he said.

He knew how stubborn Margaret could be when her mind was made up.

The church was full and people were beginning to whisper impatiently. Father Devin walked up to the podium. He began talking about the importance of marriage and family life in relation to the church. Father Devin was good at this sort of thing, but Kevin knew he could not ad lib for long.

"I'll take care of this," he said. He marched resolutely toward Margaret's dressing room.

"Is she serious, Mary?" Jack asked.

"I'm afraid so."

"Maybe Kevin will change her mind," Jack said.

"No chance of that," Mary replied. "I can tell you what will happen. She will say, 'Oh, Father,' and start to cry. Kevin will then turn to mush, and he will be back here convinced the wedding was a bad idea in the first place."

Kevin knocked on the door.

"Come in," Margaret said.

She was brushing at her hair. She saw her father's reflection in the mirror. "Oh Father!" Margaret got up and ran to him. She put her arms around him and started sobbing on his shoulder.

Kevin patted her back. "There, there," he said soothingly. "Don't cry now. Tell me what this is all about."

"I don't know, Father. Everything was all right until we got to the church. Now I have this overpowering feeling that I'm making a big mistake."

"What you're feeling is not a bit unusual," Kevin said. He took his handkerchief out of his pocket and gently wiped the tears from her cheeks. "I felt the same way when I married your mother. I was afraid of losing my freedom, but in the end it turned out to be the best thing that ever happened to me."

"That's because you're a man," Margaret said. "I don't imagine Robert's life will change much, either. Oh Father, I was so excited and happy, and now I feel like I'm walking into a trap."

Kevin sighed. He could see that her mind was made up. "Is there anything I can do?" he asked.

"No, Father. You and Mother are both so supportive. I'm so sorry to put you through this."

"Well, if you're sure about this, I'll go tell Father Devin to call off the service."

"I think that would be best," Margaret said.

Kevin kissed her on the forehead. "Now, don't you feel bad. Everything will work out for the best."

Jack and Mary were waiting for him in the lobby.

"Well?" Mary asked.

"Maybe this wedding was not meant to be," Kevin said.

Mary and Jack smiled at each other.

"Did I say something funny?" Kevin asked.

"No dear," Mary said. "What do you suggest we do now?"

"I guess I will have to make the announcement to call off the wedding," Kevin said. "We can't keep Father Devin and our friends waiting any longer."

"Hold off for another few minutes," Jack said. "I want to talk to Margaret."

"I don't know what good it will do, but you go ahead and I will see how much longer Father Devin can stall the service," Kevin said.

Margaret opened the door. "Uncle Jack!"

He leaned over and she kissed his cheek. "Your wedding dress is beautiful, Margaret."

"Thank you. Mother used pieces of her wedding dress to make it." Margaret scrutinized Jack. "I see my parents have called in the city's number-one negotiator."

Jack laughed. "No, this was my idea. Your parents are taking this quite well. Most parents would be in here screaming at you and trying to pull you to the altar. May I sit down?"

"Of course." Margaret offered him a chair. She pulled the dressing-table stool over to the chair and sat down facing him.

"As your godfather, Margaret, I feel a responsibility to you, so I want you to listen to what I have to say."

Margaret nodded. Jack had always been a second father to the Donavan children. As a little girl she could remember how in awe she was of this huge man who came to the house with her father. Jack was always kind and generous and the Donavan children were not the least bit intimidated by him.

Jack leaned over and looked directly into her eyes. "Now I want you to forget about the wedding, and your parents, and I want you to tell me about the hopes and dreams of Margaret Donavan."

"What . . . do you mean?" Margaret stammered.

"How do you see yourself ten years from now?" Jack asked.

"Will you be rich and famous? Will you marry and have children? What is your plan for Margaret Donavan?"

Margaret looked away from him. "I guess I don't have one," she said. "Although I've always dreamed of having a career."

"Doing what?" Jack asked.

"Well, I . . ."

"Come on, out with it," Jack said. "Let's be honest with each other."

"It's just a dream," Margaret said. "But I've always wanted to design and sell my own fashions. I've been interested in fashion since I was a little girl. I guess it came from watching Mother make clothes all these years."

"Okay," Jack said. "Do you see yourself married?"

"Yes," Margaret said. "but only if I can have a career."

"Who would you marry?" Jack asked.

"Well...Robert of course."

"Why?" Jack asked.

"Because I love him, Uncle Jack."

Jack leaned back in his chair. "So your decision to call off the wedding has nothing to do with Robert."

"No," Margaret answered.

Jack studied her for a moment. "What you're afraid of, Margaret, is that marriage will require so much of you that you will never realize your dreams."

Tears welled up in Margaret's eyes. "I feel so selfish, Uncle Jack."

"You are not selfish," Jack said. "If you don't act on your feelings, you will never be happy. Now, you listen to me. You have already said that you will eventually marry Robert. Is that correct?"

Margaret nodded.

"All right then, your marriage is settled, so let's go to work on your career. I've always had a dream of my own, Margaret. You four girls, and Joey, are the only children I will ever have. I've hoped that one day I might help you get started in business. Your sisters seem to be content as housewives and Joey still has to get through his schooling, so I guess it's up to you to fulfill my dream."

Margaret looked at him questioningly.

"Here's my proposal. I have some good friends who work in the garment district in New York City. After your wedding and honeymoon, I will send you there to learn all you can about fashion merchandising. Kansas City is attracting business from all over the Midwest, and my plan is for you and I to open up an exclusive dress shop on Petticoat Lane."

Margaret stared at him, speechless.

"Well, what do you say?"

"Uncle Jack, it's everything I ever dreamed of, but it would cost thousands of dollars for a shop and inventory. I can't take your money."

"It's not my money, it's *our* money. When something happens to me, you kids will inherit most of what I have, anyway. This way I get to see some of it put to good use. But I also want you to understand that I'm not giving you anything. I will finance your fashion education and put up money for the business. You will start out with twenty percent ownership, and if you work hard and make the business a success, you can buy my share."

"Oh, Uncle Jack!" Jack was startled as Margaret jumped up and threw her arms around his neck. "I love you so much."

Jack gave her a hug. For the first time in his life he felt the pride and satisfaction of a parent. He cleared his throat. "Do we have a deal, Margaret Donavan?"

"Yes we do, Mr. Hannon."

Jack held out his arm. "All right, then, let's get this marriage under way so you and I can start a business."

Margaret took his arm and they went out the door.

She was smiling and radiant as Jack escorted her into the lobby. Kevin and Mary saw them coming and looked at each other, mystified. Mary hurried down to take her seat in front of the church. Margaret took her father's arm. Jack motioned with his hand for Father Devin to start the service. The organist struck up "Here Comes The Bride." Kevin leaned behind Margaret and looked at Jack. "How did you do it?" he whispered. Jack waved his hand as if it were nothing more than a trifling matter and went to take his seat with the Donavan family in the front of the cathedral.

### FROM ADAM QUINT'S JOURNAL — December 2, 1896

*All of the Donavan girls are now married. It seems like only yesterday they were little girls, running and laughing through the house. We thought we had lost them to the natural progression of life, but we are asked to babysit the grandchildren quite often, and we are included in most of the Donavan family functions. Much to our surprise, Margaret went into business with Jack. No one had the slightest inkling that Boss Hannon would one day own a dress shop. Jack has had to endure some good-natured kidding about it from his friends.*

*Red and Melissa really are living happily ever after. Red's ranch is prospering and Melissa continues to expand her lumber business. If one of them has to leave town on business, the other always goes along, as they refuse to be separated even for a day. They dearly love their granddaughter, Becky. She looks a lot like Beth and Red.*

*Melissa confided to Bonnie that she is worried about Beth and Michael's relationship. I'm sure there are conflicts, for they come from such totally different backgrounds. Michael has always been an enigma to me. There are those who say he controls the Kansas City underworld, but I've never known him to be anything but a perfect gentlemen. Perhaps I'm being naive, but Michael has never been convicted of a crime, or harmed anyone that I know of. There are those in Missouri politics who say I don't see all that I should, and perhaps they are right, but over the years Jack Hannon, the Farrels, the Donavans, and their extended families, have become part of our own, and I would not abandon a part of my family without just cause.*

*After the Moses Cobb incident two years ago, Jack is now firmly entrenched as the undisputed leader of the First Ward. The Republicans are still in the shadows licking their wounds. I have yet to understand why they keep attacking Jack. It is obvious to everyone that the people of the First Ward are prosperous and happy, and whenever the Republicans attack him, they always come away looking foolish.*

*The city is still slowly recovering from the real estate crash of 1888, and also from a trade depression in 1893 that caused a national panic. I remain optimistic, however, and see nothing but good things ahead.*

# 11

## JOEY

AUGUST, 1897

Joey Donavan's parents and older sisters doted on him. Rather than make him egotistical, or spoiled, it had the opposite effect. No young man was more considerate of his family or others, than Joey.

By the age of six, Kevin was taking him everywhere. Joey became a familiar figure in the West Bottoms and the levee district as he followed his dad around. He even carried his own small pad and pencil. Joey was known by every policeman, fireman, and elbow bender in the district.

His Uncle Jack loved to play a game with him. Every Saturday when Joey followed Kevin into O'Shea's tavern, Jack would yell, "Who's that you're with, Joey?"

"That's my dad," Joey would answer.

"What's he do?"

"He's a reporter."

"What's he report?"

At this Joey would shrug his shoulders.

Jack and the rest of the saloon would howl with laughter. It earned Joey a sarsaparilla, so he never questioned the reason.

In the third grade he started bringing home his classmates. They were from every part of the city. Their only common denominator was their need for a hot meal. Joey would watch with satisfaction as his mother placed hot food in front of an appreciative friend.

"What do you make of him, Mary?" Kevin would ask.

Mary would just smile and shake her head.

"Do you remember that rough-looking kid he brought home the other day?" Kevin asked. "What was his name?"

"Skronsky," Mary replied.

"Skronsky, that's right. I asked him if Joe ever got into fights at school. Skronsky got the most incredulous look on his face. He looked at me as if I had committed blasphemy. 'No one would bother Joey!' he said."

Mary laughed. "That will teach you to be so inquisitive."

At the age of eleven, when Joey started bringing home derelicts from the levee, Mary had had enough. She called Father Devin, the priest at her church. Father Devin enlisted Joey to work in the church-sponsored soup kitchen down in the levee district.

Joey spent most of his time following Father Devin on his rounds. He had little time for his family.

"Don't you want to play ball and be with your friends, Joe?" Kevin admonished him.

"I like to help people, Father."

"I'm sure you do, but couldn't you spend less time with the city's derelicts and more with your family?"

"But there's so much to be done."

"The gandy dancers were getting along just fine before you came along, young man."

Joey loved his father, so he tried to keep their disagreements to a minimum. He would make himself visible around the house for a few days until the magnetism of the destitute and downtrodden pulled him back into the poor districts of the city.

At sixteen, some of the curl was leaving his hair and the cluster of freckles under his eyes was fading with the years.

* * *

Joey walked down Main Street toward the levee. The street slanted quickly away from the new city, down the hill to the older section of town. You could walk down the incline into the city's past as easily as you could turn the pages of a history book.

The river districts had given birth to the new metropolis up on the bluffs. Tall buildings now dominated the skyline overlooking the West Bottoms and North End. Cable cars moved through the streets, collecting and depositing passengers who darted in and out of stores and office buildings. There was a constant hum of activity as new construction reached for the sky and the city expanded outward in every direction away from the river.

In contrast, there was a sense of history down below in old town where the city had begun. There was a feeling of permanence in the time-worn streets and weather-beaten buildings. Unlike the bustling activity of the offspring up on the bluffs, everything moved slower in the river district. To Joey, old town was like an aged grandfather who had completed his task, and now just wanted to sit by the river and be left in peace.

Joey stopped at the Ninth Street juncture where Main and Delaware Streets formed a Y.

Ollie Thompson was shouting at the pedestrians to watch out for cable cars. The Civil War veteran, wearing his Confederate cap, limped around the street. He was the picture of a commander frustrated at the movement of his troops. Ollie was a familiar figure around town. When he wasn't directing traffic, he delivered telegrams for Western Union.

Joey looked up at the diamond spire on the Times building. This was his favorite spot in the city. From his position under the Owl Cigar sign, he could view the city's populace darting among the cable cars. Carriages deftly moved along the street, somehow avoiding pedestrians and cable cars alike. The junction cleared for a moment. Joey continued on his way.

**The junction at Main and Delaware**

"Good morning, Mr. Thompson!" he yelled.

Ollie whirled around on his good leg. He tipped his hat. "Morning, Joey. Are you headed for the mission?"

"Yes, sir."

Ollie spotted an offending pedestrian. He hobbled away, yelling and waving his arms.

Joey walked beside the shiny rails. The hot August sun would soon turn them a fiery white. He turned east off Delaware Street into Market Square. The sound of vendors hawking their wares intermingled with men shouting and swearing as they loaded produce wagons for delivery around the city.

Joey stopped at Frank Pacini's small warehouse. A stream of profanity filtered out into the square. Joey stuck his head around the corner of Frank's office. Frank covered the telephone with his hand.

"Joey! Take a piece of fresh fruit."

"No, thanks, Mr. Pacini."

"Do it, I said!"

You didn't refuse Frank Pacini. Joey picked up an apple. He waved a thank you. The happiest day of his life had been when he was allowed to ride on the Christmas wagon with his father, Uncle Jack, and the Pacinis.

He walked away from the pleasant scent of fruit ripening in the open air. He continued on toward the Catholic Mission on Second Street. Industrial smells from the West Bottoms crept around the bluffs. They hovered over the North End, clinging to the mist that blanketed the river.

Joey stopped walking. A derelict lay in the street. A wine bottle protruded from beneath one of the man's legs. Joey pulled him into the shade of an alley. He propped the man against a building. When he reached the mission, he sent two men back for the derelict.

Sister Margarite was in the kitchen. "Good morning, Joey."

"Good morning, Sister. What needs to be done?"

"You may set up the serving line."

Joey nodded. "What's for lunch?"

"Soup, soup, and soup," Sister Margarite answered.

"Sounds familiar."

Sister Margarite smiled.

Joey went to work. He covered the long wooden table with a tablecloth, then carried the plates and bowls from the kitchen and stacked them at one end of the table. When he had finished he went to the kitchen to help Sister Margarite peel potatoes.

"Should I make collections today, Sister?"

"Would you mind, Joey? The food supply is getting short again. Father Devin says that you're so much better at it than the rest of us."

Joey smiled.

"That's because I know whom to put the bite on."

Sister Margarite laughed. "And all this time I thought it was your sweet, innocent face."

Joey expertly split a potato into four pieces. He dropped it into the pot.

"Have you thought anymore about our discussion, Joey?"

"It's been weighing on my mind, Sister."

"No decision, then?"

"No."

"To train for the priesthood is something you have to want very badly, Joey. If it's right for you, God will point the way."

"I hope so, Sister Margarite."

"It's a decision that will affect the rest of your life. You have the benefit of time. Use it wisely and you will make the right decision."

Sister Margarite plopped the last potato into the pot. Together they carried it to the stove.

Joey helped serve the noon meal. It was late afternoon when he and Sister Margarite finished cleaning up the kitchen.

"I'm going on my rounds, Sister."

"May God be with you, Joey."

He crossed Market Square. He was careful not to ask donations from anyone who had recently donated. Joey Donavan was no amateur collector.

After soliciting from several businesses on the market, he worked his way east into the fashionable neighborhoods along Independence Avenue. He saved this district for lean times when money was hard to come by.

Joey reviewed the names of the residents as he moved along the street. He went up to the first house and knocked on the door. "Good evening, Mr. Cohen. I work for Father Devin at the Catholic Mission on Second Street. I'm asking for contributions to help feed the less fortunate."

Mr. Cohen reached into his pocket. He pulled out some change. He handed it to Joey.

"Thank you, sir. And God bless you."

He went on to the next house.

"Good evening, Mr. Baxter. I'm Joey . . ."

"Save your speech, Joey. I know it by heart." Baxter took a dollar bill from his pocket. He handed it to Joey.

"Thanks, Mr. Baxter." Joey continued collecting down the street.

In the twilight he noticed lights burning in a house that had just been constructed. He walked toward the light at the end of the block. The Queen Anne style home was similar to the one the Donavans had purchased two years ago. It combined brick, fish-scale shingles, Gothic chimneys, and porches. The only difference Joey could discern was porch design and a semicircular turret on this house that culminated in an open-air porch on the third floor.

Not one to miss a donation, Joey bounded up the steps. He knocked on the door. A man answered. He was dressed in an elegant maroon silk robe tied with a black sash at the waist.

"Yes, what is it?"

"My name's Joey Donavan, sir. I'm collecting for the Catholic Mission."

The man's eyes flashed from above cheekbones that dominated his face. "Come inside so I can get a look at you," he commanded.

Joey entered the house. He held out his hand. The man shook it reluctantly.

"I'm Robert Sieben," he said. He rubbed his well-trimmed mustache. "Now tell me what you want."

Joey glanced into the parlor. A girl was watching him. She had her father's features. Her face was expressionless but her eyes were smiling at him. He felt very uncomfortable.

"Well, what is it, young man?"

Joey was startled into speech. "My name's Joey Donavan . . ."

"You mentioned that. What is the Catholic Mission?"

"The mission is a place for the hungry and destitute to come for food and shelter." Joey's eyes moved back to the girl.

"How do I know you're not keeping the money for yourself, Mr Donavan?"

Joey was not offended by the question. "You can ask anyone on the block about my credibility, Mr. Sieben."

"You're well known in this neighborhood?"

"Yes, sir."

"You don't look destitute, Mr. Donavan."

"No, sir. I work at the mission in my spare time."

"You're the solicitor."

"I do a bit of everything, sir. Whatever is required."

"Are you paid a wage?"

Joey felt the girl's eyes boring into him. He pulled at his collar. "I don't work for money, sir. It's a charitable organization."

"I take it the money will be well spent, Mr. Donavan?"

"We squeeze every penny, sir."

"Oh, all right." Mr. Sieben seemed satisfied. "Wait here. I'll go upstairs and get the money."

Joey watched him vanish at the top of the stairs.

He turned to the girl. "Have you lived here long?"

"No. Just for a few days."

She moved away from the chair and approached him. Her straight black hair was cut neatly at her shoulders. She was thin, dark, and very attractive.

"I'm Jill Sieben. Don't let father scare you, Joey. He questions everyone. It's the attorney in him."

"That's okay. I'm used to it."

Jill smiled. "What you're doing is very noble," she said.

"Have you seen anything of the city?" Joey asked.

"No. We've been so busy with the move. I'm hopeful Father and I will get out soon."

Mr. Sieben walked down the stairs. Jill went back into the parlor.

"How long have you been at this business of charity, Mr. Donavan?"

"I've been doing it for five years, sir."

Mr. Sieben cleared his throat. He handed over the money.

"Thank you, Mr. Sieben."

Joey stole one last glance at Jill Sieben. He backed toward the door. "Good night."

Out on the street he looked back several times before the Sieben house disappeared from view.

* * *

"Joey, eat your breakfast."

"I'm not hungry, Mother."

"You, not hungry?" Kevin looked at the full plate of food in front of his son.

Joey picked at a waffle with his fork.

"You must be coming down with something," Mary said.

Joey pushed the plate of food away.

"I think I'll run down to the mission, Mother. I'm sorry about the food."

Joey got up from the table. He went out the door.

"I wonder what's the matter with him?" Mary asked.

"I'm sure it's this business about becoming a priest," Kevin answered. "He must be close to a decision."

"Do you think he's really serious about it, Kevin? Maybe you received some wrong information."

"You know my sources are correct."

Mary sighed. "He will discuss it with you when he feels he's ready."

"That, my dear, is what I'm afraid of. What will I say to him?"

Mary started gathering the breakfast dishes. "I don't know. We both feel he's too young for a commitment on that grand a scale. Raising a child without interfering is very difficult."

Kevin wiped his mouth with a napkin.

"We had better be ready, Mary. He's on the verge of something."

* * *

Joey Donavan leaned against a lamp post. The Sieben house loomed large in the twilight.

He hadn't slept well the last two nights. The dark hair and brown eyes of Jill Sieben were keeping him awake.

Sister Margarite had even commented on his lack of enthusiasm. That had never happened before.

The thought of Mr. Sieben answering the door was not a pleasant one. The confidence he had pumped himself full of was starting to ebb.

On rubbery legs he walked across the street. He knocked on the door. His worst fear was realized. Mr. Sieben answered the door. He eyed Joey coldly. "Am I required to give to your organization daily, Mr. Donavan?"

"No, sir."

"Then why are you on my doorstep?"

"Well, sir . . ."

"I don't have all night, Mr. Donavan."

"I wonder if you might permit me to speak with Jill?"

"What about?"

"Well, sir, she's new to the city and if someone her own age could tell her a bit about it, the town might not seem so foreign."

"Is this part of your missionary duties, Mr. Donavan?"

Joey flushed.

"I suspected as much. On any other occasion, Mr. Donavan, I would refer you to the street. It so happens my daughter is having a difficult adjustment to our most recent move. A conversation with one of the locals might lessen some of her loneliness."

Joey breathed a sigh of relief. He took his hat off and entered the house. Mr. Sieben pointed to a chair in the parlor. "Jill!" he called up the stairs.

"Yes, Father?"

Joey swallowed. His throat was dry.

"You have a caller."

Jill bounded down the stairs.

"Who would be call —," She spotted Joey sitting in the parlor. Her smile made all his discomfort worthwhile.

"Hello, Joey."

She had remembered his name.

"Hello, Jill."

She walked into the parlor and took a seat across from him.

Mr. Sieben stationed himself on the couch, newspaper in hand.

"I wanted to stop by and see if you were getting settled," Joey said. He flushed again as Mr. Sieben eyed him from over the paper.

"That's very kind of you, Joey. I'm sure we won't be completely finished for another week."

An embarrassing silence followed. Mr. Sieben dropped the paper into his lap.

"How old are you, Donavan?"

"Seventeen, sir."

"Do you participate in sports?"

"No, sir."

"Why not?"

"I'm busy with other things."

Mr. Sieben snorted. He went back to reading his paper.

"Do you think New York will win the pennant for the fourth time in a row?" Joey asked. "It looks like St. Louis is out of it."

Mr. Sieben peered from around the paper. "No, I don't think New York will win. And you're right about St. Louis. The sports page isn't foreign to you then, Donavan?"

"No, sir. It's required reading at our house. My father's the assistant sports editor for the *Times*."

"Is he now?"

"Yes, sir."

"Do I assume that you plan to go into journalism when you finish your schooling?"

"No, sir."

"Then what vocation will you pursue?"

Joey hesitated.

"I'm considering the priesthood."

"A priest?"

"Yes, sir."

"And what does your father think of your plans?"

"Not much, I'm afraid. However, my parents will back whatever decision I make."

"Do you go to the Catholic school, Joey?" Jill asked.

"No. I attend the public school."

"I'm going to have coffee in the kitchen. I trust you won't be long, Mr. Donavan?"

"No, sir. Thank you for letting me call."

Mr. Sieben retreated to the kitchen. Joey was visibly relieved.

"I'm sorry," Jill said.

Joey looked at his arms and legs. "I think I'm still intact."

Jill laughed. "Don't be too hard on Father. I'm all he has and he can be overly protective."

"Your mother?" Joey asked.

"She died when I was ten."

"I'm sorry."

Jill studied his face. "I'm glad you came back," she said.

Joey searched for something to say. "It must have been difficult to leave your friends in St. Louis."

She smiled. "Yes, that was the hardest part. Father and I are Jewish, and we lived in a close-knit neighborhood."

"I have an idea," Joey said. "Let me take you to Troost Park on Saturday."

"Troost Park?"

"It's our local amusement park."

"I'd love to, Joey, but Father might not approve."

"Your father can chaperone."

"Oh, that should make it all right!" Jill said excitedly.

"Then we have a date?"

"Oh yes, Joey!" Jill put her fingers to her lips. "Oh," she said.

Joey laughed at her enthusiasm. Jill dropped her hands into her lap. She laughed with him.

"If we're to pull this off successfully," Joey said, "I had better be going." Jill followed him to the door.

"Thank you for being so kind, Joey. You're making me feel welcome here."

"I can't take credit for that, Miss Sieben. My motives were entirely selfish."

Her cheeks turned red.

"I'll see you on Friday, Jill."

"Good-bye, Joey."

* * *

Jill and Joey stepped off the streetcar.

"Oh, I wish Father could have seen this," Jill said.

"Yes. Too bad he had a meeting," Joey answered.

She looked at him out of the corner of her eye. They laughed together.

Their footsteps were muffled as they walked into the sawdust at the park entrance on Twenty-ninth Street and were surrounded by guns popping and rides whirring.

Jill looked around, her eyes sparkling. "I love amusement parks," she said. "What shall we do first?"

"You're the guest. You decide."

"The Ferris wheel."

Joey handed over the tickets. The operator put them in a seat. He clanged the bar shut. The wheel shuddered into movement. They held on tightly as the seat reached its peak and went over the top.

Jill laughed excitedly. "I get such a hollow feeling in the pit of my stomach!" she shouted.

It took them another hour to work their way through the shooting galleries and ball-throwing establishments.

"Come on." Joey took her hand. "We'll get some food and go listen to the band."

Joey purchased hot dogs, sodas, and peanuts. Jill helped him carry the food through the park. They took a seat facing the band shell. Sorrentino's band tuned their instruments.

"Having fun?" Joey asked.

Jill had a mouthful of hotdog.

"Sorry," he said.

She swallowed. "I've never had so much fun!"

Sorrentino's band was ready. In honor of John Philip Sousa, another Troost Park favorite, the band struck up "King Cotton." They followed with the "Washington Post March."

The chairs and open areas in front of the band shell began to fill. Joey took off his suit coat. He loosened his string tie. He was beginning to feel very comfortable with Jill Sieben. He leaned back in his chair and stole glances at her as he listened to the music. As darkness fell, Sorrentino's band closed the concert with "Stars and Stripes Forever."

"Should we be going?" Jill asked.

"Come on!" Joey grabbed her hand. "The best is yet to come." He led her over to a large lake. Electric fountains spewed rainbow-colored water high in the air. The colored droplets fell glistening into the lake.

"Joey, it's beautiful!" Jill pointed to wooden platforms in the lake. "Look at the statues!"

Joey laughed. "They're not statues, they're real." The women on the platforms were dressed in white lights and classic draperies.

"Are you sure?" Jill asked.

"Come on, I'll show you." Joey led her around the lake for a closer look.

The announcer's voice followed them, describing the dresses and what each girl represented. They moved close to one of the statues.

"Watch her eyes," Joey said.

The girl remained motionless. Jill followed as Joey moved to the edge of the lake.

"If you don't blink, your eyes will water!" Joey yelled.

The girl remained unperturbed.

"Watch closely, now," Joey said. He smacked his hands together.

"She blinked!" Jill shouted. "I never would have guessed it."

They took a seat on the bank and listened to the commentary.

After the water spectacular they walked out of the park hand-in-hand.

The streetcar ride back to Jill's house seemed too short. Joey walked her to the front door.

"I had a wonderful time, Joey."

"So did I."

"I wish there was some way I could repay your kindness."

"It just so happens there is."

She looked at him questioningly.

"Come to my house for dinner on Sunday afternoon. I haven't been spending much time at home. It would get me back in my parent's good graces."

"Are you sure it will be all right?"

"Yes. You can invite your father as well."

Jill smiled. "I would love to come."

"Good. I'll pick you up at noon on Sunday. Good night, Jill."

"Good night, Joey."

* * *

Kevin sat at the head of the table. Jack sat next to him. Mary and the girls were scurrying around trying to get dinner ready.

"Now, remember, Mary, you and Jack have to back me up. These priests are connivers. They have a way of getting you around to their way of thinking."

"How could you say such a thing, Kevin Donavan!" Mary admonished him. "There's no finer man than Father Devin. And what makes you think it's Father Devin who's coming to dinner?"

"Who else would it be? Joe's been moping about all week. I'm sure the decision concerning the priesthood is at hand."

Anna came out of the kitchen. "Why don't you want Joey to become a priest, Father? He would make a good one."

"He's not ready," Kevin insisted. "I want him to experience the world before some holy order picks him off the street like a sacrificial lamb."

Jack sipped his glass of wine. "Would you feel that way if Baron Billy Nelson, the distinguished owner of the *Times,* picked him off the streets to become a cub reporter?"

"That's different," Kevin said.

Jack laughed. Molly started placing the silverware on the table.

"You're trying to influence the boy as much as Father Devin," Jack said.

"Don't you think Joey should make the decision, Father?" Teresa asked.

"Now, all of you listen to me," Kevin said. "We have to remain united in this endeavor. Joe is fond of his sisters. He will respect your opinion."

"What if it's different from yours, Father?" Teresa asked.

"Then kindly keep it to yourself, Teresa."

"That's why our husbands were not invited," Margaret said. "Father can't control their thinking."

Mary placed the last dish of food on the table. She took her seat. "Poor Father Devin. It will be like Daniel in the lion's den."

"For which he has been well trained," Kevin countered.

The screen door slammed. The gathering tensed. Kevin nodded at them confidently.

Joey walked into the dining room with Jill Sieben on his arm. "Hello, everyone. I'm sorry we're late."

Kevin stared at Jill. His mouth dropped open. Having Father Devin replaced by a young lady was too much for him.

Joey introduced Jill around the table.

"We're so happy you could come, dear," Mary said. She gave her husband a smile of satisfaction.

Jack recovered his composure ahead of the open-mouthed head of the household. "You will have to forgive us, Miss Sieben. We're used to Joey dragging in derelicts from the levee. We were unprepared for a young lady, much less one so lovely."

Jill smiled. "It was kind of you to invite me."

"Jill recently moved here from St. Louis with her father," Joey said.

"Are you enjoying the city?" Molly asked.

"Oh, yes. Joey took me to Troost Park on Friday night. We had a wonderful time."

Kevin looked at Mary, mystified.

What business is your father in, Miss Sieben?" Jack asked.

"He's a lawyer. He's joining the firm of Stein and Rothman."

"A prestigious firm," Jack said.

"You should have invited Mr. Sieben, Joey," Mary said.

"He had prior commitments, Mother."

"I'm sorry he couldn't come," Jill said. "He enjoys your column very much, Mr. Donavan."

Kevin recovered his tongue.

"Your father's a sports fan?"

"Fanatically."

"How did you meet my son, Jill?"

"Joey was collecting for the mission."

"I see. We're glad you could come, Jill. You've brightened our table considerably."

Jill turned to Jack. "Are you the Mr. Hannon of political fame?"

Jack cleared his throat.

Kevin grinned. "He's the one, Miss Sieben."

"Are you familiar with politics, Jill?" Jack asked.

"Somewhat. We studied Missouri politics in school last year. My instructor said you're the most powerful man in the state. Is that true, Mr. Hannon?"

"Of course not, Miss Sieben. The governor retains that distinction."

"My instructor called the governor's mansion 'the house that Hannon built.' "

Jack flushed. Kevin roared with laughter. "Jill, that remark just earned you a permanent place at my table."

"I didn't mean any disrespect, Mr. Hannon. Your works of charity are well known in the St. Louis area."

"You're kind to say so, Miss Sieben."

Jack turned to Kevin. "What's the latest on the newspaper war?"

Kevin grinned. "I assume you're speaking of the delicate situation in Cuba?"

Jack snorted. "That's the one, all right. The newspapers are whipping public opinion into a fury with these unsubstantiated stories."

"Do you think the reports of atrocities committed by the Spanish are true?" Mary asked.

"No, I don't," Jack replied. "Hearst and Pulitzer are determined to lead yellow journalism to its finest hour."

"And what profession rescued the beautiful Evangelina Cisneros from the hells of a Spanish prison?" Kevin asked.

"Rather than an act of humanitarianism, I'm sure the main objective was to sell newspapers."

Jill was amazed that Kevin took no offense at the remarks.

"Do you think we will go to war, Uncle Jack?" Molly asked.

"I'm sure of it, Molly. There's strong sentiment in the country to annex Cuba. This gives us the excuse we need."

"Don't you have any sympathy for the plight of the Cuban revolutionaries?" Mary asked.

"Of course. Like most Americans, I champion the underdog. All I'm saying is that if we're going to liberate a people from an unpopular government, let's do just that and quit trying to make the Spanish appear subhuman."

"What do you think, Father?" Anna asked.

"Your Uncle Jack is right. This country hasn't had a war to support in over thirty years. Most of the country's Civil War veterans are rattling their sabers. If McKinley doesn't declare war soon, the American public may attack Cuba en masse."

"You make us sound like warmongers," Mary admonished him.

"It's human nature," Kevin answered. "War starts out as a noble enterprise. We forget, with the passage of time, how horrible it really is. Nothing quiets the nationalistic furor quicker than a casualty list. The public will sober quickly when the war starts."

After dinner, Kevin and Jack retired to Kevin's den.

Joey and Jill started helping the Donavan girls clean up the dining room table. "If you want to go in with the men, Joey, I'll be okay," Jill said.

"Don't worry about him, Jill," Molly said. "Joey likes to stay out here where the interesting conversation takes place."

Everyone laughed.

The Donavan girls returned to the roles they had performed since childhood. Teresa carried the serving dishes into the kitchen while Margaret scraped and stacked the dinner and dessert dishes. Anna removed the cups and saucers from the table. After Joey and Jill cleared the silverware, Margaret gathered the dirty linen into her arms and headed for the kitchen. Molly pulled a white lace tablecloth from the top drawer of the hutch. Joey and Jill helped her smooth it over the table. Molly blew out the candles and they all retreated into the kitchen.

"The dinner was delicious, Mrs. Donavan," Jill said.

"Thank you, dear. We're delighted that you came tonight."

"Yes," Teresa concurred, as she pulled a sudsy plate from the dish water. "Not only is she charming and lovely, Joey, but for the first time on record, someone has rendered Father and Uncle Jack speechless."

Joey smiled. He leaned against the doorjamb and watched Jill move confidently around the kitchen.

"I can tell that you are no stranger to hard work, Jill," Mary said.

"No, ma'am. I keep house for my father. Although sometimes I must admit that I would like to be."

"Amen to that," Margaret said, as she carefully placed Mary's rose-patterned Bavarian china in the cupboard above the sink.

"Okay, little brother," Molly said. "Now that we have you all to ourselves, we want to hear about you and Jill."

"Yes," Margaret agreed. "Seventeen years without so much as a glance at the feminine species, and before we know it, you're already out on your second date. What magic did you weave over him, Jill?"

Jill laughed good-naturedly as Joey cringed in the doorway. Mary read the pleading look in her son's eyes and came to his rescue.

"It's such a lovely evening, Joey, why don't you and Jill go out on the porch swing?"

Jill nodded her approval.

Against the rhythmic chirping of locusts, Joey creaked the swing into motion. The smell of Mary's lilac bushes permeated the evening air.

"You have a lovely family, Joey. Everyone seems to have such a good time just being together. I've always longed for a brother or sister."

"Sometimes I've wished for a few less," Joey said.

Jill laughed. "You don't mean that."

"Not really. After my sisters moved out I missed having them around. I get more attention from Mother and Father than I want."

"They're wonderful people, Joey."

"Yes. And I love them dearly. I can also understand some of the disadvantages of being an only child."

"Amen to that," Jill said.

It was Joey's turn to laugh.

"Your father and Mr. Hannon seem to have a very special relationship," Jill said.

"Yes. My father and Uncle Jack grew up taking care of each other. They were orphans with no one else to depend on. To this day, if anyone speaks ill of Uncle Jack, my father will invite him out into the street."

Jill slid her hand into his. "And here we are complaining about too much parental attention. We should be ashamed of ourselves."

Joey's heart raced at the touch of her hand. Anna's statement was not true. He had noticed girls before; but he had never felt like this. In the twilight, Jill looked as dark and enchanting as an Arabian princess. Captivated by the smell of rose water from her hair, Joey Donavan felt contentment for the first time in his life. He squeezed Jill's hand gently in his. Out on the horizon the evening sky had never seemed so blue or the stars so bright.

## SEPTEMBER 6, 1897

Michael sat at a table with the other members of his organization. He listened as a district chief went over a report. As the years passed, business seemed to be playing a less important role in his life.

More and more, he found himself wanting to be at home with Beth and Becky. They seemed to be the only meaningful part of his existence. His ambition had waned with time, and he was beginning to wonder if it was worth being on top of his chosen profession. There was always someone plotting against him, or clawing and scratching at the throne to bring him down. He had discovered that being on top was also a trap; he had nothing to strive for. He had lost that sharp, driving edge that had put him on top in the first place. Beth wanted him to just walk away from the business. It sounded so simple, but what would he do? Through the years, he had purged all the feelings of inferiority he had known in his youth. To a degree he had put the poor Italian immigrant boy to rest. But he could never forget what it was like to be hungry, and he would always remember the cold streets of the tenement district. So in spite of Beth's feelings, he could not walk away from the business, because the business was all he had. He was too comfortable to throw everything away and start all over again. And besides, his associates would not take kindly to his departure. He knew too much, and his motives would always be suspect. They preferred that a pine box and a trip to the cemetery be included in any of his retirement plans.

The maître d' motioned to him.

"Telephone, Mr. Pacini."

Michael picked up the receiver.

"Yes?"

"Just wanted to remind you that we're celebrating your daughter's fourth birthday party tonight."

"I haven't forgotten, Beth."

"Eight o'clock. Becky told me to call."

"You tell her I wouldn't miss it for anything."

"Hurry home, Michael. I miss you." The phone clicked.

Michael went back to the table. "Let's call it a night. We'll go over the remaining reports at the next meeting."

He waited until the last district chief had left Latta's restaurant. Then he grabbed the package containing Becky's doll and followed his two lieutenants to the door. They checked the street outside before motioning for him to follow. He walked outside. A freight wagon was passing next to his carriage.

Where was a freight wagon going this time of night? he wondered. The thought registered at the same time the canvas on the wagon rolled up.

"Watch it!" Michael screamed.

The wagon recoiled as shotgun blasts flashed in the night.

The package exploded in Michael's arms. The blast hit him in the chest, knocking him backwards. His two lieutenants fell to the ground, mortally wounded. Michael fell into the stairwell outside the restaurant door. Glass exploded above his head as the barrage continued. Customers were screaming hysterically.

Michael pushed open the door. He crawled into the restaurant. He rolled over and jumped to his feet, then ran through the kitchen and out the side door. Someone was sure to be in the restaurant to finish the job. Warm blood flowed down his side and stomach. The doll had taken the brunt of the buckshot and saved his life, but he had a bad chest wound. He ran through the alley and headed down the hill to the levee. His only hope for survival was to make it to O'Shea's. Jack Hannon would protect him.

Halfway down the hill, he fell. The blood continued to flow. He knew he wasn't going to make it. He spotted a newsboy walking along Seventh Street.

"Hey there!" Michael yelled.

The boy hesitated.

"Come over here!"

The boy walked cautiously toward him. Michael worked his wallet out of his coat. He took out a ten dollar bill.

The boy stopped under the streetlight a few feet away.

"Want to make some money?" Michael grimaced against the pain of his wound.

"Yes, sir."

"Do you know where O'Shea's tavern is on Delaware Street?"

"Yes, sir."

Michael held out the money. "Here's ten dollars."

"Ten dollars!" The boy stared at the money.

"If you have Mr. Hannon or his bartender here in ten minutes there's another ten waiting for you. Just say 'Michael is hurt.' Can you do it?"

"I can do it, mister." The boy grabbed the money. He took off running.

Michael crawled back into the alley. He passed out.

Someone was shaking him.

"Michael!"

He opened his eyes. Jack was kneeling over him.

"Hello, Boss," he said weakly. He passed out again.

* * *

Red picked up the telephone.

"Yes, yes. How bad is it, Jack?"

Melissa read his expression.

"I'll be right there." He hung up the phone.

"What is it, Red?"

"Michael's been shot."

"Oh God! Will he live?"

"I don't know. We have to find a safe place to take him. You'll have to tell Beth."

Melissa picked up the birthday packages. She went quickly to the door.

* * *

Michael peered out the window of Adam Quint's old cabin in Crackerneck. For two weeks he had hovered near death. It took him another month to feel well enough to move home. From his sources, he learned the attack had been ordered from outside the city. Chicago, most likely. The Italian grapevine had spread the word that Angelo Banetti wanted to increase his sphere of influence out of Chicago into Kansas City.

He watched as Beth pulled the carriage to a halt in front of the cabin. She walked inside.

"You're looking better today."

"What? No hug or kiss?"

Beth pecked him on the cheek. "All ready to go?"

"Yes."

On the way home Michael made plans for his return to work.

The carriage stopped in front of the house.

"You'll have to stay with your folks for a few days, Beth."

Beth looked at her husband. "I'm leaving you, Michael."

Michael stared at her. "Just like that?"

"Eight years of wondering if you're going to stay alive is not 'just like that.' "

"You're overreacting, Beth."

"No, Michael. You're already plotting revenge. I can see it in your eyes. I love you, Michael, but I can't take it anymore. I can't live like this."

Beth reached over. She adjusted the sling on Michael's arm.

"Out of love for you these past years, I've suppressed how I really feel. I hate violence. I hate your way of life. When you were shot, it confirmed my worst fears. Uncle Red was right. You do have the ability to carry on business at any cost. I don't have that ability, Michael."

"Where will you go?" he asked.

"I've rented a small house on the East Side for Becky and me to live in. I'm returning to my teaching position."

"What can I say that will stop you, Beth?"

"Say you'll change, Michael. Say you'll get a decent job and start leading a normal existence."

"I've told you before, Beth. I can't change what I am." He stepped off the carriage.

"I hope that when you finally realize you can, Michael, it won't be too late for us."

"And one more thing," Beth said. She fought the urge to cry. "I've always known about Maria Ramponi. If you don't feel you can give her up, then I don't ever want to see you again."

Michael stepped back as the carriage lurched ahead. He stared after her as she moved the carriage out the gate and down the street. So she had known about Maria all along. How difficult it must have been for her to remain silent all these years. There were some difficult decisions to be made in the days ahead. He could see in Beth's eyes that she had meant every word she had said. Somehow, he had always known that it would come down to a choice between his family and the business. However, remaining alive was his first concern. Everything else would have to wait.

Willy was waiting at the base of the steps.

"Give the staff the night off, Willy."

"Okay, Michael." Willy disappeared inside.

Michael looked up at the tower on his Victorian house. It seemed to spin up and up like a tower in a fairy tale. A lookout would have to be stationed in the tower. He walked around to the south side of the house. A red brick driveway ran through to the carriage sheds at the side of the property. A portico jutted out from the house. It was built so that guests could depart from their carriages in inclement weather without getting wet. A high hedge ran next to the driveway. It would be easy cover to get close to the house, Michael thought. He walked to the rear of the grounds. The house sat on a sloping hill two hundred yards from the nearest neighbor. The rear of the house concerned him the most. In daylight the hill could be watched easily. After dark was something else. The outside shutter doors leading into the study would not keep out a determined intruder. The north side of the house was well fortified. The windows were high enough off the ground to give adequate protection. When the attack came, feints would be made at the front of the house with the main assault at the rear.

Michael finished his survey. He returned to the front of the house. He climbed the steps. The two wolf heads carved into brick above the door seemed to have a sinister look.

He entered the house.

Willy handed him a double-barreled shotgun.

"Barricade the south portico door, Willy."

"Okay, Michael."

In the kitchen Michael grabbed an ice pick and shoved it in his boot. Willy and four of his best men in the house were all he needed. Any more men, and they would be shooting each other in these close quarters.

Willy finished barricading the south portico door.

He gathered the men around Michael.

"I want a man on the second and third floor of the tower," Michael said. "Keep your heads down and don't strike any matches. You have a good field of fire but you're also exposed in the windows. Two more men will guard the study doors at the back of the house. One of you stand watch at all times next to the window. The other man will be ready for an assault on the doors. Willy will keep an eye on the north side. I'll roam the house and help out where I'm needed. Keep plenty of ammunition with you. You won't find any in the dark."

He listened to footsteps as the men took their positions in the house.

"Will they come tonight, Michael?"

"Yes. Angelo knows I'm wounded. He will try to finish the job."

"Will he send Johnny Sotta?"

"Yes."

"Remember the old days in the Toad-a-Loup, Michael?"

"I remember, Willy."

"I was never as afraid as I am right now," Willy said.

After serving five years in a hospital for the criminally insane on a murder charge, Johnny Sotta had been released. Angelo Banetti hired him as a weapon of fear against would-be opponents. Sotta's only reason for existence was to stalk and kill. He was insane, but he was also crafty. No one had lived to tell about an encounter with Johnny Sotta. He was always lurking somewhere in the shadows near Angelo Banneti.

"We'll keep him out of the house, Willy," Michael said.

The guard on the third floor tower called down.

"A carriage is coming, Michael!"

He looked out the window, then walked out on the front porch carrying the shotgun. Jack Hannon pulled his carriage to a halt in front of the house.

"Hello, Michael. I stopped by to see if everything is all right."

"Everything's fine."

Jack glanced at the shotgun. "If you need help, all you have to do is ask."

"I know that. This is a private matter."

Jack nodded, then turned the carriage around and headed out the gate.

Back inside, Michael went into the parlor. He sank into a chair facing the fireplace. A picture of Becky painted on one of the fireplace tiles stared back at him. His wounds were healing, but he still felt weak. Twilight's shadows chased the light from the room. He closed his eyes and waited. Down the hill a dog was barking. Michael's head fell slowly to one side. He dozed off.

The dog yelped in pain. Michael's eyes snapped open. It was dark. All was quiet again.

He sprang to his feet. "They're coming!" he yelled to the others.

He held the shotgun tightly and slipped out of the chair. He crept quietly up the stairs to a back bedroom. He sank to his knees and laid the barrel of the shotgun on the sill under the open window.

Clouds had blown in from the west. They blocked the light of the moon. The lace curtains on the window blew against his face. A low rumble of thunder could be heard in the distance.

He kept his eyes on the area leading up to the back of the house. The grandfather clock at the base of the stairs ticked steadily against the quiet. Suddenly a man broke from the darkness and ran through the open area. He made it to the side of the house.

"Damn!" Michael said. He turned the shotgun to the right. Another man darted into the open area. Michael fired both barrels of the shotgun. Someone screamed. Michael ducked down. The window exploded above his head. He crouched low and ran from the room. Outside the door he reloaded the shotgun. He ran down the stairs. He heard rifle fire from the tower. Windows shattered as the front of the house was assaulted. He heard the railing on the third floor of the tower snap. He stepped against a wall. A body fell on the marble entryway with a sickening thud.

Michael knew his neighbors would dismiss the first few shots, but not a full-fledged battle. Johnny Sotta had twenty minutes before the police arrived, and Johnny knew it.

Michael ran for the study. He braced himself against the doorjamb. The room exploded. Michael covered his face against the flash. "Dynamite!" he screamed. "The sonofabitch threw dynamite!" Wind rushed through the gaping hole in the house. Three men stormed the gap. Shotguns went off in a deafening roar. The men rushing at him seemed to disintegrate. Two more intruders followed closely behind. Michael saved a shell. More shots exploded. One of his men screamed. The two intruders were cut down. Johnny Sotta would be next. Michael waited. A man slipped through the hole. Michael fired from point-blank range. The man went down. Michael reached in his pocket for two more shells. He saw a man slip catlike through the hole. The man disappeared into the kitchen. Johnny Sotta was in the house. Johnny would have sacrificed his men in the initial assault and been the last one to enter the house. Michael backed out of the study. He ran to the front of the house and up the tower's spiral staircase. On the second floor he stumbled. He reached down and felt the cold face of his second-floor guard. Michael caught his breath. He waited and listened. Several minutes passed. A scream from the study shattered the stillness. Only Willy and Michael were left.

"Michael!" Willy called from the stairway on the north side of the house. His voice was filled with terror. Michael kept quiet. A flash of lightning illuminated the tower, revealing his presence. He crouched low and ran down the stairs. He stood next to the grandfather clock, as close to the wall as he could get. The tick-ticking of the clock sounded like gunshots against his ear. His breath came in short gasps.

An insane laugh sounded somewhere in the house — the icy sound of a demonic madman. Michael held his breath for fear of making a sound.

"Help me, Michael!" Willy cried out. "He's in the house, Michael!" Willy had lost control. He was sobbing on the stairway.

Footsteps sounded on the marble hallway. Michael fired both barrels of the shotgun. A man was blown across the room. Michael stepped away from the wall. A blow knocked the shotgun from his hands. A pair of vise-like hands went around his throat. The hands squeezed tighter and tighter, paralyzing him. He felt too weak to fight back and fell to his knees. Lightning flashed through the windows. He looked up into the yellow, fiendish eyes of Johnny Sotta. Michael was losing consciousness.

"Michael!" Willy shrieked.

With his last ounce of strength, Michael reached into his boot. He pulled out the ice pick and thrust it upward into Johnny Sotta's groin. Johnny screamed. He fell to his knees. Michael plunged the pick into the side of Johnny's neck. Johnny pitched forward on his face.

Michael rubbed his throat. He gulped in the air.

He got up off the floor and lit a kerosene lantern. Willy was sobbing on the staircase. Michael walked up the stairs. He put his hand on Willy's trembling shoulder.

"I'm sorry, Michael."

"It's all over, Willy." Michael heard the police wagon speeding down the street.

"Take Sotta's body out back, Willy. When the police leave I want you to take him down to the freight yard."

"What will I do with him, Michael?"

Michael studied the body sprawled on the floor.

"Nail him to a boxcar and send him back to Chicago."

Willy stared at Michael.

"Send the boxcar in care of Angelo Banetti."

# 12

# The Spanish American War

February, 1898

For the next six months Joey saw Jill whenever he could. On a cold day in February he stopped by her house and the two of them went outside, more than willing to fight the elements in order to be away from the prying eyes of Mr. Sieben.

Out on the porch Joey tucked a scarf around Jill's neck. He gripped her mitten-covered hand and led her out into the falling snow.

"Isn't it beautiful, Joey?"

"Ya . . . ya . . . yes," Joey answered, clicking his teeth as Jill laughed.

Giant snowflakes drifted down, covering the ground. The falling snow filled their tracks as they moved along the street. Smoke poured out of the chimneys along the way. Joey led Jill around the corner, away from eyes that might be peering from behind parlor curtains. He glanced over at her. Jill's face was red against the cold. His decision about the priesthood had been complicated by this lovely girl. She seemed content to be his best friend and made no other demands on him. Experiences he once found so fulfilling alone now seemed incomplete without her.

He squeezed her hand. They stopped walking. She saw the strained look on his face.

"What is it, Joey?"

He looked into her eyes. "I love you, Jill."

"You do?" she asked, surprised.

"Yes, I do." He pulled her close and kissed the red tip of her nose.

She put her arms around his neck. "I've wanted you to say that." She kissed him. "I've complicated your life these past few months, Joey. It hasn't been easy watching you struggle with yourself. I'm glad you told me how you feel."

"So am I. I have to talk to your father, Jill. One night a week together isn't enough."

"I feel that way too, Joey, but I'm afraid father won't relent. You know how protective he is. As much as I care about you, I can't go against his wishes."

"I won't ask you to."

"I know you won't. Maybe if we talked to him together."

Joey shook his head.

"No, I should talk to him alone."

"I've loved you since the day we first met, Joey."

He pulled her close and held her tightly to him.

The snow was falling harder as they returned to the porch.

"Are you sure you want to go through with this?"

Joey nodded.

They entered the house. Jill took his coat. He walked to the study and knocked on the door.

"Come in!"

Joey entered the room. Fresh from Jill's embrace, he had his courage up.

"May I speak with you for a moment, sir?"

Mr. Sieben was still in his business suit. He sipped a glass of sherry. "What is it, Mr. Donavan?" He did not offer Joey a seat.

"I want to see Jill more often, Mr. Sieben."

"I was under the impression you were seeing a lot of her now."

"Only on Saturdays, sir."

"You're both attending school. I would say that is sufficient, Mr. Donavan."

"I thought we might study together on Wednesday evening," Joey persisted.

"I'm afraid that's out of the question. I've been meaning to speak to you, Donavan." Mr. Sieben refilled his glass from the sherry decanter. "I was under the impression that you and my daughter were just good friends. Obviously it has developed into something more."

"That's true, sir."

"What are your plans after the school year?"

"I haven't decided."

"Don't you think it's time you did?"

Joey remained silent.

"With this infatuation, you've obviously given up the idea of becoming a priest?"

"Yes, I guess so."

Mr. Sieben eyed him coldly.

"You guess so? You don't know what you want, do you, Donavan?"

"No, sir. I guess I don't."

"Then let me tell you what I want. I want my daughter to go to college. I want her to be able to support herself in this world in case something should happen to me. After she's educated, I would like her to marry someone from her own faith. Someone who has the means to support her in the fashion she's accustomed to. What I don't want is for her to get mixed up with some frazzle-brained boy who doesn't know what he wants. So many young women are misled by a simple case of infatuation. They end up getting married and leading a life they can't possibly be separated from. Like her mother, my daughter is a fragile person. What could you possibly offer her? Six kids, a mortgage, and thirty years of hard labor?"

"I hadn't thought that far ahead, sir."

"Well, perhaps it's time you did! I want this relationship halted before it goes any further. You and my daughter are from different cultures."

Joey was sweating uncomfortably, but his love of Jill overcame his fear of Mr. Sieben.

"You mean different religions."

"Call it what you like. I'm sure you get the point."

"You're telling me that I can't see her again?"

"No. I don't want you martyred, Mr. Donavan. You can see Jill on the present schedule. I'll let this case of infatuation run its course."

"And if it doesn't?"

"Then you will have no doubt as to the ultimate outcome. My daughter won't go against my wishes. And you, Mr. Donavan, are now well aware of those wishes."

"Don't you think Jill should have something to say about her future?"

"With my guidance, she will have."

"You don't like me much, do you, Mr. Sieben?"

"You as an individual have no meaning whatsoever to me, Mr. Donavan. Good evening to you."

Joey flushed with anger. He turned on his heel and walked out of the study. He grabbed his coat and scarf from the closet and headed for the door.

"Joey!" Jill bounded down the steps.

Joey gained control of himself.

"What did Father say?" she asked.

Joey kissed her cheek. "He said it would be best if we kept to our present schedule."

Her face clouded with disappointment.

Joey winked at her. "It's okay. We'll make better use out of the time we have."

Jill smiled. "You find something positive in everything, Joey Donavan. I'll see you on Saturday."

He hugged her. "I love you, Jill."

* * *

Joey sat at the kitchen table sipping a cup of tea. He watched his mother clean the kitchen counters.

Mary looked out the kitchen window. Snow was drifting down in the light of the lamp post.

"I wonder how much snow we'll get this time?" she asked.

Joey remained silent, staring at his tea.

Mary turned around. "Is something the matter, Joey?"

"I'm sorry, Mother. I was just thinking."

Mary sat down next to him. "Do you want to talk about it?"

He watched her neatly fold the dish towel and place it on the table next to her.

"Are you happy, Mother?"

Surprised, Mary stared at him. "Why do you ask?"

"I just wondered. You always work so hard. Do you enjoy your life?"

"Of course I do."

"It hasn't been easy," Joey said. "Do you ever wish you had married a rich man?"

Mary laughed. "What's gotten into you, anyway?"

"Just curious."

"For your information, according to my economic situation at the time, your father was a rich man."

"Was Father's success in business important to you?"

"Only in its importance to him," Mary answered.

"What about religion?" Joey asked.

Mary leaned back in her chair. "Jill's father?" she asked.

Joey nodded.

"Religion is a problem only if those involved choose to make it so. I assume that is the case."

"Yes."

"Is it an issue between you and Jill?"

"No, it isn't."

"Then don't worry about it. Those situations have a way of working themselves out."

"Mr. Sieben seemed pretty firm about it."

"I would suggest that you give it some time, Joey. If differences aren't magnified, they have a way of working themselves out."

Joey leaned over and kissed his mother on the cheek.

"Thanks for the tea and the advice, Mother. I'm going upstairs and get some sleep."

"Good night, Joey."

Mary listened to his footsteps go up the stairs. As Joey's door clicked shut she hoped the advice she had given proved to be correct.

* * *

The winter of 1897-1898 gave way to spring.

With Jill at his side Joey drove the horse and buggy out of the city. The April sun was partially dulled by large white clouds that drifted across the sky.

The horse was breathing hard after the long pull out to Swope Park.

Joey brought the horse to a halt. He helped Jill out of the wagon. They carried the picnic basket and blanket to the crest of a grassy knoll.

Jill spread the blanket beneath a giant elm tree. The buildings of the city looked miniature in the distance.

Joey peered into the basket. "Want something to eat?"

"No, thank you, Joey. I'm not hungry."

He reached into the basket. "I brought something that will wash the dust out of our throats." He pulled out a bottle of wine.

Jill gave him a conspiratorial smile. "I've only had wine at the dinner table," she said.

Joey poured the wine. He handed her one of the borrowed glasses from Mary's cupboard.

"A toast to spring." Their glasses touched.

Through the trees they caught glimpses of other couples strolling in the park. Jill reached for his hand.

"Of all the months of the year, I love April the most," she said.

"If it didn't put us closer to your departure, I would agree."

Jill squeezed his hand.

"We have the summer, Joey."

Joey nodded. "Yes, we do have the summer."

Jill looked out across the meadow. All the colors of spring were alive in the sunlight. "It would be a comfort to me if I knew your plans for fall, Joey."

"Will Stephens College accept me?"

Jill laughed. "Males are not allowed, I'm afraid."

Joey leaned back on his elbow.

"We've had so much fun. The city won't be the same without you."

"Columbia isn't that far away, Joey. We can see each other on holidays and during spring break."

"It isn't enough."

"I know, but it's all we have. You have to decide what you want to do and we have to give father time to mellow."

Joey sat up. He pulled her close to him and kissed her lightly on the lips.

"Above all else, Miss Sieben, I want you."

"And I you, Mr. Donavan. After two years of college, I'm yours."

"Two years won't change your father, Jill. He will still be against the marriage."

"Perhaps, but I will have fulfilled my obligation to him."

Joey took her in his arms. He pulled her down on the blanket.

"Forget your obligations, Jill. Marry me today."

"Joey, please."

"We'll start out fresh with the new season — facing the world together, with no obligations to anyone."

"Oh, if only we could. I feel so selfish. You've given up all thoughts of becoming a priest, and I've given up nothing. I just can't go through life with the guilt of having betrayed my father's wishes."

Joey ran his fingers through her hair. "I understand. I just don't want time and a separation to destroy what we have."

"My father hopes that will happen, but it won't, Joey." She hugged his neck and kissed him. "The time will pass quickly, Joey."

He pulled her into a sitting position and handed her the glass of wine. "Two years is a long time, Jill."

"Joey, please?"

He nodded.

After lunch and another glass of wine, Jill lay back on the blanket. Joey lay down beside her. She rested her head in the crook of his arm. He kissed her eyelids.

He watched the clouds pass overhead. Jill's breathing became slow and steady against his neck. He brushed back a strand of hair that had fallen across her face. What will you do, Joey Donavan? The question seemed to be on everyone's lips. A legitimate question for a young man graduated from school, but one Joey could not yet answer. He closed his eyes and dozed off.

When he blinked his eyes open, he looked up into Jill's face. His head was cradled in her lap. She bent over and kissed his nose and began to recite:

My dreams live on
out beyond the summer sky
as I awake, they slip away
and I have failed to say good-bye.

"From?" Joey asked.

"From Jill Sieben to Joey Donavan. In a field of clover on this glorious day of April 19th, 1898."

Joey pulled her head down and kissed her lips.

* * *

The next day as Joey worked his way down Main Street toward the mission, he wondered at the crowds of people lining the streets. All north- and south-bound traffic was blocked from entering the thoroughfare. Joey could hear the faint sound of a marching band in the distance.

Women waved scarves and children sat on the motionless trolleys waving in joyous anticipation.

"What's going on?" Joey asked an old man standing next to him.

"Look!" The old man pointed up the street. "Here they come!"

A line of soldiers crested the hill. They marched down into the throng of cheering people. Line after line of soldiers followed.

"We'll show the goddamn Spaniards!" the old man shouted. He had tears in his eyes. "The blue and the grey together again," he muttered.

The soldiers marched smartly past, proud to be the object of this burst of patriotism. They were dressed in blue sack coats with sky blue trousers and canvas leggings. Their khaki campaign hats gave them the appearance of cowboy soldiers.

Joey watched as each unit marched past.

Two hours later, Joey Donavan walked into Jack Hannon's office.

"Hello, Uncle Jack."

"Joey! What brings you here on such a fine spring day?"

"I thought you might like to have dinner with us this evening."

"That's kind of you, Joey. However, I don't want to wear out my welcome. Sunday is my day at the Donavans."

Joey fidgeted with his hat. "I would like for you to come, sir."

Jack studied his godson. "Are you all right, Joey?"

"Yes, sir. It's just that I . . . I joined the Army today, Uncle Jack."

Jack whistled softly. He got up from his chair and put his arm around Joey's shoulder. "You're right. You do need me to come to dinner."

* * *

The sound of the train impatiently chug-chugging played in the background.

Joey stood next to his parents on the station platform. He spotted Jill pushing her way through the crowd of people.

She had a bewildered expression on her face.

She wore a light brown dress with a high neck and leg-of-mutton sleeves. Her dress formed an hourglass, with the trumpet-shaped skirt flaring out at the hem.

Joey thought she had never looked more beautiful.

He reached for her. She put her arms around his neck. Her breath caressed his cheek. He held her tightly against him.

"You will be careful?" she asked.

"Yes. I'll be assigned to a medical corps. I won't even carry a gun."

"I'll miss you terribly."

"And I'll miss you. Just remember that we have a commitment two years from now."

"You're my life, Joey. I won't forget."

"All aboard!" the conductor called.

Mary moved over. She hugged him tearfully. Kevin shook his hand. "Take care of yourself, son."

Joey dutifully kissed each of his sisters on the cheek. He shook hands with his Uncle Jack.

He hugged his mother one more time. "Good-bye, Mother."

"Be careful, Joey."

Jill walked with him to the steps of the train.

"Have fun at school," Joey said. "And remember, two years will pass awfully fast."

"My words have already come back to haunt me," she answered. He wiped the tears from her cheek. She sobbed as he held her tightly. "I was going to be so brave."

"You are brave. I love you, Jill."

"And I love you, Joey Donavan."

He pulled away and bounded up the steps.

Jill moved back from the train. She searched the windows until his face appeared.

With the rest of the recruits and soldiers Joey waved until the station was lost from view.

* * *

Joey had been accepted and trained as a corpsman. He was assigned to the Twelfth Infantry Regiment, a part of the Third Brigade. The Brigade had been sent to Tampa Bay, Florida, to take part in the invasion of Cuba.

The transport ships loaded with troops for the invasion had languished in Tampa Bay for five days awaiting orders to disembark. If orders were not forthcoming, heat and disease would soon decimate the invasion fleet.

Joey moved through the stifling heat of the hold, administering aid to the stricken men. He carried a water bucket and dipper, moving among the triple-deck bunks serving water to those men too ill to move. Dressed in woolens, the men were ill-equipped to live in the ovenlike conditions of the ship's hold.

His uniform was soaking wet by the time he made it back to the ship's deck. He moved over to the railing and took a deep breath of fresh air.

The other ships of the invasion force lay low in the water from the weight of troops and supplies. All the euphoria and anticipation of the invasion force had evaporated, with days of waiting in the boiling sun. The men looked dazed and beaten as they went about their daily tasks on troop ships that were an inferno.

"How are the men holding up, Donavan?" Sergeant Morgan, the burly First Sergeant of B Company, moved up to the rail next to him. He took off his campaign hat and wiped the sweat from his brow.

"Five more cases of malaria this morning, Sergeant." Joey reported.

Sergeant Morgan shook his head is disgust. "Donavan, we are witness to the most monumental blunder in military history. This army may be defeated before it ever leaves this goddamn hellhole of a port." The sergeant's face was red enough to explode.

"Do you have any idea what one case of typhus in this cesspool of an environment would mean?" he looked at the weariness in Joey's face. His voice softened. "Yes, you do know, Donavan."

In the distance, Joey watched breakers run onto the beach. The first sergeant had every reason to vent his wrath. If it were not for the human suffering, the incompetency of the War Department would be laughable. In every direction leading to the harbor, trains were lined along the keys. The quartermaster corps hadn't the slightest idea what they contained or where they should go. All supplies were hopelessly mired. Only recently had the docks been cleared of tents and luggage, which were placed aboard the transports.

The heat had also taken its toll on the twenty-three-hundred horses and mules of the invasion force. The animals looked tired and haggard from days in the ship's hold. Joey thought of Red Farrell every time he saw one of the poor creatures. Red would be incensed at the treatment they were receiving.

"I'm sure we'll be sailing soon, Sergeant," he said.

Sergeant Morgan grunted. "If we don't, the United States will attack Cuba with a fleet of ghost ships."

The sergeant put his hand on Joey's shoulder. "You had better get some sleep, Donavan." Sergeant Morgan walked away.

"Hey, Joey." Jebadiah Tyree walked up and leaned on the ship's rail. "What was the Sarge steamin' about?" he asked.

"The mess on the docks," Joey answered.

"It sure is a logjam," Jeb agreed as he looked out at the docks.

Jeb was a rifleman in the infantry company Joey was assigned to. He had latched onto Joey after discovering they were both from Missouri. Jeb was from the Ozark country south of Springfield, in the southern part of the state. His uniform looked one size too big for his thin frame, and his eyes had that sunken, hollow look of someone who had known hard times. Jeb looked a lot older than his twenty years.

Joey had seen the look on many of the men who had passed through the mission. Jeb's frail appearance was deceiving, for he could outrun and outshoot any man in the regiment.

"You ever been any place this hot, Joey?" Jeb asked.

"Yes, Kansas City in August."

"It's all them city buildings what holds the heat," Jeb said. "You come down to the Ozarks in August. We'll lay ourselves out under a shade tree next to a cold runnin' stream and watch the world go by," he said.

Joey laughed. "I'll take you up on that, Jeb."

"Most of the city boys are layin' down below, pukin' their guts out," Jeb said. "You must come from sturdy stock, Joey."

Joey wiped the sweat from his brow. "Sometimes I don't feel so good myself," he said.

"Me neither," Jeb said. "It's like everthing else in this here life. If ya give in to it, it'll get ya fer sure."

In the distance they could hear shouts from men of the Quartermaster Corps as they did battle with the mountain of supplies lined along the docks.

"You know, Joey, I ain't never even seen a Spaniard before," Jeb said. "How we goin to know who to shoot at?"

"I don't know Jeb. I guess we'll find out when we get to Cuba. I know I wouldn't want your rifle pointed at me. Where did you learn how to shoot?"

"Back home," Jeb answered. "Ya learn to shoot when yer hungry. I don't reckon I would want your job, Joey, havin to go into a fight and get shot at with no way to shoot back."

Joey shrugged. "I have the job I wanted. I couldn't shoot another human being, anyway."

"Them Spaniards ain't human," Jeb said. "Have ya heard how they torture prisoners?"

"I wouldn't pay much attention to the rumors going around the ship," Joey said. "The men have had nothing to do during the wait but work their imaginations."

"Maybe so, but I ain't takin no chances with gettin' captured," Jeb said resolutely.

The morning sun had moved higher in the sky, warming ship decks that would soon be boiling.

"A man could go plumb crazy in this heat," Jeb said. "We got to get out of this harbor and on our way."

"It makes you wonder if anyone is really in charge of this mess," Joey said. "The Spanish may beat us by default. Most of the men in our company can't even stand up and hold a rifle. I'm hoping the fresh air at sea will revive everyone. Speaking of the men, I had better get back to work, Jeb."

"Ya better take it easy, Joey," Jeb said. "Yer gonna be flat on your back with the sickness like the rest of them fellas."

"I'll get some rest tonight, Jeb. You better get out of the hot sun."

"The sun is better than goin' down below and smellin' that puke," Jeb said.

"Suit yourself," Joey said. "Just try to find some shade," he suggested.

"If I found some, a hundred fellas would be tryin' to squeeze into it," Jeb said.

Joey smiled. "I'll talk to you later, Jeb." He took a deep breath of fresh air to fortify himself against the stench of the hold, and then entered the gangway leading down into the bowels of the ship.

The next day, much to the relief of everyone, the flotilla steamed out of Tampa Bay. There were no crowds or fanfare to see them off, for the convoy had been called back to port once before and everyone was skeptical that the ships were actually sailing.

But this time, it was for real. The transports, traveling at a speed of seven miles an hour, reached Cuba in five-and-a-half days.

Joey stood at the ship's railing with the rest of the men. The rugged mountains of the Sierra Maestra had come into view.

"So that's Cuba," Jeb said. "Except for the mountains, it don't look much different than Florida."

"It sure looks peaceful from here," Joey said.

All the men who could walk were lined several rows deep at the ship's railing watching the lush green Cuban coast drift past.

"Maybe the Spanish heard we were coming and hightailed it out of here," one of the men said. The others laughed nervously.

The transports seemed to drift along for hours before finally dropping anchor just outside Satiago Harbor.

The next day the fleet received new orders and the ships sailed fifteen miles to the east and anchored a mile offshore at Daiquiri Beach.

At dawn the next day, June 22nd, the troops prepared to disembark. The invasion was to begin on the Daiquiri and Sibony beachheads.

Sergeant Morgan scanned the shoreline with his binoculars. "I don't see any fortifications, but they may have set up their defenses back in the tree line," he said to a sergeant standing next to him. "Check your equipment and get ready to disembark!" he shouted to the men.

Joey and Jeb sat next to each other in the longboat that would carry them into shore. The longboats of the fleet looked like toy boats as they bobbed in the water next to the giant transports. The troops eyed the mist-shrouded Cuban coast they would soon have to attack. Even if it meant facing an unknown beachhead, the troops were glad to be away from the stifling heat of the transport ships.

Joey ducked and held his ears as American warships opened up a tremendous bombardment along a twenty-mile stretch of the Cuban coastline. The troops in the longboat cheered as plumes of smoke appeared on the beaches and hillsides. The roar of the guns was deafening. The bombardment went on for another thirty minutes before the longboats finally pulled away from the mother ships and headed for the beach.

"This is it, Joey," Jeb said as he peered in at the beachhead. "Good luck to ya."

"You too, Jeb," Joey said.

The longboats seemed to take forever to reach the shore. In the distance Joey could see landing craft arriving at a pier that jutted out into the water. The troops were running along the pier and onto the beach.

Joey heard the thump of the longboat as it nestled against the pier.

"Let's move it!" Sergeant Morgan shouted.

Joey scrambled up the ladder behind Jeb. They ran as fast as they could across the pier and onto the beach. When they reached the tree line, Joey dove face down next to Jeb. They both gulped for air and scanned the area around them.

They stayed put until Sergeant Morgan sent scouts ahead to check the area. The scouts came back shaking their heads at the apparent lack of opposition.

"If this don't beat all," Jeb said. "We been worryin' about them Spaniards and they ain't even here."

Joey and Jeb got to their feet and looked down the beach. The troops were shouting and laughing while they waved a welcome to the incoming longboats. There was not a single shot fired along the whole beachfront.

"Well, thank God for this," Joey said.

"Yeah. I hope the war stays this easy," Jeb said.

* * *

A week later, Joey and Jeb stumbled along a quagmire of a road with the rest of the twelfth infantry. Sudden rains fell from the skies, soaking their uniforms and equipment. And just as quickly, the sun would come out and bake men and animals into submission. Steam boiled out of the jungle floor until the rains came again to quench the fires. In the middle of the day it was over a hundred degrees. The troops thought Tampa Bay was a resort, by comparison.

Dead pack-train animals littered the trail — horses and mules that had been too long in the ship's hold and had lost their stamina.

Cuban fever was spreading among the men. An all-encompassing disease, it included malaria, dysentery, and yellow fever. The men were further weakened by food that was unfit for the tropics. The quartermaster corps had sent plenty of salt pork and hardtack, but there was a shortage of vegetables, and red meat was nonexistent. And there was never enough water. Joey had never known such a craving for water. The troops emptied their canteens long before they would find another spring or stream. Joey's tongue felt swollen and he kept licking the sweat from around his lips.

As he walked along the trail he thought of the landing two weeks ago, of the troops laughing and swimming naked in the cool ocean waters. It seemed so long ago.

The Americans had finally realized this expedition was no longer a lark. They had been bloodied in their first engagement with the Spanish at a place called Las Guasimas.

"Ya want a drink of this water, Joey?" Jeb walked up beside him, holding out his canteen.

"I can't take your water, Jeb," Joey said.

"Ah, go on," Jeb said. "I've drunk all I want."

Joey took the canteen and drank two delightful swallows of the cool water.

"Thanks, Jeb." It took all his willpower not to drink it all. He was amazed at Jeb's ability to march for hours in the heat without the need for water.

They heard shouts from the men up ahead.

"There's the Santiago Road we been lookin' for," Jeb said. The infantry division moved out of the jungle onto the road. They marched ahead until they came to the village of El Pozo.

When the order to fall out was given, the troops raced to the village wells. They barely had time to drink and fill their canteens before the order was given to fall back in.

The division marched north and passed through the village of Marianage. The troops all breathed a sigh of relief when the order was given to fall out and set up camp.

Joey dropped his gear to the ground. He took the bandana from around his neck and soaked it in water from his canteen. It was the only luxury he allowed himself before he started moving among the troops administering aid to the sick and to those suffering foot damage from the long forced march from the sea.

It was after two a.m. when he drove the last stake into the flap of the battalion hospital tent. He stumbled among troops sprawled everywhere in the darkness and found his way back to the company bivouac area.

"Where ya been, Joey?" Jeb was sitting on his blanket pulling his boots on.

"Setting up the hospital tent," Joey whispered. He sat down on his blanket and started pulling his boots off.

"I figured the Spaniards had grabbed ya," Jeb said.

"Where you going?" Joey asked.

"Got the guard duty," Jeb explained.

"You keep your eyes open out there," Joey said.

"Don't worry none about me," Jeb said. "I spent more time in the dark woods than any man alive. They ain't about to sneak up on me."

Jeb grabbed his rifle and slinked away into the night.

Joey laid his head back on his backpack and stretched out his sore legs. He had never been this tired in his life.

The regiment was camped a mile from the fortified village of El Caney. To the west, beyond San Juan Hill, Joey watched lights from the city of Santiago burn brightly in the night. They reminded him of home. At night he would step outside the mission and watch the lights on the bluffs. He thought of Jill, his mother and father, and his sisters. Joey fell asleep thinking about home, and looking at the lights of Kansas City.

* * *

Artillery shook the ground. Joey sat up. The regiment's guns were firing into the hills. In the gray light of dawn, puffs of smoke were visible on the hillsides. Joey stood up and stretched.

"Short night, huh Donavan?" Sergeant Morgan walked up beside him.

"What's happening, Sergeant?"

Sergeant Morgan pointed to the high ground. A fort and a series of blockhouses were visible along the ridge.

"El Caney on the left, and El Viso on the right," Sergeant Morgan explained. "Our assignment is to take El Caney."

Joey viewed the terrain.

A steep hill rose one hundred feet above the southeast corner of the village of El Caney. On its crest there was a stone fort with the red and gold flag of Spain flying above it. Joey could see Spanish troops moving around outside the fort.

"There's a lot of open ground leading up to the Spanish fort on the summit, Sergeant."

"You're right, Donavan. If the Spaniards are well fortified, and I think they are, you're in for a busy day. The high command is giving us two hours to take El Caney. In a pig's ass," the Sergeant muttered as he walked away.

An hour later the regiment was on the move. Joey followed Jeb's infantry squad into the brush.

"Keep your head down and don't take no chances, Joey," Jeb commanded. Off to the east, heavy vollies of rifle fire erupted as American troops began the attack on El Caney.

Ahead of him in the brush the troops started to fan out as they moved closer to the fort on the summit. Joey instinctively ducked as the Spanish started to fire down the hill. The *z z z z z - eu* sound of mauser bullets whined through the brush around him. There was an unmistakable thud as bullets encountered human flesh. Ahead of him several men went down.

Joey ran up and fell to his knees next to a wounded soldier. The man pointed to his thigh. "My leg," the man grimaced in pain. Joey used his knife to cut away the soldier's pants. He dressed the wound, and made a battlefield bandage to stop the bleeding.

"Stretcher bearer," he yelled. He dressed another soldier's shoulder wound and sent the man to the rear.

The Spanish were raining a murderous fire on the Americans as they tried to make their way up the hill. More men fell, wounded. Joey ran ahead to the next man. He turned him over. The man had taken a bullet to the head. His lifeless eyes stared up at Joey. All around him men were moaning in pain. Joey worked frantically to save as many as he could. The sun had risen higher in the sky and was making the battlefield an inferno for the wounded. "Stretcher bearer," he yelled the words until he was hoarse. Artillery fire from both sides continued to explode on the hillsides around El Caney.

Joey was working on a wounded soldier when Jeb crawled up next to him.

"How ya doin', Joey?"

Joey and Jeb ducked their heads as mauser bullets sprayed the rocks in front of them. The Spanish had no respect for the wounded, medics, or stretcher bearers. They rained a murderous fire on anything that moved.

"I'm out of bandages," Joey said. "I'll have to go back for some more. What's happening Jeb? Are we winning?"

"It don't look good, Joey. We been fightin' for two hours and we ain't even close to the fort. Look over yonder."

Joey watched as a soldier fired his weapon at the Spanish. A plume of smoke rose from the soldier's rifle. The man was cut down in a hail of bullets from the Spanish fort above.

"It's these damn Springfield rifles," Jeb said. "The Spanish sharpshooters just shoot where they see smoke."

Joey finished bandaging the wounded man. "I better go back for some more medical supplies," Joey said.

"Go ahead," Jeb said. "I'll draw their fire while you make a run for it."

Jeb aimed his rifle around the rocks.

"Go!" he yelled.

Joey started running down the hill.

He heard the steady crack of Jeb's rifle, and then the return volley from the Spanish. He made his way down the hill to the hospital tent. The wounded lay scattered everywhere around the tent as the surgeons worked frantically to save them.

Joey stuffed his medical bag with supplies. He only stopped long enough for a drink of water and to fill his canteen before heading back up the hill. When he returned to the front the regiment was still bogged down, but they had moved closer to the Spanish fort on top of the hill. Joey could now see the barbed wire running across the terrain, and the entrenched positions of the Spanish. The troops had been assaulting the fort for over three hours. Orders came down to halt the attack so the troops could rest. Sergeant Morgan moved among the troops, ordering them to hold their fire and offering encouragement.

The murderous fire from the fort slacked off as well. Joey went to work clearing his sector of wounded soldiers before the battle resumed. Sergeant Morgan walked over to him as he worked on a wounded man.

"You better take a break, Donavan, or you won't last in this heat," Sergeant Morgan said.

Joey was soaked with sweat. His arms and hands were covered with other people's blood. He looked up at the sergeant.

"We're taking a lot of casualties, Sergeant Morgan."

Sergeant Morgan took a swig of water from his canteen. He looked up at the Spanish fort. "Don't I know it," he said. "The bastards are puttin' up one hell of a fight, but before the day is over we'll take that fort." He put his hand on Joey's shoulder. "You're doin a good job, Donavan." Sergeant Morgan walked away to join his men.

A half hour later the men of the Twelfth Infantry started to advance. They were met with a murderous fire from the fort. American troops were falling everywhere in the brush.

Joey ignored the bullets that whined around him. He applied a shoulder compress to a wounded man and sent him back to the rear. Up ahead of him he could hear a moan from a wounded soldier. Joey bent low and ran through the brush until he found a soldier lying face down in the grass. He dropped to his knees and turned the man over.

"Jeb!" Joey cried out. Jeb had taken a bullet in the neck, and Joey could see that he was dying.

Joey took his hand.

Jeb looked up at him. "Keep yer head down, Joey," he whispered. Joey felt Jeb's hand go slack as the life ebbed out of him.

Joey rested his hands on his knees and stared at the young man who had become his best friend.

At El Caney the men of the Twelfth Infantry had overrun the Spanish blockhouses and were assaulting the fort. Joey looked up the hill and saw American troops reach the summit.

From his position at a window inside the fort, a Spanish marksman took aim. He squeezed the trigger on his mauser.

Joey recoiled from the force of the bullet. He felt a searing hollow sensation in his chest. He reached for the spot and the palm of his hand came away covered with blood. There was no pain, but he could not seem to catch his breath. He fell on his back in the grass, and looked directly into the glaring sun. Why did he feel so cold? Snow was falling on the rooftops. Jill's cheeks were red against the winter white. Joey reached out his hand to touch her.

* * *

Ollie Thompson limped out of the telegraph office. He started down the hill to the levee. A gust of wind twisted his confederate cap, but Ollie didn't notice.

The old confederate ignored his own edict. He stepped in front of a cable car. The car almost ran him down. The conductor shook his fist at Ollie. His jaw firmly set, Ollie continued on until he came to O'Shea's place on Delaware Street.

He went inside the restaurant and walked back to Jack's office.

Jack sat at his desk. He was busy studying a racing form.

"Hello, boss."

Surprised, Jack looked up. No one entered Jack Hannon's office after two in the afternoon. He used this time to catch up on his book work and to go over racing forms.

"Hello, Ollie. Is something wrong? You don't look too good."

Jack reached into a drawer. He poured Ollie a glass of whiskey.

Ollie sat down. He downed the whiskey in two large gulps. Jack waited until Ollie caught his breath. Ollie reached into his pocket. He pulled out a telegram. He handed it to Jack. Jack looked it over.

"It's addressed to the Donavan's, Ollie."

Ollie nodded.

"I've delivered those telegrams before, boss. I thought you should have it."

Jack placed the telegram on the desk. He poured himself a drink.

"You did the right thing, Ollie." The words sounded hollow in his throat. Afraid, for the first time in his life, Jack picked up a letter opener. He sliced open the envelope and took out the telegram.

Ollie read Jack's expression.

"I'm sorry, boss."

Jack nodded. "Thanks, Ollie."

* * *

Jack stopped the carriage in front of the Donavan home. He walked slowly to the door. Mary answered his knock.

"Jack! This is a surprise. I'm glad you came by. Kevin and I were. . . . What is it, Jack?"

"I've tried to think of something to say to you, Mary. I . . ." Jack put his head down. "This telegram came for you and Kevin. It's from the War Department."

Mary's face turned pale. She took the telegram and read the words. A look of disbelief crossed her face.

Jack put his huge hands on her shoulders. He steadied her. "You've always been the strong one, Mary. Please be strong now."

Mary looked at him as if from a trance. "You'll come with me to tell Kevin?"

Jack wiped his eyes with a handkerchief. "No, Mary. I've never been able to see him hurt. I'm sorry."

"It's all right, Jack."

Jack looked at her ashen face.

"I wish there was something I could say that would help you."

Mary covered here eyes with her hand. "He was such an angel, Jack. Why did . . .," her voice broke. She held back a sob.

Jack put his arm around her. "Go and tell his father, Mary."

"Yes, I must."

Jack turned away. He walked back outside to his carriage.

"Who's that you're with, Joey?"

"That's my Dad."

"What's he do?"

"He's a reporter?"

"What's he report?"

How they all had laughed when Joey shrugged his shoulders.

Mary entered the study. She walked behind Kevin's chair.

Streaks of gray ran through his hair.

"I thought I heard the door, Mary." He turned around. "What's the matter?" She knelt down by his chair. She laid her head on his chest and started to sob as he took the telegram from her clenched fist.

Mary left him alone. She had to get away. She ran out the door.

Step after step she walked numbly ahead. The miles passed. She stopped and looked around. A feeling of panic set in. She had felt this way once before. The cyclone. She started to run. She turned the corner on Grand and ran east on Independence Avenue. She ran faster and faster. Jill's house was up ahead. Had she planned to come here? Mary stopped in front of the Sieben's house to catch her breath. The setting sun cast an eerie glow on the houses. She felt faint. She grabbed the gatepost to steady herself. If she could just make it inside. Kevin would be there. He would shake her by the shoulders.

"Mary! It's all right! I picked Joey up. He's safe at the office."

She walked into the Sieben house. Voices were coming from a room next to her.

Jill and Mr. Sieben looked up as she entered the room.

"Mrs. Donavan!" Jill said. Mary looked at those innocent eyes and knew there would be no reprieve. She tried to speak, but nothing would come. She covered her face and began to cry.

"Oh, please no!" Jill backed into the corner of the dining room. Mary hurried to her.

"No!" Jill screamed.

Mary held Jill tightly to her. She felt the sobs rack Jill's frail body. Jill fainted in Mary's arms.

* * *

Frank Pacini waited for his last driver to return from a produce run. He heard the man's footsteps crossing the hardwood floor. The driver appeared from around the corner.

"Here's my delivery book, Mr. Pacini."

Frank nodded. He reached for the light.

The driver hesitated. "Did you hear the bad news, Mr. Pacini?"

"What news?"

"I heard it at O'Shea's. Joey Donavan was killed in Cuba."

Frank stared at the driver.

"Goodnight, Mr. Pacini."

Frank watched the driver walk away. He pictured Joey leaning around the corner of the office.

"Morning, Mr. Pacini."

"Grab yourself a piece of fruit, Joey."

The phone rang. Frank ripped it off the wall.

* * *

Sister Margarite lit a candle for Joey. She knelt down and folded her hands on top of the altar rail.

"You have years and years ahead of you, Joey. God will show you the way." Sister Margarite dropped her head into her hands. She began to pray.

Father Devin, visibly shaken, held a Mass for Joey. The church was packed to overflowing.

At the Donavan home, the friends of the family came daily to pay their respects. Kevin and Mary received them all. They retained their composure until nightfall when everyone had gone. A derelict would come by, hat in hand, to pay his respects to the family. These were the moments when the Donavans felt the magnitude of their loss.

Through his political connections in Washington, Jack managed to have the body shipped back to Kansas City. On the seventeenth day of July, 1898, two weeks after Joey's death, the Donavan family once again stood on the platform of Union Depot.

Kevin felt Mary's hand tighten in his as a whistle sounded in the distance. How many times he had heard that lonely sound in the middle of the night and been comforted. It had meant that the world was awake and functioning.

The whistle sounded again, closer.

For the rest of his life, when he heard a train whistle, he would be reminded of the death of his only son.

From out of the east, a light came searching through the darkness. The clack-clacking of the train followed close behind. The train braked hard. The engine seemed to coast by Kevin into the station.

Kevin thought of Jill at home under the care of her doctor.

He watched the passengers get off the train into the arms of loved ones.

Jack had him by the arm.

"This way, Kevin."

Thank God for Jack. He and Mary would never have made it without him. Jack had made all the funeral arrangements.

With the help of the local police force, Michael Pacini had provided men and transportation.

The procession moved down the station platform to a baggage car.

An Army honor guard was there to receive the coffin.

Two freight clerks slid the flag-draped coffin out the door. They lifted it carefully onto the station platform. The colors of the flag were stark against the lantern's light.

From every section of the city people came to the Catholic church. The rich, the poor, different races and religions. They all filed past the flag draped coffin before taking seats in the church.

Father Devin watched in wonderment. How could Joey have touched so many?

Jill Sieben sat in the front row with her father and the Donavan family. Her hands were folded neatly in her lap.

She refused to look around her or acknowledge the comforting words of others.

Father Devin vowed to check on her in the days and weeks ahead.

After the solemn ceremony, the flag-draped coffin was placed on a caisson in front of the cathedral. Red Farrel steadied the horses.

The Army Honor Guard marched alongside the caisson as it moved east on Eleventh Street to Main. At the request of the family, the funeral procession turned north and headed for the levee. At the juncture of Delaware and Main the procession stopped for a moment before heading down into the older district. The coffin rested under the diamond spire on the Times building.

Red coaxed the horses ahead, down into the levee.

People ran from doorways and market stalls to place flowers on the caisson. It was covered by the time the procession reached the old Catholic mission.

Sister Margarite, the staff, and the mission's residents stood outside. Sister Margarite made the sign of the cross.

Father Devin conducted the solemn ceremony at the Elmwood cemetery.

Kevin looked around him at the trees basking in the warm sun. He vaguely listened to Father Devin's words. He glanced at Mary. She had a strong faith he often envied. It carried her through the hard times. They were going to put his son in the ground and he had nothing to sustain him. Perhaps like the trees of spring, Joey would bud again in another time and place. Kevin wasn't as sure of it as Mary seemed to be. . . . He turned away before the coffin was lowered into the ground. The family moved through the green of the cemetery. Jack was at Kevin's side. He helped the family into the carriage.

"I'm sorry Kevin, but I have to get your approval on the headstone. It will read 'Corporal Joe Donavan, born January 10, 1881, died July 2nd, 1898.' "

Across from him, Kevin looked at the grieving faces of Anna, Teresa,

Molly, and Margaret, and he remembered the nursery rhyme the girls used to sing to his baby boy. "Roll it and roll it and mark it with a T, and put it in the oven for Joey and me."

"His name was Joey," Kevin said. "Put Joey Donavan on the headstone."

For the first time since Joey's death, Kevin Donavan put his face in his hands and wept.

# 13

## The Flood

November 21, 1900

Michael stepped off the train. Dressed in a flannel shirt, work pants and boots, he looked like any other laborer as he hurried across the station platform. He put on his heavy coat. Dusk was settling over the city of Chicago. As he moved through the Loop he passed groups of Friday night revelers.

Michael walked deliberately through the Loop. He changed streets and directions several times to see if he was being followed.

Satisfied that he was alone, he headed south on Michigan Avenue. It was dark by the time he reached the Gold Coast mansions on South Michigan. He stayed in the shadows and finally stopped across the street from a large Gothic-style mansion. Snow-covered walls surrounded the grounds. He pulled his collar tight against the chill November wind.

Cigarette embers glowed in the darkness. Two men were guarding the gate. Michael crossed the street. He walked along the side wall until he found a tree. He climbed up, and moved along a lower branch and dropped onto the top of the wall. All was quiet. Jumping down, he hurried across the grounds. He opened a downstairs window in the mansion and crawled in. Laughter drifted from a room down the hall. Michael sat down. He removed his boots, then walked softly past the marble statues guarding the hallway and peered into the room. Angelo's bodyguards were busy playing cards. Michael slipped past the room. He moved quickly up the spiral staircase. At the end of the second floor hall he stopped. Pleasurable moans were coming from the master bedroom.

Angelo lay naked on the bed. A girl had her head between his legs. Michael walked into the room. He crept silently over to the bed. Angelo's eyes were closed. His mouth pursed open as he emitted sighs of pleasure.

Michael stuffed a gun barrel in Angelo's mouth. He grabbed the girl's hair with his other hand. The gangleader's eyes jerked open. His head instinctively came off the pillow. The gun barrel cut his mouth. Blood flowed out.

"Hello, Angelo. You or your girl make one sound and I'm going to spray your brains all over these satin sheets."

Terrified, Angelo motioned for the girl to remain silent.

She began quietly sobbing.

"Your boys did a lousy job with the shotguns, Angelo."

Angelo tried to shake his head.

"I know, Angelo, it wasn't your idea. You're a dead man, Angelo."

The gangleader's eyes begged for mercy.

Michael pulled back the hammer on the pistol. Angelo went rigid.

"What would you give to have your life back, Angelo?"

Angelo's eyes pleaded for mercy.

"Here's the deal that will resurrect Angelo Banetti. I'm walking away from the business, Angelo. In the process I'm giving you your life and a multi-million dollar operation. All I want is to be left alone."

The gangleader nodded.

"If me or my family is threatened in any way, Angelo, I'll be back. I'll cut your heart out and shove it up your ass."

Michael pulled the gun barrel out of Angelo's mouth. The gangleader rolled over. He threw up over the side of the bed. Michael tossed the gun down on the floor. He could hear Angelo gagging as he walked down the stairs.

* * *

Willy was waiting with the carriage when Michael arrived back at Kansas City's Union Depot. Michael had one more piece of unfinished business to take care of.

"Take me over to Maria's house, Willy," Michael said.

"Okay, Michael."

Willy deftly moved the carriage through the busy streets. He coaxed the horses through traffic, dodging other carriages, and weaving around street cars, while keeping a watchful eye out for pedestrians.

"We've been together a long time, Willy," Michael said.

Willy glanced over at Michael. Michael was not one for small talk. Willy shrugged his shoulders. "Yeah, I guess so, Michael."

"Do you think you could get along in another line of work?" Michael asked.

"After the night we spent with Johnny Sotta, I could adjust real easy, Michael."

Michael laughed.

The horses were startled by the sound of a motor car coming around the corner. Willy fought to control the horses as they reared in the air.

"Goddamn horseless carriages," he swore.

The man driving past tipped his hat in apology. Willy quieted the horses and they continued on their way.

"How about money, Willy?" Michael asked. "Have you been putting it away for your old age like I told you to?"

Willy smiled. "I got lots of money, Michael. What do I have to spend it on? I got no family or steady girlfriend. You need a loan, Michael?" Willy kidded.

Michael smiled. "No Willy, I don't need a loan."

Willy moved the horses down Independence Avenue and turned left on Harrison Street.

He pulled the horses to a halt in front of Maria's house.

"What time do you want me back here?" Willy asked.

"I'm not going in," Michael said. He took the horse's reins from Willy.

"What do you mean?" Willy stared at Michael. "Why did we drive all the way over here?"

"You're going in," Michael said.

"I've seen the way you look at Maria. Over the years you would have given anything to trade places with me. Am I right?"

Willy was bewildered. He didn't think Michael had ever noticed.

"She's beautiful, Michael. But I wouldn't ever try anything with Maria. She's your girl."

"I know that, Willy. We've been together since we were kids, and you're the best friend I have. I give you my word that it's over between Maria and me. She needs someone to take care of her, and it's time you settled down."

Willy was dumbfounded. He could not believe Michael was serious.

"Come on, Michael, look at me." Willy jumped off of the carriage and stood in the street.

"I've gone too fat, and I'm practically bald. Maria is one of the most beautiful women in the city. She wouldn't have nothing to do with me."

"Maria and I have already discussed it. She wants you to call on her."

"Willy pointed his finger at his own chest. "She wants me to call on her?" he asked unbelievingly.

"Yes, you," Michael said. "And quit running yourself down. You have a lot to offer Maria. You have a good head for business, and you're kind and generous."

Willy stared at Michael, speechless. Michael had never paid him a compliment before.

"But if you don't have the guts to do it, I'll find someone else," Michael said. He started to move the horses ahead.

"Wait, wait!" Willy said, putting his hands up. "Okay, I'll do it. I'll go up to the door and you and Maria can have your laugh for the night. Will that make you happy, Michael?"

"That will make me happy, Willy."

Willy straightened his clothes. "You will wait for me, Michael?"

"I'll be right here, Willy."

Willy gave Michael a look that said he knew it was a game but he was going to be a good sport and play along. He turned and walked through the yard and onto the front porch. He lost his nerve and turned around.

"Do it, Willy," Michael called.

Willy turned back around and knocked on the door.

Michael waited until he saw Maria let Willy in before moving the horses down the street.

* * *

"Goddamn it!" Frank Pacini slammed the phone down. He walked out of the office. At seventy-one he was stoop-shouldered and walked with a limp.

"Where's the foreman!" Frank shouted.

The foreman came running up the stairs.

"Yes, sir?"

"Who's driving the midtown run? He's late on the last delivery."

"It's the new man I hired today, Mr. Pacini."

Frank scowled at his foreman.

"Send him to my office when he comes in."

"Yes, sir."

"Can't hire decent help any more," Frank muttered.

He went back to his office. He started checking off the daily invoices. He worked for an hour before a knock sounded on the door.

"Come in!" Frank kept his eyes on the invoice. "Young man, if you're going to work here, you're going to have to run a route efficiently."

"Yes, sir."

Frank look up. "Michael! What are you doing here?"

"The foreman said you wanted to see me."

Frank got up from his chair. He walked over and put his arms around Michael.

* * *

Red twirled Melissa to the music. They danced around Convention Hall on this New Year's Eve of 1900.

"You're still the best lookin' woman in the city," he whispered.

Melissa smiled. "You're just trying to make me forget my age."

"No, ma'am. If ever there was a woman for all time, it is you."

Melissa leaned back and looked at her husband. "I may just give you another dance, Mr. Farrel."

Red scanned the hall as they danced. The Donavans and the Quints moved along the floor with the music. Beth sat next to Jack Hannon as he held court back at the table.

Eight flatcars of evergreens had been shipped in for decorations. Ten thousand incandescent globes flashed colors around the auditorium. A century bell made of hundreds of pounds of mistletoe hung from the ceiling, and thousands of yards of white muslin lined the top of Convention Hall. The spectators' boxes were lined with chrysanthemums and evergreens. Kansas City was welcoming in the new century in style.

The dancers applauded as the music ended. Red escorted Melissa back to the table.

"Don't forget to ask Beth to dance, Red. I insisted that she come with us. This past year she's done nothing but work."

"If she feels so bad, why did she leave Michael?"

"Because she has her principles, my dear."

The throng of politicians around Jack melted into the auditorium.

"Are you planning a political coup of some sort, Mr. Hannon?" Kevin asked.

"Yes. I'm going to overthrow the Baron of Brush Creek and start my own newspaper. Actually, we were discussing the merits of buying one of the new horseless carriages. Would you like to go in with me, Donavan?"

"Why not. The ones I see on the road seem to be holding up. What do you think, Red?"

"I'm a horse lover, but I'm afraid they're the comin' thing."

The Kansas City Symphony swung into another tune.

"Mary, could I have this dance?" Red asked.

"You may, Mr. Farrel." Mary joined Red on the dance floor. Her gown of white satin brushed along the floor.

"Isn't it a wonderful night, Red?"

"Yep. And you can bet we won't see another like it. Kevin seems to be doing much better, Mary."

Mary flinched. "It was a full year before he started to come out of it. Joey's death was very hard on him. He's the same Kevin Donavan, only some of the spark is missing."

"With time he will get it back, Mary. And what about you?"

"I'm doing fine. I get lonely sometimes with the girls gone, but it doesn't last long. A visit with the grandchildren and I'm back enjoying the quiet. You seem to be the happiest man on earth, Red Farrel. I'm so glad you and Melissa were able to make a life together."

Red smiled. "Thank you, Mary. It was a long time comin'. I enjoy every minute I'm with her. I'm a lucky man, and best of all, I know it. Melissa and I are also lucky to have all of you for good friends. We've all been together for thirty years now."

"Yes. On the way to the dance this evening Kevin and I were talking about what a strong bond we all have."

The music ended. Red stepped back. He bowed.

"Thank you, Mrs. Donavan."

Mary curtsied. "And you, Mr. Farrel." Arm-in-arm they walked back to the table.

"What are you going to put in the century box, Jack?" Adam asked.

"I haven't decided."

"What about you, Kevin?"

"I'm going to drop in a note telling the world that Jack Hannon coerced me into buying a horseless carriage."

Everyone laughed.

"What is the century box?" Red asked.

"The city has a box placed in the south end of the auditorium," Adam explained. "We're all to drop in souvenirs. After the dance the box will be permanently sealed until the year two thousand and one."

"It gives me a strange feeling to be able to freeze a moment in time for a hundred years," Melissa said. "I wonder what the world will be like?"

"With the progress we've already seen in this century, I can't imagine," Adam answered. "Only sixty minutes are left until midnight, so start preparing the items you're leaving to posterity."

Michael moved through the crowd on the dance floor. He walked up to the table. Jack spotted him. "Michael! Sit down and have a drink with us."

Beth turned around. Michael stood behind her. She turned away, avoiding his eyes.

"You're sure I won't be intruding?"

"Of course not," Jack answered.

Michael pulled out a chair next to Beth and sat down.

Beth glanced over at him. It had been three months since his last visit with Becky.

"We were discussing the century box, Michael. What will you put in?" Jack asked.

"My new business card," Michael replied. "Would you like to see one?"

"Of course."

Michael reached in his pocket. He pulled out a card and pushed it across the table to Jack. Jack examined it. He raised his eyes and looked at Beth.

"Pacini's Produce Company, Market Square, Frank and Michael Pacini, Owners."

Beth turned to Michael, a questioning look in her eyes.

"A new century, Beth. And for us a new beginning. That is, if you care to have me back."

Beth searched his face. She knew how difficult it was for him to give up everything and start over again. "Oh, Michael." She leaned over and wrapped her arms around his neck.

Above the hall an hourglass filled with sixty lights marked the last hour of the century. As each minute ticked off, one of the lights blinked out.

Melissa took off her white gloves. She laid them on the table. She took a pen from her purse and started writing on the Convention Hall program. "I leave these gloves to one of the great granddaughters I hope to have. We are approaching midnight on December 31st at the Century Ball. I am having a wonderful time. I love you, sweetheart."

*Melissa Graham Farrel*

*905 Penn Street*

*Kansas City, Missouri*

Red looked at his wife. She dabbed at her eyes. He took her hand. "Are you, okay?"

Melissa smiled. "Yes. Everything is wonderful." She took a ribbon from her purse and tied her gloves inside the Convention Hall program.

Only two lights were left shining in the hourglass. Everyone rose to their feet.

"Let's join hands," Adam said.

All eyes were on the hourglass. The last light blinked off.

The lighted 1900 sign flashed 1901. Fifteen thousand voices were raised in song.

"May Old Acquaintance Be Forgot . . ."

A chill went up Melissa's spine.

After the dance they filed out of the auditorium. Melissa stopped next to the century box. She pondered for a moment before placing her gloves neatly in one of the corners.

The stonemason looked around the deserted building. His helpers carried the century box over to a specially designed corner in Convention Hall. The box was shoved in place. The stonemason began a seal that would last a hundred years.

## MEMORIAL DAY, 1903

Red folded the evening paper. He placed it on the lamp table. He got up from his chair and went to the window.

"It's rainin' harder, Melissa."

"Will you have to leave?" she asked.

"I'm afraid so. I'll have to move some livestock to higher ground. The Platte River is sure to overflow."

He went to the closet and put on his boots and slicker.

"I may have to stay at the ranch. Will you be okay?"

"Of course." Melissa kissed his cheek.

"Do be careful, Red."

He nodded. I'll make it back before dinner tomorrow. Are you going to Beth's early?"

"Yes. Don't hurry, I'll meet you there."

She held the door as he ran out into the storm.

By early evening the rain had slackened. Melissa decided to go down to the office. It had been raining intermittently for four days. With Red busy at the ranch it would be a perfect opportunity to catch up on her book work.

She guided the carriage around several large mudholes and into the lumber yard. The West Bottoms were void of activity.

She tied the horse to a ring at the curb and went upstairs to her office.

The Kaw River, flowing out of Kansas, had been on the rise for three days. It met the already swollen Missouri River at Kansas City. Out of control, the two rivers left their banks and flooded into the West Bottoms.

It was well past midnight when she made the final entry in the ledger. She took off her glasses and rubbed her eyes. The rain continued to pound on the roof. She stretched her arms and rubbed the back of her neck. Suddenly the lamp on the desk went out, pitching the room into darkness.

She reached in her desk drawer for a candle. She heard a loud rumble in the distance. She lit a candle and started down the stairs. The sound of flowing water reached her.

"Oh, my God," she whispered. Light from the candle revealed water slowly creeping up the stairs. Another rumble sounded. Railroad bridges were crumbling against the onslaught of water.

She knew there was only one way out. She quickly rolled up the folds of her skirt and stepped into the water. She managed to force the door open. Outside, the street was a torrent of water. The horse and carriage were gone from the hitching ring. She waded back through the water and climbed the stairs. She looked out an upstairs window. Fires were breaking out in the darkness as railroad cars loaded with lime turned over, soaked with water, and ignited.

The lumber yard was situated close to the mouth of the Kaw. There was no telling how high the water might rise. She stuffed all her important papers into the floor safe. With a pair of scissors she cut her bulky skirt up to her knees. She removed her mother's brooch from the neck of her blouse and placed it in the safe.

Downstairs, she waded into the water once again. Out on the street, water was up to her waist. The rain quickly extinguished the candle. Everything was black. She tried not to panic. She could hear the distressed cries of animals that had washed out of the stockyards. Off in the distance, lights were visible on Quality Hill. She started moving toward the lights.

The water rose higher. It was up to her shoulders. Fires from the freight cars burned on the water line, illuminating the rushing water. Houses and warehouses were torn from their moorings and swept away. Melissa fought against the current but it was too strong. She was swept off her feet. She grabbed a piece of floating debris and held on.

She was a strong swimmer, so with a little luck she could make it to higher ground. She let go of the debris and started swimming toward the lights in the distance. She struggled against the current with all her might. Her muscles ached with fatigue, and the water kept dragging her under, but she would not give up. She struggled on and on against the relentless rush of water. Streaks of lightning flashed across the sky, and she could hear the claps of thunder above the rushing water. She focused on the lights at the top of Quality Hill and fought hard to reach the river bank. I must be getting close, she thought. She was so cold, and her body ached with fatigue, but she would never give up.

Come on, just a little further, she coaxed herself. Lightning flashed and she could see ahead. "Oh God," she whispered. The river bank was no longer where it was supposed to be. She took a deep breath and willed her body to go on, but there was nothing left. She was so tired. "Don't give up," she whispered. "Don't give up." She turned and saw a mountain of debris sweeping toward her. Ahead there was nothing but darkness.

The lights on Quality Hill were far, far away. She thought of Red, and Beth, and Becky, as she was swept away into the night.

* * *

Red wrapped a chain around the wrought iron gate. Beth had refused to take the house and live in it. The memories were too painful. Red had not spent a night there since Melissa's death. Only thirty days had passed and yet the house seemed old and deserted, as if he were a stranger passing on the street. It was an odd feeling to have been part of something for so long and to have no affection for it. All his ties had been to Melissa.

He snapped the lock shut.

Still, he could not bring himself to sell it. Time would take care of the house, and time could have it.

He walked over to the edge of the bluffs. Down below in the West Bottoms men were scurrying around repairing the damage.

The Keeney Lumber and Brick Yard would go on the auction block. Michael was too busy with the produce business to take it.

In the distance the Kansas and Missouri rivers meandered peacefully along in their banks. Proud and defiant, the Hannibal Bridge still spanned the river.

The ninety-three million dollar loss in the flood meant little to Red Farrel. He had lost Melissa, and Melissa was everything. He was not a quitter, and he would not give up this life, but for all practical purposes he knew it was over for him. He would go on with his everyday existence, but without Melissa there would be no joy in it. She had not left his heart and mind for forty years, and he would think of her constantly until the day he died.

FROM ADAM QUINT'S JOURNAL — NOVEMBER 1903

*The flood of 1903 was the most devastating thing ever to happen to my extended family and to the city. It took all of us many years to get over the death of Joey Donavan, and now we have lost Melissa. I don't think Red will ever recover from losing her. I often wonder why there are those among us who are always asked to carry more than their share of tragedy and grief. Beth has tried to be a comfort to him, but she was devastated as well. Melissa was such a strong, vibrant, and beautiful woman it seems impossible that she is no longer with us. The more time goes by, the more we miss her.*

*She loved her family dearly, and I'm sure she put up a valiant struggle against the elements. I have driven out to the ranch several times to see Red. He is a survivor, but I could tell that he no longer has any interest in living. He and Melissa had grown very close to Becky, and perhaps in time, Becky will bring him out of his depression.*

*Jack has worked day and night as leader of the flood relief program. It will be many years before the city recovers from this natural disaster. The cost will be in the millions of dollars, and it will take a herculean effort to restore all the factories and businesses that were destroyed in the First Ward. I have introduced a flood control bill in the Missouri Senate, and I'm sure it will pass, but we always seem to do these things after the fact.*

*One tries to rationalize these tragedies as part of the human experience, but each and every one weakens the spirit. However, one must go on.*

*The burdens of public office, my advancing years, and a desire to get back to teaching have led me to the conclusion that retirement from public office would be in my best interest. I am announcing my resignation January 1, 1904, and it will become effective in November. Perhaps I can have a greater impact on society by sharing my life's experiences with young people.*

* * *

From his position on the ladder, Kevin placed the star at the top of the Christmas tree.

"Is it straight, Mary?"

She cocked her head. "A little more to the left."

Kevin made the adjustment. Mary applauded. "Perfect, my dear. You have once again won the yearly battle of the Christmas tree."

Kevin climbed off the ladder. He backed across the room to survey the nine-foot Scotch pine. The fire in the fireplace felt warm against his back.

"Not bad," he said. "Now if we can only keep the grandchildren from pulling it over."

Mary sniffed the air. "Smell the fresh pine, Kevin. It's the true scent of the Christmas season."

"After my battle with this green monster I would prefer the smell of a hot toddy."

Mary laughed. "You will have to wait until our guests arrive."

A knock sounded at the door.

"Aha!" Kevin said. "Mention alcoholic beverage and Jack Hannon will always come to the rescue."

Kevin opened the front door. Jack stood on the porch. Three young boys stood behind him. They all peered at Kevin from around armloads of packages.

"Merry Christmas!" Jack said. "Come along, lads!" Jack and his entourage walked past Kevin into the house. Mary guided them to the Christmas tree. "I give up," she said. "You spoiled the children, Jack, and you are determined to spoil the grandchildren."

Jack laughed. He placed the packages under the tree.

"Merry Christmas, Mrs. Donavan!" He kissed Mary on the cheek. "Here you are, lads!" Jack handed each of the boys a silver dollar.

"Thanks, Mr. Hannon! Merry Christmas!" The boys ran happily from the house.

Kevin helped Jack with his coat.

"I'm not too early, Mary?" he asked.

"Of course not. Come over by the fire. Kevin will fix us a drink."

Kevin poured Jack a straight glass of bourbon.

"Thank you, sir." Jack looked out the window at the snow falling intermittently against the window panes. "If this continues, we may have our white Christmas after all."

Mary took a sip of wine from her glass. "I understand Red Farrel turned down our invitation, Jack."

He nodded.

"He's been cooped up out on the ranch for six months now," Mary said. "Isn't there something we can do?"

"He's still terribly depressed, Mary. We've tried about everything. You can't force a man to rejoin society against his will."

Adam and Bonnie Quint arrived at the house. They joined the conversation around the fireplace.

"We were discussing Red Farrel," Mary said. "We're trying to figure out a way we can help him."

"I was out to the ranch last week," Adam said. "Red has always been a fighter, but I think Melissa's death was too much for him. I'm afraid he's given up."

"It's such a tragedy," Mary said. "After all they went through to be together."

"Yes, it is," Adam agreed. "I thought Beth might be able to bring him around, but so far she's had no success."

"There must be some way," Mary said.

Adam swirled the ice around in his glass. "There is a way, but I've been reluctant to discuss it."

They looked at Adam questioningly.

"Years ago, Melissa rescued Red from a life of crime. She gave him Beth. Beth still doesn't know that Red's her father. If she knew, it might make a difference. With Melissa gone I can't see what the harm would be."

"All these years and Red hasn't told her?" Bonnie asked.

"They have a wonderful relationship," Mary said. "Until now I'm sure it didn't matter. It's a delicate situation, to say the least. If she's told it will have to be done discreetly."

They all stared at her.

Mary stepped back. "Why are you all looking at me?"

"Be very discreet, Mary." Jack said.

"But I didn't . . ."

A knock sounded at the front door.

Kevin greeted the Pacinis.

After dinner the men retired to Kevin's study. Bonnie went upstairs to freshen up.

Beth looked out the window.

"It's snowing harder," she said.

Mary was reminded of another night. Snow falling in the lantern's light.

Joey sipping a cup of tea in the warmth of the kitchen.

"I hope it continues," Mary said. "I love a white Christmas."

"I assume Uncle Red turned down your invitation, Mary?"

"Yes. Through the years we've celebrated so many of the holiday seasons together. We miss him terribly."

Beth pulled a lace handkerchief from her sleeve. She started to cry. Mary put her arm around Beth.

"I miss my mother, Mary."

"I know you do. I miss Joey the most at Christmas. It's such a time of joy and celebration. If they could only be here to share it with us."

Beth wiped her eyes. "I'm sorry, Mary. I've tried to reason with Uncle Red, but nothing seems to work. He's so hardened by Mother's death. Perhaps I haven't tried hard enough. I've lost my parents in accidents that were such freaks of nature. Both times it's been such a shock."

Mary poured Beth another cup of coffee.

"Kevin and I, the Quints, and Jack Hannon have always had a special relationship with your Uncle Red and your mother," she said softly. "I want you to keep that in mind while I tell you a story."

Beth stared questioningly at Mary.

"Thirty-four years ago, a young couple were to be married. Two people who were very much in love. At their wedding accouncement party the bride-to-be found out from a newspaper reporter that her fiancé rode with Quantrill on his infamous raid on Lawrence. Her father had been killed on that same raid, killed by Quantrill's gang. She loved her father very much. In hatred, anger, and frustration, she called off the wedding. Her husband-to-be was devastated. He turned to a life of crime and became an outlaw. A month after the wedding was cancelled the woman found out she was pregnant. She married a good friend she had known for many years. I've simplified a very complicated story for you, Beth."

Beth stared blankly at Mary.

"You lost a good friend in John Keeney, Beth, but you still have your father."

"You mean . . ."

"Yes. Red Farrel is your real father."

Beth's eyes seemed to be searching the past.

"I feel so numb. All those years and I never even suspected."

"You had no reason to."

"Why didn't Uncle Red tell me?"

"I'm sure that just being with you was enough for him. He went to prison for you. We think he will rejoin society for you as well."

"I have to go and see him, Mary."

"Yes. I thought you would. I'll tell Michael you're ready to leave."

* * *

Michael braked the 1902 Model-C Packard to a halt. He turned off the engine. He helped Beth out of the bulky automobile wrap and foot muff and gave her a quick, tender kiss on the cheek.

Red opened the front door and he walked out to the car.

"What are you two doin' out here this late in the day?" he asked.

"Hello, Uncle Red. We just wanted to see how you're getting along."

"You both look frozen. Come in by the fire."

They followed Red inside.

"Sit down. I'll pour you a drink."

"You're all dressed up."

"We've had an early dinner at the Donavans," Beth said. "All your friends said to tell you hello."

Red nodded. "Here, sip this brandy. It will warm you up."

"Where's your tree, Uncle Red?"

"I haven't put one up. Maybe I'll get around to it later."

Beth knew that he wouldn't.

"We can't stay but a minute, Uncle Red. Actually we drove out to invite you to a bobsled party we're having on the 23rd. All your friends will be there. I want you to come."

Red looked away.

"It's snowing harder, Beth. We had better start back," Michael said. "I'll restart the car." Michael went out the door.

Beth took a deep breath, then plunged in. "You can't go on like this, Uncle Red. You have to start living again. With Jim gone, this place seems so lonely. I want you to come into town and spend Christmas at our house. We don't have Mother but we do have each other." Beth leaned over and kissed his cheek. "I love you, Father," she whispered.

* * *

Jack took several sips of the smooth, nankeen-colored drink.

"You can't fool me, Michael Pacini. You have stolen Connie O'Shea's eggnog recipe!"

Michael laughed. "I told you he would find us out, Beth."

"If you will forgive us, Jack, we promise not to break the sacred trust," Beth said.

Jack fluffed the crown of egg whites with a silver spoon.

"You have certainly done Connie proud. Nowhere on this night will I find a drink as delicious."

"But he will definitely try," Mary said as everyone laughed.

"Now, Mary," Jack said. "You know you love to go egg-nogging with me."

"Who else would rescue Kevin from the snow banks?" Mary replied.

Jack chuckled. "Remember the night Kevin passed out in the bobsled, Mary?"

"I try not to."

"We backtracked for five miles before we realized he was under the buffalo robes at our feet."

"That was the night I gave up trying to match the king of eggnog drink-for-drink," Kevin said.

Adam Quint took Michael aside.

"Has Beth heard from Red?"

"No, she's terribly disappointed."

"I'm sure she is."

Michael heard harness bells swing into the yard. Becky ran into the parlor.

"The bobsled's here!" she cried excitedly.

Michael helped everyone on with their coats. He wrapped Becky's scarf tight around her neck. He could hardly believe she was ten years old. "Tell the driver we'll be right out, Becky."

"Okay, Father." Becky ran out the door.

The night was clear and crisp. Frozen snow crunched under their feet as they walked toward the sleigh. Having to face the brunt of the wind, the driver was well bundled against the cold. Becky sat next to him, impatiently waiting. Adam helped the ladies into the back of the sleigh. They burrowed into the fresh-smelling straw. Everyone covered up with blankets.

"We're all set!" Michael reported.

The driver hunched his shoulders against the cold.

"Let's go!" Jack shouted.

The sleigh remained motionless. The passengers looked at each other.

"Maybe he's hard of hearing," Mary suggested.

Michael leaned forward. "Becky, would you tell the driver we're ready."

"He says he won't go until he's paid, Father."

"Won't go until he's paid?" Jack shouted.

"Now, see here!" Michael threw off his blanket. "What's the meaning of this?"

"The driver says that he doesn't trust politicians or produce men," Becky said matter-of-factly.

Michael and Jack were red in the face with anger. They struggled from beneath the blankets. The driver turned around and grinned at them.

"Merry Christmas, everyone."

Becky laughed.

"Well, I'll be damned," Jack said.

Beth scrambled to her feet.

"Merry Christmas, Father," she said.

# 14

# THE WORLD'S FAIR

JUNE, 1904

Mary met Kevin as he walked up the porch steps.

"Good evening, dear." She kissed his cheek. Kevin joined her on the swing.

Two boys flushed a girl from bushes at the side of the house. The threesome ran screaming into the backyard.

"Whose kids were those?" Kevin asked.

Mary smiled. "They're Teresa's, as you well know."

"You and I have done our share of populating the city, Mary girl."

Mary fanned herself against the heat. "How was work today?" she asked.

"I received some sobering news."

"Oh?"

"Adam Quint is retiring from the newspaper. It doesn't seem that long ago that he retired from politics."

"Will he continue to teach?"

"Yes. I've been trying to think of something we could do for him. A party, or a dinner, perhaps."

"When will he leave?"

"Next week. His last assignment is the Louisiana Purchase Exposition in St. Louis."

"Well then, it seems obvious to me," Mary said.

"What does?"

"The four of you should accompany Adam to the World's Fair. I'm sure Michael can get away. Beth says that he lets Willy Lavetti handle the day-to-day operation of the business. You have some vacation time we're not going to use. Jack has worn himself out the past year directing the city's flood relief program. And God knows Red needs to get away from the ranch for awhile."

Kevin stared thoughtfully into the twilight. "You know something, Mary?"

"What?"

"Jack's often said that for me to *achieve* brilliance all I have to do is return home in the evening."

Mary laughed. Kevin kissed her forehead. "I'll see if I can round up the old gang," he said.

* * *

The Kansas City to St. Louis Express steadily tick-ticked along the rails. From his seat inside the dining car, Red looked out at the countryside.

"Well, Captain Quint, are you sure about this retirement business?"

"Completely, Red. I can't do justice to both jobs any longer."

"I'm sorry to hear it," Kevin said. "We've had some grand times together."

"But we've also had the same problem. With Jack, Red, and Michael for friends we've been excluded from reporting most of the exciting news."

The five men laughed together.

"I wouldn't trade it for anything," Adam continued. "I've been reflecting on the famous and the infamous characters I've met over the years. Quantrill, Anderson, the James boys, the Youngers, Earp, Hickock, Cody, Grover Cleveland, Eugene Field, and George Caleb Bingham. I could go on and on. My days in city government and the state senate."

"Why quit now, Adam?" Jack asked. "We're on the threshhold of another new age. With the Wright brothers' flight last year and Fetch and Krarup's coast-to-coast auto trip, who knows what might happen next."

"You're right, Jack," Adam agreed. "The theme of this year's fair is progress. I have to quit now before I get caught up in all the excitement of the twentieth century. I want to pass on some of these mistakes I've made to the new generation."

"What are the specifics of your last assignment?" Kevin asked over the men's laughter.

"Nothing specific, Kevin. Just a capsule of daily events at the fair. An interview with President Roosevelt would put a nice cap on my career, but I'm not counting on it. After McKinley's assassination I'm sure everyone will be kept at a distance."

"Perhaps I can help," Jack said. "I've met with the president on several occasions. If the opportunity presents itself we'll try for an interview. This president isn't shy when it comes to meeting with the press."

"Speaking of my compatriots," Kevin said, "I'm going back to the press car and see if I can scrounge up any sports news."

"I believe Mary mentioned to Beth that this was to be your vacation," Michael said.

Kevin smiled at Michael. "My job is a vacation."

"You wouldn't be seeking alcoholic beverage would you, Kevin?" Jack asked.

"How could you even suggest it?"

Kevin moved back through the aisles. He balanced himself against the swaying of the train. He opened the door of the last car to the sound of voices raised in song: "Meet Me In Saint Louie/ Louie, Meet Me At the Fair." Reporters were strewn all about the car. They had gathered from the western and northwestern states, made their train connections in Kansas City, and were converging on St. Louis. Kevin walked gingerly through a poker game that was in progress across the aisle. He weaved his way back to a makeshift bar in the corner. A porter was busy dispensing drinks.

"What's your pleasure, sir?"

"Scotch, if you please."

"Kevin Donavan!" Kevin turned around. A man was pushing his way toward him.

"Barney Fisher!" Kevin shook hands. "How have you been, Barney?"

"Fine. Are you still pounding it out for the Baron, Donavan?"

"Still at it, Barney. As I recall, the editor of the *Denver Post* is an astute individual. How did you convince him the World's Fair has anything to do with sports?"

Barney laughed. "It wasn't easy. The impact of the World's Fair on baseball, or something to that effect."

"He bought that?"

"No. Actually, I think he wanted to be rid of me for a few weeks."

Kevin laughed.

Barney ordered two whiskeys.

"Let me buy those for you, Barney."

"Thank you, Kevin, but I've just met a young suffragette. I've spent the last several hours convincing her that Susan B. Anthony is my idol."

"Something tells me the women's movement is not the movement you have in mind, Barney."

Barney smiled wickedly. He picked up the two drinks from the counter.

"Satisfy my curiosity, Donavan. Tell me why you're speeding through the dusk toward St. Louis. McAleer is leading the Browns to another sixth place finish, so I'm sure it isn't baseball."

"No, Barney. I'm on vacation."

"Is Mary with you?"

"No, just some old friends."

Barney gave Kevin a curious stare. "You're never far from a story, Donavan. Don't be surprised if you see me dogging your trail."

"I assure you it's only a vacation, Barney."

"I'm off to fight for women's rights, Donavan. We'll have that drink in St. Louis."

Kevin watched Barney retreat from the car. He spotted a vacant seat and moved over and sat down. The young man next to him stared glumly out the window. Kevin sipped his drink. He glanced over at the young man and offered his hand. "I'm Kevin Donavan."

The boy shook hands. "Andy Briggs, Mr. Donavan."

"You seem awfully glum in this mass of frivolity, Andy. Nothing serious, I hope."

"I won't know that until I get back home to St. Louis, Mr. Donavan."

"Are you a newspaperman, Andy?"

"Yes, sir."

"We newspapermen stick together. Maybe I can help."

"I don't think anyone can help, Mr. Donavan. I work for the *St. Louis Post-Dispatch*. My editor sent me west for some stirring reports on the wild West."

"And you didn't find any?"

"The wild West only exists in books. You know what's going to happen to me when I return after six weeks with no story, don't you?"

"Your editor just might be understanding," Kevin said.

Andy raised his eyes.

"That bad, huh?"

Andy nodded.

"Can I get you a drink, Andy?"

"No, thank you, sir." Andy slumped down in his seat.

Kevin refreshed his drink at the bar and returned to his seat. "I'm going to help you out, Andy."

The young man looked questioningly at Kevin.

"In the process I'm also going to teach you a valuable lesson. A lesson I don't want you to forget. Look around and tell me what you see."

Andy scanned the railroad car. "A car full of reporters having a good time."

"Exactly so. Now tell me what's happening in the car up ahead."

"I haven't the slightest idea."

"Right again. And neither does this car full of reporters."

"What's the point, Mr. Donavan?"

"Do you have pencil and pad on you, Andy?"

"Yes, sir."

"Then come with me."

Kevin led the curious Andy through the railroad cars. Four cars ahead, he stopped. "Now keep your mouth shut and your mind working, Andy."

"Yes, sir."

Kevin led Andy over to the table.

"Did you bring us a drink, Kevin?" Jack asked.

"No, but I did bump into an acquaintance. I want you gentlemen to meet Andy Briggs. Andy, this is Jack Hannon, Michael Pacini, Adam Quint, and Red Farrel." Andy shook hands with each of them. Kevin saw the light of recognition go on in Andy's eyes. Andy started to speak.

"I'm going to buy Andy some coffee," Kevin said. He pushed Andy ahead of him down the aisle toward the back of the car.

"Was that *the* Red Farrel?" Andy asked. "And Jack Hannon?"

"Yes."

"I've got to get an interview!" Andy tried to push his way past Kevin.

"Interview? Think, Andy, think. You're sitting on the hottest news story in the Midwest. Did you recognize the other names?"

Andy thought for a moment. "Michael Pacini, reputed head of the Kansas City underworld."

"Former head," Kevin corrected. "And Adam Quint?"

Andy shook his head. "I didn't recognize the name."

"Infamous border gang leader. He helped mastermind the raid on Lawrence with William Quantrill."

"Of course!" Andy shouted. "Let me past, Mr. Donavan. This interview will save my job."

"Interview! I'm trying to help you, Andy. Let the society pages do the interviews. Now, what have you got?"

"Let's see," Andy said excitedly. "Red Farrel, the notorious outlaw; Jack Hannon, the most politically powerful man in the state; Adam Quint of border gang fame; and Michael Pacini, former head of the Kansas City underworld."

"What are they doing, Andy?"

"They're on a train headed for St. Louis."

"Why?"

"To attend the fair, I assume."

"You assume. You can't assume anything, Andy. Why would three notorious men and a political boss be going to a fair together?"

Andy searched for words. "I don't know, Mr. Donavan."

"Well, there's your story, Andy. Neither does anyone else. Remember, an interview with former outlaws gets buried on the back pages. Now what's your headline, Andy?"

Andy's eyes flicked back and forth. "Help me this one time, Mr. Donavan."

With his hand, Kevin traced a headline in front of him: "K.C. Gang Invades World Fair."

"The train is due for a stop in Columbia in ten minutes. Now write down everything I tell you. We're going to have St. Louis asking Why? Why? Why? We'll have their tongues hanging out panting for more."

Andy jumped to his feet. Kevin grabbed his arm. "Now remember, Andy. Go right to the top. A scoop is worthless if it isn't read." Kevin clenched his fist. "Catch your editor up in the excitement of three desperados and a political boss bearing down on the city from the west. Weave a veil of intrigue over the whole affair."

"Yes, sir. I'm on my way, Mr. Donavan." Andy ran out of the railroad car. Kevin watched him pass by the window and run into the station. His thoughts were of a day long ago and a young man walking across the Hannibal Bridge behind Octave Chanute.

The train whistle sounded. The coach lunged forward. Kevin searched the station platform for Andy. The train moved slowly ahead. Andy burst out the door of the station. He ran alongside the train and jumped aboard. When he plopped down beside Kevin, he had a smile of satisfaction on his face.

"Andy, I do believe I'm looking into the face of success."

Andy pumped Kevin's hand. "We did it, Mr. Donavan! The story seemed to flow out of me. The editor kept screaming questions at me."

"What did you answer?"

"I gave him just enough to make him want more. We're going on the front page. He says he'll ask questions later."

"Congratulations, Andy."

"How can I ever thank you, Mr. Donavan?"

"By telling me what you learned from all this."

"I learned that a story can be right under your nose as well as a thousand miles away."

"Also remember that a good reporter can create excitement and still remain true to his profession. I must get back to my friends, Andy. You're going to make a fine reporter."

"Thanks for everything, Mr. Donavan."

At St. Louis, Jack, Red, Michael, and Adam stepped off the train into a throng of reporters. Kevin kept to the rear of the procession as they pushed their way into Union Station.

"What's the purpose of your trip, Mr. Hannon?" a reporter yelled.

"We've come to see the World's Fair."

"Why are you traveling with Michael Pacini?"

"We happen to be friends."

The four men were separated by newspaper reporters. Red was completely surrounded.

Kevin smiled as Michael answered each question with a terse "No comment." Adam answered a barrage of questions about his relationship with Quantrill and his participation in the border war.

Michael ran outside. He hailed a taxi. It took him half an hour to get his friends out of the station and into the taxi.

"Where to, sir?" the driver asked.

"The Inside Inn."

The driver headed the automobile toward the fairground.

* * *

Jack laid the morning edition of the *Post-Dispatch* next to his plate.

"I assume you've all had the opportunity to read the morning paper?"

"Yes," Adam answered. "I wonder if the women and children of St. Louis will be allowed out on the street during out visit. We could sue for libel, but that would be more trouble than it's worth."

"You would think with the World's Fair in progress the newspapers would have something more interesting to pursue," Michael said.

Kevin wiped his mouth with a napkin. "Gentlemen, let's not let one unpleasant episode ruin our vacation. At our doorstep await the wonders of the world. Shall we go?"

On the way outside Jack pulled Kevin aside. "This may sound farfetched, Kevin."

"What, Jack?"

"Unless I'm terribly mistaken, the article in the *Post-Dispatch* had a Kevin Donavan flair about it."

"You thought it was that good?"

"I didn't say that. What was the name of the young man you introduced us to?"

"For heaven's sake, Jack. I can't remember everyone I meet on a train. Come on, our companions are waiting."

Jack eyed Kevin suspiciously as he followed him outside.

Back at the Union Hotel, at Union Depot, another man read the front-page story with interest. He placed his tray of food on the floor and called two men into the room.

"Read it!" The two men scanned the article.

"This is the first time he's come out of Kansas City. You make damn sure he don't get back."

"Whatever you say, Angelo."

* * *

Kevin glanced over his shoulder. "They're still behind us," he said.

The group stopped and looked back. Two young boys who were following stopped and stared.

"I'll see what they want," Kevin said. He walked back.

"Hello, boys. Could we help you with something?"

"Is that Red Farrel?" one of them asked.

"Sure is."

"Thought so. We saw his picture in the paper."

"How long did you two wait outside the hotel?" Kevin asked.

"Since sunup."

Kevin smiled. "Wait here." Kevin walked back to the group. "They're fans of yours, Red. They spent the morning outside the hotel."

Red nodded. He walked back.

"Hello, boys. I'm Red Farrel." The boys took several steps backward.

"What are your names?"

"I'm Homer Jones. He's Bud Casey."

"Pleased to meet you. How old are you, boys?"

"We're both nine," Homer said.

"Aren't you missin' a lot of fun followin' me around?"

"No, sir. We've already seen everything."

"You've been here before, have you?"

"Every day," Homer said.

"Isn't that costly?"

"We sneak in," Bud said. Homer nudged Bud with his elbow.

"He won't tell, Homer. He's an outlaw." A pained expression creased Homer's face.

Red laughed. "It's all right, Homer. Now tell me what I can do for you."

Homer shrugged. "We just wanted to see what you look like."

"Not disappointed, are you?"

"No, sir."

"I have to rejoin my friends. Boys, it's been a pleasure." Red tipped his

Stetson.

Homer and Bud watched him walk away. They waited for a moment and then continued their pursuit.

The St. Louis World's Fair was a celebration of Thomas Jefferson's purchase of the Louisiana territory. Fifty-three foreign governments were represented. One thousand buildings were constructed on one thousand two hundred and forty acres of ground. The fair was larger than the previous World's Fairs of Chicago and Paris combined, and cost over fifty million dollars. Each of the nine palatial exhibition buildings covered from four to twenty acres of ground. Nine hundred industries were represented. Individual states of the union built elaborate pavilions and foreign governments constructed acres of cultural exhibits. Seventy-five miles of walking paths wound through primitive villages and stately buildings. Elaborate gardens and monuments created a backdrop of total splendor. The fair opened April 30th and was to run until December 1st, with daily attendance averaging 100,000.

From his position at the base of Festival Hall, Jack looked north across the grand basin. Fountains spewed water sixty feet in the air. Exhibition palaces lined the waterway down a mile-long concourse.

"My God! I've seen nothing in Paris or Rome more impressive," he said.

"It has to be seen to be believed," Adam agreed.

The five men moved along the concourse taking in the sights. Jack's imposing figure stood out in any crowd. It wasn't long before the press caught up. In exchange for privacy, Jack, Red, and Adam agreed to a press conference at the end of each day. The reporters accepted the truce and faded into the crowd.

"How does it feel to be the object of the news instead of reporting it, Adam?" Michael asked.

"Very frustrating, Michael. The facts be damned. These people want sensationalism. I'm still wondering how they knew about our arrival."

"Let's tour the agricultural building and then have lunch," Kevin quickly suggested.

They toured only a fraction of the seven miles of aisles in the building before Jack patted his stomach.

"Gentlemen, the man in here is crying for attention. Let's seek out food and refreshment."

Red held back. "I have an errand to run and then I'll be along."

"We're having lunch at the Missouri pavilion," Jack said. "I promised the exposition administrators they would get a chance to meet with you, Red, so don't run out on us."

Red stepped behind a farm implement display. He watched his friends move out of the building. He had the feeling they were being followed by someone other than Homer and Bud. He left the building and kept his friends in sight as they walked down a strip of amusement and sports pavilions called the Pike. Red scanned the crowds of people as he moved along. He walked past the Wild West Indian Congress, Cairo, with an assortment of exotic animals, The Cliff Dwellers, Paris on the Pike. At Mysterious Asia Jack led the procession away from the Pike into a sparsely populated area of the park. Four men broke away from the crowd and followed. There were two of them on either side of the street.

Red wanted to be sure he wasn't imagining things. He moved up close to the men. He wanted to be able to identify them if they were still around after lunch. He followed the men through the winding paths of the Japanese Gardens. He stopped at the giant Ferris wheel. The wheel measured two hundred and fifty feet in diameter and was the park's main attraction. He noticed that Homer and Bud were still following behind and waved them over. They came reluctantly. Red looked up at the Ferris wheel. "How would you boys like a ride?"

"Okay," Homer said nonchalantly. Red purchased the tickets. He helped them into a seat. He watched as the seat swung upward and then made his escape toward the Missouri pavilion.

Lunch was attended by Missouri politicians and some of St. Louis's prominent citizens. Afterward, Red followed his friends out into the early June sunlight. He spotted two of the men. They were out in the road pointing at the dome on top of the building. The other two lounged against a Corinthian column to his right. In front of him Bud and Homer sat waiting on the stairs. They knew what Red didn't—that you could keep anyone in sight from the top of the Ferris wheel.

Red pondered as the group moved along. The men were obviously not following him. But who? Kevin and Adam were unlikely candidates. If he could separate Jack and Michael, he would have his answer.

The group stopped on the steps of the grand basin. Out on the lake, gondolas moved slowly along the water.

"Anyone for a ride?" Red asked.

"How about you, Michael?"

"Sure. Why not." Jack pointed to a grove of shade trees. "You'll find us over there."

Red and Michael stepped aboard a gondola. Two Orientals pushed the boat away from the shore.

Red looked over the umbrellas of two women sitting in front of him. He saw two of the men step aboard a gondola.

"I didn't know the fair would be this impressive," Michael said. "I'm going to bring Beth and Becky back for a visit in October."

"You should, Michael."

Red watched the other two men move around columns lining the bank. They were following the boat. There was no longer any doubt. Someone was after Michael.

Back in his room at the hotel Red rested his head on the pillow. Noise from the fair was fading with the light.

It had been one full year since Melissa's death. He closed his eyes. As always, he could see her face so clearly. Oh, how she would have enjoyed the fair. Out of respect for Adam Quint and their years of friendship, he had decided to make the trip. The years ahead seemed so bleak and void of purpose without Melissa. And now Michael was threatened. If anything happened to Michael, Beth would be devastated. Beth's happiness was all that mattered now.

Red sat up. He lifted the Colt revolver from his open suitcase. He knew Adam Quint would have a Navy Colt stuck somewhere in his luggage. He left his room and walked down the hall. He knocked on Adam's door.

"Come in."

"I hope I'm not botherin' you, Adam."

"Of course not, Red. I find that the older I get the less I like to be alone. Sit down. I'll pour us a drink. It's been an exciting day. I'm not used to being a celebrity."

"Do you miss the old days, Adam?"

"Sometimes I do. But one of the first signs of age is living in the past, so I try not to."

"I'm afraid the past is catchin' up with us, Adam."

"What?"

"Did you pack your Navy Colt?"

"Yes. Some habits are hard to break." Adam smiled. "You're not starting to believe our press clippings are you, Red?"

Red lowered his voice. "I need your help, Adam. Someone wants to kill Michael."

"Michael?"

Red explained what he had observed.

"Any chance your're wrong, Red?"

"I spent too many years on the run to be wrong."

"What's your plan?"

"Tomorrow I'll see what we're up against and then make a plan."

"Does Michael know about this?"

"We won't tell him until he has to know. He might get mad and do somethin' foolish." Red finished his drink. He went to the door.

"I'm seventy-two years old, Red," Adam said. "I don't know how much help I'll be."

"You've always been more help to me than anyone, Captain Quint." Red left the room. He walked down to the registration desk in the lobby. The desk clerk watched as Red scratched Michael's name from the register. Red handed the clerk ten dollars.

"If anyone asks for Mr. Pacini's room number I want to know right away."

"Yes, Mr. Farrel."

The next day passed uneventfully. The four men continued to follow at a distance. Red discreetly pointed the men out to Adam. Homer and Bud were still following as well. That was another problem Red had to solve.

Their visit from Kansas City had been well publicized. The men who were following knew tomorrow would be their last day at the fair.

That night Red and Adam planned their strategy.

"We have surprise on our side, Adam. They think they just have one unarmed man to deal with. Michael can pick where he wants to fight."

"I won't be much help in a running gunfight, Red."

"I don't move too fast myself. We'll have to keep up with Michael as best we can. Can you still shoot, Adam?"

"Some things you don't forget. When do you think they'll make their move?"

"Tomorrow night is the big fireworks display. Everyone will be at the Plaza of Saint Louis. If I wanted to shoot someone, I'd do it during the fireworks."

"When will you tell Michael?"

"The last possible minute. He'll do better if he doesn't have to think to much. Michael is a fighter when he has to be."

The next day was hot and windless—an August day in early June. Red and his companions spent most of their time in the shade of the exhibition palaces. As evening drew near they walked out of the Palace of Transportation. Homer and Bud were waiting.

"Let's have dinner over at the Swedish restaurant by the Ferris wheel," Jack suggested.

Red glanced over at Homer and Bud. "You all go ahead. I'm goin' to talk with my two shadows."

The men laughed. "Good luck, Red," Kevin said. "We'll meet you at the restaurant."

Red motioned for Homer and Bud. "You boys stick to a trail as good as anyone I've ever seen," he told them.

"You upset, Mr. Farrell?" Homer asked.

"No Homer. In fact, I'm glad you stuck with me. I need your help."

"You do?" Homer asked excitedly.

"Can you and Bud follow orders?"

"You bet we can!"

"Good. Before I let you help me, you have to pass a test. My friends are bein' trailed by four men. When I get to the Swedish restaurant I want you to describe each of those men to me. And don't let them see you."

"Let's go Bud," Homer said. The two boys bolted into the crowd.

A few practice fireworks exploded against a purple sky. Crowds of people began moving toward the Plaza of Saint Louis.

"Jack, I believe it's your turn." Kevin pushed the dinner check across the table.

"Thank you, Kevin. Gentlemen, shall we head for the fireworks display? A spectacle I will observe from a prone position."

Red remained seated. "I need to talk to Michael a minute. We'll follow you."

"This is my last chance to purchase some souvenirs," Adam said. "Jack, you and Kevin save us a good spot to view the fireworks."

"We'll meet at the Louisiana Monument," Jack said. He followed Kevin and Adam out the door.

Red got up from his chair. "Let's take a walk, Michael." The heat of the day had faded with the setting sun. The two men moved along the street toward the walled city of Jerusalem.

"Something on your mind?" Michael asked.

"I've never asked about your business, Michael, but there is somethin' I have to know. Have you stayed outside the organization?"

"Yes. Is Beth starting to worry again?"

"No. This has nothin' to do with Beth. Did you leave the organization on good terms?"

Michael shrugged. "That wasn't possible. Why do you ask?"

"Someone's been trailin' you since we got here. Any idea who it might be?"

"I'm no longer a threat to anyone, Red. Revenge is the only motive I can think of, and that would mean Angelo Banetti out of Chicago."

"Will it always be this way for you, Michael?"

Michael sighed. "No. I should have handled Angelo when I had the chance."

Bud and Homer walked casually up the street toward Red and Michael. They stopped in front of Red.

"The four men are gone, Mr. Farrel."

Red reached down and adjusted Homer's cap. "Thanks, boys." Red gave Homer some money. "Remember now, stay on the Ferris wheel until I come and get you off."

"Okay, Mr. Farrel." The boys ran off down the street.

"What was that all about?" Michael asked. Red guided Michael through the gate of The Jerusalem Pavilion and into the Garden of Gethsemane.

Red's voice was full of urgency. "We're up against four men, Michael. They're ready to make a move. I put a pistol above the door in the mosque up ahead. You do what you have to. Adam and I will back you up as best we can." Fireworks popped above their heads. The explosions were dull against the half light.

"When I duck to the right, you head for the mosque. Now! Run!"

A bullet zinged off the wall next to Red. He crouched down and watched Michael disappear into the mosque. All was quiet again. Red ran down one of the narrow streets of the exhibit to the back of the mosque. He was just in time to see Michael slide over the wall. Four men ran out the gate after Michael.

A scattering of women and children were still on the streets. Michael's pursuers tried to remain as inconspicuous as possible as they hurried after him. Red had to walk fast to keep them in sight.

They passed the Plaza of Saint Louis. Out on the field cadets from the

West Point Academy went through maneuvers. Shouted commands carried across the parade ground.

Michael moved through the crowds of people waiting for the fireworks display. The four men were in close pursuit. In the distance, drums carried a steady beat through the twilight. Michael headed for the Philippine Archipelago.

Groups of natives eyed him suspiciously as he moved around thatched huts in the village. He followed a bamboo fence that ran deep into the compound, to a lake. Huts of a Moro village were built on bamboo poles out in the lake. Michael stopped and looked around. He had the feeling someone was close by. He ran across a bridge into the village. As he passed a hut a glint of steel caught his eye. He ducked. A machete whistled over his head into the hut. Michael tripped as he tried to run. He fell on his face in the dirt. He rolled over quickly. The machete was arching through the air at him. He fired two shots into the face behind the machete. A man slumped to the ground.

Michael grabbed the man by his feet and dragged him to the lake, where he pushed him into the water. Then he hurried on.

Red searched frantically through the Philippine Village for Michael. He finally gave up and ran back to the Ferris wheel. Bud and Homer were spinning up to the peak. Red waited until they drifted down.

"Where are they?" he yelled.

"The Garden of Versailles," Homer pointed.

Red ran through the gate surrounding the Grand Trianon and the Garden of Versailles. The area seemed deserted. He ran up on the pavilion. He leaned against a column to catch his breath. Overhead, the fireworks were starting to shower down.

A series of shots rang out. Red looked to the east. Michael was zig-zagging through the Garden of Versailles. He ran out of the garden onto the pavilion. He was running toward Red. A man stopped in the garden and fired two shots at Michael. Red stepped from behind the column. He waved Michael past. Red dropped to one knee. The bandit was running too fast to take aim. A bullet whizzed past Red's ear. Red fired one shot from the revolver into the bandit's heart.

It was getting dark. Michael stayed just ahead of his pursuers. Close enough to be seen, but not close enough to be an easy target. He ran on. Up ahead, the ivory white of the temple of Ceylon appeared from out of the twilight. Michael bounded up the steps. He slipped quietly into the temple. He looked around. Brass lamps hung from the ceiling. In the heart of the temple a statue of Buddha rose peacefully above an altar. The walls of the shrine were painted with scenes from the sage's life.

Doors on either side of the temple slid open and closed. There was no way out. He was trapped. He backed toward the center of the temple. The statue of Buddha stared impassively down at him. Michael crouched down by the altar railing. He could hear the labored breathing of the two assassins as they moved toward him. A form moved in the shadows. Michael pointed his pistol and pulled the trigger. The hammer clicked. He tried again. The sound of metal against metal sounded hollow in the temple. A man stood up and walked toward him. He stopped a few feet away and leveled his gun at Michael's chest. Michael could feel his heart pounding violently. The man smiled. A Navy Colt went off in Michael's ear. The assassin was blown backwards by the force of the bullet. Adam Quint stepped from behind the statue of Buddha.

"Adam! Thank God!" Michael said.

"Stay down, Michael. We have one more to go."

Darkness had hidden the back of the temple.

"Red should be behind him," Adam said.

"Red! Are you there?" Adam shouted.

"I'm here!" Red's voice called from the temple entrance.

"He's trapped between us!" Adam shouted.

"Put your hands in the air and come out!" Red yelled. "You don't have a chance! Tell us what we want to know and we will let you go!" A few moments of silence passed.

"Don't shoot!" A man stepped from behind a curtain at the side of the temple. His hands were raised over his head. Red and Michael converged on him. Michael took his gun.

"Where's Angelo staying?" Michael asked.

The man hesitated.

"Angelo isn't worth dying for," Michael said. "Tell me what I want to know and you can catch a train for Chicago."

"The Union Hotel at the Union Station."

"Room number?"

"Two twenty-two."

"Hold him here for twenty minutes," Michael said.

Red grabbed Michael's arm. "Catch the express back to Kansas City tonight. I'll bring your luggage with me tomorrow."

"All right." Michael said. "Answer one question for me. Why were you two always at the right location?"

"That's easy," Adam said. "Red had Homer and Bud spinning above the fairgrounds keeping an eye on you. You're very lucky this ended before dark."

"Thanks, both of you," Michael said. "I owe you my life."

Red pushed the bandit toward the door. "See you in Kansas City, Michael."

* * *

Twenty minutes later Michael climbed the fire escape to the second floor of the Union Hotel. He moved down the hall to room two twenty-two. He knocked on the door.

"Who is it?"

"Room service." The lock snapped back. The door opened. A man leaned his head out into the hall. Michael hit him with the barrel of the pistol. He caught the guard in his arms and carried him back into the room. Michael found Angelo in front of a mirror in the back bedroom carefully adjusting his tie.

"You look good, Angelo."

Angelo spun around.

"Michael, how are you? It's good to see you again."

"Save it, Angelo."

The smile left Angelo's face.

"I gave you everything, Angelo. All I asked was to be left alone."

"We can deal, Michael."

"No more deals. You're only allowed one resurrection."

"If you wanted to kill me, Michael, you wouldn't be wasting time talking."

"I'm waiting, Angelo."

"For what?"

A whistle shrilled in the train yard below. Michael pulled the trigger.

Down in the freight yard Michael tossed his gun into a passing coal car. He walked into Union Station and over to a telephone.

"Police commissioner, please."

"Just a moment."

"Hello."

"Sorry to bother you at home, Commissioner."

"Who is this?"

"Shut up and listen. At the World's Fair there are bodies in the Moro Lagoon, on the pavilion of the Grand Trianon, and in the Temple of Ceylon. This is Chicago business, Commissioner. I suggest that you keep it quiet. The city will lose millions if people are scared away from the fair. Do you understand, Commissioner?"

"I understand."

"Good. Send your men over to the Union Hotel; room two twenty-two." Michael hung up the phone. He knew the killings would be kept quiet. The cities of St. Louis and Chicago were fierce competitors. St. Louis wanted to beat the previous World's Fair attendance record set by Chicago.

That evening, Michael boarded a train for Kansas City. He had made a mistake in thinking Angelo would let him walk away from the organization so easily, but with Angelo dead he knew he would be left alone; all his ties and commitments to the business had been through Angelo.

Homer and Bud followed Red through Union Station. Red spotted them as he was about to board the train. He walked over.

"Boys, I want to thank you. If you're ever in Kansas City I want you to come see me."

Red reached into his vest pocket. He handed each of the boys a bullet. "A token of my appreciation for a job well done." He shook their hands. "Good-bye, Homer, Bud."

The two boys watched as Red boarded the train. With the bullets clenched tightly in their fists they ran down the station platform and watched the train until it was lost from sight.

# 15

# Requiem

September 9, 1909

Miles Davis ate the last piece of trout on his plate. He leaned back in his chair and surveyed the stained glass windows and oak woodwork of the Savoy Grill.

"Excellent meal, Lawrence."

The waiter put a match to Lawrence Dubois's cigar. Lawrence inhaled contentedly. "Some brandy please, waiter." The waiter nodded and moved away.

"How quickly the years have passed, Miles."

"Yes, but somehow I've always managed to stay ten years older than you, Lawrence."

"True Miles, but you look so much younger than me. That's why I've decided to join you in retirement. One more year and I'm finished."

"I'm glad to hear it. You've had an impressive career. But why wait another year?"

"I still have something I want to do. You know what I mean."

The waiter placed two glasses of brandy on the table.

"And you know that an efficient lawyer learns from his defeats, Lawrence. Hannon's sixty years old. He's had his way in this town for twenty five years. What difference could it possibly make?"

"All the difference. I won't enjoy my retirement if Hannon is still in control of the city."

"The city? Hell, he controls the entire state. Forget it, Lawrence. Hannon's too big."

"You know the old saying, Miles."

"I do. And if Hannon falls, I'll start believing it."

"Then do so Miles, because it's going to happen."

"Not another foolproof plan?"

Lawrence laughed. "No, I've learned to take nothing for granted where Hannon's concerned. Two years ago I planted one of my men in Hannon's organization. He's now in control of Democratic campaign coffers."

"Hannon's no thief, Lawrence."

"No. But he does borrow from Peter to pay Paul. That can make for some interesting newspaper headlines. We have a governor in office dedicated to reform. Two of our newspapers have reform editors; and the clergy of all faiths are clamoring for someone to clean up the city."

"And that someone will be you."

"Exactly. Today I wrapped up my personal and business affairs. The last year of my career will be devoted to the destruction of Boss Hannon."

"I can't say that I wish you well, Lawrence. Having reached the age of seventy five, I've found that my business and political fires have cooled considerably."

"My good friend. I'm not asking that you contribute anything. I thought it might be interesting for you to follow Hannon's demise from your home in Florida. You do subscribe to the local papers?"

"Of course."

"Then I invite you to sit comfortably in the sunshine and watch the final curtain fall on my humble career."

Miles looked at Lawrence Dubois. He said nothing.

* * *

Bonnie Quint greeted Jack at the door and invited him to Adam's study.

An older man sat across from Adam. He looked vaguely familiar. Both men rose to their feet.

"Jack, you remember Miles Davis."

Jack shook his hand.

"Miles and I are old adversaries."

"*Were* old adversaries," Miles corrected.

"I'm glad to hear that, Miles."

Adam motioned for them to sit down. "Miles has something he would like to discuss with you, Jack."

Jack looked questioningly at Miles.

"These last ten years of retirement have been quite enjoyable for me, Hannon."

"With all due respect, Miles, I can't say that I've missed you."

Miles laughed. "No, I'm sure you haven't. I came here to suggest that you consider retirement."

"I believe that sentiment was first proposed in 1882, Miles."

"I had no part in the attempt on your life in '82, Hannon. And I'm not here representing anyone. I've had my successes and I've done some things I'm not particularly proud of. One of those things is the real estate crash of '87. I helped set you up, so I feel that I owe you one. I'll pay my debt to you and clear my conscience in the process. Your enemies are going to launch a campaign to oust you from government."

"I've fought that battle for twenty-five years, Miles."

"No one can lead a political organization that long and remain completely clean, Hannon. All the excesses and deficiencies of your underlings will be laid at the doorstep of O'Shea's tavern. The early years of prostitution and gambling, questionable political appointments, your relationship with Michael Pacini. A well-run smear campaign and your enemies can, and will, bring you down. You can do them one better. You can announce your retirement."

"He has a point, Jack." Adam said. "You're not one of the governor's favorite people. Once these righteous crusades catch on there's no stopping them."

"You're both talking as if I have something to be ashamed of," Jack said. "I've been elected to public office by a vote of the people for twenty-five years. And I've never walked away from a fight in my life."

Miles put up his hands in a gesture of conciliation.

"I didn't come here to offend you, Hannon. Only to warn you. You have spent forty years building your reputation in this town. Keep in mind that in a few short months it can be destroyed." Miles got up from his chair. "I've spoken my mind. You've been a worthy adversary, Hannon. I hope I can be forgiven for my one lapse of judgment."

Jack stood up. He shook Miles's hand. "Consider it done, Miles. I want to thank you for coming here. By the way, how is your daughter, Sarah?"

"She's fine. Last month she became a grandmother for the fifth time. A spring chicken, I'm not.

"I'll tell Sarah that you inquired. Good day to you, gentlemen."

* * *

"Last one up!" Kevin dealt the cards.

"Red . . . possible straight. Adam . . . no help. Michael . . . two pair. Jack . . . no help. And finally to the dealer with the luck of the Irish." Kevin turned the final card.

"Damn! Anyone care to challenge Michael's pair?" Everyone turned their cards over.

"It's time to call it a night when a pair of sevens win," Jack said. Michael swept his winnings off the table.

"It's comforting to know that my donation will bring a few more freight cars of lettuce into the city," Kevin said.

Michael laughed. "A few more dollars passing from the rich Irish to the poor of Italy."

Jack poured them the final drink of the evening. He held up his glass. "To good friends." They all drank the toast.

Red glanced at the newspaper glaring at him from Jack's desk.

"Boss Hannon Gambles Away Campaign Funds."

Lawrence Dubois's campaign had been relentless these last two weeks in his attempt to influence the early November elections. The newspapers announced new charges daily: "Hannon Featherbeds Local Government — Boss of Prostitution and Gambling? — Chief Hannon and His Police Force — Boss Hannon and Government Contracts."

Jack seemed to weather it all in good spirits.

"Is there anything we can do, Jack?" Red asked.

"No, Red. You can't fight half-truths and innuendo." Jack pointed to the paper. "The latest headline, for instance. I took a few dollars from campaign coffers to pay a gambling debt. Three days later I paid the money back with interest. Does it mention that in the newspaper? I've used bad judgment on occasion, but I've never committed a crime. I've become more notorious than our esteemed Mr. Farrel, the James Gang, and the Younger Brothers combined. No one has bothered to ask me for an interview to hear my explanation of these charges. All I can do is sit back and take it."

"And watch your reputation be ruined," Kevin said.

"My friends in the river wards will stand by me, Kevin. This smear campaign will weaken my influence around the city, but I'm safe in the North End and the West Bottoms."

"What's the reaction in Jeff City, Adam?" Red asked.

"The governor is threatening to send the attorney general to Kansas City for an investigation. So far, nothing has materialized, but I'm afraid it's only a matter of time."

"I don't suppose you would consider not running?" Michael asked.

"No. They've initiated the fight. I won't back away from it. When I win this election the purveyors of doom will be silenced for another twenty five years. I appreciate the concern you've all shown. Now I'm going to bed to rest up for tomorrows headlines."

Kevin followed his three friends out the back door of O'Shea's.

"Jack looks awfully tired, Kevin," Adam said.

"Yes. He pretends that he's not concerned, but it's getting to him. Jack has always been very sensitive. He thinks it's a defeat if there's one person out there who doesn't like him."

"I sometimes feel guilty having talked him into running for political office," Adam said.

"You made his life for him, Adam. He's often said that you helped him amount to something."

"Let's all try to think of a way we can help Jack out of this trouble," Red suggested. "Next Friday night we'll put our ideas on the poker table. Somehow we'll come up with somethin'."

* * *

Jack braked his car to a halt at the end of Bluff Street in the Quality Hill neighborhood. It was his favorite spot in the city, a place he often came in the evening to relax and gather his thoughts. From here he could watch the mighty Missouri flow past the city. He could also look out on the North End, and watch the sun set over the West Bottoms. In a way Kevin was right; he had not given birth to the city, but he did watch over it like a nervous father. He could identify every building in his district, and he knew most of the business owners by name. He was involved in every major project concerning the First Ward.

Jack moved to get out of his car. He felt the sudden surge of nausea he had been experiencing the past few days. He clenched his hand into a fist several times against the numbness in his left arm. He got out of the car and took a deep breath of fresh air. In a few minutes he began to feel better.

Down below, lights from the city began to twinkle on in the dusk.

He often thought it strange that he could become so attached to a place so far from his homeland. But from the day Hemp Cotter had first introduced him to Gully Town he had been fascinated by the city and its people. He had always done his very best to protect and promote the interests of both. Sometimes he had cut through red tape and bent a few laws to accomplish his purpose, but never to the detriment of the working men and women of the city. Perhaps he should have listened to Miles Davis and retired. He had been surprised at the visciousness of the newspaper attacks against him. Sometimes innuendo was a stronger force than evidence; it made people want to believe what was in the headlines. Perhaps he had used up his alloted share of good fortune. For almost thirty years the people had chosen him to protect and guide them in their pursuit of a better life. He felt it would be an admission of guilt if he retired. If the people did agree with the newspapers, they would say so in the next election.

The nausea returned. He felt unsteady on his feet, so he leaned back against the fender of his car. He made a mental note to start watching what he ate. The numb feeling in his arm started to spread across his chest.

He would have to get in the car and go see Doc Meade. He tried to move, but an intense pain replaced the numbness and he fell to his knees, clutching at his chest.

He tried to catch himself, but he fell over on his right side into the street. It felt like a fist was in his chest blocking the air. He closed his eyes against the pain, and took short, steady gulps of air.

After several minutes the pain began to ease. He was afraid any movement would bring it back.

He opened his eyes and lifted his head out of the street. Darkness was slowly covering the city. The early September night still carried the heat and humidity of August.

Off in the distance he could hear shouts of laughter as a cable car plunged down the Ninth Street incline. He wondered what time it was. Had he lost conciousness or had he only been here a few minutes? Down below the lights from the city looked safe and inviting. He tried to move again, but his body would not obey the command. He laid his head back down in the street. As soon as he regained his strength he would get up and drive back down to O'Shea's. But an hour passed, and then another. He felt so weak and helpless lying in the street, as though some unseen force had reached inside him and sapped his energy. His thoughts were of Kevin and Mary, and the Donavan girls. He had to get up and get moving because he was the godfather to a host of Donavan grandchildren, and there was still so much to be done in the First Ward. I'll rest a minute more, and then give it another try, he thought. He opened his eyes, lifted his head and looked around. The sound of automobile traffic on Broadway was beginning to fade, and the moon had moved higher in the sky. I must have passed out, he thought. The dull ache was still centered in his chest.

He had never kept to a set schedule, so he would not be missed at

O'Shea's. No one would find him until morning. Keep thinking about other things and don't panic, he told himself. He remembered that day so long ago when he and Kevin had first ventured up to Quality Hill. Sarah had looked so beautiful at the opera, and he had been so sure she was interested in him. He prided himself on his understanding of human nature, but he had certainly misread Sarah. But what had started out as a humbling experience ended up being the most successful trip ever for him and Kevin; they had found Mary McFarland. How could he ever explain what he felt for Mary? He admired and respected her so much, and he was grateful for the stable life she had given Kevin. Jack felt his role as a member of the Donavan family was his greatest blessing on earth. He had always been afraid that if he married it would somehow spoil his relationship with Kevin and Mary. They were all the family he had ever needed.

A noise off in the distance interrupted his thoughts. It was the unmistakable sound of a horse's hoofs striking the pavement.

Jack breathed a sigh of relief. He had forgotten that Joe Corrigan made a sweep of the bluff after patrolling the Quality Hill neighborhood. Joe knew his car, and he would stop and say hello. Hoofbeats from the policeman's horse grew louder as Joe moved the horse toward the bluff at the end of the street.

Joe Corrigan recognized Jack's model Z Oldsmobile. He wondered what Jack was doing here this late at night. Joe moved the horse closer. In the moonlight he spotted someone lying in the street. There was no mistaking Jack's huge body. Joe dismounted and ran over to Jack. He kneeled down beside him.

"Jack. What is it? What's happened to ya?"

Jack looked up at the round Irish face. He tried to speak but nothing would come. He took Joe's hand and laid it on his chest.

"It's yer heart?"

Jack nodded. Joe took off his shirt and placed it under Jack's head. "I have to run back up Bluff Street to reach a call box," Joe said. "I'll be but a minute, and then we'll get ya to a hospital."

* * *

Doc Meade sat at the bar at O'Shea's. He had been up all night. He downed his whiskey in one gulp, and felt the fiery liquid settle in his stomach. After sixty long years in the profession, these things were still not any easier. At his request the police and the hospital had kept Jack's illness quiet until after he had talked to Kevin. He had watched these two Irishmen go from hell-raising youngsters to the top of their professions. They had been his good friends for over forty years.

Doc Meade pulled out his pocket watch. He only had a few minutes left; Kevin was usually here by seven.

"Could I have another one, Harry?" the doc asked.

"Sure, Doc."

"Good morning, O'Shea's." Kevin walked into the tavern. "Hello, Doc."

Kevin moved up to the bar. "Can I have a coffee, Harry?"

"Comin' right up, Kevin," Harry said. Harry grabbed a cup and poured the steamy liquid.

"Is Master Hannon out of bed yet?" Kevin asked.

Doc Meade downed his whiskey. "Come over to a table, Kevin, I have to talk to you," he said.

Kevin followed the doctor over and sat down. His instincts told him something was wrong.

"What's happened, Doc?"

"It's Jack. He's had a heart attack."

Kevin looked stunned. He started to get up. Doc Meade grabbed his arm.

"He's not here, Kevin. We have him at Saint Mary's. I know this is difficult for you, but you must listen to me carefully."

Kevin read the look of concern on Doc Meade's face. He nodded numbly.

"Jack has had a major heart attack. He's in the care of the best heart specialist in the city, but the prognosis is poor. He's been asking for you, so I've left word at the hospital that you are to be his only visitor."

"You mean there's a chance he might not make it?" Kevin asked disbelievingly.

"I know this is difficult for you, Kevin, but I want you to leave here now and go to the hospital."

Kevin stared at Doc Meade. This could not be happening. Yesterday Jack had come for Sunday dinner. He had looked a little tired, but . . .

"Go now, Kevin," Doc Meade said firmly.

Kevin entered Jack's room at the hospital. The heart specialist had not given Jack much of a chance, but Kevin knew better. It would take more than a heart attack to stop Jack Hannon. Kevin moved over to the bed. Jack's face was ashen, and he looked very tired. Kevin reached down and put Jack's hand in his.

"So this is where you're hiding. I just left people at O'Shea's bar who look worse than you."

Kevin felt Jack give his hand a slight squeeze, and he saw just the trace of a smile on Jack's lips.

Kevin pulled a chair up next to the bed. The room was void of any other furniture and the bare gray walls seemed so stark and uninviting.

"The Doc says you're going to be okay, Jack Hannon, but he says we're in for a bit of a fight."

"I said, Doc, you are talking about the man who brought me across the Atlantic Ocean on an old freighter, put Otto Sullenburg the heavyweight champion of the world on his back, the man who has never lost a political battle, the man . . ." Jack looked up at him.

"It's okay, Kevin," he whispered. Jack closed his eyes again.

Over the next couple of hours the nurses moved in and out of the room, checking Jack's pulse and monitoring his breathing.

Kevin was afraid to leave the room even long enough to call Mary. He kept talking so Jack would know he was not alone.

"Do you remember the time we met the dude from back East outside the Goat meeting at O'Shea's? He said he was new in town and wanted to join an organization where he could meet people and get established. I told him he was in luck. All he had to do was to go into this political meeting, and when the speaker asked for suggestions, he should stand up and say the city should get rid of the wild goats that were smelling up the Irish neighborhoods. 'That's all I have to do?' he asks. 'It's their favorite cause,' I explain. 'If you show support for this issue they will welcome you like a brother.' So the dude goes into the meeting and makes his speech. It was the first time I ever heard it grow quiet at a Goat meeting. Remember the look on the dude's face when John Mulroon rushed down off the stage and grabbed him by the back of his collar and the seat of his pants? John got a running start down the aisle. We had to step aside as he threw the dude out the door and half way across Delaware Street. I felt so guilty I ended up spending half my paycheck on the dude for drinks and dinner."

Jack was not responding. Kevin was afraid to stop talking because the silence made him think, and he did not want to face what was happening.

"We only have a few months before we have to start planning for the Christmas Wagon, Jack. How many truckloads did you give away last year? Must have been ten or eleven."

Kevin looked up as the doctor returned to the room. The doctor examined Jack and then huddled with the nurses. Kevin squeezed Jack's hand tighter as he read their expressions.

A few minutes later a priest entered the room. Kevin got up out of his chair and stood in front of Jack's bed as if to shield him from the priest. Somehow he had to get Jack out of this; time had not changed a thing, they were still the two little Irish boys who had to take care of each other. The priest moved around the bed and started administering the Last Rites.

"Listen to me, Jack," Kevin said. "If you can just hold on and get some rest, we'll beat this thing. When we get you out of here you can come live with Mary and me. We'll take care of everything. Jack listen to me," Kevin sobbed. "Jack . . . Jack. . . ."

Jack could barely hear Kevin's voice. It seemed to be coming from far, far away. There was so much he wanted to say to Kevin, but he was too tired to form the words. He felt as if he were slipping down the side of a mountain. He would catch himself for a moment before his strength gave out, and then he would fall away. He made one last effort to grasp the mountain, but it was no use.

Below him he could see thatched huts and winding streets, and fields that were a patchwork of blues and greens. Kevin was at his side, and like kings in a castle, they were safe in their room high above the streets of Limerick.

* * *

Mary looked at the clock on the mantle. Kevin should have been home an hour ago. Lately he'd only been having one beer at O'Shea's before heading home. She turned down the fire on the stove. Another half hour passed. She decided to call the paper.

"Sports desk."

"Bobby?" she asked.

"Yes?"

"This is Mrs. Donavan."

Silence on the other end.

"Kevin hasn't come home, Bobby. Is he still working?"

"No ma'am."

"Did he say where he was going?"

"No ma'am."

Something was wrong. Bobby's voice was strained.

"What is it, Bobby? What's happened?"

"Hold on, Mrs. Donavan."

Mary bit down on her lip as the minutes passed.

"Hello, Mary?" She clutched her chest in fright. It was the editor of the *Times*.

"John, please tell me what has happened!"

"I'm sorry I have to be the one to tell you, Mary. Jack Hannon had a heart attack. He died a little while ago."

"Oh no," Mary whispered.

"I'm sorry, Mary." She put down the phone.

With tremendous self-control she held back a sob. Grief would have to come later. She had to find Kevin.

* * *

O'Shea's was locked up tight. Mary headed down to the river. A railroad worker saw her coming. He pointed to the Hannibal Bridge.

Mary nodded her thanks. She picked up her skirts and walked out onto the span.

Kevin leaned on the bridge railing. He watched the murky waters swirl beneath the bridge.

Mary leaned on the rail next to him. She could see that his eyes were red and swollen.

"Aren't you Mary McFarland, the queen of Quality Hill?"

Mary smiled. They stood together watching the Missouri flow from out of the west.

"It was forty years ago that Jack and I first crossed the Hannibal Bridge."

"Yes, I know."

Kevin looked to the south at the skyline of the city.

"It seems impossible that everything can go on without him, Mary. All these years the city seemed to revolve around Jack. He's gone and the buildings are still standing."

"Yes. We aren't made of mortar and stone, Kevin. It would be tragic if we were."

"He built this city, Mary. They should put up a monument to him."

"You know he wouldn't like that. Jack's monument will be in the people he helped."

Kevin watched the water flow under the span.

"When I first crossed this bridge in 1869, Mary, I felt so alive. Life was such a great adventure. It was as if the world had been created just for me. The joys and sorrows would somehow balance out. Over the years, the sorrows seem to have tipped the scales."

Mary put her hand on his arm.

"I don't know," Kevin continued. "Maybe I've gotten more pessimistic with age. Who was it that said you don't get old, you just get worn out? Something slipped away from me when Joey died. I've never been able to get it back. Now with Jack gone . . . I don't know, Mary . . . Sometimes I would just like to cross that great river myself."

Mary put his hand in hers. "I felt that way for a long time after Joey's death," she said. "But then I began to realize how much he accomplished in the short time he was allotted. And that was true of Jack Hannon. Do you ever remember either of them feeling sorry for themselves? No. They were too busy living. We should think of them with joy and laughter, not sorrow and depression. When we see them again, won't they scold us for wasting our precious time!"

Kevin looked at his wife.

"You really believe that you'll see them again, don't you?"

"Of course I do."

He looked away, lost in thought.

"Whatever happened to Jill Sieben, Mary?"

"She moved to the East Coast with her father."

"I've always regretted that I never went to see her."

"I'm sure she understands, Kevin."

"Yes, perhaps."

"Let's go home, Kevin."

He pushed away from the railing.

"I can't, Mary."

"What are you going to do?"

"I have to stay with Jack." He started to walk away, then turned around. "Have I ever told you that I love you, Mary Donavan?"

Mary shook her head. There were tears in her eyes. "No, Kevin. You've never had to."

He smiled, then he walked back and kissed her gently on the forehead.

### FROM ADAM QUINT'S JOURNAL — APRIL 15, 1912

*With each passing year, I seem to be more firmly entrenched on my porch overlooking "Reporters' Row." I don't know whether the years have sapped my energy or given me the wisdom to know there's nothing going on anywhere that I'm missing.*

*Bonnie will soon be home from work. She now has three stores in the city and a manager to run each of them. She is constantly on the go, and will not even think of retirement. I am sure she draws her strength from Margaret Donavan. Margaret has dress shops all over the Midwest, and she is very successful. Bonnie is her mentor, and she and Margaret are always in a tizzy about something to do with women's apparel. I implore them to slow down and leave some business for someone else, but to no avail.*

*Red still spends all of his time at the ranch. After Melissa's death, he poured all of his energy into raising horses. He has become one of the country's most renowned experts on the quarter horse. He has no social life, and to my knowledge he has never looked at another woman. The last of a dying breed, he still rides the range on horseback, and he has yet to purchase an automobile. However, he does seem to come alive when he is around Becky. It is good to know through her he can still have some joy in his life.*

*The city elections are here once again. After three years it still seems impossible that Jack is not around to dominate the political scene. His death was the death of the Boss System in Kansas City.*

*There are no men left on the scene with the stature, strength, and charisma to organize and dominate ward politics. City government is now run by committee. Jack could get more done for the people in one morning than today's bureaucrats get accomplished in a month.*

*In my lifetime, Jack was one of the few men who truly made a difference to those who knew and loved him, and to those he served. He was a good man, a good friend, and he is always in my thoughts.*

*Kevin and Mary still live down the street. Most of the Donavan grandchildren are now in their teens, but as always, Bonnie and I are still included in everything they do. We have exchanged our babysitting duties for ball games and picnics, and we love every minute of it.*

*Michael has been very successful with Pacini's Produce Company, and Beth is still teaching school.*

*The city has become a metropolis and has outgrown my ability to keep up with it. The southern boundary is now out to Seventy Ninth Street, and we have over two hundred passenger trains and three hundred freight trains passing through the city every day. The population is 250,000 and residential districts are springing up everywhere.*

*At the urging and prodding of my employer, William Rockhill Nelson, Kansas City has one of the largest park systems in the country, and with the advent of the automobile, miles of paved roads are under construction. It is almost too much to believe for those of us who remember the city as a bunch of ramshackle buildings set on muddy streets down by the river.*

*I have informed the school board of my retirement from teaching. I have reached an age where I want to free myself from all commitments. The only thing I can't seem to give up is my weekly newspaper column. Somehow it has become a part of my identity, and try as I may, I can't kill it off. This will also be my last journal entry. The world has turned over many times since I began keeping this journal in the age of the horse and buggy. I have been privileged to watch and record the events of the industrial revolution and all of its benefits for mankind. Those mere mortals of my past, General Shelby, William Quantrill, Jesse James, and others, have become legendary figures who will live on in American folklore. Those dearest to me; my parents, Jack, Melissa, Joey, Hester and Jake, Ben, Luke, and Jason, will always live on in my heart. So I close this journal, looking optimistically to the future, with deep respect for the past, and with a firm faith in the spirit of my fellow man.*

## APRIL, 1915

With her daughters, their husbands, and sixteen grandchildren, Mary had given up trying to have everyone over for Sunday dinner. Once a month she prepared a special meal for her four daughters, and accommodated the rest of the family only on special holidays.

"You look tired, Mother," Teresa said.

Mary sipped her coffee. "I'm fine, Teresa."

"Your mother is tired," Kevin agreed. "What she needs is a rest. It's all this extra work she's doing for the American Peace Society. I've tried to convince her the pacifist movement won't keep us out of war, but she won't listen."

"No, I won't listen," Mary replied. "Not with four grandsons to be sacrificed in another useless war. I'm going to fight with every ounce of energy I have. I thank God every night that we have a president who has enough good sense to keep us out of these ridiculous European fights."

"Woodrow Wilson has good intentions, Mary, but he will eventually bow to public pressure."

The president is a decent man, Kevin Donavan. He will do what he feels is right. The public can't change a man's values and principles."

"Maybe not, Mary girl, but Mr. Wilson won't be able to turn the other cheek forever."

"If Roosevelt would quit beating the war drums up on Sagamore Hill it might help calm the situation," Mary replied.

"You're surely not blaming Roosevelt for the war in Europe?"

"If Roosevelt were still president, our boys would already be in the trenches," Mary said. "The sentiment for peace is strong enough in this country that I can't see him being nominated at the democratic convention."

"I'm not so sure," Kevin replied.

"The Germans are acting very belligerent, Mother," Margaret said. "They're harassing our shipping on the high seas. We can't remain neutral with constant provocation."

"We can remain neutral," Mary insisted. "Why should we sacrifice Americans to satisfy a blood quarrel between the Europeans? We can keep our ships and our citizens out of the shipping lanes involved in the war zone."

"You're suggesting isolationism," Kevin said.

"Until the Europeans come to their senses, you bet I am."

"Enough of this war talk," Molly said. "You need a rest, Mother. Why don't you and Father take a vacation?"

"Yes," Anna agreed. "The American Peace Society will be able to manage for a few weeks without you. The four of us will substitute on your charitable committees."

"This is beginning to sound like a conspiracy to get rid of me," Mary said. "Besides, where would we go?"

"You must have a secret destination mapped out and tucked away in your mind," Anna said.

Mary turned away. She took a lace handkerchief from her sleeve and dabbed at her eyes.

"I'm sorry Mother. Was it something I said?"

Mary squeezed Anna's hand. "No, dear. Of course not. It's just that I've always wanted to see my mother again. It's been forty-two years since I last saw her and my brothers and sisters."

"Well, there you have it!" Teresa said. "You and Father can make a pilgrimage back to the old country. What could be more restful and romantic than Ireland in the springtime?"

"It would be too dangerous," Molly said. "The Germans have warned Americans not to travel on allied ships."

"Molly's right," Mary said. "You can make the trip after the war is over."

"Nonsense!" Kevin said. "The war might last for years. I had no idea you wanted to return to Ireland. Why haven't you mentioned it before?"

"I don't know. Over the years there were always so many other things that seemed more important." Mary could see Kevin's eyes churning with the possibilities.

"Do you really think we could go, Kevin?"

"Of course we can. I'm sure I can get a special assignment from the newspaper."

"But will it be worth the risk?"

"What risk? We'll travel on a ship flying the stars and stripes."

"Oh Mother! It will be so exciting!" Molly said. "When will you leave?"

Mary looked at Kevin.

"How's two weeks from today?" he asked.

Mary nodded. "I can't believe this is happening."

Margaret leaned over and hugged her mother. "Isn't it romantic! You can stay in one of those rustic inns nestled in the Irish countryside."

"Are you sure you can manage without us?" Mary asked.

"It won't be easy," Teresa said, "but I promise you Kansas City will be here when you return. Now the four of us are going to get out of here and let you two make your travel plans."

Mary and Kevin followed the girls out to the street. They kissed each of them good-bye and helped them into Anna's Packard.

"Don't let her have second thoughts and back out on you, Father," Margaret said.

"I won't Margaret. We're going to deliver Mary McFarland back to Kerry County."

"Good for you." Anna backed the Packard out of the driveway onto the street. Kevin and Mary waved as the car roared away to the south.

"Those girls can be very convincing," Mary said.

Kevin smiled. "Yes. And they confirmed my suspicions that you're working too hard."

Mary put her arms around Kevin's neck. She rested her head on his chest.

"The neighbors are going to talk," he said.

"You don't care anything about seeing Ireland again," Kevin Donavan. "You're only going to please me."

Kevin hugged Mary close to him. "So that's what you think?"

"Yes."

He kissed her forehead. "Shall I drive you to Mass?"

"No, thank you. I'm going to walk. Why don't you come with me?"

Kevin rolled his eyes. "Is there no end to what you'll ask a man to do?"

Mary laughed. "I'll fix one of your favorite desserts when I get home."

Mary watched Kevin go into the house. She pulled her coat tight against the early April wind. She started walking. The city had pushed to the south and caught up with her shrinking neighborhood. The Donavans and a few others had resisted the insatiable appetite of the commercial real estate developers. They would probably have to sell eventually or be zoned out of existence. She continued on for several blocks into the heart of the city. The wind seemed all the colder as it tunneled between the tall buildings. At Eleventh Street she glanced east. The activity surrounding the city's busiest hotel, The Baltimore, was at a standstill. The hotel looked tranquil on this Sunday evening. Mary turned out of the north wind and headed west on Eleventh Street.

She joined the crowd of worshippers entering the Immaculate Conception Cathedral.

Inside the church, Mary was in a world apart. A world of peace and contentment. No problem seemed too great once she was in the confines of the cathedral. She moved down the aisle to the right center of the church. She genuflected and moved on to a kneeling rail. She began to pray.

Mary had been a member of this parish since 1873. The old church facing Broadway, and the site of her wedding, had been razed in 1887. In a renovation project three years ago, stained glass windows had been installed in the new church. The six windows on either side of the cathedral rose majestically to the ceiling. Mary always sat in the pew under her favorite window. She finished her prayer and looked up at the scene showing Jesus walking on a stone path surrounded by sheep. He cradled a baby lamb in his arms. "I Am The Good Shepherd" was printed beneath his feet.

She turned and stared into the light flickering from the red and white candles at the front of the church.

Mass was over. The last person had filed out of the cathedral. Mary remained on the kneeling rail, her hands folded on top of the pew in front of her. She dropped her head onto her hands.

Father Devin slid onto the pew next to her. He knelt down beside her.

"Hello, Father."

"Hello, Mary. Am I intruding?"

"Of course not. It was a wonderful service."

"Thank you. Sometimes the repetition in my work requires a bit of encouragement. How are you feeling, Mary?"

"I'm all right, Father. By coincidence my daughters talked Kevin and me into the vacation you were suggesting."

"That's wonderful, Mary."

"I would like to think so Father, but I'm feeling very selfish about it."

"Why would you?"

"I'm asking my husband to risk the German blockade so I can return to Ireland. I want to see my mother."

"Under the circumstances you have every right to. Have you told Kevin?"

"No, Father. I've decided against it. I couldn't bear to see him unhappy or have him treat me differently."

"He will know eventually, Mary."

"Yes. But he won't have to live with it for so long. My doctors say I won't fall apart until near the end."

"Burdens are much lighter when they're shared, Mary."

"I know. I was just saying a thankful prayer that I have you and the church."

Father Devin cupped his hands over hers. "Have a safe journey, Mary."

* * *

As she stood beside Kevin on the ship's deck, Mary breathed a sigh of relief. The trip across the ocean had proved uneventful. The ship had observed a blackout as they entered the danger zone at Fastnet on the south coast of Ireland. The blackout remained in effect as the ship entered Saint George's Channel in the Irish Sea and continued until they arrived safely at Liverpool.

Horns blared in the foggy morning as tugboats guided the luxury liner toward the docks.

It had been ten days since they boarded a Pullman coach at the new Union Station in Kansas City and waved good-bye to the Donavan clan. A switch of trains in Chicago, and two days later they were in New York City. The vacant passenger compartments on the ocean liner *America,* and a notice from the German Embassy in Washington warning Americans not to travel in the danger zone, had caused Mary great concern. But now, on the last leg of the journey, she was glad they had taken the risk.

The fog was starting to lift as the giant ship was coaxed into its moorings. Down below, hundreds of people were swarming over the wharf watching the ship arrive.

"What's going on, Kevin? Why are all those people here?"

"I don't know. I've already checked the passenger list. There are no celebrities on board."

The ship was secured to the dock. The gangway was put in place. There was a great commotion as the passengers stepped off the ship into the swarming crowd.

"Stay here, Mary. I'm going to find out what this is all about." Kevin ran down the gangway. He stopped beside a young man who was busy pointing out the ship to a young lady.

"That's where she went in! On the starboard side behind the bridge!"

"Excuse me," Kevin said. "What's going on?"

"The *Lusitania's* been torpedoed. She went down off Old Head of Kinsdale on the Irish coast."

Kevin was stunned. He stared at the young man. "Was there any loss of life?"

"Yes. Hundreds. Are you an American, sir?"

"Yes."

"It looks like The Kaiser just invited the Colonies into the war." The man went back to his survey of the ship. Kevin turned and hurried up the gangway.

Mary read his expression as he walked toward her.

"What happened, Kevin?"

He wrapped his arms around her. "The Germans have sunk the *Lusitania.*"

"Oh no, Kevin. Were there any casualties?"

"I'm afraid so. There were American passengers on board. I think you know what this means?"

Mary felt too numb to cry.

"Come on," Kevin said. "I'll get you to the hotel."

She pulled away. "You'll do no such thing. You have a job to do. I'll find the hotel and get settled. After you've cabled your story you can meet me there."

Kevin kissed her cheek. "You're sure?"

"Off with you, Kevin Donavan."

Kevin ran quickly down the gangway.

Mary stared blankly out at the city of Liverpool. She closed her eyes and said a prayer.

At the hotel she knew better than to unpack. She was freshening up when Kevin burst through the door. He sat down on the bed to catch his breath.

"Are you trying to kill yourself?" Mary admonished him.

Kevin was finally able to speak. "I'm sorry Mary, but we have to leave. I've found an Irish fisherman on his way home to Queenstown. He agreed to give us a ride on his trawler. The survivors of the *Lusitania* will be taken to Queenstown. Do you mind terribly?"

"Of course not. Kenmare is only fifty miles away. I'll go on to my mother's house and you can join me later."

"It's going to be a rough ride, Mary, and you're so tired."

"Don't you think I can keep up with the likes of you, Kevin Donavan?"

"Ship space is at a premium, Mary, or I wouldn't ask you to go."

"With all the excitement going on I couldn't rest anyway. It's so ironic."

"What?" Kevin asked.

"When I left Ireland I boarded a ship at Queenstown."

Kevin picked up the suitcases. Mary followed him out the door.

The trawler pushed its way through the choppy waters of Queenstown harbor. In the distance Mary could see rows of houses stacked from the waterfront to the top of the hill. Off to the side, the Gothic columns of Saint Colman's Cathedral dominated the town and the wharf.

"I can't believe it hasn't changed," Mary said. "I remember how homesick I was when I last looked upon this scene. I almost jumped overboard and swam back to the dock."

"Lucky for me you didn't," Kevin said.

Mary wrapped her arm in his. "Will you visit Limerick while we're here?"

Kevin shook his head.

"Don't you want to see your boyhood home again?" Mary adjusted the collar on Kevin's coat. "Jack wouldn't mind, you know."

"Maybe not," Kevin said, "but somehow it wouldn't seem right."

The captain cut the engine on the trawler. The boat coasted into shore. Kevin helped Mary onto the dock.

"It looks like we've arrived ahead of the crowd. Let's secure a hotel room and get some rest."

"I'm too close to Kenmare to stop now, Kevin. If you'll get me transportation I'm going on ahead."

"You have to get some rest, Mary."

"I'll rest when I've finally laid eyes on my mother. How long will you be in Queenstown?"

"I'll join you in three days. We'll put all this war business behind us and have a real vacation. I promise."

"If you're delayed, send a message so I won't worry," Mary said.

* * *

The car hit a bump in the road. Mary's eyes jerked open. Windshield wipers were thumping away the Irish mist.

Tip Connor, her driver, apologized. "You deserve a rest after running the German blockade."

Mary smiled. She looked over at Tip. With narrow cheekbones, protruding ears and lines in his face chiseled by the wind, he could have been any of a thousand Irishmen. His tam was cocked forward above the bridge of his nose, leaving just enough room to reveal the humor in his eyes.

Mary looked out the window. The Emerald Isle was lush with the green of spring. The road weaved through the foothills leading down to the meeting place of the Iveragh and Beara peninsulas. In the distance, Mary caught glimpses of the blue waters of the Kenmare River.

"The land never changes, Mrs. Donavan." Tip read her mind.

"There's not a lovelier spot on earth," Mary replied.

"Although I've been nowhere else to compare, I would have to agree with you." Tip glanced over at her.

"There's no need to be nervous, you know," he said.

"It's that obvious?"

"Aye. In a few days you'll feel as if you never left."

"It's partly because they were not expecting me until the day after tomorrow."

"Never you mind. After a forty-year absence, no one will be standing on ceremony."

The car bumped along for several more miles.

"The farm is around the next bend in the road, Tip."

He braked the car to a halt in front of a whitewashed cottage surrounded by a white stone fence. He retrieved Mary's suitcases from the back seat and followed her through the farmyard to the open front door. No one was in sight.

"Won't you come in for tea?" Mary asked.

Tip placed the suitcases on the ground. He tipped his cap.

"You're on your own, Mary McFarland." She watched as he retreated to the car, then she stepped inside the cottage.

The forgotten smell of peat burning in the fireplace filled the cottage.

"Who's there?" a voice called. Mary turned the corner and walked into the living room. Her mother sat in a chair by the fireplace. Mary went over and stood in front of her.

The old woman searched Mary's face.

"Praise be to God," she said.

Mary dropped to her knees. Her mother cupped Mary's face in her hands. "My little Mary. I thought I might not get to see you again."

Mary dropped her head into her mother's lap. She remembered Jack Hannon's words: "You're the strong one among us, Mary." Her health, her frustration with the war, and the rigors of the trip were too much. She felt her mother's hands stroking her hair.

In her mother's arms, Mary felt for the first time since leaving Ireland that she no longer had to be strong. She put her arms around her mother and began to cry.

* * *

Before joining Mary in Kenmare, Kevin had attended the funeral for victims of the *Lusitania* in Queenstown.

Now he stood in front of the fireplace surrounded by the McFarland clan.

"Tell us another story, Mr. Donavan," the children pleaded.

Kevin smiled. He had kept the McFarlands, adults and children alike, spellbound with stories of the wild West. Mary implored him to keep the exaggerations to a minimum.

"Let me fill your glass, Kevin." Mary's brother, Pat, poured Kevin another drink.

Mary returned to the kitchen to help her mother and sisters prepare the evening meal. She and Kevin had managed to survive three days and nights of merriment. Her brothers, Pat, Dan, and James, had taken Kevin in as one of their own. Her sisters, Susan and Angela, treated Mary as if she had never left. One brother and two of Mary's sisters had passed away.

"That's a fine man you have, Mary."

"Yes, Mother."

"You've led an exciting life in America."

Mary watched her eighty-year old mother move deftly around the kitchen.

"Looking back on it, I guess we have. This trip back to Ireland is the most exciting of all."

"Maybe not so exciting, but it's given you a chance to get some color back in your cheeks." Her mother leaned over close to Mary. "I've insisted that everyone leave early tonight so you and your husband can get some rest."

"But don't get the idea we're going to leave you alone," Susan said. "Tomorrow we're going to picnic and fish on the Roughty River."

"It sounds like great fun, Susan, but you don't have to interrupt your lives to entertain Kevin and me."

"Interrupt!" Angela said. "I can't remember when we've all had such a good time. I just wish you could have brought the entire family."

"Perhaps on the next visit," Mary answered. "Although if my family keeps growing, we'll require an entire ocean liner."

Steam escaped into the air as Mrs. McFarland lifted the lid off the pot. She stirred the stew with a wooden ladle. "If you girls will seat everyone, I'll serve the stew."

After dinner the McFarland boys sabotaged their mother's plan. They hustled Kevin off to the nearest pub. It was after midnight when they all came singing up the road in the darkness.

"We'll let you sleep later in the morning," Mary's mother assured her. "With all the talk of revolution in Ireland the men need someone to talk to. All their frustrations are being poured out on your husband."

"Kevin is enjoying every minute of it, Mother."

Susan and Angela gathered up the kids and said good night.

Mary helped Kevin up the stairs to their bedroom. She managed to get him undressed and into bed.

"The world's in a mess, Mary girl," he muttered.

She slipped into bed. "Close your eyes and get some sleep. You must be exhausted."

"Whenever I close my eyes I see those coffins in the mass grave in Queenstown. Men, women and little children, all innocent victims."

"It must have been a terrible sight, Kevin."

"Yes. Even here in Ireland there's no escaping the turmoil. Your brothers will soon be fighting with the Sinn Fein."

"I assumed that would be the case. At least they have an idea of what they're fighting for."

"You're not against the Irish revolution, then?"

"I'm against violence in any form, Kevin."

"It's taken me years to come to the realization, Mary, but so am I. So am I."

Mary rubbed Kevin's arm until he fell asleep.

* * *

On their tenth day in Ireland, Mary and Kevin sat on a grassy knoll overlooking the forks of a stream. In the distance the mountains of Macgillicuddy Reeks soared into the clouds.

Kevin poured Mary another glass of wine.

"Thank you, sir. I can't believe I've had you to myself for three whole days."

"Your brothers seem to know just how much your mother will tolerate," Kevin said. "I certainly wouldn't want to cross her."

Mary laughed. "Mother thinks you're very special."

"After all these years, I finally have parental approval."

Mary looked toward the mountains as she sipped her wine.

"Do you realize, Kevin, that if we had stayed in Ireland we might never have met."

"Yes. It's funny how things work out. I'm glad we came back to Ireland, Mary. You look well rested and that McFarland glitter has returned to your eyes."

Mary lay back on the blanket. "I feel better than I have in a long time."

"Why did you want to return to Ireland, Mary?"

"To see my mother again."

Kevin lay down beside her. "I mean the other reason."

"I guess I was searching for something," Mary said.

"And you found it?"

"Yes. Ireland has given me peace of mind, and my mother has given me the strength to carry on."

Mary rolled over on to her stomach. "If you had your life to live over again, Kevin, would you change anything?"

Kevin smiled.

"Yes. Any man who says 'no' to that question must have been extremely intelligent in his youth. But I wouldn't change one thing about our relationship."

"Nor would I, Kevin. Would you mind terribly if we left for Kansas City tomorrow?"

"We have four days left."

"I know. But I miss my girls and my home."

"Won't your mother be disappointed?"

"No. We've already talked it over."

"To tell you the truth, Mary, I've been homesick since we first boarded the train."

Mary laid her head on his chest. "I love you, Kevin Donavan."

## DECEMBER, 1917

A caravan of trucks marked "Pacini's Produce Company" moved east along Fifth Street. Michael Pacini drove the lead truck.

The snow, whipped by a northerly wind, was starting to drift against the curbs and buildings. Through the frost on the windshield he could see the first gathering of people waiting on the sidewalk.

A group of children rushed out of a side street. They ran beside the trucks.

"Here comes the Christmas Wagon!" they shouted.

Michael took a sip of whiskey. He passed the bottle to Kevin. The trucks braked to a halt. Michael's men began distributing the fruits and vegetables.

With the war raging in Europe, commodities were hard to come by.

Michael turned his head as a coughing spell came on. His doctor had recently diagnosed consumption. If Michael wanted to live he would have to go south for the winters. Arizona might not be bad, he thought. Somehow it didn't seem to matter. Christmas wasn't the same without Beth. She had been taken in a flu epidemic in 1913. He had stayed by her bedside for days waiting for the fever to break. In the few hours he had slept, Red was always with her. They had called in the best doctors in the city, but to no avail. They could not break the fever. Dear, sweet, and gentle Beth, had been taken from them. His Uncle Frank had died five years ago. Only he and Kevin were left to carry on the Christmas wagon tradition.

"You had better get that cough taken care of," Kevin suggested. He returned the bottle to Michael.

He took another drink. "That should do the trick."

The two men waved through the windows as the trucks started up and continued on through Little Italy.

Children with red faces smiled at them as their parents lifted them up to be seen. At each stop, Michael and Kevin rolled down the windows so they could shake hands with the men and receive warm kisses from the women.

"How are Becky and her family, Michael?"

"Fine. I'm going to spend Christmas Day with them. Why don't you come along? We can talk over old times with Red."

"I went out to see him yesterday," Kevin said. "Your granddaughter, Courtney, is a beauty."

Michael smiled. "Isn't she something? Won't you accept the invitation, Kevin?"

"I appreciate it, but I have four households and I forget how many grandchildren to visit tomorrow."

The snow was falling harder as they finished distributing the gifts and headed the empty trucks back to Market Square.

Michael braked the truck to a halt. He expertly backed up to the dock, where he thanked the men and paid them each a Christmas bonus.

"Can I give you a ride uptown, Kevin?"

"Thanks, Michael. I think I'll walk."

They shook hands. "A very Merry Christmas to you, Michael."

"And to you, my good friend."

Michael shivered as he walked up the stairs to his apartment. He had the money to live anywhere, but he chose to live above the market.

Inside, he took off the Chesterfield coat and hung it on a hanger. He thought of Jack Hannon as he gently brushed the snow off the shoulders.

Michael knew he wasn't going to Arizona, and he knew this had been the last Christmas Wagon.

* * *

Kevin walked west on Third Street to Delaware. He wrapped his coat tightly around him against the chill from the river.

On Delaware, he stopped and looked across the street. A warehouse now stood on the ground that was once O'Shea's. Through the falling snow he could see ice flowing beneath the Hannibal Bridge. He turned and headed south, past the Pacific House on Fourth Street, and on uptown to the juncture of Delaware and Main. He turned around and looked back down the slope to the levee.

Through the falling snow he could see that hot July day eighteen years ago. Joey's casket resting on the caisson. The reins in Red Farrel's hands.

Oh, how he missed Mary. His heart ached for her every day. Sometimes he could still feel her presence beside him, and he could see those laughing hazel eyes. She had given him the strength and will to go on. Mary McFarland would not let him give up on himself. A streetcar rumbled past. Clouds of snow were blown into the air. "You really believe that you'll see them again, don't you, Mary?" Above the buildings, way down on the levee, Mary's face smiled back at him. "Of course I do."

Kevin Donavan turned and walked away. An old man trudging through the snow.

**Delaware Street**

## OCTOBER 26, 1928

"Mother! It's the game of the year," Courtney pleaded.

"We discussed this two weeks ago, Courtney. Your Father and I have to leave town. You're staying with your grandfather." Courtney's violet eyes flashed.

"But Mother!"

"I'm not going to argue, Courtney. The decision's been made."

Red looked up as his seventeen-year-old great-granddaughter plopped disconsolately into a chair. Courtney was the image of Melissa Graham.

"What's the matter, young lady?"

"Nothing, Grandpa."

"I couldn't help overhearing your conversation, Courtney. You go to the game. I'll be all right."

"I couldn't do that Grandpa. I'd worry about you."

"Don't you think I can take care of myself?"

"Sure you can."

"Well, then?"

Courtney folded her arms around her knees.

"No, Grandpa."

"It's no fun bein' a bother to people, Courtney. Suppose we make a deal."

She looked at him questioningly.

"Isn't your boyfriend the one who speeds out of here in that Chrysler six?"

"Yes. That's Jerry's car. Why do you ask?"

"I don't get to do much around here. Why don't you take me to the game?"

Courtney looked at her grandfather.

"Mother's right. She's always saying you can't stand to see me unhappy. You don't really want to go to the ball game."

"But I do. The reason I'm always stuck in this house is because everyone seems to know what I want."

Courtney crossed the room. She took his hand. She had the skin coloring of Michael Pacini.

"Are you sure you're up to it, Grandpa?"

"I feel fine, Courtney. You start makin' our plans."

* * *

"Grandpa." Red opened his eyes. Courtney was shaking his knee.

Rudy Vallee's voice filtered from the radio in the living room.

"Just Molly and me, and baby makes three, we'll hurry to my blue heaven."

Courtney took the afghan from his legs. She folded it neatly.

"We'll take this in case you get cold, Grandpa."

Red sat in the back seat of the car watching the land roll by.

Courtney was on her knees, her arms wrapped around the back of the front seat.

She listened to Jerry narrate the first two months of his freshman year.

"You'll love K.U., Courtney. I can hardly wait until you're with me next year."

Jerry glanced at the back seat. "Have you ever been to Lawrence, Mr. Farrel?"

"I was there once, Jerry. It was a long time ago."

"How long?" Jerry asked.

"Sixty five years."

Jerry whistled. "You weren't kidding, Mr. Farrel."

The car entered the outskirts of Lawrence.

Jerry gave them a guided tour through the small college town. Through Jerry's running commentary, Red could hear shouted commands and a faraway echo of gunshots.

"Has the town changed much, Mr. Farrel?"

"What did you say, Jerry?"

"Has the town changed much?"

"Yes. Yes, it has."

Jerry checked his watch.

"We'd better head on up the hill. It's almost game time."

After the climb up the stadium steps, Red took his seat. He caught his breath.

"Are you okay, Grandpa?"

"I'm fine, Courtney."

The October sun had taken the chill out of the day. From his position high in the stadium, Red could see for miles to the east. He pictured black smoke curling into the air.

The crowd roared. Jerry handed Red a pair of binoculars.

"We're going down to the student cheering section, Mr. Farrel. Enjoy the game."

"Thank you, Jerry. I will."

Red watched the action flow back and forth on the field. The game was a scoreless tie at halftime.

Courtney bounded up the steps. She handed Red a hotdog and some lemonade. She sat down next to him. "Are you enjoying the game, Grandpa?"

"Yes, Melissa."

"Courtney, Grandpa."

"I'm sorry, Courtney. I did it again."

Courtney squeezed his hand. "That's okay. Jerry and I will come up and get you after the game."

Red watched her bound down the steps.

Iowa State dominated the second half offensively but failed to penetrate the Kansas goal.

After the game Red followed Courtney and Jerry across the field. A westerly wind blew a discarded hotdog wrapper across Red's shoes. He glanced at the scoreboard. Kansas - 0, Iowa State - 0.

In the back seat of the car Courtney covered his legs with the afghan. He slept until the car came to a halt in front of the house.

"I'm sorry, Jerry," Courtney said. "We'll postpone the picnic until another time."

"What picnic?" Red asked.

"I play in a golf tournament tomorrow, Mr. Farrel. I wanted Courtney to follow me around. We were going to have a picnic afterward."

"Where are you playin', Jerry?"

"The Kansas City Country Club."

"Can I come along?" Red asked.

Jerry laughed.

"I told you he was a good sport, Courtney."

"Aren't you tired, Grandpa?"

"I'll get plenty of rest tonight. We'll see you tomorrow, Jerry."

Jerry put his hand on Red's shoulder. "Thanks, Mr. Farrel."

* * *

Courtney spread the blanket under a tree. Jerry set a chair down next to the blanket.

"Thanks, Jerry. How's your game?" Red asked.

Jerry adjusted the golf bag draped over his shoulder. "I'm no Bobby

Jones, Mr. Farrel. On a good day I'll score in the mid-eighties."

"Good luck to you, Jerry. Now you kids run along."

"Thanks, Mr. Farrel."

"I packed you a sandwich, Grandpa. There's lemonade in the picnic basket."

"Okay, Courtney." He watched them walk across the fairway. A fairway that was once a battlefield. Red looked out on the ground above Westport and pictured the thousands of men and horses lined in battle formation. Down below the bluffs, at Brush Creek, a new shopping district was taking shape. Red started walking. Alert for errant tee shots, he began tracing his steps on that fateful day.

"Sixty-four years," he whispered. "How could it have been sixty-four years?" He stopped and watched a plane fly overhead. Lindbergh had flown to Paris last year. The world was changing so fast. He continued walking. The rock fences were gone, and there were more trees, but he could remember every inch of the ground he had fought on. The initial cavalry charge. Luke, Jason and Ben. Adam Quint had been dead ten years now.

Back and forth across the fairways he walked. Everyone from the old days had gone. Why was he still left alive? Once again he followed General Shelby back up the hill. Through the leaves of red and gold he could see the roof tops in Westport. He heard the rebel yell and charged back down the hill. The battle was raging. He could hear the artillery shells explode and he could smell the acrid smoke. His breath came in short gasps. He stopped beside a green. The flag waving in the breeze was a battle flag. This was where the stallion had fallen. Red reached for the tightness in his chest. He fell forward onto the fairway.

From an adjoining fairway, Courtney saw the crowd gathered around the green. Instinctively she knew.

"Grandpa!" She ran across the fairway and shoved her way through the golfers.

"Give him some room!" A man shouted.

Courtney fell to her knees beside Red. Tears fell down her cheeks. "Oh, Grandpa." Red looked up at her. He could see his wife's broach on Courtney's blouse.

"Melissa," he whispered.

Courtney wiped the grass from his face. She stroked his hair.

"I love you, Grandpa."

Red Farrel took his last breath. The faces of the golfers seemed far above him.

"If you shoot me, don't hurt my horse," he said.

# About the Author

G. P. Schultz is a thirty-year resident of the Kansas City area. The idea for his novel, *Gully Town,* originated eighteen years ago when he was working as a produce buyer in the city market area.

Although *Gully Town* is a work of fiction, Mr. Schultz spent many years of research poring over old documents, maps, and histories of the city in an effort to make *Gully Town* as authentic as possible. He also spent a lot of quiet time on Delaware Street, and in the West Bottoms, creating the structure of the novel and trying to bring nineteenth-century Kansas City back to life.

G. P. Schultz currently owns his own brokerage business. The business is a one-man operation and allows him the luxury of doing what he loves the most, write fiction. *Gully Town* is his first novel.

He lives in the Kansas City area with his wife Vicki. They have two daughters and two grandsons.

KANSAS CITY
To St. Joseph
N
S
W
E
WYANDOTTE
THIRD ST.
SECOND ST.
FIRST ST.
FRONT ST.
MISSOURI
KAW RIVER
SECOND ST.
THIRD ST.
FOURTH ST.
FIFTH ST.
SIXTH
SEVENTH ST.
EIGHTH ST.
KANSAS CITY, KANSAS
WATER ST.
WOOD
ARMSTRONG ST.
JAMES ST.
ST. LOUIS AVE.
WEST BOTTOMS
EIGHTH ST.
UNION AVE.
SANTE FE ST.
UNION DEPOT
HICKORY ST.
MULBERRY ST.
TWELFTH ST.
NINTH STREET
INCLINE
BLUFF ST.
LINCOLN ST.
FLORENCE
JEFFERSON ST.
FRANKLIN ST.
MULKEY ST.
LAFAYETTE ST.
JARBOL ST.
ADELINE ST.
STOCKYARDS
KANSAS-MISSOURI STATE LINE
FOURTEENTH ST.
BELL ST.
TENNESSEE ST.
WYOMING ST.
OAKS HOTEL
SIXTEENTH ST.
To Lawrence